THE
SNOW
GIRL

Javier Castillo grew up in Malaga and studied business followed by a Master's in Management at ESCP Europe. His first novel, *El día que se perdió la cordura* (2017), became a true publishing phenomenon, translated into 15 languages and published in more than 60 countries. Rights have been acquired to produce the television series. His second novel, *El día que se perdió el amor* (2018), received both public and critical acclaim, as did *Todo lo que sucedió con Miranda Huff* (2019). *The Snow Girl* was the most read novel during the 2020 lockdown in Spain, and in 2023 it was released as a miniseries on Netflix, achieving great success. *The Soul Game* (2021) marked his global consolidation as one of the masters of suspense. To date, his novels have reached more than 2,000,000 readers. His sixth novel, *The Crystal Cuckoo*, was published in January 2023.

Follow the author
on Twitter @JavierCordura
and on his Instagram Javiercordura

JAVIER CASTILLO

THE SNOW GIRL

Translated by Isabelle Kaufeler

GRUPOⅢ
ⅢBOOKS

Grupo Books is an imprint of Penguin Random House Grupo Editorial, S. A. U.

©2023, by Javier Castillo
©2023, by Penguin Random House Grupo Editorial, S. A. U.
Travessera de Gràcia, 47-49. 08021 Barcelona, Spain
English translation ©2023, by Isabelle Kaufeler
Originally published in Spanish in 2020 by Penguin Random House Grupo Editorial
as *La chica de nieve*

ISBN: 978-16-447-3860-3

Printed in Colombia

To you, Grandma;
although you will never read this,
I am sure you can feel it.

And to you, Mom;
for being the example
for everything that I am.

Perhaps there is still someone out there who doesn't want to know that thorns grow fearlessly on even the most beautiful rose.

Chapter 1
New York
November 26, 1998

*You can never sense when
the worst is about to happen.*

Grace turned away from the pomp of the Thanksgiving Day parade for a few moments to look up at her daughter, who was sitting on her father's shoulders beaming with happiness. She noticed how her legs were swinging playfully and how her husband's hands held onto her thighs with a firmness she would later remember as insufficient. The Macy's Santa was approaching, smiling from his enormous throne, and every now and then Kiera would point at the procession of pixies, elves, huge gingerbread men and teddy bears walking ahead of his float and squeal with delight. It was raining. A soft, fine drizzle that dampened waterproofs and umbrellas and, looking back, perhaps those drops had always looked like tears.

"There!" shouted the little girl, "Look there!"

Aaron and Grace followed the line of Kiera's finger, which was pointing at a white helium balloon floating away into the clouds, getting smaller as it climbed between the New York skyscrapers. Then she looked down at her mother excitedly and Grace knew immediately that she wouldn't be able to say no.

Grace turned to look at one of the street corners where there was a woman dressed as Mary Poppins, her umbrella open beneath a huge bunch of white balloons which she was giving out to everyone who came near.

"Would you like a balloon?" Grace asked, knowing what her daughter's response would be.

Kiera was too excited to reply. She just opened her mouth in a delighted grin and nodded, showing her prominent dimples.

"But Santa's almost here! We can't miss him!" protested Aaron.

Kiera's dimples faded and revealed the small gap between her front teeth where food sometimes got caught. There was a carrot cake waiting for them at home, ready to celebrate her birthday the next day. At the thought of her birthday, Aaron gave in.

"Alright," he continued, "where do you get those balloons?"

"Mary Poppins is giving them out on the corner," replied Grace nervously. People had started to crowd closer around them and the peace of the previous moments began to melt, just like the butter in the turkey stuffing they were going to eat at dinner that evening.

"Kiera, stay with Mommy and you two can keep our spot."

"No! I want Mary Poppins."

Aaron sighed and Grace smiled, aware that he was about to give in once again.

"I hope little Michael will be less stubborn," Aaron added, stroking his wife's growing bump. Grace was five months pregnant, something that had worried him at first, especially with Kiera still so little, but now he was excited about it.

"Kiera's turned out like her father," Grace laughed, "and don't you try and tell me otherwise."

"Alright sweetie. Let's go and get that balloon!"

Aaron scooped Kiera back onto his shoulders and started pushing his way through the swiftly growing crowd towards the corner. He stopped after a few steps and before going any further turned back to Grace, shouting, "Will you be OK?"

"Sure! Don't be long! He's coming!"

Kiera gave her mother another big smile from up on her father's shoulders, her face radiating happiness in all directions. Years later, Grace drew consolation from this when she tried to convince herself that the void wasn't so dark, nor the pain so intense or the grief so suffocating: in the last memory she had of Kiera, her daughter was smiling.

Once they made it to Mary Poppins, Aaron put Kiera down on the ground: a decision which he would never forgive himself for. He thought she would be closer to Mary Poppins that way, and he might even be able to crouch down next to her and encourage her to ask for the balloon herself. We do things with high hopes, even when they may have the worst possible consequences. The sound of the band mingled with the shouts of the crowd, hundreds of arms and legs squeezed past on all sides and Kiera, a little scared, clung tightly to her father's hand. Then she reached out her other hand towards the girl dressed as Mary Poppins, who said the words which would forever haunt the memory of a father about to lose everything:

"Would this adorable girl like a spoonful of sugar?"

Kiera laughed. She also made a sound that Aaron would later remember as a slight snort, somewhere between a laugh and a suppressed giggle. This is the kind of memory that sticks in your mind, the kind we cling onto as hard as we can.

That was the last time he heard her laugh.

Just as Kiera took hold of the string of the balloon Miss Poppins handed her with fragile fingers there was another explosion of red confetti, the children all shrieked with excitement again, and parents and tourists suddenly got jumpy following a set of jostles that came from everywhere and nowhere at the same time.

And then the inevitable happened. Except that later, Aaron thought of so many things he could have done differently in those two short minutes: perhaps he should have been the one to take the balloon, or insisted that Kiera stay with Grace, or even approached the woman from the right instead of the left.

Someone bumped into Aaron. He took a step backwards and stumbled over a foot high barrier that surrounded a tree on the corner of 36th and Broadway. And there, at that exact moment, was the last time he felt the touch of Kiera's fingers: their temperature, their softness, how her little hand clung to her father's index, middle and ring fingers. Both their hands let go and Aaron didn't know then that it would be forever. It would have been a simple fall if it hadn't set off a domino effect of other people toppling over, and if getting up from the ground had taken just a second rather than extending to a long minute of being stamped on by people who had moved back to keep clear of the procession and get back onto the sidewalk, accidentally trampling his hands or legs. From the ground, Aaron shouted as best he could:

"Kiera! Stay right where you are!"

While still on the ground, Aaron also thought he heard: "Daddy!"

Bruised from being stepped on, he forced his way to his feet and realized that Kiera was no longer next to Mary Poppins. The other people who had fallen over struggled to their feet and tried to reclaim their spots. From somewhere among them, Aaron shouted again.

"Kiera! Kiera!"

The people around him looked at him in surprise, unaware of what was going on. He ran over to the woman in the costume:

"My daughter. Have you seen her?"

"The little girl in the white raincoat?"

"Yes! Where is she?"

"I gave her the balloon and then we got separated in all the pushing. I lost sight of her in the commotion. Isn't she with you?"

"Kiera!" Aaron shouted again, interrupting the woman and turning to look around him. He searched for her among the hundreds of legs. "Kiera!"

And then it happened. One of those things that happens at the worst moment, something that anyone with a bird's eye view could have resolved in a second. Someone let go of a white helium balloon and Aaron saw it. The very worst thing that could have happened.

He struggled to push through the crowd that blocked his path and ran towards the place where the balloon had risen from, moving away from where he had been and calling, "Kiera! My daughter!"

At the same time, Mary Poppins also began to shout, "A little girl is lost!"

When Aaron finally managed to get to the place where the white balloon had gone up, just in front of the entrance to a bank, a man and his daughter with two curly bunches were laughing as they waved goodbye to the balloon.

"Have you seen a little girl in a white raincoat?" Aaron asked in a desperate voice.

The man looked at him with concern and shook his head.

Aaron kept looking everywhere. He ran towards the corner, pushing everything out of his way. He was desperate. Thousands of people merged together around him with legs, arms and heads that blocked his view. He felt so lost and helpless that he thought his heart would disappear from inside his chest. The music of the trumpets from Santa's procession was blasting in Aaron's ears like a high-pitched doorbell that made his cries fade into the air. People crowded together, Santa Claus laughed on his float, and the whole world wanted to be close enough to see him.

"Kiera!"

He got as close as he could to his wife who, oblivious to it all, was watching some giant gingerbread men dancing with emphatic moves.

"Grace! I can't find Kiera!" he panted.

"What?!"

"I can't find Kiera! I put her down and I… I lost her," Aaron's voice trembled. "I can't find her."

"What did you say?"

"I can't find her."

It took Grace's face a moment to transition from excitement to confusion and then panic, before she began shouting, "Kiera!"

They both yelled her name all over the place, until people around them stopped what they were doing to join them in looking for Kiera. The parade continued in the distance, with Santa Claus smiling and waving at the children who followed him on their parents' shoulders, until it stopped in Herald Square and announced the official start of the holiday season.

In contrast, for Aaron and Grace, who had given voice and soul looking for their daughter, everything would change forever an hour later.

Chapter 2
Miren Triggs
1998

Misfortune always seeks out
those who can bear it,
revenge, on the other hand,
seeks those who cannot.

The first time I heard about the disappearance of Kiera Templeton was while I was studying at Columbia University. At the entrance to the School of Journalism, I picked up one of the free copies of the *Manhattan Press* they left for students in the hope that we would dream big and learn from the best. I had woken up early after a recurring nightmare in which I ran through a deserted New York street, running from my own shadow, and I took advantage of that sinister image to get up, shower and get ready before sunrise. I arrived early, and the corridors of the faculty building were deserted. I preferred it that way. I hated walking through strangers and filing into class aware of the looks and whispers as I passed. In those corridors I was no longer Miren, but instead "that-girl-who…", or sometimes "shhh-shhh-she-can-hear-us".

Sometimes I thought they were right and that I'd stopped having my own name, as if now I could only be the ghost of that night. When I looked at myself in the mirror and stared deep into my own eyes, I would ask myself, "Are you still there, Miren?"

That day was particularly strange. It was a week after Thanksgiving when the face of a little girl, Kiera Templeton, was on the front page of one of the most widely read newspapers on the planet.

The headline of the *Manhattan Press* on the December 1, 1998 was simply: "Have You Seen Kiera Templeton?" with a line below the photo which read, "More information on page 12". Kiera's face looked out surprised from the front page in a candid image, her green eyes focused on something beyond the camera. This was the image that would become engraved in the memory of the whole country. Her face reminded me of myself when I was little, the look in her eyes... that of my own as an adult. So vulnerable, so weak, so... broken.

The 71ˢᵗ Macy's parade in 1998 would be fondly remembered by Americans for two reasons. Firstly, because it is still considered to have been the best parade in history, with fourteen marching bands, performances from NSYNC, Backstreet Boys and Martina McBride, flash mobs performed by hundreds of majorettes and involving the entire cast of Sesame Street, and even an endless procession of firefighter clowns. The year before, there had been serious problems with the wind. Some balloons caused injuries and damage, and there was even an incident where Barney the purple dinosaur had to be punctured by a group of spectators to bring the balloon back under control and down to the ground. The chaos had been so bad that the organizing committee had focused all their efforts on restoring the event's mangled reputation. No parent would take their child to a parade where they might be hit by Barney or Babe, a five-story tall piglet. The best minds in the organization were tasked with eliminating every potential risk. Everything had to run smoothly for the 1998 parade. They implemented restrictions on the height and size of the giant balloons, which meant a permanent retirement for the sublime Woody Woodpecker. The participants responsible for pulling along the floating procession were given extensive training courses on how to control the characters. The show was so engrossing that, even today, almost twenty years later, the entire country still has vivid memories of the enormous procession dressed in blue that followed Santa Claus to the final destination in Herald Square. Everything went perfectly. The parade was a genuine success, apart from the fact that it was the day Kiera Templeton, a little girl of barely three years old, vanished among the crowd as if she'd never existed.

Jim Schmoer, my Investigative Journalism lecturer, was late to class. Back then he was also managing editor of the *Wall Street Daily*, a financial newspaper with more than a slight bent towards general news, and it looked like he had been in the municipal archive finding an old record. He stood in front of the entire class and, holding up his copy of the *Manhattan Press* and shaking it angrily, asked:

"Why do you think they're doing this? Why do you think they've put Kiera Templeton's photo on the front page with such a blunt headline?"

Sarah Marks, a keen classmate who sat two rows in front of me, answered in a loud voice, "So that we will all recognize her if we see her. It might help find her. If someone sees her and recognizes her, they might be able to raise the alarm."

Professor Schmoer shook his head and pointed at me. "What do you think, Ms. Triggs?"

"It's sad, but they're doing it to sell more papers," I said without hesitation.

"Go on."

"According to what I read in the paper, she disappeared a week ago from the corner of Herald Square. The alarm was raised immediately, and the entire city was out looking for her almost as soon as the parade finished. In the article it says that her photo was already on the news the night of the parade and they even began the CBS news broadcast the next morning with her picture. Two days later her face was plastered all over the streetlamps of Manhattan. They've put it on the front page now, a whole week later, not to help, but to jump onto the bandwagon of morbid curiosity this seems to be generating."

Professor Schmoer waited for a moment before responding.

"But had you ever seen this girl before? Did you see the news that night or the next morning?"

"No, Professor. I don't have a TV at home, and I live up in Harlem. Missing posters for little rich girls don't make it to the streetlamps there."

"Well then? Haven't they achieved their goal? Haven't they helped you recognize her? Don't you think they've done it to increase the likelihood of finding her?"

"No, Professor. I mean. In part, yes, but no."

"Please continue," he said, knowing I had reached the conclusion he was hoping for.

"They've mentioned that her face has been shown on CBS already because they don't want people to judge them for being the first to take advantage of the search, although that's exactly what they're doing."

"But now you're familiar with Kiera Templeton's face, and now you can join in the search for her."

"Yes, but that wasn't their end goal. Their end goal was to sell newspapers. Maybe CBS genuinely wanted to help with their early broadcasts, but now it seems like the media only want to drag it out. They're only trying to milk the story because a lot of people appear to be interested in it."

Professor Schmoer turned to face the rest of the class, and, to my surprise, began to clap.

"That's exactly what has happened, Ms. Triggs," he said, nodding his head, "and that's the way I want you to think.

What is hiding behind a story that makes it onto the front page? Why is one disappearance more important than another? Why is the entire country looking for Kiera Templeton right now?" He paused before declaring, "The whole world has joined the search for Kiera Templeton because it's profitable."

It was a simplistic view of the situation, I don't deny it, but it was that sad injustice that drew me to the case of Kiera's disappearance.

"The sad thing is… and you'll soon find this out for yourselves, the media join these searches through self-interest. When you think a story should be told because it is wrong or sad, the only question your editor will actually ask is: will it sell more copies? This world is driven by self-interest.

"Families ask the media for help for the same reason. In the end, a case in the public eye is assigned more police resources than an anonymous one. That's a fact. The politician of the day needs to win over public opinion, that's the only thing that matters to them, and that's where it comes full circle. They are all interested in moving the story; some to earn money; others to regain hope."

I stayed silent, angry. In fact, I think the whole class did. It was bleak. It was depressing. Afterwards, as if Kiera's story was already yesterday's news, Schmoer began to discuss an article which implicated the city's mayor in a possible embezzlement of funds from a carpark that was being built on the banks of the Hudson, and then finished the class by commenting on the details of an investigation he was working on into a new drug spreading through the city's suburbs that was starting to take a toll on the city's lower income demographic. The class was a ceaseless barrage of reality checks. You came in first thing full of motivation and left a while later feeling broken and questioning everything. Now I think about it, he achieved his goal.

Before finishing the class and finishing for another week, Professor Schmoer would usually assign us a topic to research during the week. Last week it had been a sexual assault by a politician on his secretary. This week, for a change, he turned round and wrote "Free choice" on the board.

"What does that mean?" called a student from one of the back rows.

"That you can investigate the topic that most interests you in today's paper."

This kind of assignment allowed us to spread our wings and discover which sort of investigative journalism best suited us: politics and corruption, social issues, environmental concerns, or the wheeling and dealing of business. One of the main news stories focused on a possible chemical spill into the Hudson after hundreds of dead fish appeared within a small radius. The story was an easy pass for the assignment and the whole class, including me, immediately realized this. All you needed to do was get hold of a water sample and test it in the faculty's lab, and you could identify the chemical that had covered the river in a carpet of floating fish. Then it would just be a case of finding out which chemical companies upriver manufactured products or generated waste that contained the substance and *voilà*. It was a piece of cake.

When we left class Christine Marks, the man magnet I had shared a table with last year, came over to me with a serious expression. We'd been good friends before, but now talking to her made me feel nauseous.

"Hey Miren, do you want to come with us to take a water sample later? It's dead easy. The others are talking about going down to Pier Twelve tonight, filling a few test tubes with water and grabbing a few beers. It's all sorted. I think there might even be some cute guys."

"I think I'll give it a miss this time."

"Again?"

"I just don't feel like it."

Christine frowned, but then she switched back to her constant long-suffering expression.

"Come on, Miren… please… I think it's time to… well, you know…"

I knew where she was going with this, and I also knew she wouldn't dare finish her sentence. We had become very distant since the previous year, well, perhaps I ought to admit that I put a lot of distance between myself and the whole world. Now I just preferred being alone to focus on my studies.

"This has nothing to do with what happened. And please don't speak to me as though I were someone to pity. I'm tired of everyone looking at me like that. I'm fine. That's all."

"Miren…," she begged, as if I were stupid. I'm sure she used the same voice for talking to children. "I didn't mean to…"

"It's not a problem, OK? Anyway, I'm not going to investigate the spill. It doesn't interest me. Since we've got a choice for once, I'd rather do something else."

Christine seemed irritated, but she didn't tell me so. She was also a coward.

"Well?"

"I'm going to investigate the disappearance of Kiera Templeton."

"The little girl? Are you sure? It's really hard to find out anything in that type of case. You're not going to have evidence or even anything resembling evidence to turn in to Professor Schmoer next week."

"So what? At least this way there'll be someone investigating the case that isn't doing it for money. That family deserves to have someone paying attention to their daughter who isn't on the make."

"Nobody cares about that little girl, Miren. You said it yourself. This assignment is there to raise your grade, not lower it. Don't waste the opportunity to get a good mark."

"It's better for you, though, right?"

"Don't play stupid, Miren."

"Maybe I always have been," I said, trying to end the conversation.

And everything could have finished there. It could have been an unsuccessful week-long investigation by an unimportant journalism student. A fail for a minor assignment that didn't affect my final grade for IJ, as we called the subject. But destiny wanted me to discover a crucial piece of information that would change both the course and luck of the search for Kiera Templeton.

Chapter 3
New York
November 26, 1998

Even at the very bottom
of the darkest pit
it is still possible to dig a little deeper.

A few minutes after Kiera disappeared, Grace called 911 from Aaron's cell phone and, disoriented, explained that she couldn't find her daughter. The police didn't waste any time, arriving just after several witnesses saw Grace and Aaron shouting at the top of their voices in desperation.

"Are you the parents?" asked the first officer on the scene after pushing his way through the crowd to reach the corner of Herald Square and Broadway.

Dozens of bystanders formed a ring around Aaron, Grace and the officer to watch the breakdown of two people who had lost what was most important to them.

"Please help me find her. Please," Grace begged. Tears streamed down her face. "Someone must have taken her. She wouldn't have gone with anyone."

"Try to stay calm, ma'am. We'll find her."

"She's so small. And she's alone. Please, you have to help us. What if somebody…? Oh my God… What if somebody took her?"

"Calm down. She'll be in a corner somewhere, scared. There are a lot of people here right now. We'll spread the word among the other officers and raise the alarm. We'll find her, I promise. How long ago did it happen? When did you last see her?"

Grace looked around her, saw people's worried faces and stopped listening. Aaron stepped in so as not to waste any time.

"Ten minutes ago, at the most. It was right here. She was sitting on my shoulders and we came to get a balloon. I put her down and… and she disappeared."

"How old is your daughter? Can you give a description to help us? What was she wearing?"

"She's three. Well, she will be tomorrow. She… has dark hair…. She had a ponytail, no, two, one on each side. And she was wearing jeans… and… a sweatshirt… white."

"It was pale pink, Aaron. For the love of God!" Grace cut in, interrupting.

"Are you sure?"

Grace sighed deeply. She felt like she was about to faint.

"It was a light-colored sweater," Aaron continued.

"If it's only been ten minutes, she must be nearby. It's impossible to move here with all these people."

One of the police officers grabbed his radio and raised the alarm:

"Attention all officers: 10-65. I repeat, 10-65. We have a three-year-old girl missing. Dark hair, wearing jeans and a light-colored sweatshirt. In the vicinity of Herald Square, 36th and Broadway." He stopped for a moment and turned to Grace, whose legs were beginning to give way. "What's your daughter called, ma'am? We'll find her, I promise you."

"Kiera. Kiera Templeton," Aaron replied for Grace, who looked like she was about to pass out. Aaron was increasingly aware of the weight of his wife, as if her legs were failing. Each second it became harder to keep her on her feet.

"The name is Kiera Templeton," the officer continued speaking into his radio. "I repeat, 10-65. Three-year-old girl, dark hair..."

Grace couldn't listen to the description of her daughter again. Her heart was pounding and her limbs couldn't take the pressure of the blood circulating through her arteries. She closed her eyes and collapsed into Aaron's arms as the people gathered around them gasped in shock.

"No, Grace... not now..." he whispered, "Please, not now..."

Aaron held her as best he could and nervously laid her down on the ground.

"Don't worry... relax, darling," he whispered into his wife's ear. "It'll soon pass..."

Grace lay on the ground with a lost expression and the surprised police officers knelt down to help. A lady came closer, and Aaron soon found himself surrounded by people wanting to know more.

"She's just having a panic attack! Please... move back. Some space. She needs space."

"Has this happened before?" asked one of the police officers. The other radioed for an ambulance. The street was crammed with people walking in all directions. The traffic was gridlocked. In the distance, Santa Claus continued to smile at the children from his float. Somewhere in all this craziness, Kiera might be huddled in a corner, afraid and asking herself why her parents weren't with her.

"Every so often. Jeez! She'd gone a month without one. It'll pass in a few minutes, but please, find Kiera. Help us find our daughter."

Grace appeared to be asleep on the ground, but her body went into light convulsions and the onlookers shrieked.

"It's nothing. It's nothing. It'll soon be over, darling," Aaron whispered into Grace's ear. "We'll find Kiera. Breathe... I don't know if you can hear me right now… Focus on your breathing and it'll pass."

Grace's expression changed from calm to terror, her eyes rolled back in her head and all Aaron could hope for was that she wouldn't hurt herself.

The knot of people around them was pressing in closer and closer, and the voices of everyone offering advice mingled with the sound of the police radios. Suddenly, the people on one side began to move out of the way and a pair of paramedics appeared with a stretcher and a first aid kit. Two police officers joined the group and began to push back the crowd, who seemed to be getting closer and closer.

Aaron took two steps back to let them get to work and held his hands to his mouth. He was overwhelmed. His daughter had disappeared a few minutes ago and now his wife was having a panic attack. He let just one tear fall. It was difficult for him. He didn't usually lose control or show his emotions in public and he felt so scrutinized at that moment that he held it all in as much as he could, but that one small drop reached the corner of his eye.

"What's her name?" shouted a paramedic.

"Grace," Aaron shouted back.

"Is this her first attack?"

"No… she has them occasionally. She's having treatment, but…" the lump in his throat stopped him from saying more.

"Grace… sweetheart, listen to me," said the paramedic in a reassuring tone. "It's nearly done… it's already stopping." He turned to Aaron and asked, "Is she allergic to any medication?"

"No," he replied, dazed. Aaron didn't know what to focus on. He felt overwhelmed. He moved one way and then another, looking at the ground and then into the distance between people's legs in a desperate attempt to spot Kiera.

"Kiera!" he yelled, "Kiera!"

One of the police officers asked him to step aside with him.

"Sir, we need your help to find your daughter. Your wife is fine. She's being taken care of by the emergency services. Which hospital would you like them to take her to? We need you to stay here with us."

"Hospital? No, no. She'll be fine in five minutes, it's nothing."

One of the paramedics came over to Aaron and the officer and said, "We need to go somewhere calmer. The ambulance is a block away and it's better for her to recover there. How about we wait for you there? We won't go to the hospital unless there are any complications. Don't worry; it's just an anxiety attack. It will pass in a few minutes and when it's over she needs to feel relaxed."

Suddenly one of the police officers who had just come over to them looked surprised and spoke into his radio.

"Central, could you repeat that last part?"

The voice on the radio was unintelligible to Aaron, who was a few meters away, but he had seen the officer's expression.

"What is it?" he shouted, "What's going on? Is it Kiera? Have they found her?"

The officer listened intently to his radio and saw that Aaron was hurrying towards him.

"You need to calm down, Mr. Templeton, OK?"

"What's happening?"

"They've found something."

Chapter 4
November 27, 2003
Five years after Kiera's disappearance

Only those who never stop looking
find themselves.

A
t the corner of 77th and Central Park West in New York at nine in the morning on November 27, hundreds of helpers and volunteers were milling around the huge inflatable figures that were about to lift off the ground. All those taking part in the launch of the enormous balloons that would travel the streets of New York until they stopped in front of Macy's in Herald Square were organized in groups, each dressed for the occasion according to which character they would be guiding. Those responsible for flying Babe, the brave little piglet, wore pink sweatshirts, those carrying the charismatic Mr. Monopoly wore elegant black suits, and there were blue jumpsuits for those accompanying the famous toy soldier. In Herald Square the morning had kicked off with an impressive flash-mob by America Sings, all in colored sweatshirts, followed by performances from some of the country's top artists.

The city had turned into one huge party, with people smiling in the streets and children walking excitedly towards various points along the parade route. Even up in the sky, the tycoon

Donald Trump flew past in his helicopter to show NBC an aerial view of the route the parade would follow along Manhattan's grid lines.

The disappearance of Kiera Templeton had slipped from the city's mind, but not from its subconscious. Mothers and fathers held onto their children tightly as they walked, taking precautions they would never have previously considered. They avoided the route's hotspots, those areas where there were likely to be the biggest crowds. Times Square, the final stop opposite Macy's, or even the areas further down Broadway were only occupied by tourists, adults and people from neighboring cities. Families with children had opted to enjoy the show near the beginning of the route up at Central Park West, a lower risk area with wide sidewalks and plenty of space to move without fear of bottlenecks or stampedes.

It was 9.53am and, just as the balloon in the shape of Sesame Street's Big Bird was taking flight while hundreds of excited, smiling children and parents looked on, a drunk burst into the middle of the street, shouting angrily as tears ran down his face.

"Watch your children! Watch your children or this city will swallow them up! It will swallow them up like it does with everything good that walks its streets! Nothing is sacred in this city! If it finds something you love, it will take it from you, like it takes away everything it sees."

Some of the parents turned away from the giant yellow bird hovering several meters above the ground to look at the drunk, who was wearing a stained suit without a tie. The man had a dark, bushy, unkempt beard; his hair was a mess. He had a cut on his lip and blood had trickled down to stain the collar of his shirt. His eyes were full of pain and desperation. He walked with difficulty as he was only wearing one shoe. On his other foot he just had a white sock which was completely black underneath.

A pair of volunteers approached the man to try and calm him down.

"Hey buddy, isn't it a little early to be in this state?" one of them said, trying to guide him to one side.

"It's Thanksgiving, aren't you ashamed of yourself?" added the other. "Get out of here before they arrest you. There are kids watching. Behave yourself."

"I'd be ashamed to take part... in this. To feed this... this monster that swallows up children," he shouted.

"Hold on a second..." said one of them who had just recognized him. "You're the... the father of that little girl who..."

"Don't you dare mention my daughter, you jerk."

"Yes! It is you... Perhaps you shouldn't come to... to this," he gestured, trying to be understanding.

Aaron held his head in his hands. He had spent the entire night drinking in one bar after another until there weren't any left open. Then he'd gone to a deli and bought a bottle of gin, which the Pakistani man behind the counter had sold him out of pity. He'd drunk a third of the bottle in one go and then vomited straightaway. He felt like crying. There were still a few hours until the Macy's parade began, marking the fifth anniversary of Kiera's disappearance, and the day before he had woken up crying, just as he had in the preceding years. Aaron had never been a drinker before losing his daughter. He'd been disciplined, had lived a healthy lifestyle and was only in the habit of drinking a glass of white wine when they had guests at their old home in Dyker Heights, an upper-class part of Brooklyn. Since what had happened to Kiera, he hadn't gone a single day without having a glass of whisky. There was such a difference between the Aaron Templeton of 1998 and 2003 that it was clear that life had given him a rough deal.

A police officer saw the scene unfolding and ran over.

"Sir, you need to leave this area," he told Aaron, taking him firmly by the arm and showing him the way to reach the other side of the barriers. "Only participants in the parade are allowed here."

"Don't touch me!" Aaron yelled.

"Sir... please... I don't want to arrest you. There are a lot of kids watching."

Aaron turned and looked at the edge of the street and saw that all eyes were fixed on him, rather than on the immense shadow cast by the yellow bird or the figure of Spiderman, which was inflating in the distance and about to take off. He hung his head. Again. He was completely defeated. Distraught and unable to cope. He couldn't deal with the emotional impact of the day of the parade, and perhaps the only thing left for him to do was to go back to his new apartment in New Jersey, to sleep and cry alone. But the police officer pulled at Aaron's arm. It was the worst thing he could have done.

Aaron spun round and delivered a powerful punch to the officer's face, knocking him to the floor in front of hundreds of astonished children and their parents, who began to jeer angrily.

"What a disgrace!" shouted one of them.

"Get out of here, loser!" yelled another.

A bottle of water hit Aaron in the face, and he looked around, shocked, unsure of where it had come from.

He didn't have time to think about why people were jeering, why people might consider his presence a bad thing, before two more police officers ran at him and tackled him to the ground. He landed face-first on the asphalt. In less than five seconds his hands were behind his back and a pair of handcuffs was cutting off the circulation to his wrists. His brain hadn't yet processed the pain of the impact, and wouldn't until a couple of minutes later. However, he was aware of the hands of the police officers and one of the volunteers who hauled him to his feet as everyone watching applauded, drowning out the shouts and cries of a father who had sunk to the depths of despair.

Once in the police van, he fell asleep.

When he woke up an hour later, he found himself sitting in the police station of the NYPD 20th precinct with his hands shackled behind him, next to a friendly-looking older man with a sad face. Aaron's face hurt and he screwed it up to try and crack some of the dried blood off his cheek, but it was a bad idea. Pain radiated in every direction.

"Bad day?" asked the man beside him.

"A bad… life," replied Aaron, who felt like he was going to retch.

"Well, life is bad if you don't do anything to change it."

Aaron turned to look at him, then nodded. It struck him that the man didn't look at all like a criminal except for the fact that he, too, had his hands tied behind his back. He imagined maybe the man was there because of a parking fine.

A woman with brown hair appeared from between the police station desks and addressed the older man:

"Mr. Rodríguez, right?" she said, taking a file out of her briefcase.

"That's right," he replied.

"My colleague from the homicide team will be here in a few minutes to ask you some questions. Would you like us to inform your lawyer?"

Aaron looked at the man with surprise.

"There's no need. I've already told you everything," Mr. Rodríguez replied calmly.

"Fine, have it your way. I want you to know you can request the duty lawyer to accompany you while you make your statement."

"My conscience is clear. I have nothing to hide," he smiled.

"Alright then," replied the police officer. "An officer will come and collect you in a few minutes. And you are… Templeton, Aaron. Come with me, please."

Aaron got up as best he could and said goodbye to Mr. Rodríguez with a short nod. He started walking along behind the officer, who went faster than him, until they reached a kind of waiting room.

"Here are your things. Call someone to come and pick you up."

"Is that it?" asked Aaron, confused.

"Look... the officer you punched feels sorry for you. He recognized you, ok? He saw you on TV when all that happened with your daughter. He says you've already suffered enough and it's Thanksgiving. He hasn't pressed charges and in the report he said that he arrested you because you were too worked up. You've just got a caution."

"So... I can go home?"

"Not so fast. You can only leave if someone comes to collect you. We can't let you leave alone while you're still so..., well, drunk. You can sleep it off in the waiting room if you want, but I wouldn't recommend it: it's Thanksgiving. Get yourself home, sleep a while and then have dinner with your family. I'm sure there's a good dinner waiting for you."

Aaron sighed and looked back over to where Mr. Rodríguez was sitting.

"Can I ask you what he did?"

"What who did?"

Aaron nodded towards the man. "He seems a decent guy."

"Oh, he is, sir. Last night he shot dead four men who had gang-raped his daughter."

Aaron swallowed hard and looked at Mr. Rodríguez with a kind of renewed respect.

"He'll probably spend the rest of his life in jail, but I don't blame him. In his position... I don't know what I'd do."

"But you're a police officer. It's your job to put the bad guys in jail."

"And that's why I said that. I don't have much confidence in the system. Those men he killed already had a history of sexual assault and... do you know where they were? On the streets. I don't know. I have less and less faith in all this. That's why I'm here at the station dealing with paperwork instead of putting my life on the line on the beat. It's better in here, buddy."

Aaron nodded. The officer took out a plastic box containing a leather wallet, a set of keys on a Pluto key ring and his Nokia 6600 cellphone, and put it on the counter. Aaron put the wallet and keys in his pockets and checked through the phone's notifications. He went through twelve missed calls from Grace and wrote a text that he deleted before sending it. He thought a call would be the quickest way out of there.

He held the handset to his ear and, a few seconds later, he heard a female voice on the other end of the line:

"Aaron?"

"Could you come and get me, Miren? I'm in a bit of trouble."

"Huh?"

"Please…"

Miren sighed.

"I'm in the newsroom. Is it urgent? Where are you?"

"At the police station."

Chapter 5
Miren Triggs
1998

A person is what they love,
but also, what they fear.

That same afternoon after class, I decided to read through everything that had been published about Kiera Templeton's disappearance. It had happened barely a week ago, but there was a steady stream of articles, news items and rumors building up around her. I went to the archive at the university's library and asked the assistant to run a search on all the news published since the day of the disappearance that included the words "Kiera Templeton".

I remember the girl's face and her cutting response: "Last week's papers haven't been processed yet. We're still on 1991."

"1991?! It's 1998," I replied. "We are in the middle of the technological era and you're telling me that we're running seven years late?"

"Afraid so. It's all very new, you know? But you can check them manually. There aren't that many."

I sighed. In a way she was right. How long could it take to find the articles that mentioned the disappearance?

"Can I see the papers from last week?"

"Which ones? *Manhattan Press, Washington Post…*"

"All of them."

"All of them?"

"All the nationals and the New York State papers."

The woman gave me a baffled look and sighed.

I sat down to wait at one of the library's tables while the intern disappeared through a side door. I waited for what felt like forever, and without realizing it, my mind went back to that night. I got up to avoid my thoughts. I wandered among the stacks for a while and lost myself whispering the titles of books written in Spanish.

I heard the sound of wheels behind me and, when I turned round, I saw the smiling face of the girl, pushing a trolley loaded with more than a hundred papers.

"All that?" I asked, surprised by the height of the pile.

"That's what you asked me for, right? The papers published in the past week. Just the nationals and those based in New York State. I don't know what you're working on, but are you sure the nationals won't be enough?"

"This is perfect."

The girl went back behind the counter, leaving me the trolley stacked with newspapers beside a table near the window. I grabbed the first paper and began to flick through the pages scanning the headlines, my eyes flying from one to the next like birds of prey over scrubland.

There are various ways you can document an investigation, and the method you choose depends heavily on your instinct and the issue you want to investigate. For some cases it's better to stick to police files, for others, municipal archives or public registers. Occasionally you'll get the critical clue from a witness or informant, and many other times it's a matter of pure instinct. Searching, digging, collating every last scrap of information that could be relevant. I was working blind on the Kiera Templeton case. It was still too early to try and get hold of the report on her disappearance and, in any case, there was no way an FBI agent would dare share information with a final year journalism student. If the FBI did collaborate, it was with the journalists from the mainstream media, and only ever when it was necessary and they thought it might help to move a case forward. It had happened before. Sometimes the police needed a thousand pairs of eyes, so they would offer the media confidential information in order to identify a killer or find a victim with help from the general public. For the most high-profile cases, like Kiera's, publishing details of the clothes she was wearing, where she was last seen, or even the things she liked could help kick-start the search and alert people in case they found any important clues.

I went quickly through the papers from November 26, the day of Thanksgiving that year, since it was the same day that Kiera disappeared. The print runs for those editions finished early in the morning and the information they contained was about news and events which had happened on the 25th, so there was no way they could contain any mention of Kiera.

After flicking through a hundred or so pages from different papers from the next day with photos of the parade and headlines about the official start of the holiday season, I found the first reference to Kiera's disappearance. In the bottom corner of page 16 of the *New York Daily News*, in a box bordered with heavy black lines, was the first photo of Kiera, the same one that had appeared days later on the front page of the *Manhattan Press*. Below it, the text reported in a clinical tone that the previous day a search had begun for a three-year-old girl who had disappeared and who was named Kiera. According to the article, she had been wearing jeans, a white or light pink sweater and a white quilted anorak. There was nothing else. Neither the time of the disappearance nor the place where she was last seen.

I was not surprised to find a more prominent article in the papers from the following day. A different newspaper, this time the *New York Post*, had dedicated a half-page spread to Kiera's disappearance. The article, credited to one Tom Walsh, read:

> Day Two in the search for Kiera Templeton, who vanished during the Thanksgiving parade. The little girl, aged three, disappeared among the crowd two days ago. Her parents are desperate to find her and request the help of all New Yorkers.

A picture of Aaron and Grace Templeton holding a photograph of their daughter accompanied the article. Their eyes were swollen from crying. That picture was where I saw them both for the first time.

I continued to read the papers and set aside the pages that mentioned Kiera or the parade, working my way through the calendar until I reached that day and the front page of the *Manhattan Press*.

I checked the time and was shocked to see it was almost nine at night. There was nobody in the library. It was open until midnight at that time of year with the mid-terms just around the corner, but still far enough ahead that nobody felt an urgent need to study.

I shouldn't have stayed so late. I quickly put the pages in my knapsack and took the trolley over to the counter. The intern grumbled when she saw the mound of jumbled paper.

I went out to the street and found myself in the darkness of the New York night. I looked one way and couldn't see a soul. In the other direction, a pair of silhouettes surrounded by smoke were chatting and smoking in the doorway of a bar. I went back inside and the girl at the counter gave me a fake smile when she saw me again.

"Please can I use the phone?" I asked. "I didn't bring money for a taxi…. I didn't plan to stay so late."

"It's only nine. There are still people on the streets."

"Can I use the phone or not?"

"Of… of course," she replied, passing me the handset.

I lived in a rental in central Harlem near the campus, in a red brick building on 115th street, barely a ten minute walk from the faculty. The faculty was east of Morningside Park, while my home was just to the west of it. I only had to cross a couple of streets, go through the park and I'd be home. The problem was that the neighborhood was tough during those years. A bunch of condos and social housing projects had brought together gangs, groups of minor-league delinquents, drug addicts and muggers on the look-out for any innocent victim, all in a single area just above the park. Attacks and assaults were virtually unheard of during the day, but the situation was completely different at night.

I dialed the only number that would be answered at that hour.

"Yes?" said a male voice on the other end.

"Do you fancy meeting up?" I asked. "I'm in the faculty library."

"Miren?"

"I'm having a bad day. Yes or no?"

"Alright. Give me fifteen minutes and I'll be there."

"I'll wait inside."

I hung up and was passing the time watching the intern trying to sort out the mess of loose sheets I'd created with the newspapers. A while later Professor Schmoer appeared in the doorway, wearing his jacket with elbow patches and his round-rimmed glasses, and signaled to me to come outside.

"Are you alright?" he asked me once we were walking along the sidewalk.

"I lost track of time."

"I'll walk you home and then head off, OK? I can't stay." He turned away and started to walk east. "I've got a problem at the newsroom. The editor in chief wants to publish something—anything—about Kiera Templeton on the front page, and I've got the feeling that all the papers will do the same thing tomorrow after the *Manhattan Press*'s front page today. They're really going to milk this story and, honestly, the thought of being part of that disgusts me."

I walked faster to catch up with him.

"So, what are you going to publish?" I asked, curious.

"The mother's call to 911. We've got hold of a copy of the recording."

"Ugh. That's pretty bad," I exhaled, raising my eyebrows. "A bit on the sensational side for the *Daily*. Aren't you supposed to be a financial paper?"

"I know. That's why what they're thinking of doing makes me sick."

I waited a moment before continuing. I focused on the sound of our footsteps on the sidewalk; and on how our shadows stretched ahead of us after we passed a streetlight, only to disappear afterwards.

"Can't you say anything? Can't you publish something else? You're the managing editor."

"Sales figures, Miren. Sales are everything," he replied, irritated. "You said so yourself today. What maybe you don't understand yet is just how much they control *everything*. The harsh reality is that they're the only thing that matters."

"That bad?"

"Today's *Manhattan Press* cleaned up. They sold ten times as many copies as they did yesterday, Miren. The rest of us have been left with surplus copies. They gambled and they won."

"Ten times?"

"We don't know what they'll come up with tomorrow, but that's how it works. Whether we like it or not, the search for that girl is going to become the hot story for all the press in the coming months, unless she reappears soon. There will even be outlets that would prefer she's never found in order to bleed the story completely dry. When people have forgotten about the disappearance and the papers have forgotten about her, there will be tributes that the whole world will ignore and then they will only resurrect the story again if a body is found or Kiera herself reappears in the middle of Times Square."

I could tell he was really down. He was so upset that I didn't dare respond.

We reached the statue of Carl Schurz, beside the park, and I asked him to go around instead of through, even though it would double the journey time; he agreed without complaint.

From that point he accompanied me in silence. No doubt it was a question of age. He was fifteen years older than me and knew that I didn't need constant conversation. He was waiting for me to slip up. Perhaps he was hoping that I'd bring up the reason I'd refused to cross the park, but it was something I didn't want to talk about. When we reached my door after going up Manhattan Avenue I said, "Thanks, Professor."

"There's no need, Miren. As you know, I'm only trying to help…"

I launched myself forward and gave him a grateful hug. It was comforting to feel a bit protected.

He quickly pushed me away, preoccupied, and I felt like shit.

"This… this is not a good idea, Miren. I can't. I've got to get back to the newsroom."

"It was just a… a hug, Jim," I told him, serious and angry. "Are you losing it?"

"Miren, you know I… I can't. I have to go. This shouldn't be happening. If anyone sees us…"

"Is it that important?" I asked, trying not to focus on him rejecting me.

"No, it's just…" he seemed to hesitate. "Well actually, yes, it is. I can't stay," he declared.

"I'm sorry, I…," I apologized, "I thought we were… friends."

"No, Miren. It's not that… I just have to get back to the newsroom. Really."

He seemed more nervous than normal and I waited for him to continue.

"It's the 911 call from Kiera Templeton's mother," he said finally. "There's something not quite right about it. And I don't think releasing it is in anyone's best interests."

"Can you tell me anything more? I've decided to investigate the Kiera Templeton story for this week's assignment."

"Aren't you going to investigate the spill?" he replied, surprised. "I thought you wanted to pass."

I was grateful he'd stopped talking about the hug, and the tension dissolved.

"And I do, but not by being the same as everyone else. They're all going to do it. It's easy as pie. Kiera deserves to have someone look at her case without dollar signs in their eyes."

Professor Schmoer nodded in agreement.

"Alright. I'll tell you just one thing from the recording."

"Go on."

"In the 911 call, the parents…"

"What about them?"

"They seem to be hiding something."

Chapter 6
Grace Templeton's 911 call
11.53 am, November 26, 1998

"911, what's your emergency?"

"I… I can't find my daughter."

"Alright… when did you last see her?"

"A… a few minutes ago… we were here at… at the parade and… she went with her father."

"Is she with her father or is she lost?"

"She was with him… but not anymore. She's lost."

"How old is she?"

"Two, nearly three. Her birthday is tomorrow."

"Alright… whereabouts are you?"

"Um…"

"Ma'am, whereabouts are you?"

"At… at the corner of 36th and Broadway. There are lots of people and she got lost. She's very small. Oh my God!"

"And… what was she wearing the last time you saw her?"

"She was wearing a… give me a moment…, I can't remember exactly. Blue trousers and… I don't know."

"A sweater or something similar? Do you remember the color?"

"Um… yes. A pink sweatshirt."

"Can you give me a brief description of your daughter?"

"She… has dark hair, cut quite short. She smiles at everyone. She's just under three foot tall. She's small for her age."

"Skin color?"

"White."

"Alright…."

"Please, help us."

"Have you moved at all? Have you looked in the immediate area?"

"It's completely full of people. It's impossible."

"Was your daughter wearing any kind of jacket or overcoat?"

"What do you mean?"

"Was she wearing anything over the pink sweater you told me about? It's raining in New York."

"Oh… yes. An anorak."

"Do you remember the color?"

"Um… white, with a hood. Yes, it had a hood."

"OK… please stay on the line. I'm going to pass you over to the police straight away, OK?"

"Sure."

A few seconds later, after several dial tones, another different woman answers on the other end.

"Ma'am?"

"Yes?"

"Did you see which way your daughter went?"

"Um… no. She was with my husband and didn't come back. She… she'd already got lost."

"Are you with your husband now?"

"Yes, he's here."

"Could you put him on the line?"

"…"

"Yes?" Aaron answered, his voice breaking.

"Sir, did you see which way your daughter went?"

"No, I didn't."

"Alright… could you confirm what time this happened?"

"Five minutes ago, at the most. There are too many people here. It's impossible to find her."

"We're going to find her."

"…"

"Sir, can you hear me?"

"Yes, yes."

"A street patrol is heading to the corner of 36th and Broadway. Wait there."

"Do you think they'll find her?" Aaron asked.

On the other end of the phone, in the background, Grace's voice can be heard saying something to Aaron, but it's unintelligible.

"Grace, not now," he said, trying to be determined.

"Don't worry, sir, your daughter will turn up."

Grace's voice is audible in the background again:

"Aaron, clean that blood off yourself."

"…"

"Sir?" the operator addresses him.

"Thank God," he says.

In the background the serious voice of someone who will later be identified as a police officer is heard:

"Are you the parents?"

Chapter 7
November 27, 2003
Five years after Kiera's disappearance

Hope emits the only light capable
of illuminating the darkest shadows.

M iren arrived at the police station dressed in a black skirt suit over a white blouse. Her brown hair was neatly tied back in a high ponytail and Aaron watched her from the waiting room as she walked decisively towards the reception desk and asked for him. The officer pointed towards where Aaron was waiting for her and, after signing a form, she turned and walked over to him, her expression serious.

"Shall we go?" she said in greeting.

They hadn't seen one another for a year, but she was not all that surprised to find him in this situation. At one stage, during the first years of the search for Kiera, she had met up with Aaron from time to time, and had watched his steady descent into the spiral of grief and hopelessness that consumed everything he touched. Over time, the demands of daily life and the fact that Miren started working as a journalist for the *Manhattan Press* made them less close and made their meetings more sporadic. The last time they'd seen each other was on the same date the year before, Kiera's birthday, when he appeared at the editorial office screaming and yelling about her and her broken promises.

"Thanks for coming, Miren… I didn't have anyone else to call."

"Sure. It's nothing. Don't mention it, Aaron. There's no need."

It was four in the afternoon and the traffic was starting to return to normal in the north of the city. The parade was over, the children's laughter had disappeared, and everyone had gone home hoping to have their Thanksgiving dinners ready on time. Miren gestured to her car, a champagne-colored Chevrolet Cavalier, which was parked in a space between two police cars. Miren got in first and waited for Aaron to join her inside.

"I'm sorry you have to see me like this," he said. He reeked of alcohol and looked terrible.

"Don't worry, it doesn't matter. I'm almost used to it," she said, annoyed.

"Today is Kiera's eighth birthday. I just… couldn't handle it."

"I know, Aaron."

"I couldn't cope with all this. The parade, her birthday, all on the same day. It brings up so many memories. So much guilt." He covered his face with his hands.

"You don't have to justify yourself, Aaron. Not to me."

"No… I want you to understand, Miren. The last time we saw each other I behaved like…"

"There's no need, Aaron. Just forget it. I know it's hard."

"How did your bosses take it?"

"Well, they weren't too happy. But you didn't leave them much choice. I guess nobody would like having the father of the most searched for girl in the United States appear in reception shouting that we invent everything we publish, because you know very well it's not true," she said, while he stared into space. His lip trembled, and so did his right hand, as if grief was randomly taking control of different parts of his body.

Miren started the car and began to head south in silence.

"Did it get you into any trouble?" Aaron continued.

"I was given an ultimatum. To leave Kiera's story alone because I would never get anywhere with it."

Aaron looked at Miren and, as if he'd been chewing it over for some time in preparation, said, "Kiera's disappearance has worked out well for you."

Miren stamped on the brake. She was already angry about having to go and get him, about having to see him drunk yet again, especially on this day, but that comment cut deep.

"How dare you say something like that, Aaron? You know I did everything I could. You know nobody has done more than I have to try and find your daughter. How could you...?"

"All I'm saying it that it's all worked out for you. Look at you... working for the *Press.*"

"Get out of my car," said Miren angrily.

"Aw, come on..."

"I said get out of my car!" she screamed.

"Miren... Please..."

"You listen to me, Aaron. Do you know how many times I've read the police report on Kiera? Do you know how many people I've interviewed in the last five years? Nobody has spent more time trying to find her than I have. Do you know how many opportunities I've turned down in my efforts to go that little bit further and find out what happened to her?"

Aaron realized he had touched a nerve.

"I'm sorry... Miren. It's just that I can't take it any more..." he faltered. "I can't.... Every year, when this day gets closer I say the same thing to myself. 'Come on Aaron, this year you're going to smile at least once on Thanksgiving. This year you're going to go and see Grace and remember what a great family you made.' I always tell myself this in the mirror when I get up, but thinking about her and everything I lost, about everything that could have been but never was, about every... every smile we lost, I can't bear it."

Miren watched him crying and clicked her tongue. However, after watching him like that for a few seconds she felt her anger subside.

"God dammit," she said, putting her hands back on the wheel and her foot on the accelerator.

"Will you take me back to my apartment? I need to sleep."

"I've spoken to Grace."

Now it was Aaron's turn to complain. "Why?"

"She's been trying to call you all day and you weren't picking up. Then she called me, to ask whether I knew where you were. She sounded bad. I guess today's emotional for her too, reopening all those old wounds."

Aaron studied Miren and noticed from her tone that she was more serious than he remembered. Her professional appearance and almost inexpressive gaze reinforced the impression he had always had of her: Miren was too cold.

"To be honest, when you called me, I picked up for her sake. I called her back to tell her where you were, and she asked me to take you to her house as soon as possible. It seemed urgent."

"I don't want to go," Aaron declared instantly.

"It's non-negotiable, Aaron. I promised her. I told her I would take you there in person."

"You're crazy if you think I'm going to go see my ex-wife on Kiera's birthday. It's the last day when I'm likely to want to spend time with her."

"I don't care. I have to take you. It will do you good. Both of you are having a hard time. Only you two can understand what each other is going through. Grace needs someone to look out for her, too. Things have been just as bad, or worse, for her and she doesn't go out and get drunk, and rant and rail against the world."

Aaron didn't answer and Miren took his silence as consent. She drove south from the 20th precinct police station on West

82nd Street, and soon arrived at the banks of the Hudson. She remained silent during the journey and Aaron looked with distaste out of the window at the city he loved so much. Before, there had been happy years of promotions at work, games in the garden of their home, touching Grace's stomach with anticipation before Michael's impending arrival. But all of it had vanished as that white balloon floated up into the clouds.

They soon entered the Battery Tunnel that passed under the river and connected Manhattan to Brooklyn. When they resurfaced, the traffic began to move more slowly, stopping at regular intervals at endless traffic lights. Aaron tried to start a conversation a couple of times, but Miren replied monosyllabically. From the outside she may have seemed angry to be wasting time with him on Thanksgiving, but in truth it was because of the barrier she had wanted to build between herself and Kiera's case. It had lodged deep inside her and now she couldn't get away from it.

When they arrived at Dyker Heights, a neighborhood of detached houses with their own gardens where the old Templeton family home was, Miren noticed that some of the neighbors were already putting up their Christmas decorations. A while later, after meandering through the streets a little, they could see Grace in the distance, waiting on the sidewalk and looking up and down the street. She seemed edgy.

"What's wrong with her?" Miren asked.

"I don't know," Aaron replied, confused. He'd never seen her like that before.

Grace was wearing a dark red dressing gown and slippers and her hair was a mess.

Bewildered, Aaron got out of the car and went over to her. "What's up, Grace?" he asked in a loud voice.

"Aaron… it's Kiera."

"What?"

"It's Kiera! She's alive!"

"What are you talking about?" Aaron demanded, struggling to understand his ex-wife.

"She's alive, Aaron. Kiera's alive!"

"What are you trying to say? What are you talking about?"

"About this!"

Grace held out her hand to reveal a VHS tape. Aaron had no idea what was going on, but when he looked at the tape more closely he saw the white sticker for the title. On it someone had written the number one in marker pen and beneath it, in capitals, was the most painful and hopeful word those parents could have read: *KIERA*.

Chapter 8
Miren Triggs
1998

She danced alone when she felt like it,
and she also shone brightly in
the night without trying.

I couldn't leave it at that. Schmoer's words disturbed me.
What could be hidden in that 911 call? Why did her parents
seem to be hiding something? In a matter of moments, the
search for Kiera Templeton began to awaken my curiosity
more than I first thought it would.

"You have to let me hear it," I begged, as though he would
easily give in.

"I can't, Miren. It's tomorrow morning's exclusive."

"What do you think I'm going to do, transcribe it and give
it to another paper or something? I'm a journalism student,
I don't know anyone in the profession other than you, and
they wouldn't pay me any attention anyway."

His look said it all. Then he replied, "I know you wouldn't,
but..."

I cut him off with a kiss. This time he went along with it.

He knew I was using him, but he didn't seem to let that
bother him. After what happened I had kept a strict distance

from men. I didn't want to get close to anybody under any circumstances. I'd built an unbreakable barrier around myself and I thought nobody else would be able to make me feel protected until one day, in a tutorial, we began to talk about that awful night as if it was something unrelated to me. He even managed to persuade me to write about it and, with time, I felt like he'd been the only one to treat me with the maturity I needed. My classmates were typical little macho guys and I saw Robert, whom I had decided to forget, in all of them. I noticed right from the start that Professor Schmoer's eyes kept wandering to me during class, and the consensus among the female student journalists was that he was the most attractive professor ever to grace a lecture hall at Columbia. You could sense his slim figure beneath the suits he always wore. His angelic good looks attracted all of us who imagined the fire under that veneer of innocence hidden behind his glasses. But the most attractive thing about him was his mind. There was a radical tone to his articles for the *Daily* which you could always identify with. He found the perfect critical focus in all his pieces and was a skilled writer whose sentences had a pace that absorbed you and drew you further in with every paragraph. Those in power were afraid of catching his sharp eye and politicians became nervous as soon as they saw him at a press conference, something which didn't often happen with politicians. His articles always focused on politics and business, and he tended to investigate stories from a distance, relying on archives, documents, accounts, and invoices. He would delve into the darker goings-on of the only two worlds that seemed to capture the country's attention—although they almost always seemed to go hand in hand—money and politics. Kiera's disappearance was going to change his world and define mine forever, although I didn't know it yet.

"Why are you doing this, Miren? I'm not sure... this is a good..."

"What happened has nothing to do with you, Jim. Don't be like the rest of the world. This has nothing to do with anybody else. Just me, and I decide how I feel, is that clear?"

"We haven't talked about what happened in a while and I don't think that pretending it didn't happen will make it go away."

"Why is the whole world so determined I should talk about it? Why the hell won't you let me decide how to deal with it myself?"

I turned round and went through the doorway of my building.

"Thanks for walking me home, Jim," I said ironically, angry.

"Miren, I didn't mean to...." He replied, bewildered, clicking his tongue and sighing.

I took the stairs two at a time, almost leaping, and disappeared from his sight when I reached the first floor landing. I could hear Jim shouting my name outside, but it was too late.

I went inside my apartment, tossed my white Converse toward the shoe-rack and disappeared into the darkness of my bedroom, unbuttoning my jeans as I went. I came back into the living room wearing my pajamas. It was always the first thing I did as soon as I arrived home: a small rental apartment in a suspect building in the most dangerous neighborhood in the city. It was a small windowless studio which had never been refurbished, had no lift, and not one single desirable feature. The kitchen was a two-ring hob that could only fit one frying pan because the burners were too close together. It was pretty much the worst apartment you could find in the Big Apple, and yet the rent was insane. As my parents put it, it looked like a hideout, and maybe I wasn't paying rent, but rather a ransom. The fact is that it was the only thing I could afford without blowing my entire college grant and what's more, it was near the campus.

The second thing I always did when I got home was the check-in call. After a few rings I heard my father pick up.

"Finally. We were about to call you. You're back a little late, aren't you?"

"Sorry, sorry. I know. I stayed on in the library working on something. Is Mom alright?"

"She's here, tearing her hair out. You need to call us earlier, OK? If you're going to be late, let us know. Your mother doesn't like you being out at this time of night."

"It's only half past nine, Dad."

"Yes, but that neighborhood…"

"It's the only one I can afford, Dad."

"You know we can help you out. We've saved up for it, and we'd really like to."

"You've already helped me out with the computer. I don't need anything more, honest. That's why I applied for a grant from the college."

I looked at the desk and saw the Bondi blue iMac my parents had given me. It had come out just a few weeks earlier and consisted of a monitor set in a turquoise blue translucent casing, a white keyboard and a round mouse that looked like it might start rolling at any moment. The best thing about it? It was seriously fast. It was easy to navigate and the sales assistant who sold it to me was really excited because he had seen the product presentation given by the founder of Apple himself. He spoke of him in such glowing terms, it was as if he'd met him in person. It hadn't taken long to get it up and running once I took it out of the box, and I'd spent a while setting up my email account and fiddling around with it until I was confident of how it worked.

"But that was only $1,300."

"$1,300 you haven't spent on yourselves."

He waited a few moments then said, "Your mother wants to speak to you."

"Fine."

She took the handset, and I could tell she was sad before she even opened her mouth. You can tell when your parents are unhappy just from their speech patterns.

"Miren," she said, "promise me you'll be careful. We don't like you staying out so late around there."

"Sure, Mom," I replied. I didn't want to upset her. She was taking things worse than me. We were more than six hundred miles apart: they were in Charlotte, North Carolina, I was in New York, and she couldn't keep an eye on what her daughter was doing or who she was going out with anymore. Her little girl had escaped from her shadow, and now she was trying to reach out her arms to make sure the sun never burned me.

"Why don't you buy yourself a cell phone? That way you can call us any time if you need something."

I sighed. I hated having to take so many precautions because of a handful of idiots who couldn't keep their flies zipped up.

"Sure, Mom," I agreed again without protest. "I'll buy one tomorrow."

In truth I wasn't all that keen on cell phones. Most of my classmates had become hooked on a game where a snake chased food round the screen and spent every break playing it. Then there were the ones who never stopped messaging all morning, paying no attention in class. It was easy to trace their interactions, who was joking around with whom, or falling in love via a 160-character message. One would type and, soon after, the other would laugh. Then the process would repeat in reverse. Nor did I like the feeling of being contactable all the time. I didn't see the need to be always available and ready to take calls when there were pay phones nearby. I felt like I would do just fine without one, but I had to give in to my mother so as not to upset her.

"I'll call you tomorrow and give you my number."

"I'm going to buy one too, that way you can call me whenever you want, honey," she said in a happier voice.

"Great. Goodnight, Mom."

"Goodnight, honey," she replied.

I hung up and sat at my desk. I took out the newspaper cuttings and saw Kiera's face looking at me expectantly. Her eyes seemed to be asking for help. I felt terrible. It looked like those parents would never see their daughter again and I felt hopeless. I picked up the phone again and, less than a minute after hanging up, I dialed my parents' number again. My mother answered, bewildered.

"Are you alright? Has something happened?"

"No. It's nothing, Mom. I just wanted to tell you I love you."

"We love you too, honey. Are you really alright? Just say the word, and we'll come and see you right now."

"No, really. That was all. I just wanted you to know. I'll be fine, OK?"

"You gave me a shock, honey. Let us know if you need anything, OK?"

"How about we see each other this weekend? I can get a flight and visit you in Charlotte."

"Seriously?"

"Yes. I'd really like that."

"Wonderful! I'll speak to Jeffrey's travel agent and book the flights tomorrow."

"Thanks, Mom."

"Thank you, honey. Speak to you tomorrow, darling."

"Catch you tomorrow, Mom."

I studied the phone, thinking about what I'd just done, but I had a lot of work to do. I sat back down at my desk and turned on the computer. While it was starting up, I started reviewing the reports I had gathered about Kiera's disappearance. In the *Daily*, the paper where Professor Schmoer worked, there was just a small column on page 12 that mentioned her and the limited progress that had been made in the search. The article also mentioned that, according to sources within the investigation, the FBI was about to take over the search for the girl to rule out the possibility of a kidnapping, but it didn't give much more information than that already contributed by other papers. As you read the article, you realized that they seemed to know much more than they were letting on but that they didn't want to share it, either out of caution or to avoid getting involved in the morbid curiosity and violence the case was likely to generate. Based on what Jim had told me, one of these further pieces of information was the additional 911 call made by the mother, Grace Templeton. But what I didn't know was that that was only the tip of the iceberg.

When the computer had finished starting up, I connected to the internet and skim-read the other pieces while I waited for the 56 kb modem to finish its connection symphony, an endless succession of buzzes and whistles in every possible frequency. When it was finally ready, I opened Netscape and typed in the address of the university's webmail provider. After logging in I saw that I only had one new message, an alert about a new internship available at an environmental magazine. I flagged it so I could answer it later and went back to the reports.

I spent two or three hours reading through them all, highlighting anything important and making a note of anything significant in a black Moleskine: "Herald Square", "well-off family", "father: manager at an insurance company", "Catholics", "happened at approx. 11.45am", "November 26", "rain", "Mary Poppins".

It struck me as ironic that Disney's perfect nanny should have been present at the moment a three-year-old girl disappeared. I underlined her name to remind myself to research who had been playing the character and what she was doing there. I went to the fridge for a Coca-Cola, the only thing I'd been having for dinner for several months. When I got back, I noticed that I'd received various new emails that stood out in bold. The first of those had "I'm Sorry" as the subject line, and the rest were simply numbered from two to six.

They were all from Professor Schmoer. He had sent them from his work email address, jschmoer@wallstreet-daily.com. I was surprised because he'd never written to me from that email address before. He wrote:

> Miren, I've attached everything we have on Kiera so far at the *Daily* to several emails. Promise me it won't leave your computer. I'm sure your eyes will see more in it than mine.
> Jim.
> Ps. Sorry for being a jerk.

The message was accompanied by an attachment named "Kiera1.rar". The following emails had no text and similar compressed files attached, and followed in numerical order. I opened the first file using UnRAR, which I was able to use as it was still in the free trial period, and I froze when I saw what it contained: two video files, dated November 26, with recordings from the security cameras in the area where Kiera Templeton disappeared.

Chapter 9
November 26, 1998

*The worst thing about fear isn't
the way it makes you freeze,
but the way it keeps its promises.*

Aaron followed a police officer through the crowd, which was beginning to disperse after the end of the parade. As he did so he could hear various sounds and updates over the radio, but he couldn't understand them because there was so much noise in the street. From time to time the officer would stop and check that Aaron was still behind him. After a few minutes the police officer turned onto 35th Street and stopped in a doorway where a group of officers was standing, looking worried.

"What's happening? Have they found her?" Aaron asked, visibly upset.

"Sir, you need to calm down, OK?" said Officer Mirton, a young, blond policeman about five foot eleven tall, who had raised the alarm following his discovery.

"How am I supposed to calm down? My three-year-old daughter is missing, and my wife is having a panic attack. I can't calm down!"

Aaron recognized this sentence in his head. He'd heard it so many times, spoken by people on the other side of his desk, that it seemed strange for him to be the one saying it. Aaron was the head of an insurance company office in Brooklyn and there had been countless occasions during his career when he'd been the one who'd had to ask the person in front of him to calm down while he confirmed that the company had just declined a policy or that the medical insurance they had taken out didn't cover some necessary treatment or other, the cost of which was unaffordable no matter what your salary. The expressions, the fear, and the desperation he saw in eyes of every shape and color in his office was the same that Aaron felt now that someone was asking him to keep calm. He found it impossible.

"Come on, sir. It's important that you focus and confirm a few details for us," said the police officer who'd brought him there.

"What?" He could barely listen. He felt overwhelmed.

The officers looked at one another as if deciding who would take the plunge.

The building they were standing in front of was an apartment block at number 225 West 35th Street, with a shop selling girls' dresses occupying the commercial property on the ground floor. The window display was full of child-size mannequins wearing dresses in every imaginable color, creating a rainbow effect that contrasted with how Aaron was feeling inside as he imagined his daughter wearing one of them. He even made an automatic mental note to tell Grace about the shop in case Kiera would like to dress up in something special for the Thanksgiving dinner they had planned at home later on.

"Follow me," said Officer Mirton in a serious voice, carefully pushing open the glass door of number 225.

Aaron followed and, once inside, he realized that there were more officers waiting for him in there, all crouching together in a corner.

"Are you the father?" one of them checked, getting up and reaching out to shake his hand.

"That's right. What's going on?"

"I'm Officer Arthur Alistair. Could you answer a few questions?"

"Ummm... yes. Sure. Whatever you need. But... could we go back to Herald Square? I'm afraid Kiera might be looking for us, but Grace and I aren't there. You see, my wife had a panic attack and I want to be nearby in case Kiera goes back there."

"Don't worry Mr.—" he waited for Aaron to provide his surname.

"Templeton."

"Templeton," he continued. "We've got officers combing the entire area around Herald Square. Rest assured, if your daughter turns up, she'll be safe. They'll let us know over the radio and everything will just have been a bad scare. Right now, we need you to help us with something."

Aaron nodded. "With what?"

"Could you describe your daughter's clothes for me again?"

"Yes... She was wearing a white down anorak and a pink sweatshirt. She was also wearing blue jeans and sneakers... I can't remember what color they were."

"Don't worry. You're doing very well."

The other officers crouching in the corner got up and stood aside. One of them headed for the exit and silently gave Aaron a couple of pats on the back as he passed.

"She has straight, dark hair, she normally wears it loose, but today she had two ponytails."

"Good. Very good," replied Officer Alistair.

"Is that why you brought me here?"

The officer waited a moment before continuing.

"Could you tell me whether the clothing over here in the corner belongs to your daughter?"

"What?!" Aaron yelled.

He took two steps towards where the police officers had been crouching a moment earlier and saw a little pile of clothing in which he immediately recognized Kiera's pink sweatshirt. The white anorak was there too, the one he had helped her put on so many times in recent weeks, after arguing with her every morning in between games because she never wanted to put it on before going out. Aaron felt the ground tremble beneath his feet and the air rush out of his lungs as he spotted locks of hair the same length as Kiera's on top of the pair of jeans he had felt against his shoulders just a short while earlier while they watched the parade together.

He cried out loudly. He shouted again, and then again, so many times that it seemed a single shriek, while the most intense pain he had ever felt catapulted him towards the depths of the darkest place imaginable.

"No!"

Chapter 10
November 27, 2003
Five years after Kiera's disappearance

A light which goes on will illuminate
your face, but also create
shadows in the corners of your soul.

Grace walked inside quickly, saying, "You have to see her, Aaron. She's alright. Our little girl. Kiera's alright."

Aaron and Miren followed her, completely stunned. They looked at each other as if poor Grace had crossed the line into madness.

"What are you talking about, Grace? What is that videotape?"

"It's our little girl. It's Kiera. She's alright. She's alright," she repeated in a whisper he could barely hear.

Aaron went inside and searched for his ex-wife, who seemed to have disappeared. Grace spoke again and he followed her voice.

"You need to see her. It's her, Aaron. It's Kiera."

A lump formed in Aaron's throat for the second time that day. He didn't like what was happening at all. His ex-wife was behaving in a very strange way. From the doorway he beckoned to Miren, who had stayed out by the mailbox, to come in.

She did as he asked but she still didn't understand what was happening.

"Grace, honey," Aaron said, going into the kitchen, where Grace had set up a television on a small stand with wheels that also housed a video player, "What's on that videotape? Our Christmas vacation? Is that it?"

Miren arrived in the kitchen and leaned against the door-frame in anticipation.

"I checked the mailbox today and this envelope was inside, Aaron. Someone left this tape of Kiera for us."

Miren interrupted, confused:

"A lead about Kiera? Is that what you're saying? A new recording from the security cameras? I've checked them all, over and over, frame by frame, second by second. The images from that day are all already in the police file, Grace. I checked all the streets and stores in the area. All the recordings from that day have been checked. There's... there's nothing else, Grace... The investigation hit a dead end."

"No," Grace said abruptly. "This is something else."

"What is it?" Miren asked again.

"It's Kiera," Grace murmured, her eyes opened wide in an expression Aaron would remember for the rest of his life.

The videotape was a 120-minute TDK with a white sticker perfectly positioned in the center, absolutely straight within the indent provided for fixing the label. On it was the word *KIERA* written in clear capital letters using a marker pen.

Grace put the videotape in the VCR and turned on the television. The screen immediately turned snowy, black and white flickers dancing in every direction. White noise came from the speakers of the gray Sanyo television and reminded Miren of an unforgettable horror movie she had seen once. Grace turned up the sound and Aaron looked at his ex-wife, not sure what to expect. Miren didn't like this business at all and was about to leave. She remembered the words of her boss, the legendary

Phil Marks, who had been responsible for the investigative journalism articles that covered the 1993 truck bomb attack on the World Trade Center, when he had urged her to stop working on Kiera's case:

"I know an investigative journalist's best qualities are tenacity and perseverance, Miren, but Kiera's case is going to end your career. Leave it alone. If you make a mistake, you will always be the journalist who messed up the case of the most famous missing girl in the United States. Don't be that person. I need you in the newsroom, catching corrupt businessmen, writing stories that change the world. You've already spent too much time on this."

The snowstorm continued swirling on the screen, crackling, filling areas that had been full of black spots a moment before with white ones and the white ones with black spots. Miren had once read in a pseudo-scientific magazine that the white snow that appeared on TV screens was, in part, the remains of the Big Bang and the origin of the universe. It said that the radiation from that time, in the form of microwaves, affected the cathode ray tube which created the image on the screen, resulting in those dancing sparks that the ghosts in eighties movies seemed to like so much. She watched the snowy screen, and thought of Kiera and what could have happened to her. That static yet moving image seemed to encourage sad thoughts, as if it were looking for the mind's most painful memories, and she understood why Grace was so upset. Miren was about to say something, but suddenly an image from the videotape replaced the snowstorm on the screen.

"Kiera?" Aaron gasped, stunned.

The image, recorded from a single viewpoint in one of the upper corners, showed a bedroom. Its walls were papered with a repeating pattern of orange flowers on a navy blue background. To one side was a single bed with an orange bedspread that matched the flowers on the walls. The fine curtains that covered a window in the center of the picture were motionless and it was evidently a clear, still day outside. But the most tragic thing, the thing that would make Aaron and Grace weep tears of joy, was hidden in the bottom right-hand corner beside a small doll's house: a dark-haired girl aged seven or eight, crouching down and playing with one of the dolls.

"It can't be," whispered Miren, her heart thumping in her chest, just as it had on the night that had changed her forever.

Chapter 11
October 12, 1997. New York. One year before Kiera's disappearance

Sometimes the darkest night lies in wait
after the brightest day.

When class finished Christine skipped over to Miren, who was still taking notes from the blackboard several minutes after their Public Archives professor had left.

"Miren, you have to come with me. There's a party at Tom's apartment and... I have an invite."

"A party?" Miren asked without much enthusiasm.

"Yes. You know what a party is, right?"

"Ha ha ha."

"Those things that college students have that... oh, wait, you're one of them," said Christine in a jokey tone, snatching the biro Miren was using to write with and putting the end in her mouth.

"You know I don't really like parties."

"Let me finish," Christine insisted. "Tom... asked if you're coming. He likes you. He really likes you."

Miren blushed pink and Christine saw her chance.

"You like him! You like him too!" she shrieked immediately, before lowering her voice so the others couldn't hear them.

"He's… cute."

"Cute? Are you saying that this guy…" Christine sat on the desk, on top of Miren's notes, and nodded towards Tom Collins, "… is cute?"

"Fine, he's okay-looking."

"Say it. Say it loud and clear that you'd hook up with him. Enough acting childish, Miren. You and I are both the same."

Miren smiled back at her. "I would never say something so gross," she said, sitting back, then adding, "I'd hook up with him and never even mention it to you."

Christine burst out laughing. "What are you going to wear to the party? We should meet up beforehand."

"Meet up?"

"You aren't really planning to go like that, in jeans and sneakers, are you? You know, meet up and get ready like normal girls do, Miren. You're a little… unusual."

"Unusual?"

"Look. I'll come round to your apartment later and bring some clothes. I bought some dresses at Urban Outfitters—you really should check out the brand, I just adore their stuff—and I'm sure they'll suit you. You're a small, right?"

"Um… there's really no need… I'm fine going like this, in jeans and a sweater."

"I'll be at your apartment at five," Christine added with a smile, ignoring Miren. "We'll get changed and go together. Deal?"

Miren smiled and Christine took it as a yes.

Classes finished for the day and Miren went home to pass the time. She took a shower and spent a while playing with her hair in front of the mirror, not sure how to style it. She had dark hair which, when loose, reached halfway down her back. Her eyes betrayed a mass of different insecurities, the fruit of years spent being ignored at high school in Charlotte. She'd always been considered a nerd there, the goody-goody, the teacher's pet, the girl nobody wanted to be friends with. When she got her place at Columbia, she had made an effort to be more open to try and fit in, but in a city with a very different rhythm to her own she was finding it difficult to come out of her shell. The year had passed quickly and, just like at high school, the only people with whom she built any kind of relationship were her teachers. Christine, who'd sat next to her since the first day of college, seemed to be the perfect counterpoint. They were very different to one another and perhaps that was the very reason they'd clicked. The other students saw Miren as the smart one who always had the right answer. Christine never answered in class and didn't take her assignments seriously, but stuck close to Miren with the simple goal of finding out what she needed to do at any given moment, even though she always wound up taking the easy option. If they had to write an article, Miren would choose a specific piece of news or a place and would build her article around it, using examples and points of discussion that left her readers wanting to know more. Christine, on the other hand, would complete her assignments with minimal effort and without getting her hands dirty, reporting events in a superficial manner without going beyond the basic facts. They were two very different approaches to journalism, but also to anything important. If you wanted to achieve something in life, there were two approaches: get stuck in up to your neck in order to emerge triumphant from the mud, or skirt around the puddle so as not to have to wash your clothes later.

The bell rang and Miren rushed to the door.

"Ready to become a cute chick?" Christine asked in greeting. Miren laughed.

"Come on in," she replied with a smile.

Christine had a suitcase in her hand which she tossed onto the couch and opened straight away, revealing a bundle of clothes covered in sequins, glitter, prints and leather.

"Do you have any music?" asked Christine, looking around.

"I have an Alanis Morissette CD that was already in the apartment when I moved in."

"What kind of shit do you listen to? Well, it doesn't matter. Put it on. Tonight, my little bumpkin is going to hook up with Tom."

Miren didn't know how to interpret the fact that Christine considered this a done deal. To tell the truth, the whole idea was starting to make her nervous. So much so that she didn't answer and just went along with it.

They spent an hour trying on dresses, giggling as they put on lipstick and singing *Walking on Sunshine* without any accompaniment for their tuneless screeching. Before Miren knew what was happening, Christine had grabbed her waist from behind and she was looking at herself in the mirror, surprised at the change she saw. She had never worn so much make up; she didn't like to, she believed that hiding behind war paint was a symbol of weakness, a way of hiding behind a mask and not being your true self.

"Check you out, Miren. You're stunning!" whispered Christine.

Miren swept her hair to one side, revealing her face, confused and surprised to see herself like that. She was wearing an orange strapless dress that stopped halfway down her thighs. She noticed the eyeshadow Christine had applied with the skill of someone who had been wearing make up for years and was surprised by the result. She saw herself as attractive for the first time ever. But then her shy side came out in a single sentence:

"I don't like wearing so much make up... I don't feel... comfortable."

"For God's sake, Miren, I've only put on a little lipstick and eyeshadow. You don't need anything else. It's just... a touch of glamor."

"A touch of glamor..." Miren repeated uncertainly in a low voice.

"A touch of fucking glamor!" crowed Christine, euphoric, with a whoop that sounded like a battle cry. Then she started to hum a song that Miren had never heard before in her life.

They set off together around seven and walked for a while until they reached a building on West 139th Street made up of modern apartments with views of the Hudson. They found some of their classmates smoking in the doorway holding cups full of some kind of liquor. A guy leant out of one of the windows and yelled that somebody with a name Miren couldn't hear had accepted a ridiculous dare. As they went upstairs together a drunk guy who neither of them recognized breathed into Miren's ear as he said something she chose to ignore.

"Is it always like this?"

"What?"

"The feeling of being checked out."

"Isn't it great?" Christine replied.

Miren looked at her, incredulous.

Once they reached the party it didn't take long for Christine to go and say hi to people Miren didn't recognize. It really wasn't hard. Miren didn't know a single person there. She looked all around her and only saw girls in the year above hers flirting with boys in the year above them. She sighed. She couldn't see Tom, the host, either, although she could hear his deep, enthusiastic laugh, which seemed to fill the apartment despite the fact the music was playing louder than any neighbor was likely to tolerate. Miren sat down by herself on a bench in the kitchen and pretended to be busy with some glasses every time somebody came over to get another drink or put more ice in the one they already had.

A dark, clean shaven boy came over and offered her a drink with a smile so wide it almost reached his ears.

"Don't tell me. It's Miren, right?"

"Er... yes," she replied. It was reassuring to have a conversation with someone. She didn't feel so alone. "Christine sent you over to speak to me, right?"

"I've no idea who Christine is," he replied with a smile.

"Let me guess, you're one of Tom's friends. One of his crew," Miren said.

"Ooh, someone's observant. Nearly, but not quite."

"We're all friends of Tom's here. Who isn't? He's popular and the one all the girls want to… well, you know."

"Well, I met him by chance."

"How come?"

"Well, I was driving along the street and I knocked him over. We've been friends ever since."

"Seriously?" Miren asked, her eyes wide with incredulity.

"No, not really," he replied immediately, smiling again. "I've no idea who Tom is. I came because my friends invited me."

Miren burst out laughing. Then, knowing where things were heading, she looked around and couldn't spot either Tom or Christine.

"It's not a bad party," Miren said, trying to break the three-second silence.

"No, it's not. A toast to good parties?"

That empty cliche flicked a switch in Miren's head. She had been about to say goodbye.

"I don't think I'm going to stay that long. I don't normally…"

"Have fun?" he asked, confused, raising his eyebrows and causing his forehead to wrinkle in a way that only made him more attractive.

"I don't normally drink much," Miren replied. "I usually prefer to read or hang out at home."

"Tell me about it. I study comparative literature. I spend every day reading and re-reading the classics. But one thing doesn't cancel out the other. I like to have fun. Just as much as I like Bukowski or… well, all writers."

"You mean you don't even study journalism?" Miren looked at him, surprised, happy he'd mentioned the name of one of her favorite authors, and added, "Find what you love and let it kill you."

"Bukowski also said, 'Some people never go crazy. What truly horrible lives they must lead,'" he said, smiling. "I'm Robert," he continued, clinking his glass against Miren's, which he had set down on the kitchen counter.

"I'm Miren. Nice to meet you," she replied, smiling and picking up the glass.

Chapter 12
Miren Triggs
1998

*Creativity is hidden in routine and
it is only when you've had
enough that it escapes
in a spark that changes everything.*

I started to explore the files attached to the emails Professor
Schmoer had sent me. I discovered that there weren't just
videos, but also documents: the statement made by Aaron
Templeton, Kiera's father, and the recording of the 911 call. It
seemed like part of the official police file, or at least what the
Daily had been able to get hold of.

The files were named in a code I quickly worked out, which
used the street, the number and the time at which the recording
began. For example, the first was BRDWY_36_1139.avi. No
doubt it referred to the corner of Broadway and 36th Street near
Herald Square and the end of the Thanksgiving parade. Another was called 35W_100_1210.avi, referring to West 35th Street
and number 100. And so on, for eleven different videos.

I opened the first without really knowing what to expect or
what to look for. According to what I'd read, Kiera had disappeared at around 11.45 am near the junction of Broadway and

36th Street, so if the numbering of the file was correct, whatever it was that had happened was due to take place a few minutes later.

The first thing I saw was umbrellas. Hundreds of them, everywhere. I didn't remember it raining that day, but that detail seriously complicated what the security cameras were able to record.

The video was recorded by a camera positioned several feet above the umbrellas awaiting the parade. The image was of a compact layer of them, like a blanket of bright colors, shimmering and swaying from one still to the next while, a little further away, you could just make out the gingerbread men trooping down the middle of the street. On the far side of the parade, people dressed in waterproofs stood under umbrellas, waiting behind a metal barrier. Above them I recognized the Haier Building on the other side of the sidewalk and was easily able to recognize where in the city this was. The camera had recorded the scene by taking a photo every two seconds, so there were long gaps from one photo to the next.

In the middle of the image a motionless light-colored umbrella stood out, surrounded by various black ones, in the area near the camera. I skipped the video forward a few times, certain the entire recording would be the same. I discovered that the only thing that changed was the composition of the carpet of umbrellas and that the gingerbread men gradually became majorettes. I looked for the Mary Poppins who was giving out balloons on the corner of 36th Street, but the camera didn't cover that area.

I noticed that a majorette had approached the barrier nearest the camera and stopped there for a few frames, as if greeting the person carrying the white umbrella. I watched six full minutes of the recording, trying to deduce more than what the camera showed: gestures, changes in the positions of the umbrellas, the speed at which they moved, but nothing noteworthy happened.

Then a man suddenly ran through them towards the place where the majorette had stopped a few minutes earlier. The umbrella disappeared, I suppose it must have fallen to the ground in the seconds that elapsed between one photo and the next, and I saw the face of Grace Templeton, Kiera's mother.

The quality of the photo wasn't particularly good, but I could discern an expression of disbelief. In the next still, Grace's expression was one of complete terror. Aaron Templeton appeared by her side, and I had the impression he was telling her something. Next, they appeared again several feet to the right, between two green umbrellas, and then they disappeared out of shot.

It was like a blow to the stomach. I couldn't imagine what they were feeling in that moment. Afterwards, I reviewed those seconds again in case I'd missed something, but I didn't discover anything new.

I opened a PDF document and discovered that it was part of a medical admissions form for Bellevue Hospital Center with Grace Templeton's details. It looked like she had experienced a severe anxiety attack and been taken there by ambulance. Time of admission was recorded as 12.50pm, so it must have been shortly after Kiera disappeared. It included her social security number, her address in Dyker Heights, and the phone number of her next of kin: Aaron Templeton.

I made a note of the names of the other video files and searched my apartment for a map of the city that I knew I had put away somewhere. When I finally found it, I marked on it the exact points where the security cameras had been recording. I didn't know why they had focused so much on 35th Street, which seemed to feature in a dozen recordings from different points along the street from the minutes just before and after the disappearance. Everything seemed to suggest that the investigation was focusing on that area, so I circled the entire street on the map.

Another document attached to one of the emails caught my eye. It was a JPG file, and it took me a couple of seconds to identify the image once it was open.

It was a photograph of a small pile of clothing thrown onto a beige marble floor. Small locks of dark hair were visible on top of it. I found the image disturbing. Could they have found a body but not yet informed the press? Was there something else in the investigation that hadn't yet come to light? In those days, the desire for the morbid details of cases was much less than it is nowadays. The information released was always the most appropriate and relevant to help, although that seemed about to change for good. Kiera's case was going to be the foundation stone on which the journalism of the following years would be based, and the *Press* had started it all with that day's front cover, which lay next to my computer. From time to time, I would glance at Kiera, who seemed to watch me, whispering:

"You're not going to find me."

I spent the next few hours opening video files and analyzing what I saw in the images, but I didn't manage to find anything relevant. The truth is that what I had wasn't much use in terms of finding a clue or anything concrete. It was as if the items Professor Schmoer had given me were chosen to distract my attention, or as if the person within the police who had given that package of information to the *Daily* was saving the bombshell for later.

I looked at my watch and realized it was almost three in the morning. I'd crossed out and discarded the points on the map where the cameras didn't seem to offer any clues. I'd already watched the clips of the recordings from the two delis in which you could see people pass in front of the store but nothing more. I'd also seen one from inside a grocery store where nothing relevant happened, and one from a Pronto Pizza that had just opened on the corner of Broadway and 36th Street.

84

One of the video files had a slightly different format. It was called CAM_4_34_PENN.avi and I couldn't work out what the title was referring to until I opened it. I took a few seconds to process the image: it moved more smoothly than the previous videos, but the quality was much worse. The lens seemed to be dirty, which cast a blurry fog over the image which was difficult to see through. In the shot a subway station platform was visible in black and white with various people waiting for the train to arrive. The video was only two minutes forty-five seconds long and I didn't expect to find anything relevant in such a short recording. A woman in a Santa hat was waiting by one of the iron columns, a couple of men dressed in suits were chatting in the background, and a tramp was slumped against a bench three pillars further along than the woman. Various other groups were waiting for the train, but in the top part of the image the camera only captured their legs.

Soon the train arrived, making the camera shake as it braked. While it pulled in, a middle-aged couple with a little boy dressed in white trousers and a dark jacket also appeared in shot and I counted a total of sixteen people leaving the carriage that was framed in the center of the image. Then the family, the woman, and the two men in suits all got on. The train left the station, the people disappeared and only the tramp was left, staring into space as if nothing had happened.

Chapter 13
November 26, 1998

It's only when you lose a piece
that you realize the puzzle
doesn't make sense anymore.

Aaron spent the next few hours walking all over the area, looking everywhere and nowhere at the same time. Each time he came across a family travelling with a small child he would hurry over, trying to find Kiera's gaze in the child's eyes. Several witnesses later told the police that they had seen a desperate Aaron yelling over and over, while the entire city seemed to ignore him. The members of the New York Police Department were also searching every corner of the city, dropping to the ground to look under vehicles, opening doors in the hope of finding Kiera abandoned on a landing. But as the hours passed and night fell over the city, the lamps and lights came on one by one in stark contrast to the darkness in Aaron's heart. His voice was no longer capable of more than a hoarse whisper.

The police found Aaron at the junction of 42nd Street and Seventh Avenue at one in the morning, slumped by a fire hydrant, weeping uncontrollably. He didn't know where else to look. Jogging and yelling, he had covered the area east to west from 28th Street to 42nd Street. During the search, he had kept going back to the corner of 36th Street, the place where it had all happened. He had checked in the local parks, he had hollered Kiera's name into the entrances of the subway, he had begged a god in whom he didn't believe for mercy and made pacts with demons that didn't exist. Nothing had worked, as always happens in the real world, where lives are cut short, and your dreams can turn on you without warning.

A CBS reporter who had intercepted the police radio frequency and heard the general alert about Kiera while packing away the camera set up to film the Macy's parade had filmed a distraught Aaron running this way and that. The clip was used the next day to open the morning news bulletin, on which a female newscaster would read in a mechanical and detached voice: "The search continues for Kiera Templeton, aged three, who disappeared yesterday during the Thanksgiving Day parade in central Manhattan. If you've seen her or have any relevant information, please contact the AMBER alert service for disappeared minors using the number displayed at the bottom of the screen". Immediately afterwards, without changing her expression or tone of voice, she would go on to speak about a traffic jam on the Brooklyn Bridge due to roadworks on the other side of the East River. At that moment, teams from every media outlet in the city would start looking for images of the distraught father, setting the machinery of sensationalism in motion.

As the police officer helped him to his feet Aaron looked at his phone, which was ringing loudly. He saw various missed calls from an unknown number.

"Yes?"

"I'm calling from Bellevue Hospital. We had to transfer your wife here to monitor her anxiety levels. She's been stable for the last few hours and is asking us to discharge her. Sir? Can you hear me?"

Aaron had stopped listening after the first sentence. Standing in front of him was the police officer who had shown him Kiera's clothing in the lobby of 225 West 35th Street and, although Aaron had forgotten his name, his face with its serious and sad expression took away all his remaining hope.

He wept.

He continued to do so while several police officers led him away and put him in a car with its sirens on. The officers had offered to take him to the hospital to be reunited with his wife and had promised that all available units would be combing the area and continuing the search for Kiera. On the way to the hospital, Aaron couldn't think of a word to say and instead studied the shadows on the street in search of his daughter, who he dreamed of seeing at every crossroads. When they arrived, the officers silently led him through the hospital to where Grace was waiting on the opposite side of a corridor with white floor and walls, standing seriously until the moment she saw and understood that Kiera was not walking alongside her husband. Grace ran towards him shouting, "My baby, my baby!" The echoes of her screams reverberated through the whole building as only the very worst news can. The shrieks of that mother would be forever etched in the memories of the patients and the nurses and doctors who had treated her, and they understood that for those parents, their pain was the purest and most tragic they had experienced in their lives. They were used to death there, used to fighting illnesses, and used to witnessing the slow decline that gradually extinguished a person's life, but they never got used to that inconsolable wailing, to seeing how parents went from being so full of hope to having none left. When she reached Aaron, Grace thumped his chest over and over again, and he absorbed the blows without feeling any pain, because he already felt dead, as though he'd drowned in the depths of himself. He waited wordlessly with tears pouring down his face while Grace shouted and blamed him until she ran out of breath.

When Agent Alistair shook his head, Aaron interpreted it as the most painful encrypted message he could possibly have received.

Chapter 14
November 27, 2003
Five years since Kiera's disappearance

Often, all hope needs to provide
is a little straw for you to grasp.

Grace, Aaron and Miren waited impatiently for Agent Benjamin Miller, who had been in charge of the investigation in 1998 when Kiera disappeared. He finally arrived two hours after Aaron had made several calls to the only number he had for him. It had been answered by a secretary who kept Aaron on hold for several minutes listening to frustrating hold music, only to cut him off without putting him through to anyone. It wasn't until the fifth time Aaron called that the secretary finally listened properly to the words he was saying:

"It's Kiera! She's alive! You have to put me through to Agent Miller, please! Kiera's alright!"

"What did you say?"

"My daughter, Kiera Templeton, is alive!" Aaron repeated, yelling into the telephone.

"Look, Mr. Templeton... we can't review her case right now... there's nothing new and Agent Miller was very clear that we shouldn't put any more of your calls through until there were additional leads. You ring us on Thanksgiving ev-

ery year about something. You ought to get some professional help."

"You don't understand... Kiera is alive! We've seen her! On
a video! They sent us a videotape of her. She's alive!"

The secretary didn't answer for a few seconds, then added
a brief: "One moment, please."

Seconds later a low voice came on the line, which was
breaking up. "Mr. Templeton? Is that you?"

"Agent Miller, thank God! You have to come. Someone left
a package at the house containing a videotape. Kiera's on it."

"A new recording from a security camera? We have several
from the moments immediately after she disappeared and none
of them showed anything conclusive."

"No. It's not a recording from the street. It's in a house.
And it's Kiera. Now. Aged eight. Playing in a bedroom."

"What did you say?"

"Kiera is alive, Agent Miller. She didn't die. Kiera's alive!"
Aaron shouted, euphoric.

"Are you sure of what you're saying?" Miller was cautious.

"It's her, Agent Miller. I'm one hundred percent certain."

"Does your wife agree? Does she think it's her?"

"You have to see for yourself."

"I'm on my way. Wait there and don't touch the tape again.
There could be... something else on there."

While they waited Grace kept smiling and weeping with
happiness at having seen Kiera playing peacefully in the bedroom. Aaron sat at the kitchen table, gazing into space. From
time to time his emotions would rise to the surface in a happy
sob. But that image of Kiera left Miren shocked and silent. She
had spent so long analyzing leads, interviewing people and reviewing a police file more than two thousand pages long without finding anything, that the simple image of the girl playing
was almost too much to handle.

In the recording, scarcely a minute long, an older Kiera played with a doll in a wooden house before getting up and leaving the doll on the bed. A few seconds later, after hesitating for a few moments, you could see her walking towards the door and putting her ear against it. She was wearing an orange knee-length dress. Then the image seemed to be frozen, but the timer continued to count. After 35 seconds, Kiera stopped listening at the door as if it had been in vain and trotted over to the window. The she moved the sheer curtain aside and looked outside with her back to the camera.

Just as the timer hit 57 seconds, Kiera went back to the bed and, for a couple of frames, looked at the camera with a blank expression. Before she could pick up the doll she had left on the mattress, the VCR ejected the tape and the screen filled with the snow that would soon flood the Templeton family's world with white noise.

"Are you absolutely sure it's her?" asked Miren, despite already knowing the answer. She had seen hundreds of photos of Kiera in different family albums, and in truth, the resemblance was undeniable even considering the difference age had made to her appearance since she disappeared aged three years old.

"It's Kiera, Miren. Can't you tell? Look at her face... God... I would recognize my daughter even after 50 years. It's our daughter!"

"I'm only saying that the quality of the recording is not that good. Perhaps we ought to..."

"It's her! Got it?!" Grace interrupted angrily.

Miren nodded as if it had nothing to do with her and went to wait outside. She lit a cigarette and realized that night had already fallen. She took her cell phone out of her jacket pocket and called the newsroom to apologize for not returning in time to finish the article she had been working on.

She looked at the rest of the houses on the street and noted that several families were hanging strings of Christmas lights from the eaves of their houses. She thought it must be hard for the Templetons to see how Christmas, with its excess of happiness and gatherings of loved ones, surrounded and besieged them like that, thousands of tiny lightbulbs unwittingly highlighting the only home that didn't have them up. In an illuminated world, an area of shadow is a signal. The Templetons' house was the only one in street that didn't go in for that crazy waste of electricity and was also clearly the one that spent least on garden maintenance. The lawn was dry with bald patches of earth all over it. She remembered the first time she'd visited the house, not long after beginning her own investigation into Kiera's disappearance, and how the immaculate state of the lawn was the first thing she'd noticed. She remembered the feeling of being in a home belonging to a comfortably well-off family, with a nice car parked in the driveway and a mailbox with a little flag to complete the picture of the perfect family. Now all that had disappeared in a puff of smoke, and pain had permeated every corner of that family's life, staining not just the façade, garden and windows with gray, but also the souls of everyone who set foot inside those four walls.

A while later a gray Pontiac with its headlights on appeared at the end of the street, and a man in his fifties wearing a suit, a green tie, and a gray coat got out of the car.

"Well, am I glad to see you again!" said Agent Miller in greeting.

She raised her eyebrows in reply and threw her cigarette butt on the ground.

"Is it genuine?" asked the FBI agent before going in.

"Looks like it," Miren replied dryly.

Aaron came out to meet and welcome him.

"Thank you for coming, Agent Miller," he said, his voice desperate.

"My wife is waiting for me with the turkey in the oven. I hope this is important," said Miller, trying to justify the fact he didn't expect to be there long.

Grace was in the kitchen, her eyes red from crying. They went into the house and Miller greeted her with a hug.

"How are you doing, Mrs. Templeton?"

"You have to watch the videotape, Agent Miller. It's Kiera. She's alive!"

"Who gave you this video?"

"It was in the mailbox, in this envelope," Grace pointed towards the padded envelope lying on the table and Miller studied it without touching it, reading the number one written on it in marker pen.

"Have you touched it?"

Grace nodded and covered her mouth with her hands.

"Where's the videotape?"

"In the VCR."

The cassette stuck out half an inch from the VCR slot, showing the black edge, which normally bore the sticker with the title. On the screen, the snow danced, reflecting in everyone's eyes.

Miller took a biro from his breast pocket and pushed the cassette into the machine. Grace crouched down beside him and pushed a button to rewind the tape. A few seconds later there was a click and eight-year-old Kiera reappeared on the screen again, innocent, playing with her doll, leaving her on the bed, listening at the door, looking out of the window. When she turned towards the camera, the picture stopped, and the VCR ejected the cassette as if nothing had happened.

"Is it her?" Agent Miller asked, concerned, "Do you definitely recognize her?"

Grace nodded, trembling. Her eyes were full of tears which were ready to break the tension and roll down her face once more.

"Are you sure?"

"Completely sure. It's Kiera."

Miller sighed and sat down. After wrestling with himself for a few seconds he went on: "You can't publish this." He said it in the direction of Miren who was waiting in the kitchen doorway. "This can't turn into the same kind of circus as before."

"You have my word," she replied. "But only if you reopen the case."

"Reopen it? We still don't know what this is. It's just a recording of a girl who... if we're honest, could be any little girl with a passing resemblance to your daughter."

"Are you serious?"

"I can't mobilize resources because of this, Mr. Templeton. It's all very vague. A videotape that appears out of nowhere five years later... It's all so tenuous that the FBI won't grant me approval. Do you know how many children disappear each year? Do you know how many active cases we have?"

"What would you do if it were your daughter, Agent Miller? Tell me, what would you do?" Aaron demanded, raising his voice. "Tell me. If some low-life had carried off your three-year-old daughter and you received a video of her on her birthday, playing as if nothing had happened, how would you feel? If someone had snatched away what you love most in the world and, years later, they taunted you by showing how happy she was without you?"

Agent Miller was unable to reply.

"All we have is this recording and your word that this is your daughter. It will be a real fight to convince my superiors. I can't promise anything."

"It's Kiera... Miller," Miren said. "You know perfectly well that it is."

"How can you be so sure?"

"Because when I wake up in the morning, the first thing I see is her face."

Chapter 15
Miren Triggs
1998

*The truth is more elusive than
deceit, but it hits you harder
when you let your guard down.*

The next morning the alarm clock went off earlier than my body needed. I had gone to bed late after reviewing the files Professor Schmoer had sent me and my breakfast was a vanilla latte I bought from Starbucks. Afterwards, I went to a cell phone store and used my card to pay for a black Nokia 5110, which seemed to be the model everybody else had, and a package that included fifty messages and sixty minutes of calls for free. Then I walked to the courthouse under the bright city sun. It was a beautiful day and when I arrived a friendly police officer asked me to leave my new cell phone in a drawer at the entrance so I could enter the building.

"Cell phones are not allowed in here," he told me, separating me from my new point of contact with the rest of the world after only fifteen minutes.

"Do you have the file I requested a couple of weeks ago?" I asked the legal secretary, who cursed as soon as she saw me. She was an African American woman in her forties who looked exactly like the mother of Steve Urkel on *Family Matters*.

"You again?"

"It's a right, did you know that? Megan's Law obliges the authorities to publish a list of all sexual offenders in the state, with information about their address and an up-to-date photo."

"We still don't have the website set up. You know. The internet. That thing everyone's always talking about."

"That's exactly what you told me two weeks ago. You can't deny me my rights. It's a federal law, did you know that?"

"We're working on it. I promise. It's just that there are a lot of records."

"Really that many?"

"You have no idea," she said, gesticulating with her hand.

"Could I take a look at the records themselves?"

"At the sexual offender records? You've got to be joking."

"What part of 'made public' do you not understand?"

"Alright, fine. Let me check," she eventually gave in. "Wait here please."

The legal secretary disappeared down a corridor and returned a while later. While I was waiting for her, I went back to the entrance for my phone and called my mother to give her the new number. She didn't answer, so I left it there again and went back to the secretary.

"Miss? Come with me please. I'll take you to the archives."

I followed her for a few minutes until we reached the basement of the court building. A man dressed in a short-sleeved shirt and tie who was reading the paper received us as though he was surprised to see any visitors down there.

"Hi Paul. How's your day going? I've brought you a girl who, well... she's here because of Megan's Law."

"Sexual offenders? We're up to our necks in that. We're digitalizing the archive but... there are thirty years' worth of sexual assaults to deal with. It's a mountain of work."

I raised my hand and gave a fake smile.

"Let's see... sign here and here," he said. "It's a document that promises you won't use the information you gather for the purposes of harassment, persecution or to take the law into your own hands, and that you are aware of the penalties should you do so."

"Of course," I replied. "Makes absolute sense. They may be criminals, but they still have their rights, y'know?"

Paul led me down a yellow-tiled corridor lit by fluorescent strip lights and stopped in front of a door.

"This section here is everything we're digitalizing. Assailants from category one through three," he said, before opening the door to reveal a gigantic maze of metal shelves full of cardboard boxes. "There'll be a little less information available on the internet, but this is what we're working with right now," he continued. "Perhaps we'll have it all finished and summarized in a couple of years but... well, Christmas is coming... and who wants to type files into a computer."

"All this? You're joking, right?"

He shook his head, his lips pursed. "You'll find files from the seventies up to the start of the eighties on those three shelves. And, well, the other two are in blocks of five years. As you can see, it's all pretty intuitive. The boxes with yellow stickers contain the Level 3 files: the most dangerous offenders. Rapists, murderers, serial pedophiles. The rest... stalkers and lower level abusers."

I swallowed.

A couple of years ago, Megan Kanka, an eight-year-old girl, had been raped and murdered by her neighbor, a repeat-offending pedophile. Megan's parents argued that had they known that their neighbor was a dangerous sexual predator, they wouldn't have let her play alone near his home. The case shocked the entire country deeply and a federal law was quickly passed, although not without controversy, that obliged the state authorities to make public a list of freed sexual offenders along with their photos, current addresses and victim profiles with the objective of informing the population if one of their neighbors was a potential sexual assailant. It was all about knowing who you had living around your house. But in New York the implementation of the law was still in its infancy, and it would take some time for this public, easily accessible register to become a reality. Instead, I had this room full of files to waste hours looking through.

"I'll be at the desk outside. Let me know if you need anything else."

Paul closed the door and left me alone there, surrounded by those folders that reeked of sexual violence.

I grabbed the first box and was surprised by how heavy it was. There must have been at least two hundred yellow cardboard files inside. I took out the first record and instantly felt sick. The photo in the top right hand corner was of a white man in his sixties with three days of stubble and a blank stare. The record was a simple form with fields that had been filled out by hand. My eyes immediately skipped to the box entitled "convicted of": sexual abuse of a six-year-old minor.

I closed the file and moved onto the next one. It wasn't what I was looking for, and I chose not to spend my time on thinking about what I'd like to do to that son of a bitch. I spent several hours moving from one archive box to the next, glancing at the photos and reading what I found. The country was foul. Well, the men were foul. After over five hundred records, I had only come across six women. Of course, what those six women had done disgusted me as much as the atrocities committed by the men, but it was obvious that sexual assaults were a predominantly male crime. Some of them had accumulated a progressive history of offenses: a groping, a more serious sexual assault, a rape, a rape and a murder. Others exhibited repetitive behavior that appeared pathological: an unhealthy obsession with a specific type of girl, with a certain kind of hair, always the same height and within a similar age range, growing worse with time, repeating after their release, having served jail time for the original crimes committed twenty or thirty years earlier. But the ones that shocked me most, and which constituted the majority, were those where the victim and perpetrator belonged to the same family. The records included a profile of the abusers' victims and it wasn't uncommon to read the term "immediate or close family member" among the descriptions.

"Bastards," I said aloud.

I went out to ask Paul how late I could stay. The task ahead was going to take me a lot longer than I'd anticipated. He told me that I was welcome to stay until six in the evening. I decided to eat something somewhere near the courthouse and then come back, and while I was waiting for my food, I called the second of the two cell phone numbers I knew by heart.

"Who is it?" asked Professor Schmoer.

"Professor Schmoer? Can you hear me? It's Miren."

"Miren. Were you able to take a look at what I sent you?"

"Yes... well, not all of it. But... thank you."

"I think the more people that get to see this... the better. And I think your input will be invaluable. I know you're different. This might not be over after all."

"Thanks, Professor. Over?"

"Where are you calling from? The connection's not great."

"From my new cell phone."

"Well, the connection's terrible."

"Great. It cost me more than two hundred dollars. I love throwing money away."

He paused, serious. "I guess you're calling me about the news."

"I haven't seen today's papers yet. Did you publish the 911 call?"

"Yes... but nobody's read the article."

"What?!"

"Nobody's read it. The call doesn't matter, Miren. Nobody's interested in it anymore," said Professor Schmoer, with the sound of cars in the background. He must have been in the street. "It's yesterday's news. The *Press*... well, I'm sorry, haven't you heard? What planet are you on?"

"I've been at the courthouse dealing with something personal," I replied, trying to explain myself.

"Personal? What about? Are you involved in a case? Have they caught whoever was responsible for... that? You could have told me. You know I would have gone with you."

"No, no. I'm looking through the archives myself."

Professor Schmoer sighed and then added in a kind of reprimand, "Fine... If you need help with it, let me know, OK, Miren?"

"Sure. I'm alright for now, honestly," I lied.

"Fine. Have you really not heard?"

"Heard what?"

"Take a look at today's *Press*. It's incredible. I don't know how they do it, but..."

"What's going on?" I felt nervous. All this suspense was killing me.

"Read the front page of the *Press* and then call me," he hung up.

"What's happened?" I asked, just before realizing he was no longer on the line.

I asked the waiter if they had a copy of that day's *Manhattan Press*, but he said no. Before I put my phone down I called my parents again, but nobody answered. What was Professor Schmoer talking about?

I waited for my food, spaghetti carbonara that cost just $7.95 and came with a free drink, then wolfed it down so I could get hold of a paper quickly. The restaurant was shabby, with mirror-covered walls and clientele that was mainly made up of criminals and their families who'd spent their morning at the courthouse. I looked at the wall next to where I was sitting and saw Kiera's face in the reflection of the television. I looked the other way, but I couldn't work out where the screen really was in that maze of mirrors.

"Could you turn the volume up?" I asked the waiter.

After a few seconds Kiera's face disappeared and was replaced by that of a grim-faced white man in his fifties with graying hair. I'd never heard of him before, but I read the headline that accompanied the image, running from right to left across the screen: "PRIME SUSPECT DETAINED".

When the waiter finally turned the volume up, I heard the anchorwoman finish her sentence, only to immediately move on to another subject.

"... married with two children, he is the prime suspect in the abduction of little Kiera Templeton and has already been detained by the authorities."

Chapter 16
October 12, 1997. New York.
One year before Kiera's disappearance.

Speaking about pain is a sign of
strength; not doing so is a sign of
bravery, because when you remain silent
it stays inside, fighting against you.

Miren didn't fully understand what was happening, but somehow, she found herself feeling dizzy, making out with Robert in Morningside Heights Park. They were sitting on a bench under a streetlight with a fluorescent bulb that flickered constantly and seemed about to go out.

"Stop… please," she murmured, dazed.

"Come on…. don't go all tight on me."

Robert continued kissing her and she closed her eyes so as not to vomit. Everything was spinning and she found it difficult to orient herself beneath the flickers of the lamp which intermittently lit up the shadow of the man on top of her. She didn't remember having drunk enough to be in this state. She wondered whether she just wasn't used to alcohol since she didn't normally drink, but whatever the cause, she was upset.

"Please STOP!" she shouted, pushing him away.

"Are you some kind of idiot, or what?"

"I can't… I don't feel well," she said, feeling disconnected from reality.

She was suddenly aware of the cool New York air on her thighs and, looking down, was horrified to find her dress yanked up to her midriff and her torn panties hanging from one of her legs.

"Please… stop," she said. But Robert ignored her and put his large hands between her legs. Miren tried to resist with what little strength she had, but she couldn't get away from him as he moved his hand rapidly.

Miren heard a male voice in the distance. In fact, it wasn't just one but several, mingled together, and she screamed with her last remaining energy in the hope that they would hear her. She didn't realize that it was the worst thing she could have done.

Afterwards there were a few more voices, a few laughs, and male shadows that blended into the darkness that replaced the streetlight every couple of seconds. She heard Robert arguing with someone. Then she saw an image of him lying on the ground unconscious, his face covered in blood. She saw three men in front of her whose smiles were the only bright part of their dark souls. She saw a fly unzip. And then another. And yet another, or perhaps it was the same one.

She closed her eyes, crying and wishing the time would pass more quickly. She understood what she had once read about Einstein and his theory that time is relative. And it turned out it really is, but in proportion to how much you're suffering.

A while later—she could never work out how much later —she awoke in complete darkness in the park. She was in pain and her dress was torn across the chest. Her lipstick was smeared, and the eye shadow Christine had done had streaked with her tears, giving her the saddest face in the whole of New York. The streetlight had finally died and she couldn't see more than a few feet in front of her. She hunted around on the ground, and it took her a few moments to find her small bag which contained her door keys. She was frozen stiff and shivering with cold. There was an icy wind blowing from the west that day and she remembered she'd worn a fur coat to the party, but she couldn't find it anywhere. She wrapped her arms around herself and tried to stand. She realized that she had lost one of her heels and took off the other shoe, instinctively gripping it like a weapon. All her bones hurt. She could feel her waist grind every time she put her right foot onto the stony ground. Her knees were covered in grazes, and she could feel a painful burning sensation between her legs. She started to cry.

She walked through the pitch-black park for several minutes before she finally found the stairs on Morningside Avenue, and came out at the corner with 116th Street. She realized she was nearly home. She looked at her wrist, but they'd stolen her watch. She checked her bag and found that her wallet was also missing.

She heard another man's voice, offering her help: "Hey! Are you alright, sister? What happened to you?"

But before she could work out where the sound was coming from, Miren had thrown her shoe on the ground and begun to run. She was dazed, like a rabbit that'd heard a hunter's gunshot and was afraid the next bullet would hit the mark. She looked all around her as she ran barefoot, and when she finally reached her front door, she noticed the taste of blood in her mouth. She went upstairs, clinging to the banister, and felt a warm trickle running down her thigh. She looked down and saw it was blood. She continued crying, almost silently so that nobody would hear her, afraid someone else might see her like that and decide to join the free-for-all on her body, which felt as if it was broken into a thousand pieces.

It took her several attempts to get the key into the lock. She couldn't stop her hands shaking, making the keyring vibrate like the tail of an agitated rattlesnake. She swallowed and when she finally managed to get into the apartment, she slammed the door behind her and threw herself against it, crying out again and again with all the energy she had left.

She looked up and saw the telephone on the table beside the couch. She dragged herself across the floor, crying and moaning, and put the handset to her ear. After a few seconds' wait she heard a woman's voice answer sleepily:

"Hello? Who's calling at this hour?"

"Help me, Mom," she whispered between sobs.

Chapter 17
November 26, 1998

*It's possible to hide an enormous
scar on your skin, but impossible
to hide a small dent in your soul.*

Officer Alistair waited at a polite distance while Kiera's mother and father slumped to the hospital floor and held one another tightly, thinking through everything they could have done differently that day. Grace remembered that as they were leaving the house, she'd noticed it was raining, and that it had crossed her mind that it might be better not to go to the parade. Kiera had had a slight cold the past couple of weeks and she hadn't wanted it to get worse, but her doubt had disappeared when the saw how happy Kiera was as she left the house, on the way to watch her first Thanksgiving Day parade. Then she remembered that Kiera had been a bit disappointed getting up that morning because they were out of Lucky Charms, her favorite cereal, and she'd told her off because she should be eating a healthier brand for breakfast than those brightly colored little sugar bombs. Aaron's mind tried to replay each moment of the morning, every gesture Kiera had made, every instant when he could have changed the course of her disappearance, and found so many small decisions that could have avoided the tragedy that it seemed unbelievable it could have actually happened at all. Then he remembered how he'd got home late from work the previous night and that Kiera had already fallen asleep so he couldn't play with her or read her a story as he almost always did before she went to bed. Kiera's disappearance had pressed the self-destruct button in both their minds, and they found themselves involuntarily searching every tiny detail for moments that could make them feel worse. The missed seconds, the kisses not given, the days at work, the small punishments.

"Mr. and Mrs. Templeton…" said Officer Alistair, "I know it's difficult to go home as if nothing had happened, but please trust us. We will find your daughter. I give you my word. All our available units are combing the area and reviewing information from the security cameras to see if they can find anything. You must trust us."

"But… the clothes… and the hair… Someone's taken her, Officer. Our daughter is with somebody against her will. Please, you have to find her," said Aaron, wary at having revealed this shocking information to his wife, who still knew nothing.

"Hair? What are you talking about?" asked Grace, surprised.

Officer Alistair pursed his lips. He wasn't used to communicating information to the parents of missing children that suggested such a negative outcome, and he tried to measure his words.

"That's something else we wanted to discuss with you. We are keeping all lines of investigation open at this point and that's why the FBI will be taking charge of the case. We need you to answer some questions for Agent Miller from the FBI's Missing Persons Department, who is waiting for us to let him know where he can meet with you."

"The FBI? Of course. Yes. Whatever's necessary to find Kiera. Where is he now?"

"I need you to formalize your statement at the station and answer a few questions. What do you say to talking to him there? I'm sure he'll be able to help you. He's one of the best."

Officer Alistair offered to take Grace and Aaron in the police car. When they arrived, it was almost three in the morning and the South District police station was deserted. There were barely half a dozen officers around, all with exhausted faces and red eyes. The basement, on the other hand, was a hive of activity. Almost 30 people had been arrested and were spending the night down there, mainly pickpockets and petty thieves waiting to appear before the judge in the morning. Aaron and Grace sat at a desk and gave their statements to Officer Alistair, who seemed more interested in passing the time until the FBI arrived than asking anything that might cause them further pain.

According to the official police statement taken by Officer Alistair, both the mother and father had been at the corner of Broadway and 36th Street with their daughter between 9.45am and 11.45am, when Aaron left his wife waiting and went with his daughter to get a balloon. It was during the following minutes that she disappeared. Aaron identified a woman dressed as Mary Poppins and everyone else who'd been in the area as potential witnesses. He tried hard to remember a specific face so they could be identified, but he couldn't. Everybody had been complete strangers and, at that time of night, especially following the stress of the previous day, it was impossible for him to recall their faces. Grace mentioned a family who'd been standing near them with a little boy of Kiera's age. She remembered them because she'd imagined Michael, the baby they were expecting, at that age and had got a bit teary. Then Grace remembered that one of the majorettes had come over to high-five Kiera, because the girl had seen Kiera's smile and thought it was cute how excited she was. Aaron agreed with Grace's memory of the events up to this point. Then, she suddenly reiterated that she hadn't been there when Kiera got lost, which unsettled him a great deal.

Officer Alistair finished writing up the statement and then asked them for a photo of Kiera. Aaron was carrying a passport photo in his wallet that showed Kiera looking at the camera with a surprised expression. It was the very same image the *Press* would carry on its front page a week later, distributing it across the country beneath the headline: "Have You Seen Kiera Templeton?"

Agent Miller arrived just as Aaron was signing the statement. He greeted them with a "Mr. and Mrs. Templeton?" which seemed to come from deep inside him. His voice was husky and low, but when they turned towards him, they saw a friendly face.

"Are you the FBI agent?"

"Agent Benjamin Miller, Missing Persons Department. I'm very sorry about what's happened to you. We've put together a specific team for this case and we're already working on finding your daughter. Don't worry. She'll show up."

"Do you think someone's kidnapped her?" asked Aaron, genuinely worried.

"I won't sugar-coat the situation, Mr. and Mrs. Templeton, because I think that would do more harm than good. The FBI only takes on this kind of case when kidnapping is considered a possibility. That's why we also need you to be at home in case you receive a call demanding a ransom. It's a high risk case and… the captors will try to make contact somehow."

"A ransom? For the love of God," Grace covered her mouth with her hands.

"It wouldn't be the first time that… well, that something like this has happened. It's more common here than it seems to be in other countries. Do you have any enemies? Anyone who might want to hurt you? Do you have the means to pay a potential ransom?"

"Enemy? Money? I'm the head of an insurance office! I sign off on insurance policies," Aaron replied, exasperated. "It's... a totally regular, commonplace job."

"Have you refused anyone a policy recently?"

Grace looked at Aaron with an expression of disapproval.

"What?" Aaron asked his wife. "Surely you're not blaming me for what happened?"

"Your job, Aaron. This has happened because of your damn job. All those people... all those helpless people," she declared angrily. "I'm sure that..."

"That has nothing to do with this, Grace," he interrupted. "How can you suggest that? Of course I refuse policies, Agent Miller, but it's not my decision. It always comes from higher up. There are certain parameters, you know? If the client isn't profitable, we can't take them on. Would a hotel accept a booking from a guest they know will destroy a hotel room?!" he replied, enraged.

"I'm not criticizing your job, Mr. Templeton. But the facts are undeniable: your job has the potential to create enemies. And in this sort of case... One possibility is that this involves someone who wants to do you harm. It could be a matter of personal revenge or a financial motive."

Grace sighed and pressed her lips together.

"We'll need a list of the clients who've been refused a policy or cover for a specific type of treatment in the last few years," said Agent Miller, making a note on a piece of paper.

"I told you, Aaron. You're always going on about your damn profit margins. But how could you..."

"Will you be able to get me that list?" Agent Miller persisted, trying to bring the subject to a close.

Aaron nodded and swallowed to loosen the knot which had formed in his throat. He was finding it hard to breathe.

"In any case, we're keeping all lines of enquiry open right now. If there's no news tomorrow, you should consider putting up posters and moving the situation on a bit. Perhaps some-body saw something."

Grace nodded, taking comfort from the words spoken by Agent Miller, who struck her as the only person in control of the situation.

"Please, find her soon," she begged.

"She'll turn up. The vast majority of these cases are solved within the first 24 hours. It's only been...," he paused and checked his watch, "14, unless I'm mistaken. We still have 10 left and, in a city like this with so many eyes all over the place, that's more than enough."

Chapter 18
November 27, 2010
Twelve years after Kiera's disappearance

*As I dug through my ruins, the only thing
I found was the wreckage of my soul.*

The bell rang loudly at the end of the hall and interrupted the silence that had crushed the life from the house. A fine layer of dust had conquered everything, and the atmosphere was so gray it was as though the ashes of a fire were the cause of that sad and depressing state. But that wasn't the case. The framed photographs that stood on the mahogany table in the living room shone as though they were polished every day. They were the only thing that shone in the whole living room. The images showed a young, happy couple: he couldn't have been older than thirty; she was slightly younger. Others depicted the same couple with a happy looking girl of about three, with dark hair and green eyes. The little girl was laughing in every photo, showing her gappy teeth.

The doorbell rang again, for longer this time, and Grace Templeton got up from the kitchen table to go to the door. Perhaps it was apathy, perhaps it was hopelessness, but she no longer walked as quickly as she had in those first years. It was the 27th of November and the phone call from her ex-husband had reawoken all her deepest fears.

Grace had got up that day with a dark mixture of feelings: anticipation, hope, bitterness, sadness and desperation. Each of those feelings was caused by the same parade that every year reminded her of her misfortune. Grace Templeton put her aging hand on the door handle and opened it shakily to find herself facing a man in his late forties with a worried expression.

They looked at one another in silence and she looked down at the man's hands, which held a padded envelope.

"Where was it this time?" Grace asked in greeting, her voice tired and disconcerted.

"In the mailbox of our old house, like the first time. The Swaghats called me. I've told Miller. He's on his way. He asked us to be careful and to wait for him and the forensics team to arrive."

"On her birthday again, Aaron. Like the first tape. What the hell do they want? Why are they doing this to us?" she asked.

Aaron's expression remained blank. The pain was already so deep that it no longer registered.

"I'd already taken the cake out of the freezer before... before I knew another tape had arrived. I ordered it from that bakery we used to see when we went for walks along the west side of Central Park. They've done a beautiful job. They've decorated it with little orange fondant flowers. You have to see it."

"Grace... please. Could you stop making Kiera's birthday into a party? There's a new tape today. Please... not this time. I know that we meet up to spend her birthday together every year, but... there's a new tape. It's too much all at once, too many emotions. I'd rather... see her and leave it at that. Don't you agree? It's the fourth tape of our daughter. I need to see her and then cry in peace."

"The cake is the only thing that stops me thinking I've gone crazy, Aaron. Don't take that away from me too. You've already done me enough damage, don't you think?"

He sighed in response and Grace turned around and disappeared into the kitchen. She soon returned carrying a white box and took it into the dining room. Aaron followed her and found her opening the box to reveal the cake inside.

"Isn't it beautiful? Kiera would love it."

"I'm sure she would, Grace," he replied quietly.

"What are you waiting for?" she asked, taking a box of matches from a wooden box full of neatly ordered rows of them. "She's turning fifteen. One-five."

Grace went into the other room and came back almost immediately with two number-shaped candles that Aaron was sure she had already prepared. He stood still, watching his ex-wife rush from side to side, going in and out of the room manically. He had to hold back his tears so that he didn't fall apart in front of her.

"Would you like a chocolate milkshake?" asked Grace, moving back towards the kitchen again.

"I've told Miren, too. I think it's important that she's here. Perhaps there's something new in this tape and it could be useful for her to see it."

Grace left and came back again shortly afterwards, her expression unchanged.

"Chocolate or vanilla? It's a carrot cake with buttercream filling."

"Did you hear me? I told Miren. She'll be here any moment now."

"Vanilla it is, then," Grace continued, feigning deafness and beginning to fill a glass with yellow milkshake.

"Grace. Please. Perhaps she'll see something different in this tape. Don't give up hope. She's good, I really believe that. It's the closest we're going to be to…"

A glass tumbler suddenly shattered against the wall just behind Aaron, who didn't even have time to duck.

"Over my dead body, Aaron. Do you understand? Call her

right now and tell her not to even think of coming. I can't take any more of the press and their need to stick their noses into everything."

Aaron sighed again. The day became harder for them both with every passing year. It was an unbearable burden for anyone, but for them, this pain had become insufferable. Superficially, Grace appeared to behave normally. She smiled, she spoke calmly and only mentioned Kiera very occasionally. With Aaron, on the other hand, there was only one possible topic of conversation. They hadn't spoken about anything else in years. When they were together, the only thing that existed was the one not at their side: Kiera.

"OK. I'll text her and say it was a false alarm. I'll show it to her another time."

Grace nodded. Her eyes were already full of tears.

Aaron put the package down on the table and sent a message to Miren: "Don't come. Grace doesn't want to see you."

Miren didn't seem to have read that message, or the previous ones telling her about this fourth tape in 12 years.

"Shall we get started?" Grace asked, turning on a 26-inch TV that stood on a metal stand facing the kitchen table. On the bottom of the stand was a silver Sony VHS player, an antique that only still worked thanks to the personal efforts of Grace and Aaron. They'd bought it in 1997 when Kiera was two so they could play her the collection of children's movies they had given her for Christmas. Her favorite was Mary Poppins, whom Aaron had now come to hate, with her songs, her strictness and correctness, and her infernal happiness. If he thought of Kiera, what he saw was the image of Mary Poppins offering her a balloon. If not for a balloon, Kiera would still be with them.

Aaron opened the envelope labelled with the number 4 and tipped its contents onto the table: a 120-minute TDK cassette tape with a white label on which *KIERA* had been written by hand.

Grace had to sit down. She'd got up feeling happy that day, feeling that this time she would manage to bear the emotional turmoil of Kiera's birthday, but Aaron's call to announce the arrival of a new video had destroyed all that in a single stroke.

"Are you alright?" asked Aaron, on the verge of tears.

She nodded vaguely, and took a sip from a glass of water that was on the table.

"Can we just get on with it, please?"

Aaron took a pair of white latex gloves from his bag and put them on. Then he carefully picked up the videocassette and slid it into the VHS machine.

He sat at the table, behind the cake and beside Grace. She struck a match and lit the candles that said "15", their warm light illuminating the orange flowers that decorated the cake and the sad hearts of the two parents. They held hands.

It was the only time they allowed themselves a truce. They met up each year on their daughter's birthday with the sole intention of watching the most recent tape they had. Then, if they had time, they would chat and tell one another how their lives were going before saying a drawn-out goodbye. It was different this time. They'd sat down together with a new tape they hadn't yet seen, and perhaps neither of them was prepared for the buildup of different emotions colliding on the same day: their daughter's birthday, and seeing her again after several years.

They looked at one another, overcome, then closed their eyes to release the tears that they could no longer hold back. There was silence, interrupted only by their breathing, until they finally began to sing Happy Birthday.

When they finished, they both leaned closer to the cake and blew the candles out for Kiera.

"What did you ask for this time?" Aaron asked his ex-wife.

"The same as every year. That she's alright."

Aaron nodded.

"How about you?"

"The same as every year. That she'll come home."

Grace gave a long, gentle sigh, laden with all her sadness, as if a stream of ghosts were flowing from her mouth. Then she rested her head on Aaron's shoulder. He reached his hand towards the table, picked up the remote control for the TV and turned it on, revealing a screen full of dancing black and white snow. He turned up the volume until they could hear the white noise that accompanied the image. That old cathode ray television didn't have a single channel programmed. It was a black 4:3 26 inch Phillips, a relic that had a direct port for the VHS player and still worked in spite of its age and the beating it had received from Aaron the night the first tape arrived. Two scratches were still visible in the upper right hand corner of the plastic casing, the result of a fall from the very same stand which now held it. Aaron changed remotes and turned on the video player. The screen turned a pure black, showing Aaron and Grace's melancholy reflections as they watched the TV. Then in the right hand corner a counter appeared, frozen on 00:00.

Grace squeezed Aaron's hand as they saw the counter begin to move. A few moments later, which seemed like an eternity to both of them, when the counter showed just 00:02, the black screen was replaced by a bedroom identical to the one Grace was expecting, but with a single difference that made their hearts freeze.

"What's going on?" Grace yelled.

In the image, filmed from a single perspective high in one of the corners, was a bedroom whose walls were papered with a repeating pattern of orange flowers on a navy blue background. To one side of the room was a single bed with an orange quilt that matched the flowers on the walls. On the other side, a pile of folders and notebooks lay beside a biro on a wooden desk, beside which there was a four-legged chair that looked better suited to a kitchen than to studying. The sheer curtains at the single window, in the center of the image, did not move.

"Where's Kiera?" asked Grace. Aaron sat very still.

They expected to see her at any moment, as usual. In each of the three previous tapes Kiera had always been there, a few years older from one tape to the next. The time counter continued, relentless, undeterred by their disbelief.

"No! There has to be a mistake," screamed Grace. "Where's my daughter?"

The doorbell rang, but they were both completely absorbed as they studied the image of that empty room, with no trace of Kiera anywhere.

When the counter reached 00.59, the image froze, and the VHS machine immediately ejected the tape. The screen turned blue for a moment, then reverted to the snow of the interference, black and white flecks dancing across the screen.

"No!" they yelled in unison, with a sudden feeling that Kiera had just disappeared all over again.

Chapter 19
November 28, 2003
Five years after Kiera's disappearance

*Could there possibly be any-
thing more powerful than
the hope of finding what
you're looking for?*

A gent Miller agreed to reopen the case on the condition
that Miren didn't publish anything for a week. Miren had
agreed that after the initial week had passed, she would give a
summary of progress on the case in a way that wouldn't endan-
ger the investigation and give her opinion in an initial article
that would set the rhythm and tone for the country's press
during the events which followed.

The videotape dropped a bombshell in the FBI's New York
office, where various agents volunteered to help clarify the or-
igins of the video and analyze, frame by frame, whether there
was anything to be found. Multiple copies of the Kiera tape
were made, and the original case was dismantled in order to
look for any trace of fingerprints on it, and to analyze the magnetic tape. The package in which the tape had been delivered
was also sent for analysis. It didn't have a postage stamp, nor
had it been processed by any post office, which meant that

somebody must have left it in the Templetons' mailbox by hand.

A team was dispatched to the Templetons' neighborhood to ask the neighbors whether they had seen anyone lurking around the house the previous day, but their statements only confirmed that, as it was a national holiday, there had been several children playing in the street, but nobody suspicious.

It was understood that Grace's fingerprints would be on both the cassette and the packaging, and her prints had been taken that same day to distinguish them from any others. The cassette was a 120-minute TDK, of which only 59 seconds had been recorded. The rest was blank, with no useful magnetic information. Nothing had been recorded in any of the remaining 119 minutes. The tape was a common brand and the most popular length, and it was still available to buy at numerous stores around the city despite the somewhat abrupt arrival of the DVD.

VHS tapes were clearly destined to disappear due to their limited quality, length and, in particular, their lack of durability. It was inevitable that the magnetic charge of a VHS tape would slowly decrease until whatever had been recorded disappeared. In effect, they would suffer the same fate as Kiera, but at a very different speed. The new digital formats meant that a single compact disc could offer improved image quality, sound and even length, while introducing additional appealing elements such as menus, special features or scene selection. Furthermore, if well cared for, they could last more than fifty years, between two and five times longer than a VHS, whose color would deteriorate after just a few years. The digital archives stored on a DVD also provided additional information about the type of recorder used, the date it was made or even, sometimes, the place where the recordings had been made, hidden in the Exif metadata stored for each of the files copied onto the disc. But these attributes were not available for a videocassette, which made such clues impossible to trace. There was nothing on a videocassette that made it possible to find, locate or identify when or where whatever was recorded in the images had taken place. The only detail of the tapes that could be analyzed was what sort of machine they had been recorded on by collating the magnetic details on the band, in the same way that a pistol leaves a unique fingerprint on each bullet it fires. Based on the lateral marks on the magnetic tape, an expert managed to discover that it had been recorded on a Sanyo VCR from 1985. A well-known manufacturing defect meant that in certain models the magnetic head, which was responsible for reorganizing the particles on the tape to record the image and sound, left a repeating pattern along the edge of each tape. That information was of little use, though: Sanyo had been one of the market leaders at that time.

A handwriting team spent the week analyzing the script that had been used to write Kiera's name on the tape and the number "1" on the envelope, and the only thing they concluded following chemical analysis of the ink was that it had been written by hand using a Sharpie marker, the most popular brand in the country. Both had been written by the same person, judging by the pressure of the writing and the way in which the writer changed direction at the top of the A and the 1. When the scientific report of the traces on the tape arrived three days later, Agent Miller lost hope. There were no fingerprints other than Grace's. The results for the envelope wouldn't arrive until the end of the week, but Agent Miller visited the Templetons in person to update them on the lack of progress in the investigation.

Aaron and Grace were excited to see him. He got out of his car with a serious expression, looked around and saw that the neighborhood radiated happiness. Two children were playing together on a bike, riding in and out of some cones they had set out on the sidewalk. An older woman was pruning hydrangeas in her garden; a middle-aged man was just finishing arranging some life-sized nutcracker dolls along his front fence. It was a supremely Christmassy neighborhood, and Agent Miller swallowed before walking towards the only house that seemed overcome by sadness.

"Have they found anything?" asked Aaron as soon as they saw him.

"It's still early days. At the moment we're taking things step by step. We're trying to find gold among those fifty-nine seconds."

"Are there any fingerprints? There has to be something."

"Not on the tape. We're waiting for the results from the envelope, but it's not looking good, Mr. and Mrs. Templeton. If this person took the trouble to avoid leaving prints on the tape, it's likely he would have done the same with the envelope."

"And the images? Isn't there anything that could help identify where they're from? She's our daughter… and we have to find her," Grace interrupted.

"The quality of the image is so poor that it's impossible to identify what's visible beyond the curtains, which makes it difficult to find where she is and with whom. We think it's a house, the green tone beyond the white curtain could suggest a yard, but… this won't help us much. Not even the direction of the light in the room will help us with its position; if we knew the time of day, we might at least work out the orientation, and perhaps the approximate latitude of her location. It's going to be very difficult to get much more from it. I know it's early to tell you this, but if we don't find anything else, the only use this video will have is to let you know that your daughter is alive and well, even if you don't know where she is. Consider it… proof of life."

"What do you mean?"

"In kidnapping cases, proof of life is used to show that the hostage is well and demand a ransom. This could be something similar, although… although they haven't asked for a ransom."

"Well then we'll have to get them to ask," Aaron said, seriously.

"Are you suggesting doing a press conference?"

"Why not?"

"The media will slow our work down and… I don't want the same thing to happen as happened five years ago."

"If it will help find my daughter, I'll do it. Have no doubt about that."

"A person died, Mr. Templeton. Something like that can't happen again."

"That wasn't my fault, Agent Miller. Remember that. I wasn't the one who lit that flame."

Chapter 20
Miren Triggs
1998

*You can never be certain where that road
you take in the middle of
the night may lead.*

I had always been disturbed by what happens in someone's soul when a loved one disappears as though they'd never existed. I'd played with the idea of searching for years. Perhaps that's why I decided to study journalism, maybe that's why that world appealed to me. Because at the end of the day, journalism is all about searching. For what the powerful hide, what politicians hide, what anybody who prefers that the truth remain unknown hides. Searching for hidden corners of a story, the enigmas, the people lost in your mind. It's about searching and finding.

As a little girl I would read the Sherlock Holmes books, not to find the culprit, but the truth of what had happened. Most of the time I would enjoy trying to work out what was going to happen before the end, but the story would always surprise me, and I never settled on the right answer. Kiera's case had caught my attention right from the start because maybe, just maybe, part of me knew that I wouldn't find her.

The image of the suspect on the screen had made me genuinely happy. I'd spent just one night searching for her myself, but now I was somehow involved on a very emotional level. Perhaps it was because of her gaze, because I saw my own eyes in Kiera's: fearful, surprised, and shocked when faced with the evil in the world.

That day the front page of the *Press* carried a photo of the suspect below the headline: "Did He Take Kiera Too?" The details of the case were on page 4, after the editorials, and consisted of a long report covering two entire pages. It contained an account of how the previous night, the man on the front cover, whose initials were J.F., had been arrested for the attempted kidnapping of a little seven-year-old girl in the Herald Square area. According to witnesses, the man grabbed the girl by the hand and led her north along Broadway in the direction of Times Square until she began to scream when she realized that her parents were not nearby and that she didn't recognize the man who'd said he'd take her to them.

Several people worked together and caught the suspect following the little girl's screams. The explanations he gave were not at all convincing, claiming he'd acted after finding the girl disoriented among the crowd and separated from her parents, and that he had decided to take her to the nearest police station at the corner of Times Square. The tension caused by Kiera's disappearance and the fact that it had taken place in the same area had raised the alarm as soon as the girl's screams were heard. It was reported that she was now safely reunited with her parents.

The parents also gave statements, featured in the article, in which they expressed gratitude for the efforts of all those who had helped detain the suspect and encouraged other parents to be on the alert for sexual predators. According to what I read, the police did not delay in connecting this incident to Kiera's disappearance. The journalist responsible mentioned that this had taken place in the same area one week later, once the suspect had confirmed that his modus operandi worked. Surely, he had done the same thing with Kiera, and now it was just a question of extracting a confession from him in order to finally find the little girl.

According to the final paragraph, all suspicions had been confirmed when the police had found that the suspect featured on the sexual offenders list for a crime committed twenty-six years earlier, when he was convicted of having sexual relations with a minor.

I closed the paper, surprised and happy that Kiera's case was about to be solved. I called Professor Schmoer again and he picked up after just a couple of rings.

"I suppose you've already heard," he said as soon as he picked up.

"It's good news. The *Press* is very good, you can't deny it."

"I suppose not. They've done a good job. I'm... I'm alone on this. My entire department is analyzing the accounts of the NASDAQ or Standard & Poor's 500 companies, and I'm the only one who occasionally tries to follow up more... human stories, if you want to call them that."

"Someone has to do that too, right?"

"Perhaps so, Miren. In any case, it is good news. And... don't worry about the assignment. You still have time to write an article about the spill. Like the others."

"They haven't found Kiera yet. My investigation still isn't over, Professor. I can turn in an assignment that covers the evolution of the case up to that point although, to be honest, there's still a lot to find out."

"Well said, Miren. An investigative journalist's most valuable quality is tenacity. That's what I always say. You're either born with it or you're not. It can't be taught. Curiosity is what defines us, the desire to put things right, however difficult that may be."

"I know. You're always saying it in class."

"It's the only thing worth learning from all this. This job is more about passion than talent, more about perseverance and effort than brilliance. It all helps, of course, but if a topic gets you excited enough, it's impossible to leave it alone until you know the truth."

"And the truth is that Kiera still hasn't reappeared."

"Indeed," he replied.

He seemed slightly strange during the conversation. His voice was shaking, but I put that down to the poor sound quality of my cell phone.

After hanging up I went back to the courthouse with a pretzel for Paul. He seemed like a decent guy. He was the classic admin assistant that nobody seemed to appreciate, and I felt quite sorry for him sitting down there on his own in the archive. I'd bought it from a street truck that no doubt got them from the same place as everywhere else and he thanked me with a smile.

"You're going to spoil me," he said, grinning. He remained seated at his small desk, and I asked him a favor before immersing myself once more in that room full of filth.

"Could you help me find something?" I asked, putting on my most persuasive expression.

"Of course. Whatever you need. I don't exactly have a ton to do, other than filing this heap right here, which doesn't have to be done this second."

I smiled. I placed the *Press* on the table, with J.F.'s face filling the front page, and took the plunge:

"Is there a way to find his record among all the files for sexual aggressors?"

"If he committed the crime in New York State, it has to be here."

"And could you help me find it?"

"What's he called?"

"I don't know. According to the article... J.F., and he was convicted 26 years ago."

"I'll take a look."

"Thanks Paul."

"Sure."

We went together into the room full of files and I continued where I'd left off. He began to look through the box files dating from the seventies. At one point he asked me what I was looking for in the nineties, but I gave him an evasive answer, transferring files from one pile onto another once I'd looked at the photos. I found it difficult to be alone with unknown men after what had happened last year. I'd stopped trusting them, and the contents of those archive boxes didn't exactly relieve my inner fears. That situation with Paul, who was opening boxes and reviewing their contents on a table, just like I was, made me tense.

A while later, I heard him shout:

"I've got it! Here it is! James Foster. J.F. Accused of… consensual sexual relations with a minor in 1972."

"Consensual?"

"Uh huh, that's what it looks like. The victim was… where does it say?"

"Under 'Victim's Age'," I replied, seriously.

"Oh, right. 17 and he was… 18."

"What? There has to be a mistake…"

"He's married and lives in Dyker Heights with his wife and two kids, a 12-year-old and a 13-year-old."

"Are you sure it's him? Dyker Heights?"

He showed me the file. It was the same person. Based on the photo, he looked like a normal guy. But it was difficult to judge this kind of thing based on appearances. He seemed to be an entirely regular, normal parent. He didn't seem dangerous, and he had no clear history of child abuse. But according to what I'd read in those pages, that didn't matter. They hid themselves well. It was their biggest advantage. Many of them were judges, doctors, police officers or priests, and their façade was so innocent that nobody could spot them unless they caught them in the act. Even if they managed to catch them, their completely normal appearance became disconcerting in interrogations. It was repugnant.

"Is there any further information?"

"Not under Megan's Law. In this room you can only consult the summary of convictions and sentences, which is what will be available on the digital register."

"Aren't you able to get hold of the full file?"

"I'm afraid not. It's a restricted document, only available to his lawyer and… well, the State."

"Alright," I conceded.

"Do you need anything else?"

"For you to leave me alone," I snapped, with a forced smile. That sentence seemed to take him by surprise, and he looked rather shocked. I felt bad. I felt kind of stressed out by his presence and knew why I had reacted in that way. Just as he was about to leave the room, a little annoyed, I raised my voice.

"Thanks, Paul. I'm sorry."

He gave me a resigned smile and disappeared into the corridor, leaving me alone once more. I felt terrible, standing there among all the boxes in the room.

I kept searching among the files from the nineties. One by one the boxes moved from one side of the table to the other when I'd checked them, ready to return to gathering dust on the shelves. I'd seen files for violent sexual offenders, people who'd masturbated in public, and rapists from among the dregs of society, but they all had something in common: they were men from every social class and ethnicity. I was already tired and ready to give up and come back another day to continue where I'd left off when an image from the darkest night in my memory flashed through my mind. The photo was unmistakable. It was the only indelible memory I had of those moments. In front of me was the file for one of the men who had raped me the previous year.

Chapter 21
1998

It's incredible how fast time flies
when you wish it wouldn't and how slowly
it goes when you need it to speed up.

The next ten hours passed in a flash. Each minute without any sign of Kiera was like a stab to the heart for her parents. At 12am the following morning, they were collapsed in the living room at home in the presence of several police officers who were waiting with them in case anybody called to demand a ransom.

"We're currently questioning all the tenants and owners of the apartments at number 225 35th Street where Kiera's clothes were found," said Agent Miller as soon as he arrived on the morning of the second day. "We're doing the same at all the stores in the neighborhood and we've asked for copies of the footage from the security cameras in the surrounding area. We're lucky that taking into account all the stores, stations and public buildings in Manhattan, there are more than three thousand security cameras. If the person who took your daughter passed in front of one of them, we'll find and catch them."

His speech sounded good, but it wasn't going to be that easy.

Most of the cameras active in 1998 consisted of small closed-circuit systems that recorded onto the same tape over and over again. In the best case scenario, the systems could record for up to six or eight hours. Basically, they were cameras for real-time security with the aim of deterring robbery or vandalism. It wasn't very often that they actually helped catch those responsible, but Agent Miller decided to keep that detail to himself, hoping to minimize the risk of admitting they were fumbling in the dark. In any case, it was something they could use for now, but which they didn't really believe was going to help.

The investigation was also focused on finding one of the few people who had witnessed the disappearance: the actress hired to give out balloons to the children near the end of the parade route. The FBI contacted Macy's, whose management gave them access to all their files, security cameras and contracts and were happy to co-operate in any way they could to help find the company responsible for hiring staff and, in particular, the girl dressed as Mary Poppins.

It was after four in the afternoon when a fragile-looking young girl arrived at the FBI office in Lower Manhattan to give her statement to one of the agents.

But that statement was just one more, among the many others they had, that didn't clarify anything or provide any insight into the case. According to the girl's account, she had seen the little girl, who she identified from a photo they showed her, smiling and with her father. She claimed there was then a small scuffle and that afterwards the father came back, searching desperately for his daughter. She had joined in calling for the girl, along with various other people among the crowd, and after that she hadn't seen anything else. They took her fingerprints and let her go home. Her version fitted perfectly with the one provided by Aaron, who at this point was putting up posters of his daughter around the center of New York with the help of a group of volunteers, neighbors, and work colleagues.

By midnight on the second day, Kiera's face was visible all over the place, attached to street lights and pay phones, at hot dog stands, on the doors of every single diner and restaurant, on trash cans and, of course, ever-present in the collective memory as the little girl who was turning into the country's biggest mystery. The days passed quickly with no news of Kiera, causing her parents' pain and fear to grow as they huddled lonely at home. A week later, when the pain was still fresh and raw, the United States woke up to find Kiera's face on the front cover of the *Manhattan Press* with the headline: "Have You Seen Kiera Templeton?"

Inside, the article gave full details of her disappearance and included various telephone numbers to report any information on her whereabouts. One of those was the number for the basic hotline that Aaron and Grace had set up at their home, with various terminals connected on a table where four volunteers, neighbors, and old friends waited and made a note of everything that came in.

The home hotline was on the verge of collapse that day. Vague clues arrived from all over the country: a girl who looked exactly like Kiera playing in a park in Los Angeles, a suspicious man walking past a school in Washington, an endless list of license plates belonging to white delivery vans parked in working-class neighborhoods that suddenly seemed to have been there several days, the adoption of a little girl in New Jersey by a couple with a low income. Kiera was everywhere and nowhere at the same time. She had become a ghost who travelled from one part of the country to another in an instant, a willful little girl everyone adored but nobody knew. During the day, missing children's charities arranged marches for that evening, in protest against the apparent inactivity of the authorities, who still hadn't said a word about the incident. Calls came into the hotline one after another, each imperceptibly sprinkling a little dust on the situation, little by little covering it up. The first few minutes receiving tips became the first few hours, the first few hours the night, by which time the entire world seemed to have seen her among the shadows. By the early hours of the morning, those initial small specks of dust had become a thick gray coat of information that offered no answers. Aaron and Grace had gone out several times during the day to speak to the media, who had taken a greater interest in the case thanks to the front page of that day's *Press,* and had made statements to various media outlets with the aim of giving a new boost to the search for their daughter. But by midnight they were exhausted and sitting on the couch at home, conscious of the whole neighborhood's Christmas lights flashing through the curtains, while the phones continued to ring with increasingly surreal messages: a medium offering her services to speak to Kiera in the afterlife, a clairvoyant who saw bodies in coffee grounds, someone who claimed to be a Spanish writer alleging Kiera had been abducted by a secret sect.

A gray Pontiac pulled up outside the house, and Aaron and Grace went out to meet it. It was Agent Miller, and his expression was serious.

"What's happening? Is there any news?"

"We think we've got him, Mr. and Mrs. Templeton," he exhaled.

"You've found her?!"

"Not so fast. Not yet. We've detained a suspect and we're questioning him."

"And does he have Kiera? Where is she?"

"We don't know anything yet. A man tried to kidnap a young girl yesterday close to where Kiera disappeared and we're not discounting anything. He must have her hidden somewhere. We're checking his statement, but we can't get ahead of ourselves. We've found various items and belongings in a vehicle, and we want to know whether any of them belong to Kiera."

Miller took out a clear plastic bag containing a glittery white leather hair slide and Grace blinked away a tear which paused on her lip, delicate as a soft ocean wave. That tear was partly from joy, partly from sadness. That tear was like no other, and that's why she let it rest there, feeling its wetness, until it evaporated.

"She has a lot of clips like that…" she said with difficulty.

"Do you think it could be hers?"

"I… I don't know. Perhaps."

"That's ok."

"Agent Miller, do you think he has Kiera?" Aaron burst out in both hope and fear.

Miller didn't reply. Any false information in his response could come back to haunt him and the parents.

"Let me go down there. I need to see his face," said Aaron, feeling bold.

"No, Mr. Templeton. That's not possible. It's too soon."

"I need to look that son of a bitch in the face, Agent Miller. Don't take that away from me."

"We're not sure yet that it's him."

"Please."

Agent Miller looked at Grace and then back at Aaron. He looked terrible. He had scruffy stubble and huge dark circles beneath his eyes, which were red and full of disappointment. He'd been wearing the same clothes for several days.

"I can't, Aaron, really I can't. It wouldn't be good for you or for the investigation. We are working flat out to find Kiera. Stay here and I'll update you on any advances tomorrow. We're working around the clock. I came in person because I think it's the least you deserve. We're getting close."

Aaron hugged Grace and she felt her husband's warmth for a second. He had seemed cold towards her all week, as if each affectionate touch were meaningless or the threat of an implicit apology. But that time it felt hopeful. Perhaps it was because when you're so distraught it's impossible to feel love, because if your soul is hurting, your heart only looks for others to blame for everything that's happening to you. This latest news had bandaged the wound, as if it might be able to heal the relationship and stem the problems that had started with accusations of guilt. Grace sighed in Aaron's arms, feeling slightly relieved, as Agent Miller said goodbye and got into his car. They watched the car's red taillights move away towards the east, both of them thinking about how much they had stopped loving each other in the moment Kiera disappeared. The child's laughter that they had never needed to hear before Kiera was born had become essential since they had heard Kiera laugh for the first time, and now it echoed in their minds.

"They're going to find her," said Aaron. "And soon it'll be the four of us again." He stroked his wife's stomach. He realized he hadn't done so for a week, since just after Kiera disappeared, and felt the gentle swell discernible under the sweater Grace was wearing. "How's Michael?"

"I don't know… I haven't really felt him move for a few days."

Chapter 22
November 27, 2010
Twelve years since Kiera's disappearance

The worst thing about being in the dark is watching as the flame of your last candle flickers away.

A gent Miller arrived as fast as he could. He'd been held up in an endless traffic jam with no possible exit at the Manhattan entrance to the Battery Tunnel following a head-on collision. He called several times to apologize for not being at the office and, when he finally managed to move after two hours stuck in gridlock, he saw an enormous crane removing the wrecks of two vehicles and two ambulances removing three bodies. Paramedics were at the scene treating several patients who had been badly injured in the pile-up following the initial crash. He'd never got used to seeing the bodies of the recently deceased, and that image of a plastic body bag being zipped up as he passed turned his stomach. Most of the cases he worked on had a happy ending, with a few exceptions where the disappeared vanished without trace. Very occasionally, a body would turn up weeks or months later in the middle of nowhere, often just bones, and on those rare occasions the pain was not so vivid, although the grief it created was equally heartbreaking. He parked outside the door to a four-story red-brick apartment building beside Prospect Park where Grace had been living for the past five years.

"How are you?" he asked as soon as he arrived.

"You've taken ages, Ben. Where were you?" Aaron replied nervously, after answering the door with a speed that revealed their emotional state to Agent Miller.

"There was a multi-vehicle pile-up at the entrance to the tunnel and I got stuck, I couldn't go forward or turn back. It looked horrific. I saw a dead body on the tarmac once the traffic started moving again and lots of people injured. What's the rush? Has something happened?"

"It's different this time, Ben," Aaron explained.

'What's happened?

"It's the video. She's not on it. Kiera's not there," Grace interrupted, distraught.

"What do you mean?"

Miller had no idea what was going on, but he remained calm. He looked around and noticed that the apartment where Grace now lived was in need of a good clean.

"This has never happened before. Never!" Aaron yelled. "We've received three videos of Kiera over the years, and she always appeared in them. But now… this fourth one… she's not there, Agent Miller. The room is empty."

"Can I see the tape?"

"Of course. It's in the machine," Grace replied.

They led him into the living room and rewound the tape. When they pressed play, Agent Miller covered his mouth with his hands as he realized that what Aaron and Grace were saying was true.

"Where was it this time? Who gave it to you?"

"At home. At our old home. Like the first one."

Miller nodded his head in acknowledgement as he reviewed the facts.

"The second and third tapes appeared at your office, Aaron, and on a park bench, correct?"

"Yes."

After the couple divorced in 2000, Grace stayed on for a while in the house that used to be the Templeton family home, but she'd had to rent it out in 2007. She couldn't bear to be in that house alone, waiting in hope of a call, a lead or any piece of information that might reveal something about Kiera. The pain had been so great and the reproaches so constant that the couple only saw each other when there was a renewed hope of finding Kiera. But that hope appeared and disappeared for just a few weeks every couple of years in the form of the random videotapes. The lights of the neighborhood where they had always lived became a symbol of their lives; because they had stopped decorating their house through grief, but in spite of the sympathetic looks the neighbors gave them in the morning, they would still turn on their decorations each evening, forgetting about the pain that lived in the only house in the area whose garden had not been invaded by plastic reindeer, elves, and snowmen.

The Templeton house was rented by an Indian family with two children whose father ran a couple of grocery stores downtown. On the day they signed the contract, Aaron and Grace said goodbye to the couple to the sound of the laughter of their two children playing and singing in Hindi in the room which had once housed the Kiera hotline. Mr. and Mrs. Swaghat promised to try and live happily in the house and inform them immediately if any parcels arrived for them. They had agreed to that strange condition in exchange for a small discount on the rent but, apart from the first year, the only items of mail they had received at that address were letters from the federal government about local taxes.

The first tape appeared in the mailbox in 2003, on Thanksgiving, while Grace was still living there, but the two following tapes appeared randomly in different locations where they would be easily found. For example, the second tape, sent in 2007, was waiting in the bushes by the insurance company office where Aaron used to work for an entire week in August. A former colleague spotted it and called Aaron because she'd read Miren Triggs' article in the *Manhattan Press* when the first tape had arrived.

The third and last tape appeared in February 2009 on a bench in Brooklyn's Prospect Park, close to where Aaron had moved to, and only came to light three days later when a tramp gave it to CBS in exchange for a couple of hundred dollars.

The three tapes of Kiera Templeton had become news in themselves, to the point where the third tape was broadcast on the news before it had been seen by her parents or analyzed by the police. A local satirical magazine even published a highly criticized cartoon in which they invited readers to search the image of a crowded beach with the message "Where's the tape of Kiera?" in reference to the popular *Where's Wally?* books. That was the height of the sensationalism and the final straw that made Aaron and Grace decide to keep out of the spotlight.

The search for Kiera, which had once united half the planet, had become a spectacle that was gradually crushing two devastated parents. The state of New York passed an urgent law that prohibited the exhibition or broadcast of key evidence in open investigations to try and put an end to the media circus surrounding the disappearance. "Kiera's Law" came into force in March 2009 without opposition and helped change the way investigative processes were covered in the media, although it was also sometimes used by politicians and businessmen to protect themselves when they were accused of irregularities. People began to criticize Kiera's Law for its implications for freedom of information and it soon had to be repealed in order to calm the press, who were demanding increased transparency during investigations. The result was an adaptation of an existing law, which became known as the Kiera-Hume law and was adopted in mid-2009. It was originally named for a business-woman who had denounced the *Wall Street Daily* for publicly exposing serious irregularities within her company relating to falsified blood tests which were being investigated by the Federal Trade Commission. The final version of the law forbade revealing or spreading information that was the subject of open criminal cases related to offenses such as kidnap, murder, or rape, but allowed it in cases of corruption, fraud, or other serious financial crimes. In this way, if a new tape of Kiera were to appear, the media circus would be avoided. The whole affair had also seen the emergence of people who collected Kiera tapes, in a kind of murky business that entailed increasingly astronomical bids on the SilkRoad online marketplace.

With each of the three tapes, efforts were made to find any clue that could help the investigation, but the three attempts made in those twelve years appeared to be in vain: fingerprint and DNA tests were run, witnesses were sought, and the footage from the camera was studied in search of common elements in the videos from different years.

The second tape in 2007 seemed to bring a glimmer of light. It had been delivered to the insurance office where Aaron used to work, which had security cameras at the front and on the corner of the building. When the images from the month of August were reviewed, a silhouette, which appeared to be a woman with curly hair, was spotted approaching the office before dawn and leaving a brown padded envelope in the bushes by the door, which was later discovered to contain the videotape. Footage was analyzed from other security cameras from the surrounding area, from banks, grocery stores and shops, even from the entrances to tunnels and highways, but there was no further sign of that silhouette.

At the time Agent Miller explained the developments to the Templeton family and gave them various images of the dark silhouette that appeared in the shot, but it only served to turn that already broken couple into two suffering souls who saw similar silhouettes in everyone they knew. It didn't bring about any more advances in the investigation and only succeeded in rekindling the hope and pain of two parents who had felt the time pass with stones in their stomachs. The first tape, in 2003, had been different. That time, the emotions lasted longer and were stronger than they would ever be again, because hope was like a blade with no handle that made them more afraid to grasp it each time. Later, whenever a new tape appeared it lit a small flame that lasted just long enough to illuminate the darkness in the hearts of Aaron and Grace, who couldn't get over what had happened.

"What do you think this means, Ben?"

"I don't know, Grace. But perhaps this is the last tape we'll receive."

Chapter 23
Miren Triggs
1998

And what is a person always running from,
if not the monsters from the past?

It was night by the time I left the courthouse archive and I felt unsafe as soon as I stepped onto the sidewalk. After turning onto Beaver Street in Lower Manhattan, I hesitated for a moment over whether to call Professor Schmoer again. He was always willing to walk me home, but for some reason, I didn't dare. Part of me had forgiven him for rejecting me, but another part of me didn't want to see him again in person. I was too far away from home to walk, and the subway was the only viable option. The nearest subway station was Wall Street, and the journey would take forty-five long minutes heading north to 116th Street. Once there, I would only have to walk one block and I'd be home. It seemed easy, but it wasn't.

I walked to the entrance of the subway, fighting against the icy air of the southerly wind that blew through Lower Manhattan and froze my eyelashes, and I started to feel anxious as soon as I started down the stairs. A couple of boys were leaning against either side of the doorway, sheltering from the cold while they chatted about baseball or basketball or whatever. There was no way to pass but between them, so I steeled myself and when I walked between them they stopped talking. I was aware of their eyes on me, their tongues licking their lips, ready to launch themselves at their prey, and I sped up until I left them behind.

I spotted a young couple going through the turnstiles and caught up with them. I slowed down to their pace and walked alongside them. As if having witnesses would save me from my fears. The two boys walked quickly towards me, and I sped up again towards the platform for the Uptown 3 train towards Harlem. I realized the two boys were almost right behind me and beckoning to me. I noticed a look pass between them and looked all round in search of someone who would help me.

There.

Was.

Nobody.

I needed to run. I needed to get out of there. For a moment I felt like jumping onto the tracks and running into the darkness of the tunnel, but I knew that would be certain death.

I couldn't let it happen to me again.

I looked up and checked that there was a security camera pointing right at where I stood. If I waited there at least a security guard would see what was happening and would come to my aid.

I took a deep breath.

The blue columns stood every six feet along the platform between the two lines, and I leaned against one of them with my back to the boys, hoping they would lose sight of me and leave me alone.

"Hey! You!" one of them shouted.

"Hey, lady! Why are you running?" said the other.

Their voices were less than thirty feet away. I checked again that I could see the security camera. "If you can see it, it can see you," I told myself. I mouthed 'help' several times, hoping the person on the other side of the screen in the control room would come and help me, but those seconds seemed endless. I felt defenseless and alone.

Again.

I closed my eyes and I saw the lights of that park flickering again, the face I had just seen in a file smiling down at me, the warmth of the trickle of blood I felt between my legs when I got home.

The sound of an approaching train filled the station, and there was a squeal as the wheels braked against the steel rails. The two boys stopped beside me, looking baffled.

"Are you alright?" one of them asked me.

"You dropped this," explained the other, holding out his hand and showing me the file with the name of my rapist that I'd just stolen from the courthouse.

It took me a moment to react, but then I nodded.

"Are you sure you're alright?" the boy insisted, confused.

"Um… sure. It's nothing," I replied, wiping away a tear with one hand and taking the file with the other. "I just had an argument with my… boss."

One of them snorted; the other one smirked and said in a comforting voice, "Don't worry, you'll find another job. This is the city where dreams are made, girl! Only good things happen here," he added.

I didn't reply. The train had stopped and opened its doors, so I slid inside to put an end to the conversation.

I spent the entire journey re-reading the guy's file. Jeremy Allen, divorced (son of a bitch). Accused and found guilty of the sexual assault of a drunk girl outside a club in the Bronx. Victim profile: twenty-one, person of color. He seemed to like them defenseless. He did four months in prison and twelve of community service. Current address: Fourth Floor, 176 West 124th Street, New York.

That bastard only lived ten blocks away from me.

I got off at 116th Street, dialed my parents' phone number before leaving the station, and my mother finally answered.

"Mom? It's about time. I've been trying to call you all day."

"Oh Miren. I'm sorry. Your grandma had a little accident coming down the stairs, and we've been at the hospital all day."

'Grandma? Is she alright?'

"Well, she's got a few bruises on her face and her back, and she's fractured her arm. Your grandpa found her unconscious in the lobby. One of her shopping bags broke, she lost her balance, and fell from the top of the stairs. You know how it is. She always has to use those paper bags, all that fuss about the environment that she's obsessed with."

"But why is she still doing the shopping? Why don't you help her? Couldn't you hire someone to help them out with the heavier stuff?"

"Help them? Your grandpa doesn't like having strangers in the house. You know that."

"Who cares what Grandpa thinks? He says that because he never does anything. And he doesn't need anybody to help him scratch his balls."

"Miren, don't talk like that. He's your grandfather."

"And a misogynist," I continued sharply.

"He grew up in a different era, Miren. That's how he was brought up. Men back then were raised to be... well, men."

"Men? Since when is that part of being a man? He grew up without a TV in his house and he definitely has one now. He's adapted well when it suits him.'

My mother sighed. It irritated her when I spoke about her father like that, but I didn't see him the same way she did. It had always bugged me ever since I was little that when we went to visit them, I had to clear the table while my male cousins could go and play. I even complained once and he responded with a sharp, "Boys don't wash dishes, Miren."

My grandma accepted it and, although I admired them both, I felt angry inside about the situation.

"I heard something in the background, Miren. Did you buy a cell phone?"

"Yes, I'm using it now."

"Can you give me the number?"

"Um… I don't know it yet. I'll check as soon as I get home and call you back."

"Are you out on the street at his hour?!" she exclaimed, horrified.

"It's not that late, Mom."

"Yes, but it's already dark. That's why you called me, isn't it?"

The sound of my footsteps on the street was audible on the call. Various cars passed in different directions and there were groups of men chatting on the front steps every two or three doorways. Every time I passed one of the groups I would ask my mother a question so they would know I was talking on the phone.

"Yes…" I admitted. "I'm… I'm nearly home. I didn't want… to feel alone this last little bit."

"You can call me whenever you want, OK darling?"

"I know. How's Dad?"

"Have you got much further to go?"

"Two minutes."

"Alright. He's here watching TV. Have you bought your ticket to come home at the weekend? I'm sure your grandma would be excited to see you."

"I've been busy. I promise I'll do it tomorrow."

"Alright."

"Is there any trouble in the street?"

"There are people, nothing's going on, though, I'd just rather keep talking to you. Are you sure you don't mind?"

"Of course not, sweetheart. Give me a moment while I turn off the hob."

"What are you cooking?" I asked while I passed the last group just before my own front door.

"I started cooking sausages, but your father is now saying to me that he doesn't want any dinner. Shall I put him on for you?"

"It's alright. I'm almost home."

"I'm glad, darling."

"I've arrived."

"Sure?"

"Yes, I'm just opening the door."

The sound of my keys was audible on the call, and I heard my mother breathing more calmly.

"I love you sweetheart."

"Love you too, Mom. If you buy yourself a cell phone to-morrow, call me on this one and I'll save your number."

"Alright. I promise I'll do it tomorrow. Sleep well, sweet-heart."

"Say bye to Dad for me."

"Will do."

I hung up and went into my apartment, which was as dark as the rest of the neighborhood had been. I turned around to lock the door behind me, but just as the door was about to close, a male voice came from the shadows at the top of the stairs, murmuring:

"Wait, Miren. It's me."

Chapter 24
November 28, 2003
Five years after Kiera's disappearance

Sometimes innocence plays
for evil's team.

Agent Miller's phone began to ring in his pocket, and he apologized to Aaron and Grace, who looked at him with a mixture of annoyance and hope.

"Agent Miller?" said the agent on the other end of the line. "It's Collins, from Forensics."

"Is this important? I'm with the family," he said, stepping away towards the sidewalk.

"We've found five prints on the envelope. The full right hand."

"Seriously? That's fantastic!"

"Yes. But... not so fast. You're not going to believe it."

"What is it?"

"They're a child's prints."

"A child?"

"You heard me right. They're small, made by the hand of a child aged eight or nine. At first, we even thought they might belong to Kiera herself."

"You can't be serious? It was Kiera who delivered this tape?"

"Let me finish. We thought they might be Kiera's, but they can't be. We've had her prints on file since we installed IAFIS in 1999, the year after she disappeared. We used the software to simulate the increase in size so we could compare them, but they're not hers. They don't match her morphology or the ridges on any of her fingers. We're waiting for confirmation from the lab team on the DNA on the envelope, but I can tell you now, we don't think it's hers. The prints belong to another child, I'm sure of it. Perhaps another missing child. We're checking the database for any match on the prints, and we've already run a search on the missing children's register dating back to 1990, but there's nothing. Perhaps whoever kidnapped Kiera is also holding another child.'

Agent Miller listened carefully while Aaron and Grace watched him, worried, trying to pick up any clue or hint of progress from the conversation.

"We've been discussing it here in the office and we think maybe we could put some pressure on the state government..." he continued a little nervously, "to launch a children's ID documentation campaign in schools. Perhaps that way we could... well, identify the prints on the envelope."

"But we could find that this boy or girl isn't in school or doesn't make an ID document, and then it would be for nothing."

"Well... we can't think of anything else. It's the first time the prime suspect has appeared to be a child."

Agent Miller gave a sigh. "Don't worry, I think that..." he interrupted himself and turned around, examining the street again, irritation on his face. He watched the woman who had moved on from her hydrangeas and was now busy trimming the new shoots of a hedge with some secateurs. The children had left their bicycles lying on the ground and were now playing hangman with some chalk on the ground, and the middle-aged man was taking a copy of the *New Yorker* out of his mailbox, with its cover of a famous film director who'd been jailed a couple of months earlier.

"I'll call you back, Collins." He hung up.

"What's happening? What have they found?" asked Aaron with a worried look, as soon as Agent Miller started to walk back towards the house.

Miller held up a hand, indicating to Grace and Aaron that they should wait a moment. Aaron put his arm around Grace and, although she wished it didn't, it made her feel sad. Then they saw Miller going over to their neighbor and asking to borrow the magazine. The man watched as he carried it over towards the two boys and crouched down to their level.

Aaron and Grace couldn't hear what Miller was saying from where they were standing, but they saw him put his hand in his pocket and offer a bill to the boys. One of them jumped to his feet, snatched the bill and then the magazine. The other boy got up too and they ran towards the Templetons' house. They stopped at the mailbox, one of them opened it and the other rolled up the magazine and left it inside. Then they ran back to the agent, who gave them another bill each.

The conversation with the boys seemed to continue. The taller of the two nodded a couple of times while the other one watched the conversation as though it didn't have anything to do with him. A few moments later, Miller began to walk towards the Templetons' house accompanied by the taller, darker boy. They wondered what in the name of God was going on.

"Mr. and Mrs. Templeton, I'd like to introduce your neighbor..."

"Zack. I'm Zack Rogers... I live four houses down. My parents are John and Melinda Rogers."

The boy seemed nervous, and he put his hands in his pockets.

"Alright, Zack. What do you want to say? You don't need to worry."

"I'm really sorry," he said, hanging his head, clearly nervous.

Grace crouched down to his height. Aaron frowned, leaving lines on his forehead similar to the ones that would come later with age.

"What is it, son?" she asked in a reassuring voice. "Please don't worry. Whatever it is, it doesn't matter. Did you know we have a daughter who would be about your age? I'm sure you'd get on. In fact, we'd love it if you could play with her one day."

Zack seemed to calm down a bit and swallowed before continuing.

"I'm sorry about the envelope... I didn't mean... I didn't mean to make you cry, Mrs. Templeton."

"What?" she asked, confused.

The boy got even more nervous and looked down at the ground. Agent Miller put a gentle hand on his shoulder, encouraging him to continue.

"Don't worry, Zack. You haven't done anything bad. You can tell them. They'll understand. What you did was a good thing," he said, comforting him.

Zack looked up after a couple of sniffs deep enough to clear his running nose.

"A... a woman paid me ten dollars to leave an envelope in your mailbox. If I'd known it would make you sad, I would never have done it."

"A woman?!" asked Aaron, surprised.

"Who was it? What did she look like?" asked Grace.

"I don't know. I hadn't ever seen her before. She had curly blonde hair... but she was just a regular woman. I thought she was the mail woman. She gave me the package and ten dollars, and asked me to leave it in the mailbox. I didn't think it was bad... I'm really sorry. She was crying and I wanted to help her. I gave her back the money, but she insisted. I swear I gave it back, but she told me to keep it, that I deserved it, honest."

"Alright son… you didn't do anything wrong, truly," Agent Miller repeated. "On the contrary, you're going to be a great help to us."

"How?" asked the little boy.

"Do you still have the bill? Perhaps we can get a DNA sample from it."

"Um… yes. In my money box, at home," he replied nervously.

"And can you remember what the woman looked like?"

"I've already told you, blond with curly hair."

"Yes. But… do you know what an identikit portrait is?" Miller asked with a smile as Grace stood up and covered her mouth with her hand.

The boy nodded and Miller exhaled a confident, "We've got her!"

Chapter 25
1998

*The fragility of a house
of cards only becomes clear when
somebody lightly touches one of the cards.*

The gynecologist's expression was too serious, with a
frown they'd never seen during any of their previous appointments. She sighed before steeling herself to speak. Aaron held his wife's hand tightly while she grimaced at the continual prodding of the ultrasound scanner which was sliding around unpleasantly as the gynecologist searched for the best angle.

"What's happening? Is Michael OK?" asked Grace, wincing in pain in response to another movement by the gynecologist, who was now searching harder.

Dr. Allice had treated Grace during her pregnancy with Kiera. She was sweet and warm, and seemed to address the pair of them, both mother and baby, from the very first appointment, cracking jokes as though the little embryo growing in Grace's belly could hear them. Aaron was tense. He had become alarmed after Grace had mentioned the lack of movement from Michael since it was normal for her to feel a continuous bubbling in her belly, like corn kernels popping, as a result of the kicks from the fetus just a few inches long.

"Perhaps it's your anxiety for Kiera, maybe it made Michael relax. He must be thinking about his sister too and that's why he's not as active as normal," Aaron told her as soon as he heard the news.

But as the seconds slowly passed and Dr. Allice remained serious, making no attempt to joke about how much that little tyke Michael had grown, or his position in Grace's belly, or how bold or shy he was, they both knew that something wasn't right.

After several minutes of silence, Dr. Allice turned off the ultrasound and turned to face the parents, conscious that what she was about to say was going to be a sucker punch.

"It's never easy to say this... but... you need to know that the fetus has stopped developing. He doesn't have a pulse and, based on the size of his femur and the circumference of his skull, I think he stopped growing around three or four days ago."

Grace let go of Aaron's hand and covered her face.

"No..., no... please, Dr. Allice... no... there must be a mistake. Michael's fine. I know he's fine."

"Grace... listen to me," replied the doctor in a serious voice. "I know it's difficult to understand it right now, but don't worry. You're fertile, you can have more children. This happens much more frequently than people realize, it's normal."

"But... everything was fine two weeks ago. This can't be true. What happened?" Aaron was crying, searching for impossible answers.

"I don't know what to tell you. There are thousands of possible reasons. I know that this is a very difficult time for you. It's best not to think about it and to concentrate on what's important. This doesn't mean you can't try again."

Aaron realized that the doctor hadn't called Michael by his name.

Grace hadn't heard any of what Aaron and the doctor had been saying. Her mind had gone back to when they'd done the pregnancy test one night, sure that her missed period had to be a mistake. After seeing the two lines on the test, a clear positive, that feeling of uncertainty had almost instantly become happiness at the idea of becoming a family of four. From the euphoria of knowing they were expecting a brother for Kiera they moved on to fear that they wouldn't be able to handle the situation, then to financial uncertainty as to whether they could afford another child and, finally, after realizing that Grace still had the pajamas and onesies from when Kiera was a baby, they felt a sense of love and closeness that they had never experienced before. Grace also remembered how they had gone in to see Kiera, who was sleeping in her little white bed, and how they'd kissed her and tucked her in, and whispered into her sleeping ear that she'd never be alone.

But those memories only distanced her from the drama she was living through, in which all her happiness had evaporated the moment when Santa passed by on his float, the majorettes danced and paraded happily in the rain, and some white balloons floated away into the sky.

The doctor kept talking, explaining the procedure that would happen next, but Grace just nodded and responded from the distance of those happy but unreachable thoughts that fell from her eyes as tears.

A while later Grace and Aaron were waiting on some uncomfortable plastic seats while the operating theatre was prepared for them to have the fetus removed, in the gynecologist's words, or Michael, as the two of them still called him. Grace's head rested on Aaron's shoulder. Her eyes were closed, and he faced forward, miserable, his gaze lost in a distant point where two of the corridor's tiles met: one white, like those balloons disappearing into the distance, the other gray, like the reflection of the future that awaited what should have been a family of four, and was now a sad couple.

They both looked up to see Dr. Allice returning, her eyes downcast, wearing her white coat.

"Will you come with me, Grace? Everything's ready," the doctor asked in the warmest voice she could muster.

Aaron got up with his wife and kissed her goodbye on the forehead.

"It will be quick. Don't worry, Aaron. You can wait here. In a couple of months this will all be a bad memory and you can start trying again. I know couples who've tried over and over again and suffered up to eight miscarriages before success. It's more common than you imagine."

Aaron nodded and tried to dislodge the lump of sadness he could feel building in his throat. He didn't have the strength to speak and the soft "I'll see you soon, darling" slipped out so quietly his wife heard it as a groan. Grace squeezed her husband's hand and felt how their fingers let go more easily than they ever had before.

As Grace and the doctor moved away down the corridor, Aaron watched his wife walk sadly, as if the steps she took were going to make the floor crack open, and as he watched her walk, he understood that was going to be the last time that he would feel his wife's love slip through his fingertips.

Chapter 26
Miren Triggs
1998

*We all keep secrets which we reveal
to the right people, but some
people are able to lock themselves away
and hurl the key to the bottom of a lake.*

Professor Schmoer appeared from the shadows on the staircase, looking shocked at my scream. He'd almost given me a heart attack.

"I'm sorry I scared you," he whispered.

The front door opposite opened a crack and the hoarse, high-pitched voice of my neighbor Miss Amber filled the whole stairwell as though coming from some non-existent speaker above our heads rather than her mouth.

"Are you alright, honey?"

"I'm sorry, ma'am," said Professor Schmoer, "It was me. I scared your neighbor by mistake."

"Don't worry, Miss Amber. Everything's fine," I said loudly, and then I whispered to Jim. "You almost scared me to death! What are you doing here?"

"If I hear shouting, I'm calling the police. Do you hear me, honey? Your mother made me promise her."

"Yes. Honestly, there's nothing to worry about. It's just… my friend came to see me."

My neighbor's door slammed shut. Although I knew she had good intentions, I still suspected that she was basically an old battle-ax. Whenever I met her on the landing, she would brag that she'd ticked off the mailman so many times about the mail-shots she received that companies had stopped sending her marketing material. For a while I believed that story because I'd seen her arguing with the cashier in the grocery store about the bad quality of the shopping bags, which seemed to break as soon as you looked at them, about the amount of air they put in cereal packets, or even about not greeting her by name when she'd been a regular customer there for decades. Looking at her, you had the impression she was a strong, assertive old lady, the epitome of strength and resilience who got what she wanted through protest and a stoic attitude to life. I imagined her in the sixties taking part in marches against the Vietnam War, shouting at the police cars that threatened the movement's pacifism. There seemed to be a rebel hiding behind her eyes, an old Amazon warrior who couldn't be easily beaten. But one day, when I got home, I found her transferring the junk mail from her mailbox to mine. I said hello and she returned my greeting as if the mail had nothing to do with her. That day I offered to carry her shopping bag upstairs, as I always did, and she accepted despite declaring, as always, that young people were not what they used to be. When we got upstairs, she snatched the bag, grumbled a little, and then closed the door behind her without even thanking me.

"I tried calling you but your phone was turned off," whispered Professor Schmoer. I signaled to him to come inside. I didn't want Miss Amber to overhear that conversation, especially because I wasn't sure she didn't have a hotline to my mother. He came in and I shut the door.

"I was on the subway. Maybe that's why you couldn't get through," I replied, a bit nervous.

"Well, Miren… it's over."

"What? What are you talking about?"

"The *Daily* have fired me."

"Why? Because of the *Press*? Is that why you're here?"

"Kind of, it's a combination of things. It's more complicated than that, but yes, it's partly because of the thing with the *Press*. They're always one step ahead of my articles. In the last few months we've noticed a massive drop in readership. It's partly because of the internet and partly because our readers get their financial news from a variety of different sources. The *Daily* is in crisis because of the fall in readership and the management has been looking for a scapegoat. They decided on me, since I'm the only one covering the investigations which are less aligned with the paper's editorial strategy. I've seen it coming for a few months, but… I didn't think it would happen so soon."

He seemed dejected and I didn't know what to say to him. Since the arrival of the internet, I'd read various articles about the transition of readers to Yahoo and other digital platforms for news that had appeared out of nowhere, and how the traditional dailies were looking for a way to adapt to the new world that was opening up in front of them. Some saw it as an opportunity, but others as a new market in which the lengthy investigative articles of the traditional press would have less and less of a place. People were hungry for instant news, for things to read and forget again, and that kind of content didn't require investigative teams focusing all their energies on a single multipage article. Not only that, but after each investigative article was published there was a period of legal action. The papers, with resources increasingly stretched by a falling readership, struggled to fund legal teams to defend themselves against the lawsuits brought by companies who'd been investigated.

"You've got the classes," I said, trying to make him feel better. I didn't really know much about him. In the months we'd spent talking when he'd been helping me psychologically we normally chatted about the investigations he was working on and my persistent questions about them, or how to approach certain assignments from class. But I didn't know anything about him, or his family, or even where he lived. "You can always keep teaching and make your living as an academic. You're good at it. You have to focus on the future," I told him firmly.

"It's not really something that excites me, Miren. The students just want to find the easiest option and pass the course. This week's assignment is a classic example. I've already received twelve essays about the PharmaLux chemical spill. All of them copies of copies of copies. The spill has been doing the rounds for six months already, it's an open secret among all the newspapers, and if nobody has published their conclusions yet, it's because they don't want a pharmaceutical giant as an enemy. This world is rotten to the core, Miren. So is journalism. We're cowards. Nobody is prepared to take a big enough risk to take the first step towards change. There's nothing original, and, as a teacher, I can't manage to engage anybody enough to see a light at the end of the tunnel. Newspapers have a complicated future ahead, and if the press loses its voice of dissent, then we're all lost. The powerful will win."

"Well, you inspire me to look below the surface, Professor Schmoer. And if one good journalist graduates from each class I think the world will still become a better place."

Schmoer remained silent for a few seconds, looking me in the eyes from behind his thick-framed glasses. He was less than two feet away, standing in front of me, more serious than I'd ever seen him.

He was hurt.

He was sad.

He was vulnerable.

Every gesture hinted at an inner battle, about to burst out at any moment, just like my nervous heart, but he suddenly turned around, exhaled loudly and walked to the couch. He sat down, sighing, holding his head in his hands, and running his fingers through his curly hair, which immediately sprang back into place as if he hadn't touched it. He took out a CD from the inside pocket of his jacket and put it on the table.

"What's that?" I asked.

"All the stuff from Kiera's case that I was able to rescue from the office. We had a lot of material, but it was too much for me to get through. I couldn't look through it all. This is everything. I only sent you part of it."

I reached across him for the CD and took it over to my computer.

"Are you allowed give me this?" I asked, surprised. It seemed unlikely.

"No, but nobody knows I've got it. Think of it as information from an informant to a budding journalist. Nobody can know how you got hold of it. Perhaps it will be helpful for your assignment.'

"I still haven't started it. I don't know if I dare write about this. There's a lot of information. The only thing I know is that I'm not convinced by the suspect they've detained. There's something missing…"

"Why do you say that? They've arrested a man with a history of sexual assault against minors who was with a seven-year-old girl in the area where Kiera disappeared. I'd say it's obvious he's some kind of predator."

"That's the very thing that has me least convinced. I've seen his file and he doesn't match that profile."

"You've seen his police file? Explain. As far as I know, sexual assaults aren't listed."

I opened my bag and handed him the suspect's Megan's Law file. He opened it at the first page and began to read, incredulous.

"What's this? His case history?"

"His file from the Megan's Law sexual offenders register. I stole it from the archive."

"Seriously?"

I nodded, proud of myself. He looked at me, surprised. He pushed his glasses back up his nose before looking down at the file again.

"I don't approve of sexual relations with minors," I continued, "but his file talks about a consensual sexual relationship with a 17-year-old girl when he was 18. Not only that, but if you look carefully, the charges were withdrawn a year later when the victim turned 18. It doesn't strike me as a natural evolution to sleep with a girl a year younger than you and then wait 26 years before beginning to abduct little girls."

"So, what's your conclusion?" he asked me, his interest clear. I enjoyed being the focus of his attention. It was… exhilarating. As if with that attention he could light a spark that could light up my shadow-filled insides for a moment.

"I think it's the type of charge brought by an overprotective parent when he discovers his daughter has found herself an older boyfriend and he finds them in bed together. Don't get me wrong, I don't approve, but I had a friend who had a boyfriend a year older than her, and there was a year when he'd already turned 18 and she was still 17 when I used to joke with her and say that her boyfriend would end up in jail."

"Seriously?"

"If her parents had caught them, if they'd known what their daughter was up to at that age, they would have reported him too, and he would also have a stain on his record and be listed on the sexual offenders register."

Still studying the form, I continued:

"I don't think the guy they've arrested is the person who took Kiera. In any case, I reckon this guy is now married to the 17-year-old girl he was having sex with at the time. I'd like to check that on the Civil Register. Perhaps I could find the woman's maiden name and cross-check in the register to see if it's the same as the victim's. I know the victim's name may be protected so I might not be able to access it, but I've got a feeling I'm right."

"But he did take the little girl, and he took her to Times Square, some distance from where her parents lost her."

"The nearest police station to where he found her is in Times Square. And that's exactly what he told the police."

Professor Schmoer nodded.

"What if he was telling the truth? I'd like to be proved wrong, Jim, and for them to have already found the person responsible for Kiera's disappearance, but I don't think it's him. I think Kiera is out there somewhere, hidden with her real captor, screaming that she wants to see her parents again," I declared, convinced.

"Have you told anyone about this? Do you think the police will look into the suspect's past?"

"I think so," I replied, worried, "and sooner or later I think they'll let this man go. The worst thing is that, in the meantime, while he's in custody and he's their main suspect, nobody is out there looking for Kiera."

Chapter 27
November 27, 2010
Twelve years after Kiera's disappearance

*Sometimes holding onto a bad memory
is the only way you can
create something good.*

After Miller left with the fourth tape, Aaron stayed at Grace's new apartment, silent, unsure what to say. The constant white noise from the TV with no signal was irritating, but with time they had both found it to be a kind of consolation, even company. Aaron walked around the room and looked at all the different photos on the table, which showed the two of them together, cheerful, holding Kiera in some of them.

"We were so young," he said sadly after picking up one of the frames to look at the image more closely.

Grace sighed deeply, pressing her lips together, and tried to be strong. She was fighting against her inner demons, which took the form of posters on lampposts plastered all over her mind. She continued with the routine she followed each year on her daughter's birthday.

She went sadly over to the table and started to gather the framed photos, arranging them on top of a small wooden box on the old living room sideboard. After picking up each frame she noticed that there was the same film of dust beneath each one on the table, as if they had just been placed on top of that impenetrable carpet of gray.

"Why do you keep doing this, Grace? You get them out every year, as if everything were the same, as if we hadn't changed, but look at us. Look at my gray hairs, my wrinkles. For the love of God, look at the bags under my eyes! And you… you've changed too, Grace. We're not the excited young people in those photos anymore. Stop denying what happened. Stop behaving as though Kiera were here."

"Aaron… shut up. I can't right now… I don't want to think about how much all this still hurts."

"Look at this photo. The three of us smiling. How long is it since you last smiled, Grace? How long is it since I heard your laugh?"

"Have *you* managed to laugh?"

Aaron shook his head silently.

"But… what you do every year doesn't make sense, celebrating her birthday as if nothing had changed. I come over and you behave as though Kiera were here. The cake, the photos, even this apartment you rented with an extra room so you can set it up like Kiera's bedroom. And… Kiera isn't here. Do you understand? Nothing from that time is still here. Not you, not me, not the happiness in those photos. Looking at them will make you more unhappy. Seeing you like this would make Kiera unhappy. And you know it, Grace. Perhaps…. Perhaps this thing with the latest tape, that she's not on it, is the best thing that could have happened to us, do you know what I mean?"

"How dare you say that?"

"Maybe if we don't receive any more tapes, we'll stop thinking constantly about her. We'll stop imagining the things we haven't experienced, all the things we've lost, and we'll focus on what we had. Do you remember? Do you remember what it was like reading her stories? Do you remember how you used to feel when she'd stroke your hand when she wanted to sleep? We need to focus on that and not on what we don't have now. We have to try and move on."

"Are you listening to yourself? Stop thinking about Kiera? Act as though she never existed?"

"A lot of people lose their children, Grace, and in the end... with time they move on."

"On? Move on? Nobody can move on from this. Nobody. Especially not a mother. She spent nine months inside me; she came from inside me, Aaron. But you'll never understand that. It's impossible. You used to work all day and you didn't get back until bedtime. I was the one she would spend every day with. All day," she repeated, raising her voice. "It was me she would run to when she fell over and grazed her knee. Perhaps you can move on and pretend it was nothing... but I can't, Aaron. I need to know that she's alright. I need to know she's not suffering. Seeing her from time to time gives me that hope. At least it gives me a bit of relief from the pain of losing her. Perhaps the tapes are a form of torture for you. But for me... for me they're the only minute I get to spend with her once every few years."

Grace started to cry like she had never done before. Her chest hurt so much, there was such a burning in her eyes that she couldn't stop herself. She had held these explanations in for many years, but right now she needed to shout them at Aaron once and for all, for behaving as if the pain was just something you had to learn to live with. In truth, often in life it was, when sadness was confined to a specific context: a breakup, a good-bye, an unexpected tragedy. But nothing was comparable with losing a child and, especially, with losing a child several times over a 12-year period.

"Nothing? Pretend it was nothing? Kiera is my daughter, too, Grace. I love her more than I've ever loved anybody else.

What you said is unfair. I'm just saying that… that perhaps not seeing her on the tapes might help us turn the page and stop looking for her."

"I will never stop looking for my daughter, Aaron! Not until I know where she is and who has her. Do you understand?" Grace yelled at the top of her voice.

Aaron hesitated over whether to continue with the conversation. He realized it was impossible to draw his ex-wife out of that dark place where she seemed to be imprisoned, and he asked himself why he didn't feel the same, so cursed, so lost in the depths of his own soul. He started to doubt whether he really loved his daughter and also what he had felt for his ex-wife. In that moment he doubted everything, even himself. But those doubts were really nothing new. They'd been there for years. He would block out his insecurities with alcohol as the date of Thanksgiving approached each year.

Only the day before, he had been drinking at home, as he did every year, until he'd fallen asleep on the couch at four in the afternoon while the television broadcast a replay of a 1990s basketball game in which Michael Jordan scored from a free throw with his eyes closed. This had been his routine during the weeks preceding Thanksgiving since 1999. He would ask for a few days off from the insurance company where he worked—they were happy to bring his Christmas holidays forward so as not to leave the office empty during the last few days of the year—and he would shut himself away drinking until he forgot everything. It took him a while to get used to getting drunk at home, and there was a day in 2003 when he lost his temper and got arrested, the year of the first tape. After that episode he tried to confine his drinking to within the walls of his own home. In the days leading up to Thanksgiving, he would go to a liquor store and buy cheap alcohol as though he were preparing for a hurricane, and he would sit and cry vodka tears until he could cry no more. His body had gradually

174

learned to process the alcohol to the point where he would wake up the next day with only a slight hangover and a dry throat that only lasted until he had drunk a double shot of black coffee for breakfast. He would repeat this routine from the start of his time off up until Kiera's birthday, when he would stop drinking to go and see Grace, and behave, for a few hours, like the family man he'd once been.

"What do you think will happen now?" Grace asked Aaron with difficulty.

"I don't know," he murmured. "I just hope Kiera's OK."

Chapter 28
1998
Unknown location

There are people who can maintain two contradictory thoughts in their minds simultaneously if it helps them to stay sane.

The white of the couch where Iris was sitting contrasted with the blue and orange of the walls, which were papered with a repeating flower pattern. In front of her, on the other side of the glass table marked with rings from glasses, William was walking back and forth in an attempt to control his nerves with physical movement as he considered what they'd just done.

"The little girl is asking for her mom, Will. That's not good. She hasn't stopped crying for two hours. We need to put a stop to this. There's still time," begged Iris, her eyes following her husband.

"Would you shut up and let me think?" he spat without looking at her.

"Listen to me, William, we can stop this. We can go back to the city center and leave her where we found her. Nobody will find out."

"Are you crazy? They'd see us and they'd arrest us for attempted kidnapping. We've cut her hair and changed her clothes to take her, Iris! Now you regret it? Now? There's no way back. You should have said no at the time. Why the hell didn't you say anything then? It seemed like a good idea to you. You kept quiet, like you always do. I always make the decisions and you... all you do is agree. Sometimes I wonder whether I'm married to a person or a rock."

"For the love of God, I didn't know what you were planning to do. Do you think I thought we were going to take her with us?" Iris asked.

"Oh please, stop lying..."

"She was alone, and I wanted to protect her. The little girl was lost... and... I just walked away from the crowd with her," she paused, her mind turning in different directions. "Something might have happened to her!"

"Then why did you buy children's clothes in the shop when I asked you to? If we go back, it's the first thing they'll ask you. And what will you say? Will you be able to explain to the police why you cut the hair of a little girl who isn't yours and why you changed her clothes? I'll tell you what they'll say: attempted kidnapping."

"I don't know, Will. I don't know why I didn't say anything. And I didn't cut her hair. That was you!"

"I did what I had to do, Iris. I wanted to make you happy. Isn't that what you were always saying? That you wanted a family? That you wanted to be able to read your child stories at night and cuddle them when they were upset?"

"But not like this, Will! We can't keep the girl. She's not ours. Have you lost your mind? I want to be a mother, but not like this."

"Listen to me, Iris; this is what we've always dreamed of. It's a gift that's fallen from heaven. We can't reject it. Don't you understand? This is the best gift life could have given us. How many years have we been trying? How many?"

"From heaven? She's fallen from heaven? You left the house carrying scissors, Will... This was always your plan."

"Yes. So?"

"What do you mean, 'So?' I suggested going to the parade because it would be a day for dreaming, for seeing in the other families what ours would be like if we had children. You already had it all planned out at that point, didn't you? Your plan was always to go to the parade and take a little girl. Tell me the truth, Will."

Will considered his reply before speaking.

"I didn't think it would be that easy, Iris. I swear I didn't. It was a crazy idea I had. I can't bear any more miscarriages. I can't bear to see you suffering again, don't you understand? We've had eight miscarriages in a row!"

Iris's hand trembled with fear. She looked towards the door at the end of the hallway, where they could hear Kiera's crying reverberating behind the wood. Iris' gaze rested on the shiny gold door handle for a few moments, aware that she would see herself reflected in it for much longer than she could bear if they went ahead with this.

"Iris, listen to me. Remember what Dr. Allice said. We will not be able to have children. That's a fact. We can't. You... your body... can't..."

"She never said that, Will. She said that we should look at other ways of having children. That lots of couples adopt and are happy."

"For the love of God, Iris. Are you listening to yourself? Isn't that the same as telling you that you won't be able to have children? I asked the doctor to be tactful when she told you, but I can see that you aren't able to read between the lines."

Kiera's crying became louder behind the door.

"Iris, you have to understand. Your damn ovaries don't work, and your uterus has already rejected eight attempts at IVF. We can't have children. Well, you can't have children. I could have them with another woman."

"You're a bastard, William. You're a fucking bastard."

"We're in this together, Iris. I did this for you."

"For me? I never asked you to kidnap a little girl, Will. I just…" inevitably, she burst into tears. "I just wanted to be a mother."

"And now you are, don't you see? We're finally parents to a lovely little girl, and it will be just the same as if she were ours. We'll have to get to know her gradually, find out what she likes, what makes her smile, and calm her down when she cries, Iris. We can raise her as our daughter, darling, with love, here in our home."

Iris remembered each failed attempt. Each time, her face had lit up at the positive result and the good news, only to discover weeks later from the drop of blood spreading in the toilet bowl that something wasn't right. She remembered each curettage, each fruitless implantation that her body went to such lengths to reject. Their health insurance only covered the first round, after which they'd had to get further and further into debt in order to afford the enormous medical bills. She remembered the face of the head of the insurance office, a serious guy with dark hair who behaved in such a cold and distant way that Iris couldn't help feeling pain in her chest when she learned they had been refused a second round.

"Please… William… tell me we can stop this now and keep trying ourselves. She's not our daughter."

"And keep throwing money away? Is that what you want? Iris… really, you have to understand this. We can't get any further into debt. We've taken out a second mortgage on the house to fund the treatment and it hasn't worked. We can't keep trying without knowing what will happen. With each attempt we're moving tens of thousands of dollars into the red. Do you understand that? This is important, Iris. You have to understand. We can't have children. We don't have the money to try again."

"We could sell the house…"

"Iris…" William went over to his wife, sat down beside her and stroked her face to brush the tears away. "Don't you understand? We can't sell it until we've paid off the two mortgages we took out on it. We're stuck here until we pay them. There's no other alternative, Iris."

"Perhaps the insurance…"

"Iris! Please stop. You know I'm right and you have to…"

She suddenly put her hand up to stop her husband and turned to look towards the bedroom in surprise, interrupting what he was about to say.

"She's stopped crying…," she whispered, a hint of excitement in her eyes. That part of her, the dark part, seemed to be awakening without her realizing, accepting with the girl's silence something she had wanted since the moment she'd taken her by the hand in the middle of the crowd at the parade. She'd been the one who had gone into a nearby store to buy children's clothes in an attempt to hide her and disguise her from her parents while William waited in a doorway. She'd also been the one who, as they walked along 35th Street, had told Kiera again and again that they were taking her to meet up with her parents, who had left without telling her because of a problem with the Christmas presents. As they went farther and farther from the corner of 36th Street and Broadway, the place where they had abducted her, they were both aware that they were passing the point of no return, that they were crossing lines that were impossible to explain. As they boarded the subway at Penn Station on their way home beneath the indifferent gaze of a hobo, they knew that this journey into darkness was a one way trip.

"Do you see?" William asked, with a barely perceptible sigh. "She has to get used to our home. It's just a matter of time until we're a happy family, Iris. Do you understand?" William moved closer to Iris, took her face in his hands and looked into her eyes.

181

"The poor little thing must be exhausted from all that crying," she whispered, leaning her head against his chest. "She just wants to be back with her parents. She's in shock. She doesn't know what's going on."

"Her parents? Her parents abandoned her in the middle of a crowd, Iris. Do you think they deserve to be parents more than we do? Do you really think that? Do you think that's fair?"

Iris got up and went to the bedroom door, worried in case something had happened. It was the first time she had felt that fear for someone other than herself, and she liked feeling protective of someone defenseless. She opened the door nervously, and when she looked on the floor near the door, she couldn't contain a spontaneous smile of happiness.

Kiera had fallen asleep and was curled up on the rug, her hair in a complete state with tufts barely an inch long mixed in with much longer strands. She was wearing the clothes that Iris had bought at the shop: white trousers and a badly buttoned navy blue jacket. Her little face was damp with tears, and Iris crouched down beside her and stroked away the trace of salt one had left on her left cheek.

"You can't imagine how much it hurts me to hear her cry, William. It hurts my heart to hear her weeping like that. I don't know if I'll be able to do it. I don't know if I can do all this. It's… too much for me."

"She's our daughter now, honey. The fact it hurts is normal. But gradually, it will get better. We have to be strong. For her. To protect her from the horrible, brutal world out there."

Chapter 29
November 29, 2003
Five years since Kiera's disappearance

It's difficult to ask for help and much
more difficult to admit to needing it.

At the FBI office, Zack, accompanied by his parents, was unsure about each new sketch by the identikit portrait artist. They were in a little room on the third floor, beside a member of the Facial Recognition Unit, who was outlining, sketching, erasing, and shading using more than 12 pencils of different thicknesses that lay on the table alongside various erasers made of different materials. Behind the artist, Agent Miller paced silently back and forth, looking from time to time at the boy, who seemed afraid he might be failing a test.

"What do you think now? Have I lengthened the nose enough?" asked the artist after a few minutes of silence while he modified that part of the face, having spent more than half an hour changing and adjusting the triangle framed by the position of the eyes in relation to the top of the nose.

"I… I don't know. I think… I think like it was before. I'm not really sure."

"Like before?! Like which of the previous 20 versions?" yelled Agent Miller, running out of patience.

A tear trickled down Zack's cheek and he wished he'd never admitted that he had been the one who left the tape in the Templetons' mailbox. His mother looked at the agent in horror as he began to lose his temper over the continuous changes in shape and size. They had produced so many different versions of this mysterious woman that each change to her face made her seem more unreal.

Truth be told, Zack couldn't remember much about the woman who had paid him ten dollars for the trouble. She had spoken to him from inside a white car, wearing sunglasses, and the only thing he could remember with any certainty was her short, blonde, curly hair. She was wearing a black sweater and driving a small car, but Zack hadn't paid attention to much else after the moment he saw the ten dollar bill appearing from inside the car window.

"Don't you speak to my son like that. Understand? We've agreed to help you with this, but we don't have to put up with your bad manners. He's only a child, for God's sake."

"Mrs. Rogers, if Zack doesn't co-operate, he will be obstructing a criminal investigation and he could find himself facing charges. A little girl's life hangs in the balance and she's relying on your son to decide if he wants to remember what the hell that woman looked like."

"How dare you say something like that? How dare you? You seem to be blaming us for what happened to that little girl, but look. It's awful, but my son is just trying to help. We want to do everything in our power to help, but not like this. Not being treated like this."

Mrs. Rogers stroked her son's cheek and spoke to him in whispers too quiet for the others to hear. Zack's father shook his head at the agent and then also crouched down beside his wife to comfort their son in a low voice.

"Darling… you can stop whenever you want, do you hear me? You don't have to do this."

"You haven't understood me, ma'am. Your son is currently the only lead we have in finding this little girl. You remember her, don't you? The daughter of your neighbors, the Templetons. You have to try. Kiera Templeton would be Zack's age now. Do you understand?"

The boy was scared, but nodded, and then whispered, "Well... I think her chin was more rounded, not so pointy."

The artist sighed and gave up, throwing his pencil onto the table with the others. He got up and signaled to Miller to step outside with him.

"You need to understand something, Ben. It's difficult for a child to try and remember something in detail that had little significance to him. This is very different to when a victim tries to recall an attacker, you know? In general, the stress of the moment of the attack makes the mind work unusually fast, almost making the memory almost photographic, capable of detecting all the little details necessary for an identikit. But without that stress... I'm afraid it's normal that the boy doesn't remember very well. All we'll end up drawing is a mixture of his memories and his imagination, especially now he thinks that the sooner he finishes, the sooner he can go home."

"He's all we have, Mark... you know that, right? This boy is the only person who's seen the woman who has Kiera Templeton. I can't call her parents and tell them we can't rely on the identikit portrait. I can't. It's too much for me."

"Well, you'll have to, Ben. I've never seen such a clear case of an unreliable witness statement. How many times has he changed the chin? How many has he changed the hairstyle? Blonde with curly hair. That's the description. We don't know anything more. The rest... guesses. No distinguishing marks, nothing special about the face. When I drew a prominent chin, he said it was like that. When I drew a more rounded one, he said the same. Then, when he saw the pointy chin again, he told me it was perfect. Not even the shape of the sunglasses is consistent. This is madness, Ben. I'm telling you now, this is not a valid portrait. I don't know how you're going to handle the family, but this isn't going to work."

"Fuck…" was Miller's only response. He looked at his watch and realized they'd spent six hours in the room with no tangible progress. Normally this process took barely an hour, or an hour and a half if things were going badly. He went over to the door and beckoned to the parents who were still beside their son, whispering to him and stroking his hair. The father left the room and spoke before Agent Miller could.

"We're going home, Agent. This is pointless. Zack is tired and he can't remember anything else. We want to help, truly, God knows we're good members of the community but," he hesitated before voicing his thoughts, then continued, "but she's not our daughter. We need to look after our own, Agent. The world is a terrible place, and each person has to look after their own family. My son can't take any more. We can try again tomorrow or another day if you want, but Zack will not be continuing with this today."

Miller sighed. It took him a few seconds to accept that he was in the same position as he as before, but with a videotape that proved he had been unable to find the little girl, and a little boy the same age as Kiera crying in a room in the FBI building.

"I understand, Mr. Rogers. It's late. We're grateful to you for Zack's effort and willingness to help. I'll call you if I need anything else. Please don't worry."

He showed them to the exit and ruffled the boy's hair as he said goodbye. He asked if any agents on their way home would be able to give the family a ride, but nobody offered, so he had to apologize once again. Then he went to his desk on the second floor thinking about how complicated everything was becoming. He turned on the computer screen and sat in silence for a few moments with his head in his hands.

"That pushy journalist from the *Press* has been calling you," said his workmate, who was a couple of years younger than him, but had a moustache and actually looked about ten years older. Agent Spencer was a shining light of the FBI's Missing Persons Unit, not because of his talent or his ability to analyze and solve complex cases, but because he had had the good fortune to work on a series of cases with happy endings one after another. They nicknamed him "the Talisman" because whenever he was assigned to the search for a missing teenage girl, she'd turn up a few days later at her boyfriend's house, or the case of a missing child would turn out to be a matter of one of the parents violating a joint custody agreement. He was a magnet for cases in which the missing person would appear as if by magic in some place in another state, because they'd run off with a new partner or gone to stay with another family member on the other side of the country. In contrast, despite being a competent and determined agent who always worked longer hours than anyone else, Miller had worked on a series of cases which seemed to get complicated and further from being solved.

"Did she call me here, at my desk?"

"Yes. I picked up last time and I told her you'd call her later. That you were busy with an identikit sketch.'

"I've never met anybody quite like her."

"Is she hot?"

"Not because of that, you idiot. Because she's the only person who has never once stopped looking for the little girl. She could be useful to us."

"To us? You're losing your mind, Ben. Don't go getting me involved in this business with the little girl. I've got a perfect track record. I don't want to ruin it. If I carry on like this, maybe they'll put me in charge one day."

Miller sniggered because he knew that was nothing but luck. He suspected Agent Spencer couldn't find his own balls in the dark, but he kept that comment to himself, aware that his superiors only looked at the stats, that Spencer's one-hundred-percent record was undeniable, and that one day he might have to kowtow to him.

The phone on his desk rang again and Agent Miller shushed Agent Spencer before answering.

"That'll be her again. You can tell me what you say to her later. She certainly has a sexy voice."

Miller picked up the handset hoping that Miren hadn't heard that last comment.

"Have you got anything, Agent Miller?" the girl asked in a neutral tone. After several years at the *Press* and following many encounters with the police, lawyers and the businesses which she dissected in each of her investigations, she had learned to know when she could call the shots and when she needed to cozy up to people. With Kiera's case it was a mixture of both. She obviously wanted to find the girl and to avoid jeopardizing the police investigation, but she also knew that she was in a position at the *Press* that meant she could force things with a bold article. In her conversation with the agent, she had agreed to delay publishing the contents of the video of Kiera, but after speaking with the parents that same morning she had discovered that a boy from the neighborhood had seen the person who'd brought the tape. This changed the urgency of the investigation. An identikit portrait would spread like wildfire among the media and publishing it might help to find whoever had Kiera.

"Miss Triggs... you remember our agreement. You promised me you wouldn't publish anything for four more days."

"But Agent Miller... if you have an identikit portrait wouldn't it be better for it to be published in the *Press*?"

"Yes, but the problem is we don't have one."

"What do you mean you don't have one?" asked Miren, surprised.

"What I said. The boy doesn't... doesn't remember her very clearly."

Agent Spencer thrust his hips in a manner impossible to put into words, and mouthed a crude comment that was impossible to repeat. Miller frowned and shook his head.

"What are you planning to do? What else have you found these three days?"

"It's a dead end, Miss Triggs. There's nothing more. There are no prints on the tape, and nobody saw anything apart from the boy, who can't remember the woman's face. A team is looking for information about the wallpaper with that pattern, but the quality is so poor that it could be any floral wallpaper. As a last resort, they're also looking into the model of that little wooden house in case it's something unusual and if we can work out where it was bought, but I can tell you now it's a job for a much bigger team than we currently have available. After what happened to that poor devil my superiors are very cautious with this case, and with just three people helping me, and no more than a week left to spend on it, the case will go cold again."

"You're already thinking of closing it? Are you really not able to put more resources into it?" asked Miren, amazed. Her deep voice seemed to attack him from the other end of the line.

"Miss Triggs… this is more complicated than it appears. Do you know how many children disappear each year in New York alone? At the moment, there are more than a hundred missing children's cases open where we have found no trace of them. And I'm just talking about the cases that have been open for a year or more."

"One hundred?"

"It's terrible, isn't it? Reports of missing children increase that figure by at least 20 every day. Most missing child cases have a happy ending, but these hundred gradually grow up, year after year, getting a few inches taller. There is a whole team whose sole job is to produce simulations of how these children evolve, trying to establish what they would look like today in case anyone comes across them in the street. This is a much bigger issue than just Kiera's case, Miss Triggs, and you really need to believe me when I tell you I'm doing what I can. I don't have more eyes to put on it. My hands are tied."

"You need eyes to review that tape? Is that what you're telling me?" asked Miren, an idea forming in her head.

"I'm just saying there's a lot to investigate, and we have limited resources. We're doing the best we can with the small team available."

"If what you need are eyes, Agent," Miren declared, "you'll have two thousand of them watching that damn tape tomorrow."

Chapter 30
Article published in the Manhattan Press Thursday November 30, 2003 "The Snow Girl" by Miren Triggs

You may remember little Kiera Templeton, who disappeared in the center of New York in broad daylight during the Macy's Thanksgiving parade, aged just three. According to her parents, Kiera was a happy, cheerful child who liked Pluto the dog, and wanted to be a shell collector on the beaches of Long Island when she grew up. Ever since her disappearance, my life has been closely linked to hers; after all, part of the reason I'm a journalist at the *Manhattan Press* is due to a piece of luck that put me in the right place at the right time, and, I should add at this point, with the right beliefs and lifestyle. And I'll tell you why.

I was raped.

Yes, you read that correctly.

It's difficult to write that word without shaking and feeling as though the keys of my keyboard almost want to escape from beneath my fingertips. Not only was I raped, but they never arrested my attacker. It was as though I was assaulted by a ghost that October night in 1997, when I couldn't see the jaws of the tiger in front of me, disguised as a smile, when he grabbed me by the hand and dragged me into the darkest cave of my life. It was difficult to get out of that cave. For a long time, I couldn't do it. Nobody tells you how, nobody shows you how. Even you yourself don't know how to act after something like that happens to you. You look at yourself in the mirror and search for what's wrong with you. Search for the reason you don't cry like you did before, or why you can't stop crying. You think about revenge and buying yourself a gun, as if this would protect your soul from the harm it's already suffered. As if, were the situation to repeat, you'd be able to pull the trigger and put an end to the trauma.

The first time I read about Kiera, I imagined her letting her hand be held by that same tiger, a smiling flatterer who told her that everything was going to be fine. Then I imagined her agreeing to play at hair salons and dressing up, just like I agreed to walk to that park in the middle of the night, as if it were something fun that I didn't think through when dizzy with alcohol, as if I were that three-year-old girl who didn't know that smiles can hide sharp teeth. That haircut and change of clothes made her invisible in a city of eight million people and, even today, nobody knows where Kiera Templeton is, just as I don't know where the Miren Triggs of six years ago is after she disappeared at the moment a shadow led me into the darkness.

Today, for the first time, I am making that rape public because, unwittingly, it connected me to Kiera Templeton and because since I learned of her story, I've seen in her the little girl I once was, who nobody found in the dark depths of the cave. And because, as was the case for me, Kiera needs your helping hands to escape that darkness.

I have looked for her for the last five years, trying to find myself along the way. Last week, as incredible as it may seem, I saw her again.

Yes. Once again, you read that correctly.

And when I say I saw her, I don't mean she appeared to me in my dreams one night, but that I saw her alive, in a room, recorded on a videotape sent to her parents five years later. It is the most macabre game I've ever seen. She has become a mirage that is both awful and hopeful for the parents who have already lost everything and now only have the hope that she may one day be reunited with them.

In the first of the images that accompany this article, you can see a freeze-frame in the best resolution possible of what Kiera looks like now, aged eight, extracted from the videotape sent to her parents, in case somebody recognizes her or has seen her at any point in the last few years. In the second image, you can see the room in which Kiera plays peacefully, in case anybody recognizes an object or anything else relevant that might help find her. On the following two pages, you will find every recognizable object found in that room and visible within shot, enlarged as much as possible: a bed, a mattress, some curtains, a door, a dress, a wooden house, and the tiles on the floor.

When I finished watching the tape sent to her parents, which is just 59 seconds long, recorded on a 120-minute tape, the screen was filled with endless white noise, the ceaseless snowstorm that invades our television sets when we have no signal. I also saw Kiera in this, but this time, I admit, in a metaphorical way. It was as if the little girl I have always searched for had been turned into snow, not the kind that melts on warm fingers, but the kind that is impossible to catch, with black and white points jumping from one place to another. Kiera Templeton is lost in that snow right now and she needs your help.

If you have information about Kiera Templeton, please call 1-800-698-1601, extension 2210.

Chapter 31
Miren Triggs
1998

Although you may not know it yet,
sadness circles around your companions.

Professor Schmoer stayed with me for a couple of hours while I looked online for information about James Foster, the suspect detained for Kiera's kidnapping, and his wife. He also provided brief explanations as I made my way through the contents of the CD he'd brought, in an effort, I suppose, not to feel alone. He'd been unsettled since I'd shared my concerns regarding the arrest of the suspect, nervous about that doubt, and he had exchanged his enthusiasm for a caution I attributed to him considering what to do about it.

After waiting for the outdated Civil Registry webpage to load, so slowly it almost seemed pedal-powered, we managed to access the suspect's civil status among the public records. There were almost four hundred James Fosters in the state, but only 180 of them lived in zip codes corresponding to central Manhattan. His date of birth was listed on his Megan's Law file, and it wasn't difficult to find his civil record after half an hour checking each name via its link, with visited links turning purple to help us keep track.

James Foster was married to a Margaret S. Foster, and Schmoer celebrated with a whispered "Yes!" when he saw that she was exactly a year younger than him. My hypothesis seemed to be growing stronger. If I was able to confirm it, I would somehow find myself with an interesting piece of information, perhaps before a lot of other media outlets. I might even be in a position to exonerate him before the police did, who I was pretty confident would use the full 72 hours they had to interrogate him before holding him on remand for the attempted kidnap of the other little girl in the city center. Although it may have been due to good intentions, this mistake could temporarily halt the search for Kiera. I didn't really know how to confirm that his previous convictions for abuse of a minor were due to a particularly strict interpretation of the law, but my head was insisting that I put all the pieces of the puzzle in place and keep moving forward. As I had learned from Professor Schmoer himself, investigative journalism wasn't something quick. Each time an investigative team from a paper decided to research a topic, they might work on it for months before publication, sometimes even years, and they always kept several articles on the go, making small amounts of progress on each, putting each small cog of a complex Swiss watch in place so that it would eventually give the exact time in an article that would have repercussions, many of them unpredictable. This required following a line of investigation until it was completely exhausted before moving on to the next and draining that as though it was a lake containing a hidden monster. The monster was the truth, often painful, often insignificant, often so simple and elegant that it resembled the famous equation of a certain white-haired scientist.

"How can we confirm that Margaret S. Foster was James Foster's so-called victim, Professor?" I asked him, at something of a loss as to how to progress.

"Please, call me Jim. I don't know why you keep calling me Professor."

"I don't want you to stop being a Professor. I wouldn't like it at all. It's… my favorite subject.'

"Don't you prefer Interview Techniques? I've heard it's taught by the legendary Emily Winston."

"It's extremely boring. All she does is go on and on about how good she was at the *Globe*. It's a subject exclusively about her and her hundreds of interviews. And she doesn't actually seem all that good at it to me. Sure, she succeeds in extracting information, but it's usually irrelevant. In the last interview of hers, I read she was in conversation with a handsome serial killer jailed for murdering several women, and do you know what she achieved? She got the killer to show her the fan mail he received from his admirers and how he sent loving responses to them. She wrote a lovely article, accompanied by charming photos, about how attentive he was to his dozen admirers and how much he seemed to care about them. I'm sure that after reading that article, a few women would be impressed by how handsome and considerate he seemed. I don't know. Humanizing criminals doesn't strike me as being in journalism's best interests."

"They're still human, even though they're criminals."

"Some of them are monsters," I said firmly and seriously, "and no article will change that."

He nodded and pushed his glasses back up with his finger, a gesture he repeated every so often. He was quiet for a while, and I realized he'd noticed my anger about the topic.

I despised that kind of person, killers and rapists capable of doing such damage without feeling the fear in their victims' eyes. I'd read a lot about them. At some point over the last few years, it had become fashionable on television to discuss the atrocities they had committed, and some journalist or commentator would always highlight, with a clear combination of admiration and disgust, how extremely distanced these psychopaths were from other people's feelings. That was how I'd felt after what happened to me: distanced from my body, from my sexuality, from my emotions. Somebody had crushed my soul and turned me into a quivering wreck who hid at home as soon as night fell. Part of me wanted my emotions to be back where they always used to be, close to my heart, and not where they seemed to have ended up: in a dark corner of a park I still couldn't walk through, even in broad daylight.

"You'll see, Miren," he said finally, "perhaps your hypothesis would be a good follow-up article for a paper. So far none of them have considered this possibility. I'm sure of it. Nobody dares contradict the *Press*."

"What do you mean?"

"If it turns out you're right that James Foster is innocent, as he seems to be, whoever breaks the story will rise so high in public opinion that no editor would turn them down. Believe me. I was managing editor of the *Daily* until today. I know what matters to the management at those papers. Image, credibility. That's why I'm not there myself now. I was always a step behind and I paid for it. That kind of forward step is what any newspaper looks for in its journalists."

"But what if he is guilty?"

"We're very close to knowing, Miren. The ball is at the edge of the hole, all you have to do is nudge it in. Don't you see?"

"But... how?" I asked, looking but unable to see.

"Using any journalist's most valuable weapon: the source. You have his address from the sex offender's register. You can ask his wife and confirm your theory. It's not something to do cold. You can't just turn up there and ask for her story. That's what a sensationalist would do. You are an investigative journalist working to confirm a hypothesis, Miren. And all you need is a yes or no from Margaret S. Foster. It's something you can get just by asking her and observing her reaction."

I remained confused. I had never taken the step up to face-to-face investigation before. We had done assignments where we interviewed our classmates or professors as part of our course. Sometimes, the interviews had even been with writers or politicians, but those had always been over the phone.

"You can do it, Miren," he said firmly.

I hated going out at night and it must have been past nine. We still had time to reach the Fosters' home, and try and talk to Margaret before the main papers' first edition deadlines. Professor Schmoer had promised me that if I confirmed my theory and wrote a sufficiently high quality article about the arrest without any holes, he would send it to his colleagues at other papers to see if I got lucky and had my first article published. If my hunch was correct, Margaret S. Foster would either be at the 20th Precinct police station waiting for news of her husband, or at home with her two children, crying over his arrest without understanding what was going on or why they were taking so long to release him following what could only have been a misunderstanding.

"Do you want me to come with you?" Schmoer asked me.

Part of me was about to say no, but I saw how dark it was outside the window and I could only agree.

According to the form, the Foster's home was in Dyker Heights, and Professor Schmoer persuaded a taxi to take us there for a small fortune. That taxi ride was the first time I felt like a real journalist. I watched the streetlights go by outside the car window and I felt like the city was one enormous story to tell. We passed through the clouds of steam from the drains as though they were giant curtains hanging from the skyscrapers. We followed the driver's chosen route without difficulty, and I was left with the memory of a city made up of lights and shadows, bold yet frightened, as if it wanted me to reveal what happened around each corner and at the same time prayed the world would never find out what it was hiding. We crossed the Brooklyn Bridge and, after arriving on the other side, I felt my emotions begin to change as we drew closer to our destination. Everything was slightly darker and hid something that reminded me of that park in the middle of the night. Schmoer remained silent for most of the journey, but at that point, and I think in part because he was aware that my fears were beginning to surface, he asked me:

"Have you forgiven that guy… Robert? The one who took you to the park that night."

"What?"

"Have you been able to forgive him for… for not doing more to protect you? My understanding was that he ran away, leaving you on your own with… with those guys."

"According to his police statement, they beat him and left him defenseless, but I don't remember any of that. I remember a fleeing coward. He wasn't even brave enough to identify the only one they arrested in an identity parade."

"I know he identified a different man to the one you did. Then he said it was too dark to be sure and identified someone else. I read the report. He made everything more complicated by doing that," Professor Schmoer said in an understanding voice.

"And thanks to him… he's still on the street. A rapist is on the loose. Another one out there."

"Did he apologize to you?" Schmoer asked.

"It took him several months to do so. He turned up at the classroom door and… he read me an Oscar Wilde quote about forgiveness. It was the most childish thing I'd seen a grown man do in some time. I told him to leave and that I never wanted to see him again."

"I guess he didn't want to help you, just himself," responded Schmoer, reading the situation.

"That's what I thought."

The taxi stopped in front of a house with its Christmas lights half put up. The entire street seemed to have finished the job apart from one other that stood in complete darkness some distance away, and the huge buildings shone so brightly it was almost like daytime. Christmas always came early in that neighborhood, a tradition that had been started by a neighbor on 84th Street in the mid-sixties and which soon spread among the rest of the locals.

"Kiera's parents live around here somewhere in the neighborhood," Schmoer said after getting out of the car.

"It must be awful feeling that somebody so nearby has taken their daughter."

"But that may not be the case. That's why we're here. To at least address that doubt."

"Yes, but they still don't know that."

The fact that there wasn't a single person on the street, although the neighborhood was considered something of a tourist destination at this time of year, made me dizzy. I walked along the sidewalk to the front door of the Foster family home, a light visible inside, as though I was crossing a rope bridge. I gave three firm knocks with the golden door knocker and a dark haired woman with dark circles under her eyes opened it wearing a dressing gown.

"Who are you? What do you want?" she asked, her expression suggesting she had no idea what we were doing there.

Chapter 32
1998

Happiness makes you believe you
have company, sadness, on the other hand,
that you've always been alone.

Aaron began to weep as he collapsed exhausted onto the couch at home after taking Grace up to the bedroom to rest following the procedure at the hospital. On one side of the living room, on a table that was normally full of framed photos of the three of them, were the telephones of the little hotline they had set up, which had been abuzz with calls over the past few days, but had now fallen silent. The volunteers had gone home hours ago once they were sure the influx of calls had slowed. One of the phones began to ring insistently as Aaron lay there and he leapt up, letting the tears that ran through his beard fall onto the handset.

"Hello? Do you know anything about Kiera?" he asked hopefully.

But the only sound on the other end of the line was the echo of the laughter of a couple of teenagers who were calling as some kind of sick joke.

"They should have kidnapped you, you sons of bitches," he shrieked, disgusted. "My three-year-old daughter has disappeared. Don't you understand?"

He thought that perhaps one of the voices would apologize, but a couple of seconds later he heard the painful sound of two giggles once again, moving away from the telephone.

Aaron yelled.

He did it so loudly that a dog in the street howled in sympathy. Then, unable to bear it a second longer, he grabbed the telephones and yanked on them, pulling out the cables of the splitter that connected them to the hotline. He threw the phones into the trash can and cursed himself for ever having sought the world's help.

Throughout the years he had worked at the insurance company he had always tried to help his clients out in some way. He would slightly alter the forms so his bosses would rubber stamp them, he would turn a blind eye when it came to initial questionnaires for health insurance, he would invent damage to pristine vehicles with the sole aim of changing the color of the car's paintwork. It wasn't a job that excited him, but it allowed him to pay the bills and live comfortably, with the only downside being that sometimes he had to be accountable and turn down policies when his superiors passed on complaints to him about his office's low profit margins. He was happy to meet the minimum quota, reaching but never exceeding the goals he was set. This meant he was popular with his clients, although obviously not with all of them. It was impossible to be loved by absolutely everybody when he had to refuse an expensive cancer treatment or explain that, after an accident in which a man had lost both his hands while working on his car in his garage, the insurance would only pay for one to be reattached.

He considered himself a good person and helped out wherever he could: he gave thirty dollars a month to an NGO working to improve the lives of children in Guatemala, he kept his recycling in perfect order, and he tried to help out with local charity collections. Perhaps that's why his neighbors helped him: because they knew he was a good man. But the people who didn't know him, all those people who only sympathized with him due to the morbid fascination generated by Kiera's disappearance, just wanted some kind of spectacle: a surprise here, a run-down of the facts there, an on-screen breakdown during peak viewing hours. But finding Kiera was the equivalent of that daring triple somersault between the trapezes without a safety net at the end of a circus performance. If they succeeded, it would be cheered and applauded. If not... the people would still go home happy because they'd already seen the lions jumping through the flaming hoop. He still couldn't believe what had happened, and he spent a while contemplating how much had changed in the space of a week. Kiera's disappearance, Grace's miscarriage. The touch of Kiera's fingers, the sound of her voice shouting "Daddy". He went out into the street to try and control the awful thought that was creeping up from his stomach towards his mind, like a dark gargoyle that wanted to climb up onto the top of his head to better survey the desolation of his family.

Then his cell phone rang. He took it out of his pocket: the display showed Agent Miller's number. At that moment he'd have taken anything that gave him something to cling onto so he didn't fall into the void, even if it was just a tiny flicker of hope: a small advance or a contradiction in the suspect's statement would be enough to hang on to.

"Tell me that son of a bitch has confessed where Kiera is," he said as soon as he answered.

"I can't do that, Mr. Templeton. And... we believe he is innocent. I had to tell you."

"What?!"

"His story matches up. He seems a good guy. An average Joe who works at Blockbuster, married with two kids."

"But... but that doesn't mean anything. Just because he seems a good person doesn't mean he is."

"We know that, and I know you need him to be the kidnap-per, but he wasn't even in the city when Kiera disappeared."

"Are you telling me it wasn't him?"

"I know it's difficult to take in, Mr. Templeton. The public wants justice, and the front page of the *Press* has made things a bit complicated for us. But it seems like the guy just wanted to help."

"Help? He tried to take a girl away in the same area where Kiera disappeared. It has to be him, Agent Miller. This can't be happening," Aaron exhaled, almost begging.

"Didn't you hear what I said? He wasn't in the city when Kiera disappeared."

"Have you checked? How can you be sure?"

"He has a record, but the accusation was dismissed. He was in Florida last week. We checked the passenger records and it's true. He got on a plane on November 24th and arrived back the day before yesterday. We've checked the cameras in Times Square and at no point does he seem to be taking the little girl by force. It's just that... the parents got panicky and overreact-ed when they saw her with a stranger... his record and the hysteria about... about Kiera did the rest."

"And the little girl? What does the little girl say?" Aaron asked desperately.

"I shouldn't be telling you this, but I'm doing it anyway because I sympathize with what's happened to you Mr. Templeton. I have a niece Kiera's age and it's all very upsetting, but we can't just grab anyone."

"But what does the little girl say?"

"The little girl says she was lost and that he said he would help her find her parents. Whether you like it or not, we have no evidence that suggests he's the one who has Kiera."

"Let me speak to him. Please."

"We're going to release him, Mr. Templeton. That's why I was calling. So the press doesn't find out. I think it's the least we can do. We're doing all we can and… that article in the *Press* was a real shit-show. It's really tied our hands. His lawyer has made a complaint that we don't have anything concrete against his client and… he's right."

"But you could interrogate him for longer."

"We can't. It's better for the investigation. Every moment we waste on him we're not exploring other avenues. Do you understand? I know you're desperate, but please trust the police. Perhaps it's for the best. We'll keep on with the search, we'll analyze new leads, and we'll review what we already have, but this is a dead end. The guy is innocent."

Aaron had moved the cell phone away from his ear as soon as he heard Agent Miller ask him to trust the police. His only hope had evaporated during a three-minute call. He felt the chill of Dyker Heights hit him in the face, saw how the lights on the house of one of his neighbors, Martin Spencer, suddenly went out, no doubt at the time they had been programmed to do so, and spotted the outline of a yellow cab from the city center crossing the street in a southerly direction. He noticed it because it was unusual for anyone to travel there by taxi from Manhattan, but he forgot about it when he felt a snowflake land on the end of his nose. He let his cell phone drop onto the lawn and went back into the house, which felt even emptier than it had a few minutes earlier.

He immediately heard a sound coming from the bedroom where he had left Grace resting, and he rushed upstairs. As he got closer he recognized the creak of the bedsprings, like when Kiera snuck into their bedroom and bounced on it. For a moment he imagined that it was Kiera, doing what she always did when they weren't watching her. He even imagined he heard her giggle, her almost uncontrollable laughter that had always reminded him of fingers running over a piano's high notes. But when he arrived upstairs and reached the doorway, he realized that Grace was having an epileptic fit in her sleep.

It was normal for it to happen at night. Grace had even faked a fit occasionally as a joke to annoy her sleeping husband, although really her fits were infrequent, occurring only when she was stressed or worried about something that made her feel threatened. Grace's mother also suffered from epilepsy and, along with her brittleness, it was the only thing she had left her daughter before she died.

Aaron sat down beside Grace on the edge of the bed and stroked her hair as the episode continued, whispering to her that it would soon be over. When the fitting finally stopped, Grace half opened her eyes, sleepy, aware that she had just had a fit, and gave her husband an exhausted smile. Aaron whispered in her ear that he would always love her, and she closed her eyes again, knowing it was true but that she no longer cared.

Chapter 33

1998

Unknown location

We lie to hide the truth
or so as not to hurt people, but also when
we wish the lie were true.

William arrived home carrying several plastic bags and still wearing his work overalls. His hands were dirty, with black lines of grease under his nails. He waved hello and stopped in the doorway when he saw that Kiera was sitting on Iris's lap watching television. The little girl looked towards the doorway and then turned back to Iris, who churned out non-stop excuses, one after another, with increasingly contradictory reasons as to why she couldn't see her parents.

"How was your day? Better?"

Iris sighed and hugged the little girl affectionately as she sat absorbed in the stampede scene from *Jumanji*. They had bought the video a couple of years earlier and had never got round to watching it at home. A group of monkeys broke into a store selling televisions and stereos, and leapt about while they ransacked it, and Kiera let out a laugh that was like heavenly music to Iris's ears.

"Are you crazy? Shut the door right now. It's freezing and Mila will catch a cold."

"Mila?" he asked, surprised.

"Yes. She's called Mila. I've always liked that name. Isn't that right, Mila?"

"Nooo! Me… Kiera," she protested with concentration and a cheeky smile on her face.

"Don't say that! It's a bad word! Don't say Kiera. Say Mila. You're called Mila."

"Mila?" asked Kiera, confused.

"Yes… that's right," Iris said happily, with a small jump that must have felt like a rollercoaster beneath the child.

"Look, monkey!" the little girl pointed to the screen again and laughed. She had been through several ups and downs that day. She'd woken up on the couch confused, having spent the entire night curled up next to Iris, who didn't stop stroking her head for a second, watching her sleep in the moonlight that shone through the only window in the room. When she woke she'd asked for her mother several times, just as she had on the previous days, but later she'd acquiesced to Iris and they'd played together with some porcelain figures from the lounge sideboard. At lunchtime, Kiera had cried for a while, asking to see her father, asking why he didn't come home to have lunch with her like always. Those questions hurt Iris, and deep inside she got angry and part of her questioned the situation, but she'd noticed that as the days went by, after the first week or so, Kiera seemed to be asking for her parents less and less. She was starting to get used to Iris's company, to her invented games using all kinds of objects from around the house, like a juicer, a photo frame, or an imitation Chinese lantern they'd bought from the same hardware store as the wallpaper. When Kiera asked for her parents, Iris would tell her that they'd had to go away on a journey, and they wouldn't be back for a while. Once, she had told her that her parents were very angry with her for asking for them so often and that they didn't want to see her again, but the little girl had responded by sobbing desperately.

Iris looked at her husband and, with a tone of voice three octaves lower than the one she used for Kiera, asked almost in a whisper:

"Did you bring it?"

"Yes. I bought a bit here and a bit there in different shops."

"Did anybody see you?"

"Of course, Iris. How else could I have bought it?" he whispered.

"I mean anyone from the neighborhood."

"I went to a shopping mall in Newark and only bought one thing in each store. I told the assistants I was buying it as a gift."

"Did you go like that? All dirty from work?"

"How did you expect me to go? I went straight after I left the workshop, for the love of God. You're turning into a psycho, Iris. Nobody is going to find us out. Nobody needs to see her. She's our daughter."

"It was on the news, Will. They're looking for her everywhere."

"What?"

"They're looking for her. The FBI gave a press conference with the latest progress. They're going to find us, Will."

"Listen to me. Nobody is going to take our little girl away from us. Do you understand? She'll never leave this house if that's what it takes. She can be our private treasure. Nobody needs to come into our home."

"We can't raise a little girl without her leaving the house. All children need to go outside and play and interact with other children. Mila is a happy girl, and in time she'll want to go out. To play in the park or to run about on the lawn."

"She'll do as we say, because she's our daughter," he said, raising his voice, which made Kiera turn to look at him in surprise.

"Where's Daddy?" the little girl asked, her face lit up by the screen.

"Mila… honey… I've already explained it to you," Iris whispered, turning to Kiera and stroking her short hair. "Will is your Daddy, too. He loves you very much and is going to take care of you like I do."

Kiera looked into Iris's eyes and whispered, "I'm tired… can… can you tell me a story?" tripping over her words in the middle of the sentence.

Iris looked at Will, swallowed and sighed.

"Of course, sweetheart. Which story would you like to hear?"

"The one… the one where Mommy and Daddy come."

Chapter 34
November 30, 2003
Five years since Kiera's disappearance

People read the papers to
find answers and not questions,
and perhaps that's the problem.

Miren Triggs' article was a media bomb across the country. Although other papers had covered Kiera's disappearance during Thanksgiving with short articles a few paragraphs long, nobody had been expecting anything like this. All the news channels tried to get hold of a copy of the tape during the morning it was published in an attempt to jump on the media bandwagon that this unknown journalist had set in motion.

Kiera's face on the cover of the *Manhattan Press* had caused a huge reaction five years earlier, but at the end of the day, people were used to the idea of a child disappearing. It was a sad fact, but it had been just an initial frenzy which had calmed down before the end of the year. The country had got used to seeing the faces of missing children on milk cartons, enriching the breakfast cereal of the United States with desperation throughout the eighties and the early nineties. This system of adverts on milk cartons had been superseded by the introduction of AMBER alerts, but was so embedded in America's subconscious that everyone knew about it, even though few people had actually seen one of those milk cartons displaying a black and white photo of a child's face.

When a paper like the *Press* adopted the polar opposite of its previous stance, asking for help and publishing several key pieces of a seemingly unsolvable puzzle, people were taken aback. The world reads the papers to find answers, not questions, and perhaps that was the problem. Maybe that was the reason the entire country was stunned by the article.

When Miren reached the office that morning, she found the smiling secretary at the front desk listening to a call with her headphones on.

"Is Phil in?"

"One second," she said, addressing the person on the other end of the line. "He's already in and he's asked for you three times. He wants to see you. I took the kids to your desk. They're waiting for you there."

"How many have come?"

"Two."

"Just two?"

The secretary nodded with a smile. Miren looked up and saw a girl and a boy slightly younger than she was in the distance, waiting by her desk.

"Is Phil angry, Eli?"

"Oh, who knows. He always seems to be."

"When were you planning on leaving?" Miren asked as she took off her gray coat, trying to buy herself some time.

"Before Christmas. We'll see how it goes."

"I'm sure it will be fine. You'll be missed."

"Humph, I don't think so, not so much. They hardly look up to say hi when I arrive."

"It's.... it's a pretty tense job. But don't worry. Once you're famous I'm sure they'll call and request an interview. Then you can wait for them with your biggest smile, and they'll have to come and see you wearing their most forced smiles. I'd love to be a fly on that wall."

Elizabeth smiled and looked down.

"Is he in his office?"

The secretary raised her hand, gesturing to the side, and nodded. Then she continued dictating the address of the office to the person on the phone and Miren stopped listening to her.

She hurried to her desk, aware of her colleagues' eyes on the back of her neck as she made her way across the office, and raised her hand to wave hello to the two youngsters. Then she pointed to the phone on her desk, which had been ringing for the past few seconds, and addressed them:

"Hi, I'm Miren Triggs. Do you see that phone there?" she asked with a forced smile.

They both nodded, nervous.

"If anyone calls, answer it and note down everything they say. Everything," she reiterated.

"Which of us should answer? There's only one phone," said the boy.

"Good point," Miren hadn't considered this detail. "Take turns and make a note of everything that's said. I'll hire whoever has better handwriting."

"What?!"

"It's called meritocracy, kids," replied Miren, before turning round. "Welcome to the *Press*."

The girl looked at her with excited eyes and nodded; the boy with a look of incredulity, before looking at his friend.

Miren made for the office belonging to Phil Marks, the Editor in Chief of the *Manhattan Press*. His door was open, and he was talking with one of the editors about the documents relating to the invasion of Iraq by the Bush administration. She waited for them to finish, leaning against the cold frame of the glass door, and Phil gestured for her to come in as the editor walked past her on the way out of the room.

"Miren, you need to explain to me what you did yesterday. That article about Kiera was not approved, it didn't go through review, and your senior editor told me that he had already warned you that you had to drop the topic. We're not a sensationalist paper and we can't stoop to this."

"Mr. Marks, just let me tell you…"

"No, let me finish, please."

Miren swallowed, trying to rid herself of the guilt she felt, although it was almost gone anyway. Phil could be sharp, but he was also one of the most rational people in the country. If he published something, it had to be in the interest of the general public. If something appeared on the pages of the *Press*, it was because it was going to bring about change.

"You can't send an article to print without review, Miren. We're at war with Iraq. The government says that Saddam has weapons of mass destruction, and we are the *Press* and we have to check that the government's claim is true. That's what the entire investigative team is working on right now."

"I understand, sir."

"However, I have a daughter the same age as that little girl. She's called Alma and… if I was going through the same thing as that family, I wouldn't want to hear a deafening silence from a country focused on what's happening thousands of miles away from home rather than fighting the enemies who live next door."

"I'm not sure I've understood you."

"There will be other parents like me who feel their pain. Everyone knows someone around that age: nieces, cousins, daughters, granddaughters. That little girl needs help too, not just our servicemen on the other side of the world."

"I'm afraid you've lost me, Mr. Marks."

"We already published the picture of Kiera on our front page back in the day. It would be selfish not to continue helping now that the case is lower profile. You can continue with the investigation. But don't mess it up. This coverage of yours is causing a real impact. Good luck."

"Th… thank you very much, Mr. Marks."

"You're most welcome. Do you have everything you need?" he said, looking for some papers on his desk.

"I took on two interns from the university. I think I can manage them."

"Fine. Start there. I want two articles about the girl per week. And I want you to find her, Miren."

"To find her?" Miren asked, tense.

"You don't think it's possible?"

"I didn't say that. It's just that… that I've never seen anything like it."

"Nor have I, Ms. Triggs, and that's the very reason you need to deal with this story carefully. That tape… I don't like this case at all."

"Thank you very much, Mr. Marks."

"Don't thank me. You're doing a good job. Jim was right."

"Professor Schmoer was always a good friend."

"How's he doing? We were rivals, but I've always admired him. I think the world of journalism is worse off without him."

"He's focused on teaching and… he has a regular slot on university radio that he records each morning and is broadcast in the evening. He hasn't changed at all. It's good to hear him. You can almost take notes from each show."

"That's good. It'll be a good sign if he manages to get more journalists like him graduating from that university. Perhaps he's doing more good there than he was at the *Daily*, looking for financial swindles and pyramid schemes. I don't really think it was the kind of article he should have been writing, you know? A journalist needs to find an area they're passionate about and immerse themselves in it, get really stuck into it. I always knew that he'd never found the area that fulfilled his sharp eye and critical focus."

"It was him who started me off on the search for Kiera," said Miren, trying to recommend him a bit more.

"Maybe the search for this little girl is up his street. I could hire him so you can work together here. After all, he was the one who recommended you with that exclusive on the release of the guy who tried to snatch that other girl, with those tapes he was recording."

"I'll ask him. I haven't spoken to him in a while. Perhaps he'd like to give me a hand."

"Keep me updated, please. Two articles a week. And we'll see how much material we can get to go on with."

"Thank you very much, Mr. Marks."

"One moment... I haven't finished," he continued.

"Yes?"

"Is what you wrote about the rape true?" he asked, catching her by surprise. His eyes locked with Miren's as he was waited for her answer. She didn't know whether it was compassion or curiosity.

Miren nodded silently, serious. Almost so serious that Phil Marks felt uncomfortable at having raised the subject.

"You didn't need to share it in the article," said Mr. Marks.

"I know."

"So why did you do it?"

"Because I needed to get over it."

"I understand," he said, nodding, but then he continued, "Is it true they didn't catch the guy who did it?"

"The police? No," said Miren, as she left the office.

She went back to her desk, where the new intern was listening to a call and her colleague was attentively watching what she wrote down in a spiral-bound notebook. He realized that Miren had come back, and he tapped his colleague on the shoulder. The girl turned round and continued listening carefully to the caller, nodding, while Miren watched her. Then she turned back to her notebook with a look of surprise and wrote something in it. She asked for the caller's name and phone number in case she needed to speak with them again and then hung up.

"I've just spoken to senior management," said Miren, seriously, "and I have good news."

"You get to speak with Phil Marks, the Editor in Chief of the *Press,* in person?"

"Yes, sometimes. But only when someone screws up, or does a really good job.'

"What did he say?"

"In summary: that today's edition is selling like hot cakes. I'll explain later. The good news is that both of you can stay. You get three-month training contracts. Five hundred dollars a month plus travel expenses. You buy your own meals. You can bring a packed lunch. There's a kitchen on the next floor down. Good luck, you've just taken your first steps in the world of journalism. You'll need to give your details to Human Resources, two floors up. OK... have there been any calls other than from head cases with ridiculous tip-offs?"

"What counts as a ridiculous tip-off?" the boy asked. "Only two people have called so far."

"Good question. Tell me what we've got, and I'll tell you. I'm sure they'll be good examples."

"The first call was from a lady in New Jersey who says the girl in the photo really reminds her of her niece."

"That probably counts as ridiculous. What about the second one?"

"I don't know whether it's relevant," the girl hesitated.

"Go ahead and tell me."

"It's about toys."

"It might be ridiculous, but it might not. Go on."

"The owner of a toy store says that the doll's house in the photo looks like a Smaller Home and Garden made by the Tomy Corporation of California. It's not a very common model nowadays, but it was popular in the nineties."

"Interesting. And not ridiculous. Perhaps we could go somewhere with that. Look online for a list of all the toy stores that sell doll's houses. Keep waiting for calls. I've got a few things to do. If you need anything, ask Eli on reception. Miren wrote down her cell phone number in the notebook. "Call me on this number if there's anything interesting."

"Until when? How late do we wait for calls?"

"How late? Didn't I tell you that you're part of the world of journalism now?"

They looked at one another confused, but they took the hint. Miren smiled and left, leaving them at her desk. The telephone rang again and this time it was the boy's turn to answer the call. His colleague watched Miren as she moved away towards the door with a sort of admiration, surprised at the confidence with which she walked.

Miren thought about whether she might have made a mistake in what she'd said to Phil Marks and repeated it to herself in her head: "The police? No."

Chapter 35
September 12, 2000
Unknown location

*Love blossoms even in
the darkest corners.*

William opened the front door wearing a grin that stretched from ear to ear, dressed in jeans and a blue polo shirt, and carrying an enormous box wrapped in red paper. It was eleven in the morning, and Kiera came running out of her bedroom to greet him with a hug and cries of excitement.

"Is it for me? Is it for me?" she kept shouting.

Iris came out of the kitchen and smiled.

"What's that?"

"I saw it in a window display and thought she'd like it."

"What is it?" shouted the little girl happily.

"Happy birthday, Mila," Will added.

"Is it my birthday?"

"Of course, honey," he replied, knowing it didn't matter. "You're five. You're a little lady today."

Iris was a bit annoyed, but she didn't want to say anything. Last year they'd given Kiera a doll that she'd got bored of after just two days. If the toy was anything like as big as the box, it must have cost a fortune which they absolutely couldn't afford, especially if Kiera was going to tire of it as quickly as she had the doll.

"Don't worry, OK? It was on sale," Will whispered to Iris while Kiera bounced around in excitement.

Will put the box on the glass table in the living room and watched as Kiera laughed non-stop to see a present in front of her that came up to her forehead.

"It's really not that big. A lot of it is the packaging," Will said, making excuses.

"It's enormous!" yelled the girl, "It's the biggest present in the world!"

Little Mila tore through the paper and saw a massive box with a clear plastic front, inside which was a toy house, complete with furniture and garden. 'Smaller Home and Garden' in bold type announced the contents of the box, but Mila didn't know how to read yet and merely stared at what was inside.

"A doll's house! It's a doll's house!"

Iris looked at Will and couldn't help smiling. It seemed to have made Kiera happy, in contrast with recent weeks. Kiera had nightmares at night, and seemed withdrawn and unwilling to do anything at home during the day. Iris, who had tried to homeschool her and teach her literacy and math as best she could, found herself faced with a brick wall and felt like she was failing as a mother. Seeing her happy was a consolation and relieved some of the weight of her guilt.

"It's a doll's house, Mommy! Look! It has a little tree!"

"Yes sweetheart. It's a doll's house! Happy birthday!"

"I love you! I love you very much!" shouted Kiera, and she really meant it. She was euphoric, and Iris was on the verge of tears after hearing those words. Will went over to the little girl and kissed her on the forehead. Then Iris did the same, and they spent several minutes together opening the huge cardboard box and removing the house. They arranged all the miniature furniture on the glass table, and Kiera arranged them in size order from left to right before carefully putting them in the right places inside the house: kitchenware, chairs, tables, couches, wardrobes and beds. Then Kiera checked the box again and found a narrow little hallway. She couldn't decide whether it should go next to the couch or the bed. Will gave his wife a complicit look and a half smile, and, slightly worried, she signaled to him that they needed to talk in private. They left Kiera in the living room and went to the kitchen to argue in whispers.

"How much did it cost you?"

"It really wasn't that much."

"More than a hundred dollars, right?"

"Four hundred."

Iris covered her mouth with her hands.

"Have you lost your mind?"

"It'll last her a long time. It's a toy for life. It's cheap. She'll still be able to play with it when she's older."

"She won't want to play with it when she's older. It's too much money, Will. We can't afford it. We owe the bank a lot of money and you're the only one working."

"You could work."

"I already do, Will. Taking care of her and the house. You're a goddamn sexist."

"Don't talk to me like that. Don't be unfair," William snapped.

"You know I'm right. And you're the one who's unfair. If I worked, who could we leave her with? We can't take her to school. People are looking for this little girl, Will. You're just mouthing off. You don't think before you speak."

"Can you keep your voice down? She's going to hear us," Will replied, "although maybe it's time she learned where she came from."

"Don't you dare tell her anything of the kind. I don't want

to see her cry anymore. It's bad enough with her asking again and again to go out into the street and having to tell her no. I'm the one who has to deal with how sad that makes her, you know? You're not here to see her begging and pleading."

"So what do we do? Go out with her anyway? We'd be in jail in less than ten minutes, Iris. There's no going back."

Iris took a deep breath, trying to relieve her anxiety and the tension in her chest. Will went over to her and gave her a conciliatory kiss on the forehead. Then he hugged her tightly before moving away just far enough to take hold of her face and look her in the eyes.

"She's our daughter and I will do whatever is necessary for her. And if I have to tighten my belt so she can have a nice toy... then I'll do it, understood?"

Iris felt her husband's embrace. Sometimes she doubted him and questioned whether he was doing enough for the family, but then she remembered that it was thanks to him that Kiera was there with them, having walked with her through the Thanksgiving crowd until they reached Penn Station subway stop.

"I know, Will... It's just that this... is really difficult. I spend hours here with her. And... when I look into her eyes, I feel like she knows the truth."

"She doesn't, sweetheart. How long is it since she stopped asking for her parents?"

"Almost a year."

"You see? Relax. We're her parents and we always will be, understand?"

Iris made a strange face and Will looked at her, upset.

"What's up?"

"I can't hear her playing."

Will and Iris left the kitchen, concerned, to check that Kiera was alright. Iris had once read in an article that nothing was more terrifying for parents than when their children fell silent, but just as they reached the living room, they realized there was: the front door was open and there was no sign of Kiera anywhere.

"This can't be happening," said Will.

"Mila?!" screamed Iris at the top of her voice.

Chapter 36
Miren Triggs
1998

The devil sometimes lives
a quiet life in the morning only to
make up for it at night.

Margaret S. Foster was a warm, sweet-natured woman who invited us in out of the November cold. She led us into the living room and invited us to sit down, but we declined her offer so as not to waste too much time. Inside, the house was beautiful, as you might expect from the neighborhood: floral wallpaper, a pink velvet couch, molded ceilings, and a parquet floor. She apologized for the fact the children were already in bed and couldn't come down to say hello. I felt uneasy. Really uneasy. There was a strange, sharp pain in my chest when I thought of the reason for our visit. Schmoer and I exchanged awkward looks, then he took the lead, since I hadn't:

"You know your husband has been arrested, don't you?"

"What?"

"You didn't know?" asked Professor Schmoer in surprise.

"Your husband. He's been arrested for the attempted kidnapping of a seven-year-old girl."

She stayed silent, but much could be read from her silence. They say a person is a slave to their words but a master of what they don't say. This was the perfect example of how this saying was not true. There was regret and sadness in that silence.

"Haven't the police come to speak with you? Do you really know nothing?" I asked, confused.

Schmoer gestured to me with his hand, and I understood.

I could tell she was nervous, and I knew something was wrong. It was as though she was about to fall apart—all we had to do was touch the weak point in the structure then stand and watch.

"I've been calling him all day, but he hasn't picked up. Nobody's told me anything."

"What do you mean? Are you trying to tell me nobody's informed you that your husband has been arrested?" Schmoer asked again.

She shook her head and began to cry. I didn't understand. I tried to catch Schmoer's eye, but he was focused on the woman's sadness.

"But... there's no need to worry. I'm sure it's a mistake," I said, trying to join the conversation. Without knowing why, I felt an urge to comfort her. "I'm sure it will all be cleared up and they'll release him. Your husband doesn't seem to be a pedophile. We've come to confirm that. We've come to ask you to tell us the details of his previous conviction."

She nodded, swallowing as she stared into the middle distance as if she were opening a dark box of secrets. All of this was filling my own box with pain.

"We know he was arrested at the age of 18 for sexual relations with a minor who was 17 at the time," I continued, "and we deduced that you were the minor and that you were boyfriend and girlfriend back then. We know the law can sometimes be rather unfair and... well, if the girl's parents make a fuss you can get into all kinds of trouble."

"I always told him he had to stop. That it wasn't right. That God was watching, and it wasn't right. But he was carried on," she said finally.

We remained silent, inviting her to continue, and realized that her eyes had glazed over with a thin but growing film of tears, the accumulation of many years' sadness.

"That was… the start of everything. We started dating when we were just kids, he was 14 and I was 13, although he was always very mature. You might say he did grown-up things. He would smoke and drink. And I liked that. I showed off about him to my friends, you know?" she looked at us but then her eyes drifted back to her memories. "We began to have sexual contact very early and my parents caught us the very day we did it for the first time; there was a lot of shoving and yelling. They kicked him out of the house and for a while they forbade us from seeing one another. But that wasn't going to stop two teenagers full of hormones, and we began to do it in secret. My parents had never liked James. They said he acted strangely, that he behaved like a womanizer. But I loved him. He looked at me with a desire that made me feel truly alive."

I nodded, because that was what she expected me to do, then she went on:

"One day, when I was 16, he asked me to shave my pubic hair. It seemed really daring to me and it was nothing compared to the kind of stuff we were already doing together, but over time it became a condition, and he would refuse to sleep with me if I didn't do it. He found it gross, he considered it insulting that I didn't want to shave my private parts. I gave in. I was in love. It seemed unimportant. We were still seeing each other in secret when he turned 18 and it was around that time that my parents caught us together. I was still only 17. My father reported it, got a restraining order for a few months and James was sentenced to attend a course on which they told him that what he had done was bad."

"Then it's true that his previous offences were for consensual sexual relations with you."

"Yes. That's right."

"If that's the case, I'm sure they'll release your husband. You need to stay calm. No doubt the kidnap attempt is just a misunderstanding and he just wanted to help a lost child and take her to the police station."

"Where does your husband work?" asked Schmoer.

"At a Blockbuster. You know, the video rental store. It's two minutes from here."

"Haven't they asked where he was? He's been in police custody since last night," Schmoer interrupted with the question I had been about to ask.

"That's why I'm telling you this. So that you know, and you can include it in the statement." She put her head in her hands and then looked up at the ceiling, as though she could see what was happening in the bedroom upstairs. "How am I going to explain all this to the kids?"

I realized that Margaret thought we were police officers. Neither of us had said anything one way or the other. Schmoer put his hand inside his jacket and took out a tape recorder, which he turned on and set on the table. A 60-minute cassette began to roll, involuntarily recording the woman's worsening sobs and, no doubt, the pounding of my heart.

"Please go on," Schmoer said in a serious voice. I just swallowed, nervous, learning at that moment that it's better to listen to stories until the very end.

"But on that course... he met more people. It was a kind of group therapy and all of them had committed the same kind of crime: they were sex offenders. Almost all of them were older than James, who was still 18 and was really just a child still. According to what he told me when I turned 18 and we started to see each another again, they had been convicted of more serious crimes but were out on parole. It was a program to... help with rehabilitation." She paused, trying to order her thoughts, and then went on, "And that was when he started to change. He started to meet up with these older guys. He spent more and more time with them. Every so often I would get angry because he didn't seem to want to see me and when he did it was just for the sex. My parents disapproved of my relationship with him—they were very traditional—but I was over 18, and they couldn't tell me what to do. It didn't take long before I got pregnant and my parents made us get married. He didn't want to, he said he hated priests, that he'd met plenty of them and they weren't trustworthy, but in the end, he gave in. Then he got a job at a Blockbuster, and everything went smoothly for a while. He received several promotions, and he would always come home with a smile. We had our daughter, Mandy, and then we made a lovely family of four."

I sighed. I didn't like where this was heading.

"And then what happened?" Schmoer asked.

"Then I found the tapes in his office," she said in a rush.

"The tapes?"

"Videos. Dozens of them, of girls filmed outside schools. Of groups of girls walking down the street. They weren't sexual, I wouldn't have tolerated that at all, but when I saw them, I asked him for an explanation. Do you know what he said?"

"What?"

"That they were for his friends, the ones from his course. That he filmed the videos for them and they paid him serious money for those images of teenage girls in short skirts. He told me that he did it because he was the only one who knew how to use a video camera and he had all the equipment at the store to make as many copies as he needed. He'd set up an illegal business selling videos of young girls, recorded without their consent."

"That's disgusting," I declared, overcome with anger.

"Your husband would film girls wearing miniskirts in the street without their knowledge, and sell those images," Schmoer said, trying to summarize.

Margaret covered her face with her hands, and I watched her break down to the point where she could barely speak. She seemed to be fighting with herself for a few seconds and then she continued between sobs.

"He promised me it would end there. That it wasn't a crime because there was nothing sexual about it. And that he could get rich off the fetishes and perversions of a bunch of lowlifes that he'd met at that group."

"But it *is* a crime," I interrupted, angry.

"You have to understand, I'm not a lawyer. I... I focused on caring for my children and ensuring they had everything they needed. He was earning so much money with those tapes that we had enough to buy this house. How else could a manager at Blockbuster earn enough to live in this neighborhood? With time I got used to the idea, and that was when James began to spend several days at a time away from home, travelling to other states. He would often go to Disneyland because he said it was easy there, and when he got home he would make several videotapes that he kept in the basement. That's why I didn't know they'd arrested him. Because I thought he was on one of his... trips."

"And then it all moved onto another level, right?" I asked, scared of finding out the truth. "And you didn't dare report him then. When all is said and done, you're complicit. You were afraid... of losing what you had."

"I was afraid of losing my children," she whispered.

"And what about other people's children? Did you ever think of them? What do you have to say about Kiera Templeton, the three-year-old girl who disappeared a week ago? Do you think your husband kidnapped her?"

"Kidnapped her? James has never... has never done any-thing against... against someone's will."

"Your husband was arrested for the attempted kidnapping of a minor, Mrs. Foster," I repeated, trying to get her to understand the facts.

"I don't know why he'd do something like that. It's not... not like him at all."

"Not like him?" I asked. "Mrs. Foster, what your husband is doing is accelerating his journey into a dark world, can't you see that? It's pathological. He wasn't doing it for the money. Open your eyes. He was doing it out of his own desire."

She didn't reply, instead her lower lip began to tremble, and a tear rolled down onto it.

"Hold on a minute.... Your children...did he...?" Schmoer asked.

She shook her head and I sighed, somewhat relieved.

"He never crossed that line, thank God. I've never left him alone with them. Never."

"Alright," said Schmoer, looking dejected.

"And Kiera. Do you know anything about Kiera Templeton?"

"Come with me, please. I need to show you something."

She got up from the couch and led us to a door beside the bottom of the stairs. When she lifted the latch, we discovered it was the entrance to the basement, a hole disappearing into darkness. She turned on a light, a single lightbulb hanging from a cable, and went down the creaking stairs. At first, I didn't see anything unusual when we reached the bottom, but then I realized I was mistaken: there was a metal shelving unit full of videotapes with labels showing different numbers: 12, 14, 16, 17, some of them even a 7 or a 9, and I realized that all the numbers were below 18. There were also a couple of wooden tables with cardboard boxes on them and several posters of Californian beaches were tacked to the walls.

"These are all..." said Professor Schmoer, trying to authenticate the evidence.

233

"Recordings, yes," she confirmed curtly.

Margaret went over to the shelving unit and crouched down by one of its corners. Then she pulled on a rope and lifted a wooden trapdoor that revealed the way down to somewhere even darker. She pressed a switch, and Professor Schmoer and I leaned forward, not wanting to go down. At the bottom was a small single bed and, facing it, a video camera mounted on a tripod.

"He started to pay teenage girls to... to come here so he could film them."

I started to feel ill and had to lean against the table for support. I was nearly sick.

"You knew about this and didn't say anything?" I asked, shocked.

"I knew about it, but they came voluntarily. Lots of them were even friends with my children."

"What?"

"They would come over and... well, James would offer them 30 or 50 dollars and... they would go down there without complaining. The girls wanted to. And... so did the boys."

"Boys too? Did your children know about this? Did they know he was paying their friends to... to record them down here?"

She nodded, compliant. Professor Schmoer took out a disposable camera that he always carried with him and took a photo of the depths of the basement, focusing on the bed and the tripod. Then he took another of the shelves with the videotapes.

"You're going to arrest me, aren't you? It's the end. I've been thinking for years... if only it was over, but... I didn't want to lose my children, do you understand?"

"We're not police officers, Mrs. Foster. We're not going to arrest you and nor do we have to understand."

"What do you mean you're not police officers?" she cried, surprised.

"We're not. But if I were, I wouldn't even let you say good-bye to your children," I said grimly.

We went up to the living room and from there Professor Schmoer called the district attorney's office to inform them of all we had found, and to report that horrible case. After many years working at the *Daily* and reporting dozens of cases of corruption and fraud, of uncovering society's hidden scams, and of being a confidante and support when it came to documenting stories that often ended up in court, he had reached a mutual understanding with those high up in the judiciary and the police. He came back with a detached and rather worried look on his face.

"Did you tell them? Are they sending the cops?" I asked, confused.

"They've just released him without charge..." he replied, leaving me in shock. I couldn't believe it. My faith in justice and the system were destroyed with a single sentence. How could I have been so naïve? How could I have believed the system worked?

"Without charges? What are you talking about? The basement is full of evidence!" I yelled.

"Somebody hasn't done their job properly, Miren," he replied seriously.

"Properly? They haven't even come to this house to check anything. They haven't done anything!" I shouted. I noticed that my voice was about to crack. "And what did the attorney's office tell you? Did they tell you they're going to arrest him again?"

"They asked me to turn on the TV."

Chapter 37
1998

Some people are like
fire: others need it.

The flames filled TV screens across the entire country. Then they jumped to the front pages of newspapers across half the world and soon that image became the symbol of a justice the authorities failed to enforce but which the people demanded: the hypnotizing dance of the flames consuming James Foster right outside the police station.

The authorities had decided against pressing charges just one day after his arrest. The girl he had supposedly tried to kidnap near Times Square confirmed James's version of events, none of the cameras in the area showed any sign of attempted kidnapping, and the previous convictions for sexual relations with a minor turned out to be those instigated by the parents of the woman who was now his wife when the couple had both been young. The police didn't want to appear influenced by the front page of the *Press*, which implied that James Foster could also be responsible for Kiera Templeton's disappearance, and a deadly hatred of him had arisen among the public from the very moment his face flooded newspaper kiosks throughout Manhattan. At midday, a crowd of people gathered outside the entrance to the police station where he was being held and subjected to an intense interrogation by the police. At six in the evening as people left work, the crowd, which had started to attract news attention, had swollen to hundreds. The demand for justice gradually diminished and by midnight there were only 30 people left, mainly activists waiting for a statement from the police to inform their next steps. Over the course of the day various news reports and daytime talk shows had spread details of the case, constructing theories and creating sinister scenarios and endings in which James Foster could have killed Kiera Templeton but had not, thank God, done the same to the seven-year-old girl he'd tried to kidnap.

When Foster finally appeared on the street, escorted by two officers assigned to get him home safely, there was such a commotion that somehow, nobody was sure how, among all the pushing and shoving, everyone suddenly realized James was covered in the stench of gasoline. The two police officers quickly found themselves overwhelmed and knocked over. From the ground, as various people set upon them for protecting a killer, they saw James's expression of terror as he looked everywhere and nowhere at the same time. A ring formed around him and when statements were taken later from all those who had been part of the mob, nobody was sure who had struck the spark that had precipitated the most powerful image in the nation's living memory.

The fire quickly spread from his feet to his face. Some witnesses recall James's cries, begging for mercy, kneeling with his hands raised, but they all agree they stopped watching as soon as they realized things might have gone too far. After barely a minute James was lying lifeless on the street, continuing to smoke until another police officer finally arrived with a fire extinguisher.

The stories carried by all the newspapers the following day confirmed James Foster's innocence, accompanied by a large photo of the man in flames and subtitles such as: 'Innocent

Man Burnt To Death', 'Sole Suspect In Kiera Templeton Case Burns Alive' and 'Mistaken Justice'. The photograph, the only one in which James Foster is pictured with upraised hands, in profile, the fire illuminating the anonymous, blurry faces of the people who watched him burn, was taken by a photographer affiliated with the Associated Press, a not-for-profit news agency, who had waited there to observe the crowd at the police station door with their demands for justice. Months later, the image won that year's Pulitzer Prize for Photography.

Every newspaper led with the story, proclaiming the innocence of a man who'd been released having been found innocent of all charges of attempted kidnapping. Every newspaper but one.

A few hours before the newspapers reached the streets, Phil Marks, head of the *Manhattan Press* received a call around midnight from Jim Schmoer, a former classmate at Harvard with whom he had attended more parties than lectures back in the day. They had pursued similar careers but with different papers, and they had kept in sporadic contact. They both worked in New York and both had risen quickly to the top of their chosen areas. Jim had earned a reputation as an investigative journalist, feared by corporations and the powerful; Phil had struck it lucky in the articles he had got involved with, plus he had sufficient funds available to him to study for a MBA while he worked, which gave him the opportunity to get into newspaper management.

"Phil, I've got something really juicy."

"How juicy? I've just pulled tomorrow's front page to kick off with James Foster on fire outside the police station. They burned an innocent man alive, Jim. And we put him in the spotlight yesterday. It's our fault. We need to seek forgiveness."

"That's exactly what I wanted to talk to you about. He's not innocent. He doesn't deserve to be seen as the victim of injustice."

"What makes you say that?" Marks asked, interested to

hear more.

Schmoer summarized the situation for Phil. He told him that the prosecutor had just sent officers to the Foster's house, and they were there waiting.

"And do you think he could have the little girl, too?"

"Kiera? No. We've already searched the whole house. They don't seem to have any other properties. They don't have her. That part is still up in the air."

"And why aren't you telling all this to the *Daily*?"

"For two reasons. Firstly... I don't work there anymore. They fired me today for always being one step behind. It's ok, it wasn't really for me."

"You're one of the best there are, Jim. It's just that... you haven't found your niche. Nobody's given you the freedom you need."

"The second reason is that... this discovery wasn't mine. It's the work of my best student and I think she deserves a chance."

"A student? Is she there with you?"

"Yes."

"Alright. Come to the offices right now. You already know the address. It's going to be a long night," he declared.

"We're on our way."

Miren had been walking around the garden, trying to process what she had just discovered and how she herself had undermined her own theory with such a horrible truth. She realized that part of her wanted people to be good, for there to be no evil in the souls of men, and that this had been the goal of this visit to the Foster home: to confirm that it had been a mistake to arrest him. But when you shine a light on a shadow, sometimes you find that what's hiding in its depths is darker than you could have imagined.

Professor Schmoer had just hung up and was waving Miren over as three police cars arrived in front of the Foster's house, their blue lights off.

"I called the *Press*."

"Why?" asked Miren, surprised.

"You've got a probationary period there starting in 45 minutes. We need to go now. There's no time to waste."

"What?"

Miren Triggs arrived at the *Press* offices with Jim Schmoer at one in the morning with the intention of writing the article there and then. There was no time to go home, send it via email and trust in a reliable internet connection.

"Miren Triggs, right?" Phil Marks greeted her as soon as he saw her come in. "We've been waiting for you. If all this about James Foster is true, tomorrow we'll have the only front page that tells the full story and not just a tiny fragment that twists the truth, and that, Ms. Triggs, is what ought to guide a good journalist. Thanks for this, Jim."

"My pleasure. It's always great to visit you here. And, having just been fired, I didn't feel like giving this story to my former bosses. Just another part of my endless fight against injustice!"

"We'll give this the profile it deserves, provided Ms. Triggs can prove she knows how to write a good enough article to make the front page of the *Press*."

"The front page?" Miren was astonished.

"Don't you think your story is good enough for the front page? Because if it's not good enough for the lead article, it wouldn't stand up to scrutiny as a simple column on page 30. We make sure all our stories are strong enough to feature on the front page. Take a look at any of them and tell me which one you wouldn't put there."

Miren didn't reply and Phil Marks led her to a desk at the far end of the office. There was already a copy editor waiting there on standby to review the article as soon as it was ready, and a layout editor was waiting in the design office ready to add the finishing touches. In a side room, Jim handed over his disposable camera with the images that were due to accompany the article. Miren sat down in front of the computer, more nervous than she had ever been before.

"You've got 25 minutes, or we won't make it."

Miren's fingers began to fly over the keyboard, from one side to the other. As she typed, she felt as if the nerve endings in her fingertips were directly connected to the rage and impotence this story made her feel.

In the article she told the unvarnished story of the path of perversion and descent into darkness taken by James Foster, an employee at a suburban Blockbuster. She also detailed how he had set up a kind of production and distribution empire from home working with pedophilic images, along with the statement made by his wife, Margaret, in which she explained how he blackmailed and bribed minors with the intention of filming them for his clients scattered across the world. The article was accompanied by one of the photos taken by Professor Schmoer with his disposable camera in which a bed with a rusty frame and rumpled sheets was visible in front of a tripod. While Miren wrote the article at top speed, the printing presses waited to get rolling, Phil suggested various titles, sent the copy editor out for a couple of coffees, and told the layout editor to be ready and waiting at his desk for when it was ready. After a tense few minutes when they didn't think they'd make the strict deadline they had to meet if they wanted to get the paper onto the streets first thing, Miren said a simple "finished". The clock showed just 21 minutes had passed.

After a quick read through by Phil Marks, Professor Schmoer began to applaud and was soon joined by the copy editor and Phil himself, congratulating her on joining the *Manhattan Press*.

The next morning when all the other papers demanded justice for an innocent man, an article in the *Manhattan Press*, under the byline of one Miren Triggs, stood out, providing the details of the life of James Foster, who had gone up in flames upon his release, and his wife, Margaret S. Foster, who was currently in police custody without a single paper knowing who she was, why she had been arrested or that her children were being cared for by Children's Services. The scandal would go on to prompt a lengthy debate about the death sentence in New York State, about how far justice should go in such cases, and the incompetence of the police force who had released a man with such a chilling room in his house. The feeling on the street, though, was that the flames had been the most fitting punishment for somebody like James Foster.

Chapter 38
November 30, 2003
Five years after Kiera's disappearance

Perhaps there's still some-
body out there who doesn't
want to know that thorns grow fearlessly
on even the most beautiful rose.

Miren left the newsroom and walked to a nearby parking lot where she paid a monthly fee of almost three hundred dollars. It was extortionate, but she had stopped using the subway some time ago and had accepted the outlay as a way of not having to share a crowded space with strangers. Hardly anyone in New York travelled the city in their own cars and for a while she had managed to deal with the issue by using taxis, but as soon as she started having to leave the office for stories, she realized this was unsustainable. She knew it was contradictory; it often meant it took her longer to get to places and in journalism that was inconceivable. But she had joined the *Press* not as a successful journalist, in that world where stories churned out at an unrelenting pace, but as a member of the investigative team, where she had to deal with topics that had gone unnoticed or been hushed up, digging into them to find the truth. This type of journalism moved at a steadier pace, although it was not without stress. Miren always had the feeling that another paper would steal her story before she could publish it, and, in practice, having to work on several complex stories at the same time and visiting archives, attending court proceedings, going to government offices and public registers, was a mountain of work that was only made worthwhile by the potential impact of the articles she was publishing. She would often work in a team when what she was investigating took on a bigger dimension, a crew of three or four journalists and additional collaborators, but she undertook other investigations alone, following a trail without anybody else at the paper knowing. One day, without anybody asking or suspecting what she was working on, she arrived at the office with an article written in a sharp, emotional style about a 16-year-old girl who had disappeared in a mysterious rural town called Salt Lake whom nobody seemed to be searching for. In contrast, on another occasion she turned up with a story that seemed to suggest that senior members of the Justice Department enjoyed themselves fooling around with underage girls at a Caribbean nightclub.

Miren gradually managed to cultivate a reputation and, although Kiera Templeton's disappearance had reached a dead end at the moment when the sole suspect went up in flames, she never stopped looking for her.

She had rented a unit in a red-brick warehouse by the river. There, she stored all the reports and files she had gathered, which she had already read through so many times that she didn't think she could find anything useful in them. Before raising the shutter that allowed access to the unit, she looked both ways to make sure nobody was watching her. The street was deserted, and the rest of the garages were closed. She pushed hard and the screech of the rusty metal filled the air, disturbing the calm of the place.

Inside, there was dust everywhere, but the accounts and

records were stored in a dozen well-ordered metal filing cabinets arranged around the walls. On the front of each drawer there were numbers written on small pieces of card indicating the relevant decade, spanning from 1960 to the fourth cabinet on the right, labeled with a simple '00'. The rest of the cabinets had names written on the drawers including Kiera Templeton, Amanda Maslow, Kate Sparks, Susan Doe, Gina Pebbles, and many more. This was where Miren kept all the information on the open cases that didn't seem to have a solution, in the hope that finding a new lead might suddenly clarify what had happened.

She opened Kiera's drawer, took out several folders and a box, and arranged them on one of the cabinets. She crouched down to put everything in a canvas bag and, perhaps due to the silence, perhaps due to the tension she experienced whenever she was in that unit full of sad, difficult stories, she jumped out of her skin when her phone began to ring in her jacket pocket.

"Mom? You've no idea what a fright you just gave me."

"Me? You're not doing anything dangerous, are you?"

"Of course not. I'm... at the office. Do you need something? I'm busy."

"Um... no. I just wanted to see how you are."

"I'm fine, Mom."

"The house felt a bit empty on Thanksgiving this year without you here."

"I know, I'm sorry Mom. I had to work, honestly."

"And I'm glad, sweetheart. You're doing what you love, what you studied to do, but..."

Miren closed her eyes. She felt awful.

"I know, Mom. I'm sorry. I'd been trying to finish an article for weeks and... things got complicated at the last minute. A source pulled out, recanted their story, and we couldn't publish anything like that without confirmation. It was a race against the clock to find a new witness to verify the story. I really am sorry."

"You celebrated Thanksgiving at the office, didn't you?"

"If it makes you feel better, I promise I didn't spend it alone. The paper has to be at the kiosks and on people's front doorsteps every day of the year. The office was full of people just like me. The bosses ordered in turkey and peas for everyone. Don't go imagining I ate a pathetic sandwich in front of my computer."

"That's what you do almost every other day," her mother shot back.

"Yes, but not on Thanksgiving."

"I'm glad they're treating you well, honey. You deserve it."

"We all have to pitch in. The internet has meant big changes and some departments are downsizing. I guess it's the moment to go the extra mile. What would the world be without journalism?"

"I don't know, honey. What I do know is that we miss you. Your father told that terrible joke about cashew nuts over dinner and he almost wound up with one stuck up his nose."

"Again?" Miren laughed.

"You know your father."

Miren was so absorbed in the conversation that she didn't notice the sound of footsteps behind her or the movement of the shadow looming over her shoulder until a strong hand grabbed her from behind and covered her mouth, causing the cell phone to fall to the floor with the call still in progress and Mrs. Triggs listening in astonishment to the fall of the phone and her daughter's muffled screams:

"Miren? What's going on? Are you still there?"

For a few seconds the man holding her did nothing, just squeezed her tightly, silently, trying to assess Miren's reactions and how strong she was while her heartrate soared as her defense mechanisms kicked in. For a second, the image of herself lying sprawled across the bench in that torn orange dress in which she had run home, panic-stricken, played on repeat in her head. Her breathing sped up as she realized her mother was still on the line.

"This is going to be quick... I've got... a little something for you," threatened a hoarse masculine voice behind her.

"Miren? Who's that man? Miren!" Mrs. Triggs was shouting.

Her attacker began to pat down her jacket pockets until he found her wallet and slipped his hand in to take it. As he did so, Miren opened her mouth and bit down hard, trapping the man's index and middle fingers, causing him to shout so loudly it was audible on the phone call. Before he realized what was happening, he was on the floor with his head against one of the metal filing cabinets and the barrel of a pistol in his mouth.

"I've got something for you, too," murmured Miren, releasing the safety.

Chapter 39
November 27, 2010
Twelve years after Kiera's disappearance

*You can find yourself yearning for pain
if it's the only thing that brings you hope.*

Agent Miller arrived at the FBI office with the tape and immediately tossed his gray raincoat onto his desk, which housed a framed set of photos from his daughter's graduation, before heading for the forensics lab with the goal of confirming that, as with the others, there were no prints on the tape other than those belonging to Grace, Aaron and the person who'd found it. The first time, the prints had proven a false lead and upset a young boy whose sole contribution had been to mess up the identikit portrait, which indicated only that the suspect was a woman with curly hair. That identikit portrait hung on the wall of Miller's cubicle beside his computer monitor, only part of the face showing, the rest covered by a file of cardboard files full of papers.

The other two tapes that had appeared since 2003 had been handled so frequently that the prints found on them were useless, having passed through the hands of countless random strangers before finally reaching the police or the family.

At first glance, this fourth tape was just like the others: a 120-minute long TDK cassette, no case, placed in a buff-colored padded envelope of the kind available in any convenience store in the country. There were no postage stamps, no stains or scratches, just a number four written on it. The package seemed intact, and perhaps the fact it had been found in the mailbox of the Templetons' former family home meant that the sole piece of evidence they had might not be contaminated.

"Would you mind taking a look at this, John?" Miller asked the agent in charge of the forensics team.

"A new Kiera tape?! Has it been handled much?"

"In theory only by the Templetons, and perhaps by the tenant who lives in their old house. Let me know if you find anything."

"Are you in a rush?" John asked, worried.

"I'm almost 55. Of course I'm in a rush."

"Alright. I'll get back to you in a couple of hours."

"Could you digitalize it and send me a copy first, please? And for the love of God, don't let it leave this room."

"Alright," John agreed. "Is there anything noteworthy on it? Any change to the furniture or anything else? It was the third one where she was wearing the orange dress, right?"

"This one, she's just… not there."

John Taylor held his breath for a moment then continued in a determined voice:

"Alright, I'll get straight on it."

"Thanks, John. I'll be at my desk. Let me know what you find."

"Of course."

Agent Miller went back to his desk with little hope. After turning on his computer and entering his password, he accessed the department's intranet to review the three previous tapes and analyze the evidence for the umpteenth time. In the folder entitled 'Kiera Templeton' he had organized all the files relating to the case after a recent effort by the FBI to digitalize its archives and reduce the massive amounts of paper that accumulated with each new investigation. Forms, paperwork, reports, photos, negatives, physical proof. Each disappearance he dealt with required ever more space, gathering dust and increasing the risk of something being overlooked when it was needed. He opened the folder entitled 'Videos'. The originals were under guard in a room in the basement, inside a cardboard box he only visited to add a new original. The family received a VHS copy of each of them, at their own request, with the symbolic goal of holding on to the nearest thing they had to seeing their daughter. Inside the folder he found an extensive list of files corresponding to security cameras in the area where Kiera disappeared, along with others from later years, the result of efforts to clarify who was leaving the tapes at the different locations.

Whenever a new tape appeared he followed the same protocol: he would watch the previous videos of the Kiera tapes one by one, each filmed in that same sad room, so as to feel the impotence that made him move forwards and not give up. He opened the first one, the one he had watched the most times, and which had started everything off. After an eternal minute, during which endless questions presented themselves, he put his face in his hands.

This was the tape on which Kiera played with a doll in the wooden house, after which she got up and left the doll on the bed. Then she went and put her ear to the door before going to look out of the window. Later she came back, looked at the camera and the video finished.

In the second tape the Templetons had received, which was left at Aaron's office one day in August 2007, Kiera was already twelve and had a slender figure and skinny legs. Agent Miller tried to continue watching the images. In this tape Kiera, her expression serious, spent the entire recording writing something by hand in some kind of notebook. At no point did she look directly at the camera. The image quality was the same in both, and other FBI experts had deduced that the same recording equipment had been used for both, positioned on a fixed mounting, its image appearing directly on a nearby screen connected to a Sanyo video recorder, to judge by the magnetic pattern that had been left on the tape.

The third tape, which was found in a park in February 2009, was the worst one for the Templeton family and was the one they found most painful to watch. It showed Kiera, aged about fourteen, in her room with the door shut, sitting at her desk and writing something by hand in a set of black notebooks, crying and moaning as she did so. She stood up for several moments and seemed to yell something in the direction of the door, but her back was to the camera and it was impossible to guess what she was shouting. The language experts had deduced that it was a single, four-word sentence by analyzing the movement of her jaw in the video based on the movements of the bone below her ear. This implied that Kiera was not alone and that whoever was holding her was nearby in these moments and Kiera knew it, but it wasn't much further use. Four identical notebooks which appeared to be personal diaries were visible on the table at which she was writing. Aaron and Grace always observed these with pride and fantasized about what their daughter might have written in them.

On one occasion Grace Templeton had spent an entire night watching the video on repeat, weeping with her daughter, keeping her company in her sadness and whispering to the screen that she shouldn't worry, that one day her mother would be with her and would always look after her, that her shoulder would be there for Kiera to cry on, even if Kiera didn't know it, even if she didn't remember her existence. Kiera also looked different in the video: she wore her hair loose and had moved on from the braid she wore in the others, showing a mane of hair that already fell below her well-developed breasts.

The love Aaron and Grace felt for her as they saw her grow up so much from video to video grew and changed each time, because now they not only shared their memories of the first three years of her life, but also of being there with her when she cried, or the excitement if she laughed in any of them, or sensing her grow and mature as if she were a free spirit, even if she were shut up like a beautiful parrot in a gilded cage.

Special Agent Spencer, who had previously occupied the desk opposite Miller, got up from his desk at the far end of the office and went out to meet Ben.

"The girl again? A new tape?"

"That's right."

"We're already working on the other girl, Ben, the one from Pier Fourteen. We can't dedicate any more resources to this. You know that. Her search has already used the same resources as 30 disappearances put together. No."

"Just give me a day. Just for the usual processing: fingerprints, DNA, and to go over the camera footage from the area. Everything seems… different this time."

"We can't, Ben. We're close to finding the girl from the pier and I need you. The boyfriend's already confessed. Now we need all the eyes we can get to reconstruct where he could have dumped her. I want you to go down there and take part in the final stages. There's a team of divers on standby to search the areas we flag up. It's a done deal, but we need to narrow down our focus."

"I promised the Templeton family I'd review this."

"I can't divert one of my agents to go on a wild goose chase, Ben."

"I've never been one of your agents, Spencer. We've always been colleagues, nothing more."

"Well, you're one of my agents now, however much that bothers you. Whatever you believe about my not deserving my promotion, my record is 114 cases solved out of 120. You waste your time on cases that don't go anywhere and… everybody deserves to be found. Not just Kiera Templeton."

"You're an asshole."

"Don't make me start disciplinary action against you, Ben. Don't go there."

"Go ahead if you want. You've always been a dick and that will just prove it."

Special Agent Spencer's expression changed, becoming one of regret, and he said in formal tone, good and loud so the rest of the office could hear it:

"Agent Miller, you are suspended from duty for one month, during which you will not have access to the building, any resources or any material relevant to open cases. Your cases will be passed automatically to Agent Wacks."

Ben nodded, looking incredulously at the rest of his colleagues, who looked down. It seemed unfair that someone like Spencer had been elevated to such a position as a result of avoiding problems rather than confronting them like he did. He got up, grabbed his gray overcoat and fired his parting shot:

"You know what makes us different? The fact that you have always focused on your damn success rates, while I have worried about each and every one of the lives of those who disappeared without a trace."

"Well, don't make your career here disappear in the same way, then," Spencer declared.

Ben turned round and left Spencer standing there, unsure what the future held for his career as an FBI agent.

A while later a file entitled 'Kiera_4.mp4' appeared in one of Agent Miller's intranet files where he kept all the content relating to the Kiera investigation, but he had already been out on the street for a while, wondering what the hell to do.

He dialed the cell phone number belonging to Miren Triggs, that journalist at the *Press* who he had always considered an annoying fly in summer, but she didn't answer. Then he decided to call the *Manhattan Press* and ask for her, but a pleasant girl with a sweet voice told him she hadn't come into the office that day.

"Dammit, where the hell are you?" he asked, after hanging up.

Chapter 40
Miren Triggs
1998

We all have shadows
inside us of various shapes and sizes,
and when the moment comes, some
grow so big they cover all the others.

However harsh it seems, watching James Foster in flames on television in 1998 as I sat on his couch talking with his wife and almost able to hear his children sleeping upstairs, I didn't feel sorry. It was… as though for once in my life I got to see the bad guys get their just desserts. Finally.

I don't remember whether I snorted or gave a smile at the sight of that image, but that's how I was feeling inside. After the initial impact of the image and reading the tagline that was running across the screen (BREAKING NEWS: J. F. burned alive after being released without charge) on the 24-hour news channel, Professor Schmoer told Margaret he was sorry about what had happened to her husband, and I went outside so as to say nothing and avoid being a hypocrite.

I felt fucking fantastic, and I didn't want to ruin the feeling. Especially after Professor Schmoer told me I had my foot in the door at the *Press* if I managed to pass the test and write an article about James that very night. I was nervous and euphoric. It was a sweet mixture of emotions. Even though I hadn't found Kiera, this feeling of justice was pleasant and, although this route to finding her had become a dead end, I wasn't going to give up easily.

We reached the office after waiting for the police and telling them what Jim had already shared with the prosecutor. And there, in that office, magic happened. There were hardly any editors still in and the boss welcomed us with a powerful and sincere handshake. I wrote the article—which my parents hung in their living room with pride—against the clock and while I did so, I remember my only concern was not to acknowledge even a shadow of a doubt as to who the real James Foster was. When I finished and everyone applauded, that moment of connection occurred, that spark that transforms nervousness into happiness, and that was the first time that I managed, for a few hours at least, to erase from my mind what had happened to me that night in the park I no longer dared cross.

We left the newspaper office around three in the morning with a request from Phil Marks, the Editor in Chief, that we should come back the following day for the editorial meeting at four in the afternoon. I would start off on an evening contract after class until my studies were complete. Jim and I got in the elevator without speaking a word, the atmosphere serious, almost avoiding each other's gaze. We hailed a taxi that was heading in the opposite direction to where I was going and, once we'd both got in, Jim gave the address of my apartment without hesitation.

"Congratulations," he said. "You're in."

"Yes..." I replied.

I was about to explode, nervous, aware that it was a mistake I had to make, both inevitable and catastrophic. He was looking straight ahead, silent and I saw that his brown shoe was tapping on the car floor.

"You…"

And then I leaned over and kissed him, interrupting whatever he was about to say.

After a second of feeling his lips, I noticed how they separated like two lovers saying goodbye at an airport. He was moving me away, but in order to look at me. His eyes fixed on mine in the darkness of the taxi, the lights of Manhattan flickering through the window, illuminating his lips and his stubbly beard. I drew closer again and kissed him once more. He stayed still for a moment and seemed to enjoy it, but then he moved me away again, and I thought I had made a mistake and that this was the end of things.

"This isn't right, Miren," he whispered, in the gentlest voice I'd ever heard him use.

"I don't give a damn," I replied, in my own most determined voice.

We kissed for the entire journey. And in the stairwell of my apartment building. And while I wrestled with my front door. And while we took our clothes off. And while his glasses went flying to the ground, cracking one of the lenses, and, irreversibly, while our naked bodies lay on the bed in my tiny studio apartment.

We both regretted what had happened pretty quickly, but were both convinced that it was inevitable. He got dressed in silence, in the shadows. I was the first to speak.

"It won't happen again, Jim," I said in a low voice.

"Why? I like being with you, Miren. You're… different."

"Because you can't lose your only remaining job," I replied.

"Nobody needs to find out."

"You teach Investigative Journalism. You have an entire class full of people primed to sniff out the truth."

Jim laughed.

"So do we say goodbye now, as if nothing happened?"

"I think that's for the best."

He nodded, his back to me. He crouched down, still shirtless, to pick up his glasses and put them in his pocket.

"You'll go far, Miren. There's something different about you. I've never met anyone else like you."

"The only thing that makes me different from the others is that I'm stubborn."

"And that's a key quality for an investigative journalist."

"I know. I learnt it from you."

He finished dressing and I stayed in bed. Then he kissed me goodbye. During the years which followed I would often remember the way the beard that had pulled me out of my dark hole scratched.

The next morning the front page of the *Press* with the story of James Foster flooded the country and, for the first but not the last time, my name was bound with the Kiera Templeton case, for revealing the real story behind the only official suspect that would ever be linked to the case following the little girl's disappearance.

I called my family in the morning and told them the good news. My parents wasted no time in going out to buy several copies of the paper, which they distributed around Charlotte, boasting that their daughter was famous.

My mother asked whether I'd go and visit them that weekend as I'd promised, but joining the newspaper staff cancelled all my plans at a stroke. Years later I'd regret cancelling those spontaneous gatherings, especially following what I went on to discover, but back then I was just a girl who, heaven knew how, had managed to get a job at the *Press*.

I was going to take the morning off, but a hopeful seed, a burning flame, had taken root in my mind. Before I knew it, it was ten in the morning and I was walking through the door of a gun store, which looked more like a pawnbrokers from the outside.

"What model would you like? If it's to defend your home I'd recommend one of these," an older man who looked like a proud member of the NRA suggested. He took a sawn-off shotgun that looked like it weighed a hundred pounds out from under the desk.

"No... I... I just want a pistol. It's to defend myself."

"Are you sure? The bad guys will be carrying these if they break into your house."

"I'm sure, really. A pistol will be fine."

The store's walls and display cases were packed with weapons, displayed as if they were shoes. Rifles, pistols, revolvers, assault weapons. It was impossible to see all that and not experience genuine panic.

"If you spend more than a thousand dollars, we give you a 25-bullet box of ammunition for free."

"Oh... yes. Alright, a pistol and a box of ammunition."

The guy gave a kind of chuckle and pointed me towards a display case containing a dizzying array of different models and calibers of pistol. Then he told me I'd have to fill out a form and wait for the result of a check on my criminal record. Then he asked me for my firearms license, and I found myself in a corner.

"License?"

"You have to have one here in New York, sweetheart."

"I don't have one. I'm from North Carolina... there, well, it's normally easier there."

"You ought to buy a gun there then, if..."

"Can you really not turn a blind eye? I want it to protect myself and my home. I live in Harlem and it's crazy up there right now. They've already broken into my building six times," I lied.

"Blacks, right?"

I nodded. How easy it was to manipulate someone like this.

"The bastards think they're the kings of the city and wreck everything. I'll give it to you for six hundred if you promise me you'll shoot if they enter your home. Better them than you, sweetheart."

"Of… of course," I said. The idea of actually using the gun made me panic.

He put it in a bag and made me promise I wouldn't carry it on the street. Leaving the shop and walking along with it in my backpack made me feel odd. It definitely wasn't the same as carrying pepper spray, which I always carried, and which gave me about the same sense of safety as an umbrella. The weapon, on the other hand, gave me a different feeling, even though, according to statistics, carrying one increased your likelihood of winding up dead. No small number of arguments, attacks and struggles ended up with the weapon in the wrong hands, and a flash and a bang ended the life of someone who should probably have just handed over their bag or their wallet. But I needed that security, even if I didn't leave home with it. I needed it. I wasn't looking for revenge, that wasn't why I was doing it, but because I needed to relive the sense of justice I had felt on seeing James Foster in flames. Sometimes the bad guys have to pay, don't they?

When I got home, I hid the pistol beneath my pillow and checked that the CD Professor Schmoer had brought me was still on my desk.

I had until four in the afternoon before I was due back at the newspaper office, so, expecting more of the same, I put the CD into the computer to take a look before arriving for what would officially be my first day at work.

On the CD was a folder with recordings from almost a hundred security cameras in addition to the ones Schmoer had already sent me by email. In one of the subfolders were another hundred documents containing transcripts of interviews with the various inhabitants of the building where the pile of Kiera's clothes and trimmed hair had been found. If my deductions were correct, it was a complete copy of the police investigation. I don't know how Jim got his hands on it, but it seemed to be everything the investigators had so far.

I read the transcripts of the interviews the police had conducted and none of the more than fifty people living in that apartment block had seen anything. On that day, at that time everybody was out in the street enjoying the giant inflatables, trying to see the street performers or doing their last-minute food shopping for that evening's dinner. Those who hadn't gone out and were at home hadn't heard anything strange in the lobby of number 225. The folder also contained scanned copies of signed statements from two officers of everything on sale at any shop or grocery store in the area around Herald Square. East 35th Street was home to 57 stores of various types, but only the convenience stores, a small store selling gifts and sundries, and six takeout food joints, including a kebab shop, a place selling pizza for a dollar a slice, and four hot dog stands all around the junction, were open that day. Once again everything seemed impossible to solve, and I felt hopeless faced with so much information that didn't seem to lead anywhere.

The next time I checked the clock it was three in the afternoon, and I headed to the newspaper offices where everything had changed forever the previous night. I read the name of the paper on the front of the building nervously when I arrived and asked at reception for my ID pass to access the building.

"Miren Triggs," I said proudly when the receptionist asked my name and which floor I was heading to.

While she checked everything was in order, a hoarse male voice spoke behind me:

"Please, Miss, you have to help me find my daughter."

A hoarse voice was one thing, but his sounded like it had been shattered into a million pieces that could never be put back together again. I turned around, surprised. That was the first time I saw Aaron Templeton in person. He was holding a copy of that day's paper, the one with my lead story, looking completely desolate and with tears pouring down his face.

Chapter 41
September 12, 2000
Unknown location

Are thieves somehow not
afraid that someone might rob them?

"Mila!" Will yelled again as he left the house, looking in every direction. "Mila!"

It was almost midday, and a brilliant sun was bathing the neighborhood in white light. A chilly autumn breeze was moving the leaves on the hedges.

"Is everything OK, Will?"

A bolt of electricity flashed through his body as he realized that his neighbor, a retired man from Kansas who lived in the house next door, might have seen Kiera and discovered her story.

"Who's Mila?" he asked from his porch, surprised. He was wearing denim dungarees with a white polo shirt underneath, along with a red cap bearing George Bush's campaign slogan and a confused expression.

"Oh… um…She's… She's our pet cat."

"You have a cat? I've never seen her around here."

"Yes… she's an old gray cat. She's been with us her whole life, but she never leaves the house. We can't find her. She must have escaped."

"I haven't seen her, but I'll let you know if I do, OK neighbor?"

Will nodded and looked at him for a couple moments longer, questioning his cheerful but serious expression. Iris and Will separated to cover more ground and look in both directions down the street. If anyone else found her, it would be the end for both of them.

Iris was running, nervous, looking behind every tree, container and bush and around each corner in the neighborhood. Will felt anger and shock as he searched, unable to stop thinking that the delay of just a few seconds could condemn them to a lifetime behind bars.

As they ran, little Kiera carefully watched a butterfly that had landed on an orange flower in the back yard. It was the first time she had been outside in a long while, she couldn't remember how long, and the brightness of the sun made her look around with her eyes half-closed. The blue of the sky was different to the shade she could see from her bedroom window. Even the back yard itself, which she had become accustomed to seeing through a pane of glass, seemed so different, so vividly colored that it seemed unreal.

She started to feel dizzy. Then she felt a strange tingling throughout her body. She sat down on the lawn, thinking that perhaps that would make it pass, and she scratched her arms as though the sensation was the result of something external. She suddenly had to close her eyes because her eyelids were heavier than they'd ever felt before. Moments later as Iris arrived, almost out of breath, Kiera began to have convulsions identical to those her mother suffered from time to time.

"Mila? What's happening?"

Iris shook her hard, horrified to see her little girl like that, trying in vain to wake her from what seemed like an endless and uncontrollable trance.

"Mila!" she screamed again, desperate, "Wake up!"

On hearing his wife's screams, Will began to run towards his house, running past it down the side alley that led to the backyard, guided by the sound of his wife's cries. When he arrived, he raised his hands to his head at the sight of Mila lying on the ground, her head to one side, her fists clenched and her body rigid as she shook violently.

"What's happening, Iris? What have you done to the girl?"

"What do you mean?"

"Do something. She's shaking," he said, as if Iris knew the solution.

"This isn't shaking, Will. It's something worse, for God's sake. We need to get her to a doctor."

"Are you crazy? I'll let her die first."

Iris turned on her husband, her eyes full of rage.

"How dare you say something like that? Help me get her inside. I can't do it by myself."

Will picked Kiera up as best he could. Her body was like a plank, her legs stiff and frozen with tension. Her arms spasmed so powerfully that Will almost dropped her twice before he made it inside the house with her. Once inside, Will put her down on the orange quilt of her bed and, while the attack continued and Iris wept, he kept walking back and forth across the room, thinking non-stop about what the hell to do.

A few minutes later, Kiera's small, skinny body stopped shaking and Iris wept again, this time with happiness, and hugged her. She knelt by the bed and thanked God for saving her little girl. Kiera seemed exhausted, and she stroked her hair for a while, rearranging a lock of her fringe that had settled on her forehead. When Kiera finally opened her eyes, Iris was studying her closely, barely an inch from her face, with such a sincere smile, still wet with tears, that she felt at home again.

"Why are you crying, Mommy?" Kiera whispered with difficulty.

"It's nothing… sweetheart… it's just…" her mind flew from

one idea to the next, trying to find an explanation that would convince but not worry her daughter, "that I thought something bad had happened to you."

"My head really hurts."

Iris looked at her husband, who was observing the situation with a serious expression, confirming that having her there was a mistake they could no longer rectify.

"You can't go outside the house, Mila. You've seen what happens now. You get very sick," said Will, trying to take control of the situation.

"Sick?"

"Yes, darling," Iris whispered gently, "I thought that... that I'd lost you."

"You didn't lose me... I was playing by the window..."

"I know... It's just that... you can't go out. It's for your own good. We don't want anything bad to happen to you."

"Why?" asked Kiera, her fatigue evident in her voice.

"Pollution, electromagnetic waves, electronic devices. It's all very harmful and... when you go outside you get sick," Iris answered, remembering a strange documentary she'd watched about electromagnetic hypersensitivity on a pseudo-science channel and which she had come to believe.

According to that documentary, people affected by electromagnetic hypersensitivity showed all kinds of symptoms, each more difficult to diagnose than the last: dizziness, burning sensations, malaise, tachycardia, difficulty breathing, and even powerful nausea and a compulsive cough when exposed to a source of electromagnetic waves. The documentary showed the cloistered life led by a woman in her fifties in San Francisco, who didn't leave her house and almost never saw daylight because she claimed that when she did so cell phone signals, increasingly present in the street, caused her to experience burning sensations and become so unwell she passed out. The woman explained that when she saw somebody speaking on their phone in the street, she had to cross the road to avoid the roasting impact of its death rays. The documentary also featured a 20-year-old man, an IT nerd, who had papered his home in aluminum foil to avoid the suffering which the mysterious and omnipresent waves caused him. The documentary concluded with one of the reporters turning his cell phone on and off inside his pocket while he interviewed the man inside his house without the man showing any signs of dizziness or burning sensations, but Iris didn't see that bit because she had begun arguing with Will, who had just got home.

"Waves? What are they?" asked the little girl, who was too clever and curious for them to handle.

"They're… things that come from electronic devices. Cell phone masts send them out, which is why we don't have cell phones at home. The television aerial also has bad waves."

"The television? Bad waves?" she whispered weakly from her bed.

After they'd taken time to answer that question, two loud knocks came from the front door. Iris and Will looked at one another quickly. He gestured to Kiera to keep quiet. He pretended there was nobody home and ignored the knocking, but soon a voice he recognized instantly came from the other side of the door.

"Will? It's Andy, from next door. Is everything alright?"

Chapter 42
November 30, 2003
Five years after Kiera's disappearance

*Not all secrets
should come to light.*

The guy who tried to attack Miren didn't know he'd chosen the wrong victim. Minutes beforehand when she'd walked past him and disappeared into the streets that led to the storage units, he'd thought she'd be easy prey: a young girl, slim, attractive, and well-dressed. She might be carrying money that would see him through the next two or three weeks, but most importantly, she was pretty and he, a normal guy who considered himself a bit of a stud, thought it had been too long since he'd last got laid. He took out a knife and walked stealthily after Miren, glancing sideways to make sure there was nobody else around. If he managed to get her into one of the units it would be a done deal, even though it was broad daylight. He could enjoy himself and have some fun for a while.

He watched her from a distance and when he finally saw her lifting one of the shutters, he smiled, revealing yellow teeth full of cavities. In New York, a city of over eight million people, there are over two thousand reported rapes a year: roughly six a day, or one every four hours. This one would have maintained this hourly rate if not for the fact that the victim was Miren Triggs.

Miren had changed after what she suffered in 1997. For a while she was afraid to go out into the street, to go to parties, to cross the park where it had happened, but after joining the *Manhattan Press* and taking part in her first investigation, she discovered that the way to fight the fear was to move on, come out of her shell, and fight to change things. Her article, in which she revealed the truth about James Foster, burned alive in the center of New York, felt like confirmation that the forces of good could triumph, and that fear and darkness didn't always win. She bought herself a weapon to keep at home, signed up for self-defense classes, and vowed she wouldn't touch a drop of alcohol while the register of the city's sex offenders still showed a single offender at large.

When the attacker grabbed her from behind, it took Miren just two seconds to work out what to do. A bite, a yank on his arm and a quick flip, and he'd be on the floor. That was what she visualized in her head, and that was exactly what happened. Miren took out her gun and placed the barrel in his mouth.

"I've got something for you, too," she whispered, releasing the safety.

She reached for her cell phone and addressed her mother while the man looked at her with an expression of panic and the taste of metal in his mouth.

"Mom? Could you call me back later? I'm..."

"Darling? You're not buying me something for Christmas, are you? You know I don't like gifts."

"I'm just about to pay at one of the big department stores. I'll call you later." Miren's voice seemed calm, and she ended the call before her mother could reply. She sighed as she turned towards her attacker with a blank smile.

An hour later, an ambulance attended an emergency following an anonymous call from a pay phone. When they arrived at the location given by the female voice on the other end of the line, they found a man tied to a metal grille between two shipping containers with a nasty gunshot wound between his legs. When they asked him what had happened, he couldn't explain, so in the report that followed the police alleged that it was a settling of scores between rival drug dealers. Miren had warned him that they'd track him down, because she was sure that his name was already on the city's sexual offender register. He could only respond with a silence that said it all.

Miren drove back through the city to her apartment, the same studio in Harlem, with two boxes of information about the case that she spent the night reviewing in her pajamas without leaving her desk. Every now and then she would take a sip from a can of Coca-Cola and take a bite of an apple to try to make up for her bad habits. She had bought herself an iBook G3 as soon as they came out, getting rid of the larger iMac with its turquoise-shelled monitor that she'd used for the last few years. To one side, illuminated by a reading lamp, its antenna angled towards the window, she kept her little transistor radio, the apartment's last bastion of vintage technology, warding off the unstoppable advances represented by her new little laptop.

When Miren reached a point when she felt stuck, faced by a web of numbers corresponding to streets, security cameras, interviews and zip codes, she checked the time and turned on the radio.

A small red light immediately lit up on one side of it and the voice of Jim Schmoer, her former professor, filled the room:

"... the voice of hope. If not, I will tell you about some prominent cases, as baffling as the one we are dealing with here today, and which mystify police forces around the world. A good example of the kind of case I'm talking about is the so-called 'Child Painter' from Malaga, in Spain. Around 15 years ago, in 1987, a little boy whose talent for painting earned him the nickname 'the Child Painter,' disappeared in Spain. One day in April he left home to walk to a gallery and… disappeared from the face of the earth as if he'd never existed. Or the case of Sarah Wilson, who got off the bus outside her home in Texas aged just eight and never made it to her front door. Both cases have been followed closely around the world due to the strange nature of the disappearances. Or the case of the little French girl, Marion Wagon, aged ten, who disappeared in 1996 after leaving school. No child just vanishes from the world without a trace. Sadly, either they are dead, or somebody doesn't want them to be found. But the case of Kiera Templeton is different. Whoever knows where she is wants her to be found, or perhaps they want to play a game, or perhaps they want to make it known that she's alright and for people to stop looking. You never know, and you never can tell what's hidden in the mind of the person who is holding her, but the key to all investigative journalism is not to find what you're looking for, but to never stop looking."

Miren nodded and smiled. She liked to feel as though, in some way, Professor Schmoer were still there on the sidelines, guiding her career. Then she turned down the volume and continued opening files containing photos and statements. She opened the folder on her computer where she had downloaded the contents of the CD the professor had given her five years earlier and reviewed the images from the security cameras again. She was hoping for a moment of lucidity, a creative spark that would help her join the dots of that impossible puzzle, with Professor Schmoer's words repeating in her head: "never stop looking."

"What do you think I'm doing, Jim?" she asked, taking another sip of Coca-Cola and a bite of her apple.

Chapter 43
September 12, 2000
Unknown location

*Evil can sniff out others
who are also infected with it.*

"Hide the girl!" Will whispered, shocked. "Hide her! If he sees her, we're done for."

Iris closed the door of Kiera's bedroom and stayed inside with her, listening to the conversation through the door. Kiera was exhausted from the fit she'd just had and watched her mother from the bed with a worried expression.

Iris could hear her husband's footsteps on the other side of the door. She heard him rummaging among the boxes and then the metallic scrape of some keys that shook like a rattlesnake. But she didn't associate that high-pitched sound with the bunch of keys that opened the only padlock in the house. Three powerful knocks sounded at the door and Will's voice bounced off the walls.

"I'm coming! Just a moment!"

Iris realized Kiera had closed her eyes, overwhelmed by fatigue and the pain in her head. On the other side of the door, Will carefully opened the front door, sticking his head out and greeting his neighbor.

"What can I do for you, Andy?" he asked, the door ajar.

"Are you sure everything is OK?"

"Yes, of course. Why should something be wrong?" he asked, trying to calm Andy's doubts.

"If you needed anything, you'd ask me, right buddy? I like to think we're good members of... of the community."

"Of course, Andy. What makes you say that?"

"Aren't you going to offer me a beer?"

Will looked behind him, disappearing from the small gap in the doorway for a second, and clicked his tongue.

"Well... you see... it's Iris. She's.... she's not very well."

"Oh, come on! I just saw her running down the street! Stop telling me fibs."

Andy pushed the door open, taking Will by surprise.

"I don't think..."

His neighbor walked quickly inside, scanning the living room as if trying to see something that he shouldn't.

The sound of Andy's footsteps inside the house made Iris's blood freeze as she pressed her ear against the flowered paper of the wall that felt colder than it should have. From there, her eyes drifted to the doll's house that Will had already set up inside the bedroom and she lost herself in the miniature size of that little home, trying to distance herself from how big everything felt in her own home right now, where she felt smaller and smaller.

"What do you want, Andy?" Will asked, annoyed. "I think you're being... rude. Good neighbors don't barge into other people's homes and... nose around in their things."

"You're right. I'm sorry, Will. Where... where are my manners?" he said in a tuneful voice, sitting down on the couch and putting his feet up on the coffee table. "You're right. This isn't... normal."

Will swallowed before speaking.

"Andy, I think I'm going to have to ask you to leave. Iris

278

isn't well and… I want to be with her. I want… well, you know how it is, I want to take care of her."

"You know something?" said his neighbor, taking the conversation in a different direction. "My wife died six years ago. And… well, life's not fair. We never had children. We tried and tried. We did it every night, even when she had her period, just in case. I must admit that they were good times. I… I never wanted children. But she did. It was all she talked about. She would stop in front of a window display of children's clothes and she would fall apart, crying, looking at tiny little skirts and trousers that we would never buy."

"I'm not following you, Andy," Will whispered.

"I didn't really take it seriously, but she… she was always looking for ways to improve her fertility: she would suck lemon peel in the mornings, she would douche herself using vinegar at night. Going to bed with her was like eating a fucking salad. I don't know if you get my drift."

Will didn't answer.

"It was her only topic of conversation, and I… well, I used to listen to her. That's what a husband does, right? I would listen to her the whole time. You knew Karen. She talked a lot. Especially with your wife. And… do you know what she never stopped telling me?"

Will began to feel very uncomfortable.

"That she talked about the same thing with your wife. That you had the very same problems getting pregnant. They even talked about the positions you were trying. Listen, I… I didn't mind. They shared good tips. We used to copy a lot of your ideas, you know? That thing with the cushion, having sex on the cold living room floor, always doing it an even number of times. We spent the whole time doing it, and pretty much all over the house. It was like a party, you know? Or it was until the day she had that brain hemorrhage in the middle of the grocery store. Some of the doctors said it was stress. Others

279

said it was the fertility hormones. Nobody could work out the exact reason, but she died, and... well, there were no more fireworks. Do you know what I mean?"

"Yes... I remember that... it came as a terrible shock to all of us," said Will, almost whispering, extremely uneasy. "But now, if you don't mind..."

"And do you know something else your wife told mine?" Andy went on, ignoring the invitation to leave.

"What?"

"That you guys couldn't have children. That it was completely out of the question. That her ovaries were dead, and her uterus seemed to reject anything implanted in it."

"Yes.... Well. It's something that... we're still trying to make progress with. We're still t.... trying, although we've lost hope a bit. Age doesn't help either..."

"I know. I can imagine, buddy."

"Andy, if you don't mind, I have things to do..."

"And that's why I wonder... who's that little girl you rushed into the house with?"

"Little girl?" asked Will, almost shouting.

"Come on, Will... don't fuck about with me. I saw you searching desperately all around the house. Are you going to try to slip one past me? Aren't we friends anymore?"

"Look, Andy... there's no..."

"It's Kiera Templeton, isn't it?"

Hearing him say those words made Will's stomach drop like he was falling off a cliff, and he didn't know how to respond. A lump formed in his throat and a rush of rage blocked his vocal cords, so he couldn't make a sound.

"You're the ones who've got that girl. The one they've spent years searching for. It looked like her. She was a little changed... but... that face. I mean, who could forget that sweet face? What was the reward they were offering? Half a million dollars? Whoa... that's a lot of dough, right buddy?"

"What do you want, Andy? Money? Is that what you want? You know we're just getting by. We hardly have enough to pay the mortgage."

"You weren't listening to any of what I just told you, were you Will? What I want is... your wife. I want the only thing I miss. I've tried going with whores... but... it doesn't feel natural, it's not the same. But Iris... she..."

"I didn't think you were...so..."

Andy looked towards the door of Kiera's bedroom and pointed.

"Is she in there? The little girl. Can I see her?"

Will was so tense his only response was to nod his head. Andy smiled and leapt to his feet. He gave Will a pat on the back as he passed him, then turned the door handle, revealing the inside of the room where Iris waited, her face covered in tears of desperation. Then he stared at the little girl, sleepy and unaware of the hellish tension in the air. Andy smiled at Iris then went over to wipe away one of her tears.

"Andy... please... don't..." she whispered.

"You have to understand me, Iris.... You've always been so... so normal. And all those things Karen used to tell me that you told her you tried with Will... I always imagined what... I'm not going to say something like that aloud with a child in the room... but..." he quickly leaned close to Iris's ear and whispered, "I always imagined what fucking you would be like."

Iris slumped even further and leant against Andy, weeping.

"Don't worry, honey... we'll... we'll have a good time. We're... well, good neighbors."

Iris suddenly moved away from him. Andy noticed her gasp of surprise.

"Hey, Andy!" Will yelled from the doorway. Andy turned round, surprised, and saw Will in front of him holding the hunting rifle he always kept in the cupboard in the hall, the one with the padlock he'd removed just minutes earlier.

"Will!" she screamed.

The shot lodged in Andy's abdomen with a dry sound and a few moments later he collapsed onto the bedroom floor, bleeding from his mouth. A few pellets had missed him and lodged in the walls, leaving an indelible mark of what had happened there. In tears, Iris threw herself on top of Kiera, stroking her little face as soon as she realized she'd opened her eyes at the sound.

"What's happening, Mommy?"

"Nothing... darling. Go back to sleep. It's just... Daddy bumped into something."

Andy's body was bleeding by the bed, but Kiera stayed lying down, not wanting to move, not wanting to look, because part of her knew that something was badly wrong. Iris kissed her forehead, and then Kiera closed her eyes to the sound of her mother's whimpers. Iris wanted to scream with panic, but couldn't. Will stayed where he was by the door, trembling, for a long time, looking at the body of his neighbor, whose blood was spreading across the floor in a puddle that grew rapidly in the way that only our worst fears can.

Chapter 44
Miren Triggs
1998

And when has life ever treated you well?

The first time I spoke with Aaron Templeton the conversation was devastating. He had been waiting for me in the doorway to the *Manhattan Press*. According to the security staff he'd been there for two hours, staring at everyone who passed him and asking occasionally if anyone knew who Miren Triggs was, the person who'd written the article about James Foster.

"Yes, I'm Miren Triggs," I said, confused.

"Can we talk?"

"I... I have to work. They're waiting for me in the office."

"Please... I'm begging you."

I was shocked to see a man around 15 years older than me so distressed and begging me for help in a broken voice, that I couldn't refuse. Part of me was afraid to get too drawn into Kiera's disappearance. I thought that proximity might not let me be objective enough to search for her without distractions, but who was I trying to fool? I was so absorbed by that case, by Kiera's look of surprise on the posters the wind was blowing around the city, that I felt as much a part of the search as her family. I called the secretary from the security desk to let her know that something important had come up and that I was going to be late. Yes, I arrived late on my first day of work. Nothing like starting off on the right foot.

I tried to imagine the total hell Aaron Templeton must be going through based on his appearance, but however hard I tried, I was convinced that he was doing even worse than he appeared to be. He had deep bags under his eyes, a straggly beard, messy hair, and rumpled clothes. If I hadn't known anything about him, it would have been easy to imagine him lying by an ATM with a bottle hidden in a paper bag, putting out his hand to ask passers-by for money.

I took him to a café on the corner opposite the newspaper offices and he agreed to pay for the coffee. When we finally sat down, he said two words I neither expected nor felt like I deserved:

"Thank you, Ms. Triggs."

"Please, there's really no need to thank me," I replied.

"Last night a monster died, and the world is a slightly better place."

"I… I didn't have anything to do with it."

"I know. But because of you the whole world knows who he really was. If it wasn't for you, Ms. Triggs…"

"Call me Miren, please. I'm just… well, just someone who looks for the truth."

"If it wasn't for you… the whole world would have thought he was a good man who'd been subjected to an injustice. It's what all the papers say, isn't it?'

"All except the *Press*."

"That's why I came… because you're the only ones who've looked for the truth in all this. That guy didn't deserve to die a hero and… thanks to you, he won't."

"He died because people needed justice, but confused it with revenge. Not because of my article. There's no need to thank me," I replied, feeling confused. "Can I ask you something, Mr. Templeton?"

"Of course."

"Is that why you came? To thank me for uncovering James Foster's backstory?"

Aaron considered his answer for a few moments, then went on:

"Yes and…also no," he hesitated. "I came to ask what else you know."

"I can't… I can't tell you anything else, Mr. Templeton. I'm sure you understand that only the police can share that information."

"Please…"

I got up and prepared to leave. I knew that he wasn't going to be the slightest help to me.

"I have to get back to the office."

"Please… just tell me if you saw anything in that house that suggested where Kiera might be. Just that."

I sighed, but I didn't think the information would do him any harm. I shook my head in silence.

"Nothing?"

"No, Mr. Templeton. Your daughter wasn't there. And it didn't look like she ever had been. I know it would make things a lot easier for you, but I'm afraid there was nothing. Your daughter… doesn't seem to have been kidnapped or anything else by James Foster. Believe me, that is not necessarily a bad thing. Perhaps Kiera is somewhere else, better cared for than she would have been by that man."

"Thank you, Miren, that's more than I needed," he said, using a finger to catch a tear that was running down his face.

"I really do have to go. If you need more information, I think you should speak to the investigators working on the case. I… I know very little. Only what's filtered out to the press, perhaps a little more, but nothing that would help find her."

"Will you help me find Kiera?" he asked, suddenly, as if I could do something, a request so sincere it was painful to hear. I pressed my lips together and pulled a sympathetic face.

"You don't need to ask me to do that. I'm already looking for her. But… it's not easy. Nobody saw her. Nobody's seen anything. Not the security cameras and not the people on the street. There's nothing. All that we have… all that we have is hope something new will come to light. That somebody will make a mistake, or we'll find something else. But… don't stop looking for your daughter. It looks like the police will run out of options soon and then… you'll have to stay strong."

"Miren, will you promise me you'll keep looking for her?"

"Will you?"

"I wouldn't be able to live with myself if I didn't," he replied. "I owe it to my wife."

"I'm very determined. I can assure you I won't stop looking for your daughter."

"Thank you, Miren, you seem like a good person. Life must have been kind to you."

I laughed inside. How little he knew about me and how soon he had dared to make such a mistaken judgement.

"Are you a good person?" I asked him.

"I think so. At least… I try to be," he said, almost sobbing.

"And when has life treated *you* well?"

He didn't reply, but he nodded before taking a sip of his coffee. I said goodbye to him after exchanging phone numbers so that we could share any leads or information that might be helpful going forward. I liked Aaron Templeton, although it was difficult to tell whether that was due to pity or because of the hope I could still see in his gaze.

I headed back to the office, and he stayed in the café, looking blindly out of the window while people hurried across the street. Perhaps he was searching his memory for a time he had behaved badly enough to deserve what had happened to his family, but I was already sure life didn't work like that, that it would throw a spanner in the works wherever the opportunity arose. I had already discovered that even when there was no way to throw a spanner in the works, life would give you a bicycle with no brakes to break your bones that way instead.

When I arrived, I sat at my desk and pretended to arrange things. Ten minutes later, a dark-haired woman with a cheerful face came over to introduce herself, saying: "You're Miren Triggs, right? The new girl."

I nodded.

"Congratulations on that lead article. That's what I call starting things off in style. I'm Nora. According to Phil, we're on the same team and you've already arrived late. You'll fit right in. You sure are young, though. I'll introduce you to Bob later, he's a bit of a jerk, but he's a great journalist. And Samantha… where the hell is Samantha?" she said, looking up and scanning the office.

"Bob Wexter? *The* Bob Wexter?"

"Yes. Although he's not such a legend once you meet him in person. He's very forgetful when it comes to everyday stuff. Sometimes he can't even remember where his desk is."

"One second… are you… Nora *Fox*?"

Nora smiled at me. I couldn't believe it. I was talking to Nora Fox, author of a famous series of articles that exposed a CIA cover-up of alleged sexual favors received by various senators in exchange for voting in favor of specific laws concerning online gambling. She had also written articles about instances of electoral fraud in Latin America that had almost brought down more than one government. She was a journalist of considerable stature and here she was talking to me in a relaxed, spontaneous way that didn't tally at all with her ability to burrow into the dark underbelly of the system.

"Yes, you've got it. That's me."

"I've read masses of your reports," I said, so excited I could almost burst.

"Thanks, Miren. You don't mind if I call you Miren, do you? I'm going to explain a few things to you and then we'll see what to put you on."

"That would be great, thanks," I replied.

"Between the three of us, Samantha, Bob, and me, four now including you, we're investigating a specific case. In theory Bob's the boss, but not in practice. There are no bosses. We agree on a topic between us, and we dig right to the bottom of it. Right now, we're researching a story about the businessmen who seem to be disappearing all over Europe. It's something murky that nobody talks about. That's what we're working on. Do you know any French? German? OK, aside from that we each have our own project, or even two, but you have to work on those yourself. What's yours going to be? Have you decided?"

"Er… no."

"What are you interested in? What bothers you? You need to get in there, into that little journalist's head of yours, and submerge yourself in your fears. Mine are to do with freedom of expression. I'm afraid of the day when they won't let me speak out, you know?"

"Right now, I'm worried about disappearing like Kiera Templeton did," I replied.

"The little girl? Well, it's a good topic, but a complicated one. The investigative avenues are almost all exhausted already, but… listen, if you find her, you'll win the Pulitzer. It's a good idea."

"I… I don't care about the Pulitzer."

"Yeah yeah, that's what we all say. Just … don't get emotional. This is journalism. There are no legends and there's no glamour here, only the truth. Your word is worth only as much as it sells. And that's the difficult part, understand?"

I nodded again. As she spoke, I had the feeling the world had sped up around me. I realized that people moved non-stop around the editorial office. Two editors were walking along a corridor chatting about the content of some pages, others were typing intently at their IBM computers and others were on calls and taking notes between loud sighs.

"Can I ask you something?" I asked the question this time.

"Of course. Shoot. You're brave for someone so young. I like you."

I took that as a compliment, because actually, I was really nervous.

"Do you really think I'll fit in?"

"Really?"

I waited for her to go on without saying anything. I knew that she would.

"We'll be lucky if we manage to keep you for more than two weeks. This world is darker than it looks from outside."

"Well, there's no problem, then," I said.

"Why do you say that?"

"Because so am I," I said in a serious voice. Nora didn't reply.

Chapter 45
December 1, 2003
Five years after Kiera's disappearance

And one day, out of the blue, someone will
ask you to stop being yourself.

The day after the incident in her storage unit, Miren arrived at the office struggling to carry the two boxes of material on Kiera Templeton and dumped them on her desk. It was still early, and the two interns hadn't arrived yet, so she went to Nora's desk, where she was typing rapidly.

"I don't feel like talking to you, Miren," said Nora, as soon as she saw her coming over.

"Are you very angry?"

"What do you think?"

"I'm sorry about the article about the tape. I would have asked for sign-off from the team, but... it was important. I'd been waiting for something like that for a long time and it was a good opportunity to find something."

"I know, Miren, but our report on the meat industry should have been published. We've spent months on it. You skipped getting sign-off on it. You skipped everything. You sent your article to print in place of the team's."

"I know… I'm sorry… but…"

"There are things you just don't do, Miren. And you know that. I didn't expect something like this of you."

"It was important, Nora. Perhaps it might help find her."

"You only care about yourself, don't you? Don't you care about anything else?"

Miren didn't reply.

"Bob already knows. He's angry. He's on the phone to Phil right now."

"You told him, didn't you?"

"I called him in Jordan yesterday to tell him. Jordan! I didn't even know where he was, you know he's always over that way, especially now with everything in Iraq. Nobody expected you'd do something like this, Miren."

"Could the veal article really not wait one day?"

"Miren, they're feeding meat and bone meal to cattle in Washington. It's really serious. We've sent samples for analysis in the UK and… if everything's confirmed this could be one of the biggest food scandals in the States. We've got a head start on this and we can't lose it. I don't know, Miren, it was a whole-team project. Was it really that necessary?"

"I thought you'd be OK with it. Phil seemed happy with the outcome. It was selling well…"

"But this isn't about Phil or what he decides. He's still thinking about the war in Iraq or what's going on in the East. We investigate what nobody wants us to uncover. This meat story is a big one, Miren. They call it Mad Cow Disease. If the laboratory in the UK confirms our suspicions, it will be extremely serious. That's what we're about, Miren. I know you're acting with good intentions and that… the little girl is your personal investigation, but… you can't ride roughshod over the rest of us."

"So what's going to happen now?"

"We've made a formal complaint to Phil. I'm sorry, Miren."

"Seriously? He agreed! Why have you done this? Now… now I'll have to justify it to the board and…"

"I really am sorry, Miren, but… you didn't leave us any choice."

Miren looked up towards Phil's office and saw that he had just hung up. She walked angrily towards his office. As she walked past her desk, the two interns who had just arrived saw her walk by so resolutely they didn't even dare say hello.

"They've screwed me over, haven't they?" said Miren, walking through the door of Phil's office.

"Miren… you already know what I think. I gave you the green light…"

"But there's always a but, isn't there? They've screwed me over."

"But the board was not happy about this complaint. They're big fans of Bob's work and this didn't have his approval."

"But you yourself told me the story about the tape… was incredible."

"I know, Miren, but… it's bordering on sensationalism."

"Just yesterday, you told me that you liked the fact that…"

"And now you're part of a team and you have to work together. That's the way it is, Miren."

"Phil… I just want to find that girl. I came here because of her. This is our opportunity."

"The board has asked us to leave the subject alone. They believe this story about the search will be like bait and the tabloids will be all over it. And they're right, Miren. Have you seen today's papers? Have you seen the talk shows? The whole world is talking about this, dragging the family through the mud. This isn't news. It's morbid curiosity. The *Press* can take no part in it. You came here to unmask James Foster. That little girl has nothing to do with it."

"Are you serious? I took on two interns for this. You gave me the go-ahead."

"Miren, I think I've made myself clear."

"So what do I do? Do I fire them? Is that what you're telling me?"

"I'm not telling you to fire them. They could do well. We can always use an extra pair of hands around here. I'll let Casey know and he'll give them some work in his department."

"This is bullshit, Phil. I'm not going to drop this."

"Miren. Be smart: the Kiera Templeton story ends here." He paused and then went on, "You're good. It won't be hard for you to find another subject that isn't so... lurid. We're not a sensationalist paper."

"For the love of God, Phil, this isn't sensationalism. This is the life of a little girl who needs us."

"It sounds good, Miren, it really does. I know that every time we've mentioned this subject we've sold twice or three times the normal number of copies, but the board... is more concerned with our credibility and serious reputation than sales right now. You've already helped the girl. Thanks to the article and the media attention, perhaps the police will divert further resources to her case."

"Since when has the paper's reputation been more important than sales figures?"

"Since today. The board doesn't like this jockeying for position and going over people's heads. You ought to know that. And I think... you've already spent more time than is justifiable on this subject."

Miren gave him her fiercest frown. He turned away and began to read some papers that were on his desk, bringing the conversation to an end. It was his way of doing things. He always acted the same way.

"You're being unfair, Phil," she said before leaving his office, walking furiously towards her desk where the two interns who had just arrived were waiting for her with bewildered expressions.

"Hi boss," said the girl, "What's in there?" she asked, pointing to the two cardboard boxes Miren had left on her desk.

"It's all gone to shit, kids. There's been a change of plan," said Miren, pushing her hair back from her face and taking a deep breath. "We need to get going. Today is your last day with the investigative team. You're going up a level. To Crime and Local News. Perhaps you'll enjoy it," she said, addressing the boy.

"You're joking, right?" he said, incredulous.

"I wish I was, but... no."

"Shit," he said, sadly. "Just yesterday I turned down an investigative position with the *Daily*."

"Why the hell did you do that?" asked Miren, uncomfortable. "You're here as an intern. If they offer you something better, you should take it. Opportunities like that don't just fall into your lap in this world."

"I know, but... this is the *Press*. Even being here as an intern... I don't know, it's the *Press*," he argued.

"So what? It's the stories that are important, not the name at the top of the paper. If what you write is good, you'll change things, no matter where you write it."

"Fuck..." said the boy, sighing and looking at the ceiling.

"Anyway, it doesn't matter. What's done is done. It's bullshit, I know. I'm extremely pissed off; I can assure you. But... things can change overnight in this industry. One morning you're important and the next you're composing crosswords for the back page."

"Are they seriously moving us to Local News?"

"Yes. You've no idea how angry I am about it."

The boy sighed heavily. The girl seemed less upset, but she was probably just better at hiding it. Miren was less angry about having to let them go than about having had her wings clipped. Just when she was within touching distance of finding Kiera, she crashed headlong into the kind of bureaucracy that she couldn't bear. Kiera's case was high-profile and interesting, but the inflexibility of the board was a brake to progressing any faster.

"The content of these boxes is everything we have on Kiera Templeton. I want you to look over all of it, today, and tell me what you think of it. I've already seen it too many times. I need fresh eyes. Are either of you vegetarian? I'll buy you lunch. It's the least I can do. We'll have a farewell do."

"Um... but what about the calls?" asked the girl.

"I'm vegan," the boy added.

"The calls? You can do both," she replied to the girl before addressing the boy, "And why do you always have to be so pernickety?"

"But the telephone hasn't stopped ringing. We barely have time to breathe between calls."

"There are two of you, aren't there?"

"Yes... but we're also working on the list of toy stores and..."

"Have you already done it?"

"Only the ones in Manhattan and New Jersey. We still need to add the ones for Brooklyn, Long Island, Queens and... if we broaden the search a bit things get more complicated."

"That's fine for now," Miren reached out and took the map of New York, which was covered with circles and crosses.

"The crosses are the stores that sell children's toys," the girl explained, "and the circles are ones that sell miniatures and models. We called a couple yesterday and they confirmed that they also sell doll's houses."

"Well done... one moment, what's your name?"

"Victoria. Victoria Wells."

"Aren't you going to ask my name?" the boy butted in, temporarily ignoring the phone that had just started ringing.

"Not right now, no. Has anything else come up from the calls, Victoria?"

"The wallpaper. A woman from…" while she was speaking her colleague picked up the telephone that kept ringing as if there was an endless queue of people at the end of the line waiting to tell their version of events or keen to be heard.

"A woman from Newark says she has it in her home. The same kind that appears on the video. They bought it in a store in the suburbs twenty years ago."

"That's something."

"Well… wait. We then had 30 calls saying that design of wallpaper is one of the standard designs sold by the Furnitools DIY chain. They've had that design in their catalogue for the last 25 years. It's available all over the country."

"Shit," said Miren with a sigh. She got up with the map of the toy stores and walked around her desk, studying it closely. "It will take forever to visit them all to see if they have anything: a list of customers who've bought the doll's house or, I don't know, credit card receipts."

"Perhaps… perhaps you could ask for help through an article again," said Victoria, "this time asking the toy stores. I'm sure plenty would be delighted to help."

"An article? I'd find myself looking for work with you two by this afternoon. The *Press* is done with this subject, kids. And that's why you can't stay. At least not with me. I'll have to do this… the traditional way. And even like that I might not get anywhere."

"By visiting them?" asked the boy as the phone he had just hung up began to ring again. Victoria reached out and picked it up.

"*Manhattan Press*. What information are you able to provide?" she said into the handset.

"There are more than a thousand toy stores across New York and New Jersey," the boy pointed out. "And that's without including Queens or Long Island. It could easily come to two thousand stores when you add in convenience stores and department stores that also sell toys."

"I know, but… if I manage to visit or call… let's say two a day on my breaks… it would take me…"

"Three years," said the boy immediately.

"Good mental arithmetic. So, tell me now, what is your name? Actually, you know what? Better not tell me. Let's keep you anonym—"

"My name's Robert," he said without letting her finish. That name brought back bad memories for Miren, but it was inevitable she would come across it from time to time. It was incredible how every so often a new person would turn up with that name and it would still provoke an instant reaction in her, as if she still needed to learn to forgive deep down inside, or to truly forget.

"What do you do when you're not in the office?" Miren asked. She'd just had a crazy idea.

"Umm… study? We're both still at college," Robert replied.

"OK. Now you're not going to be on the investigative desk, would you like to earn some extra cash on the weekends?"

Chapter 46
November 27, 2010
Twelve years after Kiera's disappearance

Imagine for a second that no-
body is looking for you
or waiting for you. Isn't that what love is?
Feeling waited for or searched for?

Agent Miller walked around downtown for a couple of hours. He was distraught and wasn't ready to go home and tell his wife what had happened yet. He needed to think what to do. Leaving the FBI had never been a part of his plan, but perhaps that push just before Christmas would help him take the step. He considered the possibility of extricating himself from the cases in which he was so involved, but he would find it impossible to erase from his brain the happy faces from those photos that he went through each morning. He thought about Josh Armington, a little boy of just 12 years old who'd disappeared from a jungle gym in full daylight. Then of Gina Pebbles, a teenage girl who'd disappeared in 2002 after leaving her school in Queens and whose trail had gone cold just over a mile away in a park where her backpack was found. He thought of Kiera. He was always thinking of her and about the tapes, and about the Templetons' pain. He visited them occasionally to see how they were and to tell them there were no advances in the investigation, and it was clear their lives had fallen apart.

Without thinking about where he was going, he headed north, crossing SoHo as he wandered until he reached Washington Square Park. A monumental fountain dominated the center of the park. It reminded him of the case of Anna Atkins, a woman who had arranged to meet a man there back in 2008, after which both of them had vanished without a trace. Although it was so crowded, with so many thousands of people living there, the city encouraged anonymity and each corner, each junction, each tree, and each crack in the sidewalk hid stories that perhaps it was better not to find. In spite of the increasing number of security cameras in the city, which were there with the aim of recording and reducing vandalism, it was difficult for anybody to remember the face of an individual they'd seen if they were asked. If you wanted to disappear, one of the best places to choose would be New York. If the cameras didn't pick anything up, it was difficult to make progress on a case. Witnesses were notable for their absence in cases like the ones he dealt with.

Lost in thought, he arrived at Union Square Park, scene of another case that came into his head. Then he continued north, zigzagging through the streets, and decided to stop at Wildberg's Sandwich, a tiny but historic joint that served the best pastrami in the city. He sat at the bar between a man in a suit and two tourists. He was both preoccupied and thirsty. The barman greeted him with a smile.

"What'll it be, buddy?"

"A beer and… a… a…," he quickly scanned the menu, "a Mitch sandwich."

"Good choice. Bad day?"

"This time of year always… always brings back bad memories. It's not easy."

"Christmas brings bad memories for a lot of us, buddy. We've all lost someone around this time of year but... well, life goes on."

"Yes... I suppose so. But when it's a lit...," Ben didn't dare finish in case he had to explain in more detail.

"My wife died on Christmas Eve, y'know?" said the barman. "And since then... well, I celebrate it for her. You have to see it that way. Otherwise, life is empty. When there's something to celebrate, you need to grab hold of it and go for it, buddy. Because bad things are always out there, lying in wait, and if you let it, the whole calendar fills up with them without you realizing."

Ben nodded and picked up the beer the barman had just left him on the bar. A while later a plate holding an egg and onion sandwich slid towards where he was sitting, just as his cell phone began to ring.

"John. Don't tell me. You've already heard," he said, as soon as he picked up.

"Yes. It's a shit-show. To be honest, I can't stand Spencer. But anyway, treat it as a vacation to spend with your family."

"I guess. I'll call Lisa later to organize a trip or something. It'll blow our savings, but... I can't bear to be in the city right now. I can't stop thinking about work. Perhaps it will do me good."

"Well... that's why I was calling you."

"Let me guess. There's nothing on either the tape or the envelope."

"That's what I was going to ask you. Who's touched it?"

"As far as I know, the Swaghats, the Indian family who now live in the Templetons' old house, the Templetons, and... me. But I used gloves. You should only find prints belonging to the Swaghats and the Templetons."

"Well... let's see. How can I put this..." John hesitated on the end of the line. "There are two other matches. Traces of two other people on the envelope."

"Two sets of prints?"

"The first the system found belong to… Miren Triggs. We've had them on file since 2003."

"Miren? How is that possible? She… she wasn't with us."

"I didn't pay them too much attention because I know she's a friend of the family."

"It doesn't make sense."

"Well… the other one, the other print is bit less clear, but the system… picked up an even stranger match."

"Hit me with it."

"You know the software we installed to allow for the evolution of fingerprints, to minimize the distortion that occurs to the fingertips with age, right?"

"Yes. You told me something about that."

"Well, it's a kind of simulation program that runs on top of IAFIS and makes it possible to extrapolate fingerprints based on age with the aim of identifying them years later. The more time that's passed since the original print was taken, the less accurate the results are, a bit like long-range weather forecasts, for example, but…"

"Sure, just spit it out."

"There were also some prints that are a 42 percent match with those belonging to Kiera Templeton. The same grooves and bifurcations and the center of the whorl is in the same place."

"What are you saying?"

"Well… it's not definitive. 42 percent wouldn't stand up in court, to be honest, but… that's a normal percentage match given the age of the prints we have on file for Kiera Templeton. If you think about it, the ones we have on file are from when she was three and these… these are for an adult."

"Are you telling me Kiera Templeton may have touched that envelope?"

"I'm telling you that it's very likely that Kiera Templeton

touched that package, but the system allows for a certain degree of error given the number of years that has passed."

"It… it's not possible."

"Do you think she was the one who delivered the tape, Ben?"

"I don't know, John, but… it sure is hard to explain."

"What's going to happen now? Do you need anything?"

"No, not if I manage to find Miren Triggs. I need to talk to her to find out how come her prints are on the envelope."

Chapter 47
September 14, 2000
Unknown location

You cross a line,
and sooner or later, you fall off a precipice.

Will had climbed a step ladder and was in the corner of Kiera's room struggling to mount a small security camera he had bought in a secondhand shop.

"There we go," he said, once he'd turned it on and checked the red light was on.

The camera's wire ran along the edge of the ceiling cornice to the top corner of the bedroom doorframe, where Will had drilled a hole in the partition wall to feed it through, after which the cable snaked along the wall of the living room until it reached the television.

Iris was playing on the couch with Kiera and asked uneasily:

"Do you really think all this is necessary?"

"I don't want any surprises, Iris. Look, I've put the camera in Mila's room on channel eight; channel nine is the one at the front door. If you press here, you activate the sound, see?"

"How much did all this cost you?"

"Don't worry, it was less than 50 dollars. It's just… a precaution."

"She won't go out again, Will. It's unnecessary. That's right, isn't it my darling?" she said to Kiera, who was clinging to her like a frightened little koala.

"No, Mommy," said Kiera in a high, hoarse voice, "I don't want to get poorly."

"And you won't, darling. It's… dangerous outside."

"I don't want any more surprises, Iris," Will repeated.

"Wasn't it enough to move the locks on the front door higher? Like this, it…"

"I want to watch *Jumanji*," said Mila, ignoring their conversation.

"Again?"

"I want to see the lion!" she shouted. Then she roared loudly at Iris, "Raaarrrrrr!"

"Alright," Iris agreed, going over to the VCR and inserting the video of *Jumanji*.

When the script reading 'Tristar Pictures' finally appeared on the screen, Iris got up and whispered to Will:

"Do you think… she saw anything?"

"Of what happened…?" he tried not to finish the sentence. "Yes."

"I think so… she's acted as though I'm not here ever since. Haven't you noticed? She only wants to be with you."

"Yes. I know… she… never lets go of me."

"But you're happy, right?"

"Are you serious?"

"Things have worked out perfectly for you. Now the girl never leaves you."

"You're going crazy, Will. We've…" she lowered her voice even further, "we've killed our neighbor and buried him under the back patio. How the hell could I be…?"

"Lower your voice! She's going to hear you!" he murmured, glancing toward the window that looked over the back yard.

"Do you think she doesn't know?"

"Are you coming, Mommy? It's starting."

"I'm coming now, sweetheart," said Will, taking the opportunity and moving toward the couch.

"Not you. Mommy." Kiera replied, turning her back on him. Then she turned back to the television, as though neither of them were there.

Will, who hadn't yet reached the couch, played deaf and sat down next to her, putting his arm around her.

"Not you. Mommy!" she repeated angrily.

Will put his head in his hands, holding back the yell that had reached his throat. He got up and started to walk back and forth across the living room. Her rejection was too much for him. He thought of everything he had done to have her there at home: the trips to clothes stores, the sleepless nights when she cried for her parents, the toys he bought to make her happy. Nothing seemed to be enough. However hard he tried, he always felt as though the girl rejected him. Iris went over to the little girl, and when Kiera caught hold of her arm, he felt as though they'd punched him in the stomach.

"I knew this would happen. I shouldn't have thought..."

"Thought what, Will?" asked Iris.

"All this! You two! And I... it's as if... as if I were a criminal. This is my home too, you know?" he yelled at them.

Kiera looked at him and her face crumpled.

"Can you stop scaring the child?" Iris replied. "It's alright, honey... Your daddy sometimes... gets upset."

"He's not my daddy," she said, a sentence that sparked off what came next.

"What did you say?!" Will yelled, angrily storming over and raising his fist at her. Iris clenched her jaw, furious, and looked at him with more hatred than she had ever felt before.

Will's fist trembled in the air and Kiera burst into noisy sobs.

"Go ahead and touch her if you dare," said Iris.

Will was about to. He didn't know why he held back. Perhaps it was the little girl's shocked face, perhaps it was his wife's angry expression, but he felt so removed from that fake family that he collapsed to his knees and started to weep with such a sharp pain between his ribs he felt like he was about to faint.

Iris hugged Kiera, trying to calm her down, while Will wept uncontrollably. Then he reached out a hand towards his wife, whispering a timid, "I'm sorry." But she moved her hand away. That simple gesture was the start of everything falling apart. It happened gradually over the following weeks, and ended in a way that Iris could never have imagined.

Chapter 48
Miren Triggs
1998–1999

Life is only fair if you make sure it is.

My experience of joining the *Press* was more dramatic than I would have liked. As soon as I set foot in the office I joined Bob Wexter, Nora Fox, and Samantha Axley's team as an investigative intern. I was the only one whose surname didn't include an 'x', and that little bit of nonsense allowed me to make jokes for a while whilst we investigated cases I could never have imagined: the sale of arms by the Government to various Gulf states, sex scandals involving members of the Senate, government leaks of serious corruption scandals. I was swamped for the first six months and painful as it was, since it remained important to me, Kiera's case was put on the back burner. I also had exams coming up and assignments to hand in for college. I would go to the *Press* offices each evening to see how I could help. My contract with them included a raise as soon as I graduated, replacing my internship period with a contract as a full-time staff journalist, but until that happened, I had to try and keep up in the evenings, staying late at the office or working extra hours once I got home.

I barely saw my parents, who became a distant source of reassurance at the other end of a telephone line.

One morning, Professor Schmoer finally walked silently down the corridor, acting as if he didn't know me, and pinned the final grades for his subject onto the notice board, including a coveted honors marker beside my name. I was officially the holder of a degree in journalism from Columbia. We hadn't spoken again since that night and as I approached him before he left, I didn't really know what to say.

"Professor," I said.

"Miren," he replied, surprised to see me. "Congratulations."

"Th… Thank you."

"You… submitted an extremely good final assignment. I expected no less of you."

"Did you like it?" I asked, deep in my insecurities.

"Doesn't your grade reflect that?"

"Yes, I guess so. Thanks again."

"I… I didn't do anything. You know that. You deserved that grade. You're the most…." he searched for a word that could summarize a complex personality but stopped trying when I interrupted him.

"It's because of you that I have a job at the *Press*."

"You're wrong, Miren. You have a job at the *Press* because you deserve it and because they could see that too. That piece on James Foster…"

"Was sheer luck. I thought he was innocent, too."

"It doesn't matter what you think as long as you track down the truth. The problem would be if what you thought changed the truth."

"Isn't that what happens with a lot of newspapers?"

"And that's why you'll make a good journalist, Miren. Your place is at the *Press*. I've no doubt about it."

"Will you keep teaching, Professor?"

"Oh, yes. I think… it's worth the effort. It's important. I'll fill the endless hours outside teaching by contributing to the faculty radio station. Perhaps you'll hear me on air."

"Yes, perhaps I will," I said, half joking. "And... thanks again, Jim."

"Don't mention it," he said, turning and waving his arm above his head as he walked away.

"Hey, Professor!" I shouted, raising my voice as he moved away. "Are those new glasses?"

"My old ones broke," he replied in farewell in a loud voice, following the private joke only he and I understood.

Once I'd left the campus, I called my parents. I was ecstatic. I could finally focus one hundred percent on my work at the paper and resume the search for Kiera, who was still in my head, hidden and yet wandering around the corners of my mind. She had never really gone away, but daily life and the stress of adapting to the pace of the newsroom had postponed the promise I'd made to myself and to her father, Mr. Templeton.

"Mom!" I squealed as soon as she answered the phone. "I'm officially a journalist!"

I can still remember that call. How easily things fall apart. You try to be strong, to think that things happen for a reason and you will understand what it was later, that life tries to give you lessons from which you can learn something vitally important, but the plain and simple truth is that my mother was crying and whimpering when she answered the phone and, for the first few moments, I hadn't understood what was going on.

"Are you OK, Mom? What's happened?"

"I wanted to call you to tell you sooner... but... I just couldn't."

"What's going on? You've got me worried."

"It's your grandpa..."

"What's wrong with Grandpa?"

"He shot your grandma."

"What?!" I gasped, horrified.

"We're at the hospital. It's really serious, Miren. You need to come home."

"But... but why...?"

At that moment I didn't really want to know. Perhaps I didn't dare open my eyes and look in the right direction.

I requested two days off from work, I think it was the only time I ever did, and when I arrived at the airport in Charlotte my father was there to meet me with a lukewarm hug. As I recall, he barely said a word during the car journey, letting our mutual silence guide our emotions. All I remember him saying, just as he pulled up in the hospital parking lot, was:

"I need to let you know, Miren. Your grandpa is in there, too. After he shot your grandma, he tried to kill himself by jumping off the balcony. He's in a coma. The doctors say he might pull through."

"But why did he do it?"

"Miren... your grandpa's spent his entire life beating your grandma. Did you really never realize? He's a domestic abuser. Do you remember when your grandma came to live with us for a while? That was why. The accident on the stairs? Your grandpa had given her a horrific beating."

I couldn't believe what I was hearing. I froze.

"Why the fuck did they stay together?"

"We tried to get involved... but your grandma... loved him."

"But... Grandma's not like that."

"Don't ask me. I don't understand it either, sweetheart. And your mother even less so. She managed to convince your grandma to report him twice but... both times she withdrew her statement and they stayed together. Did you know that your grandfather once pointed his shotgun at your mother? She told me everything today. She's distraught. She's spent her whole life hoping you'd never see something like this. Trying to make it seem like everything was OK. Your studies, your career, your education.... But... I guess the truth always comes out in the end, doesn't it?"

I nodded. It felt like my heart had been torn out and the couple of pats on the leg he gave me in encouragement really weren't enough.

When I arrived, I saw my mother crying on a plastic chair in the waiting room. She got up, walking unsteadily, and hugged me harder than I think she ever had before. I wondered when she had got so old, although perhaps it was seeing her so overcome and devastated. She was the first to speak and she did so in a whisper, in my ear and between sobs, exhaling a hoarse, "I'm sorry." I stroked her back and couldn't help crying myself. It was the first time we'd seen one another in months, and doing it like this, having my eyes opened in such a way, made me wonder whether I was doing the right thing.

"How's Grandma?" I asked, once I'd steeled myself.

"She's not good. They're operating on her and… she might not survive. She's… she's elderly and she's lost a lot of blood. I shouldn't have let her go back to him…"

I swallowed. I was finding it hard to speak.

"It's not your fault. It was Grandpa who did it."

"But if I… If I'd paid better attention…"

"Mom… please. Don't think about that now. She'll get better. You'll see." She nodded, perhaps because she needed someone to tell her that everything would be alright. My father had gone to the hospital cafeteria to avoid the difficult conversations, and I sat down with her in the corridor to wait. I dried her tears; she wept on my shoulder. For the first time in a long while I felt like I had stopped being a burden to my mother, becoming instead a support she could lean on. After the attack in the park, she'd been there, worried, trying to protect me and make me feel better. Perhaps that's why she never told me about my grandmother's problems. She had gone through life taking on other people's problems, pouring her efforts into other people's difficulties, and, for once, she needed someone to do the same for her. In the end, they were her parents, she'd spent her childhood with them, and the worst thing is that in the bad times we always turn to our happy memories to keep us from going mad. I was sure that while she wept, she was remembering all the times when my grandfather had behaved well, when she had seen my grandmother happy with him, trying to limit the terrible tragedy of the shooting. However, in reality, each punch, yell or push had done just as much damage.

A while later I offered to get her a herbal tea, hoping that having something warm in her hands would keep her calm, and she accepted. I walked towards the cafeteria and along the way I saw the open door to the hospital rooms. There were people in all of them. In each of them, you could see from the doorway that there was somebody sitting with the person whose feet lay on the bed. In all but one. My grandfather's room.

I went in and saw him lying there, hooked up to the monitors while he slept. His mouth was open, and his weak breathing fogged up the clear plastic of the mask. His expression of complete calm turned my stomach. While my grandmother fought for her life in the operating theatre, he seemed to be sleeping peacefully.

I watched him for a while, and tried to remember a life of deceit where I'd seen him only as a misogynist, not a domestic abuser. I recalled my grandma's unexplained bruises, the looks of terror that I didn't understand back then, the uncomfortable silences when he used to arrive home while I was still a little girl, and my grandma calling my mom to come and collect me. Now I know, of course, that it was so I wouldn't see what was happening between those four walls.

Suddenly the monitor tracking his cardiac rhythm began to sound and I watched as his pulse rate shot up above 150. It continued steadily upwards to 170, progressing a few seconds later to 180 while a loud beeping increased in intensity. He was motionless and seemed unaware of anything happening in his chest. In one of the most significant moments of my life, in that lonely room with a man I had never loved or even liked, the man who had tried to kill my grandma, I went over to the monitor where the lines were drawing crazy graphs, and... I unplugged it.

The room fell silent once more.

His breathing was quicker, but the alarm intended to let the doctors know he had gone into heart failure was no longer turned on to do so.

I watched him wheeze, contorting slightly for a short time until he finally stopped. I went over to him, frightened, and saw that his mask was no longer fogging up every few seconds. I plugged the machine back in. A silent white line appeared where his pulse had previously registered, but the beeping had stopped. A message reading 'no signal' appeared on the screen. Then I walked out as if nothing had happened, but knowing inside me that everything had changed.

A few moments later I sat down beside my mother again with a herbal tea for her and a hot coffee for me.

Chapter 49
December 2003–January 2004
Five years after the disappearance

Nothing works without compromise.

With the help of the two interns who began working extra hours for her, Miren started to compile information from all the toy stores and model stores in Manhattan, Brooklyn, Queens, New Jersey, and Long Island. This was journalism the old-fashioned way, but that was how it had to be done back then. There were no extensive databases to consult; not all the stores were online. It was a case of taking the telephone book, going to the toy store section, and dialing in the hope that whoever picked up would be willing to help.

To start with, covering just the area they had decide to focus on was a mammoth task. They agreed on a plan: Victoria and Robert would call the toy stores from an improvised office consisting of two tables at the café opposite the *Press* building, the same café where Miren had once met Aaron Templeton. In these calls, made at six dollars an hour paid from Miren's own pocket, Victoria and Robert would track down the toy stores that had Smaller Home and Garden doll's houses in their catalogues. Gradually, as the weekends went by, they confirmed that very few toy stores featured it, which seemed like a good sign. The list shortened to these, and, if Miren could get hold of a list of customers who had once bought one of these miniature houses, she would have something to work with.

But Christmas 2003 fell during the investigation and the toy stores stopped answering their phones while they attended the huge numbers of customers who needed to find the perfect present for Santa Claus to leave under the tree on Christmas Day.

In January 2004, after working alone for three weekends, Miren met them at the café and suggested going through their progress.

"Is this all you've found?" asked Miren, surprised.

"Look, Miren… this… is impossible. It looks like they stopped manufacturing them years ago and… it's tricky to find places that still sell them."

"I understand," she said, a bit dazed, without looking up from the piece of paper. There were just four toy stores written on it. "How many have you called over the last three weekends?"

"About 40."

"Just 40?!"

"A lot of stores don't even answer the phone, and those that do won't even bother to check whether they used to sell this model of doll's house. They ask us to visit in person, then hang up because they're very busy."

Miren sighed. This was worse than she'd expected.

"OK, we wanted to tell you something, too," Robert interrupted, who finally seemed to be interested in the conversation. He had sat with his head down until that point, watching the steam rise from his drink.

"Go ahead," said Miren, trying not to make it quick.

"We don't want to do this anymore," he said.

"What?"

"This. Calling toy stores. I didn't study for this, you know?

I have a student loan worth two hundred thousand dollars. I think I'm worth more. That's what my parents say."

"Yes. OK… But… you have to start somewhere, right? You want to work in investigative journalism, and this is one way of doing it: putting in some extra hours and earning…" Miren paused and changed tack mid-sentence. "I just don't understand. Can one of you tell me what's going on?"

"We spoke to Nora last week," Robert finally admitted.

"Why?"

"She's leaving the paper," Robert said. "She wants to set up a freelance investigative team and sell her work to the highest bidder."

"And what does that have to do with…?"

They both hung their heads and looked at their paper cups. Miren looked at them, confused. This attitude wasn't anything like their normal cheerful demeanor.

"Ah… I understand. She's offered to take you with her."

"It's… it's a good opportunity, Miren. This… is like looking for a needle in a haystack," said Robert in explanation.

"I know, but… that's exactly what a journalist's job is. Looking for the impossible and finding it."

Victoria looked up and shook her head. "This is more than impossible, Miren. What if they bought the doll's house in another state? What if Kiera Templeton is in a different country? Will you visit every toy store on the planet? And all… for what?"

"To find a little girl who disappeared on Thanksgiving who has nobody trying to find her except out of damned morbid fascination."

"We haven't achieved anything, Miren. Surely you can see that. This is a waste of time."

"So? What do you think you'll be doing with Nora?"

"She's promised us a six-month contract with a full salary. It will be double what we earn from interning at the *Press* and the extra hours."

"But you'll work with Nora."

"And what's so bad about her?"

Miren stood up and gathered the papers from the table.

"You'll find out. I…"

"Please, Miren… try and understand. It's a good opportunity. In Crime and Local News, we carry heaps of paper from one table to another. With you… with you we make phone calls."

"Although they may not seem to be, those phone calls are important. But… it doesn't matter. I'll manage. Do you know what I think is a shame?"

They remained motionless and didn't answer.

"You two seemed different, but I don't know why I bother. Everyone in this goddamn city seems to be something they're not."

She left the café, leaving them both there before they had the chance to reply. She looked up at the *Press*'s imposing building from the street and realized that a fine drizzle had wet the ground and filled the streets with colorful umbrellas. She hurried across the road to the opposite sidewalk, navigating between honking taxis that screeched to a halt just inches away from her, and walked inside the building with damp hair and a wet jacket.

When she reached her desk, she realized that she had no choice. She dialed Agent Miller's number and waited for him to pick up.

"Is that you, Ms. Triggs?" his voice asked on the other end of the line.

"I need your help and you need mine."

Chapter 50
December 21, 2000
Unknown location

*Even among the guilty, someone who
looks carefully can find a glimmer of love.*

Will had been out of sorts for several weeks, barely speaking when he got in from work. As soon as he arrived home, he would sit down to have a drink in one of the armchairs in the living room while Iris and the little girl played with the doll's house or tickled one another on the couch. Every time his wife asked him something he would huff at her, and when she reproached him for drinking too much he would get up, ignoring her, and pour himself another. Inside, Will felt like he no longer fit in. His marriage was a failure, his fatherhood a farce. If at any point he'd thought it was all going to turn out well, he now mentally went through all the points that had proven the opposite to be true: they couldn't take the girl out to the park to play with other children, they were afraid she might fall seriously ill and they would be forced to take her to hospital, they prayed that nobody would ever see her.

During those nights when he sat in the chair until he slumped over from the alcohol without even turning the TV on, he remembered the moment when he and Iris had moved to that house in Clifton, Passaic County, New Jersey. It was a wooden-framed house of just over 950 square feet on a plot of just over 2,500 square feet, painted white with a gable roof. It was in a peaceful neighborhood that was cheap due to its location little more than three hundred feet from an electricity sub-station and, although the neighbors weren't the pleasantest in the world, that little corner had struck them as the perfect place to start a family. Will remembered how he'd carried Iris, aged barely 25 years old, over the threshold after they got married in a chapel in Garfield, where they both came from, and which was just a few miles away. They had both grown up in complex environments; they had connected while trying to save one another. Will's father had drowned in the bathtub at home when he was just a little boy; his mother had died of an overdose when he was 15. He had ended up in a foster home with parents who always tried to understand him but whom he always rejected, and he'd left home once he turned 18. He'd found a job at a garage and lived in a studio apartment for a while until, by chance, he'd crossed paths with Iris, a girl with blond, curly hair whose motorcycle had broken down. They'd fallen in love as only fools do. But there were so many faults in both their personalities that somehow, they fit together. Like Will, Iris had grown up with an absent mother and a dead father who was replaced by a series of foulmouthed men whose names she didn't even try to remember because she only ever saw them once. Eventually, she'd started working in a fast food restaurant and with her first savings, she bought the second-hand motorbike that would forever connect her to Will.

The courtship turned out shorter than either of them anticipated after she got pregnant at only 19. Will went down on one knee in front of Iris at a diner on Dahnert's Lake one evening when the golden sun shone on the tables along the little bridge that connected it to the lakeshore. They got married without telling anyone with one of Will's colleagues from the garage as the only witness. They paid the deposit on the small house with all their savings. When Iris's mother found out she hadn't invited her to her wedding she was so hurt she never went to visit her. But that stepladder which happiness allowed them to climb, step by step, out of their pit of unhappiness reached its limit when tragedy struck. One night when Iris was seven months pregnant, she woke up with stabbing pains in her stomach to find the sheets drenched in blood.

That was the first baby they'd lost, but it sowed a need in them that had never existed before. They wanted to be parents. They'd loved that little one, whose name they had already chosen, so much that it was impossible to imagine continuing to live in that house without becoming parents. But the years went by, and sadness filled their home in the form of miscarriages and ever-more daunting medical bills.

One night, after hearing the little girl laugh while Iris told her a story about witches and thieves, Will got up and left the house.

Iris was worried every minute he didn't come back. She went around the house a few times and out into the yard repeatedly to see if she could see him coming back down the street. When she didn't hear from him, she went to bed thinking that perhaps he would be home soon. Normally Will would only go out at night to take out the trash. Perhaps he had gone to the gas station to top up the tank to save time the next day or perhaps he was doing a last minute trip to a 24-hour grocery store, but he always let her know when he did that. This time, however, he'd got into the car and headed south without saying what he was planning to do. He'd simply gone over to her as she told Mila a story, kissed her on the top of the head and then left in silence.

At around two in the morning, headlights lit up the front of the house and Iris, who had barely slept, got up quickly to see whether Will had arrived safely home. She was worried about him. He hadn't been the same since the incident with their neighbor. He had become a recluse who hardly said a word to her. On one occasion she had even asked him if everything was alright only to receive a grunt in reply. His desperation had been clear.

She ran into the living room and waited for the door to open so she could ask him how he was, but then there was a knock at the door and the voice of an unfamiliar man filled the living room.

"Mrs. Noakes?"

Iris froze. She didn't know what was going on or who was at the door. She immediately turned on the television and switched to channel nine, where she could check the image on the front-door camera. It showed two uniformed police officers looking at the front door.

"What have you done, Will?!" she thought to herself. A thousand possibilities flashed through her mind. Could he have confessed? Had he turned them in? She was on the verge of collapse. She went to the cupboard where they kept the shotgun and removed the padlock. She checked Mila was sleeping soundly then closed the door to her bedroom.

They knocked at the door again and she ran to open it, feigning sleepiness and buttoning up her robe.

"Yes?"

"Are you Mrs. Noakes, ma'am?"

"Yes….," she said in a hoarse voice with her eyes half closed. "Has something happened?"

The two officers looked at one another, deciding with a glance which of them was going to deliver the news. One of them, dark-haired and scruffy looking, began:

"I'm afraid… this isn't easy… but…"

"But what? What's happening?"

"Your husband… has died."

Iris covered her mouth with her hands, horrified.

"A train hit his car on the Bloomfield Avenue level crossing. He died instantly."

"No… he can't be," Iris gasped.

Chapter 51
Miren Triggs
1999–2001

*The whole world seemed
to be disappearing down the drain
and nobody was doing anything to stop it.*

My grandfather's death was a real blow for my mother. She cried when she found out that his heart had failed and that by the time the doctors realized it was too late to do anything. He was her father and also a son of a bitch, but death often prompts deep forgiveness, even against your own wishes.

I went back to New York, trying to forget about it, and the whirlpool of journalism sucked me in entirely. There was no denying I was passionate about journalism, but each day it demanded more of me. It consumed my time and energy and, although it gave my life meaning, it also opened hidden doorways and revealed the gory details of stories that were difficult to get out of my mind: a company that exploited little girls in Asia in illegal factories by day and brothels by night; an animal rights activist who sold meat to Manhattan restaurants; a father who set fire to his children to get revenge on their mother. The deeper you went into this world, the more it changed you. When I spoke with my colleagues in the editorial office I realized that the younger members of the team were excited and enthusiastic, and the veterans were cynics who hated the world. They weren't all like that, but in their writing you could detect a cry for help in finding some good news that wouldn't torment them.

Bob had made sure I was working flat out in the newsroom on increasingly demanding and depressing tasks, reviewing stories about companies, about state budgets, about factory inventories. I would get up before dawn and, when I wasn't digging in an archive or interviewing someone, I would leave the newsroom late at night once I'd transcribed all the material I'd worked on that day.

One night in 2001 I reached my front door and realized that Miss Amber's door was ajar. That wasn't normal for her. She was so private that even the blinds on her windows onto the main street were always lowered.

"Miss Amber?" I called, gently pushing the door open to look inside.

Her apartment was almost an exact replica of mine. I'd never seen it in detail; she had never invited me in for a cup of tea to tell me her life story. The only detail I'd noticed was the light of a lamp that stood just inside the door when we happened to meet on the landing. This time, the apartment was in darkness.

"Miss Amber? Are you alright?" I asked, raising my voice.

I didn't like this at all. There are different kinds of silence. You can feel it in the air, in the muffled sounds of your steps on the floor, in the stillness of the distant curtains which I noticed move very slightly on the far side of the living room.

I went inside the apartment and tried to turn on the lamp in the hallway, but the bulb had gone. I walked in the dark, moving further inside, and my attention was caught by the photos on the walls. I recognized Miss Amber from 30 or 40 years ago, radiant with perfectly styled hair and a wide smile like a string of pearls. In one of the pictures, she was wearing a swimsuit and jumping in the air on a beach beside a good-looking young man of around the same age. In another her head was thrown back in laughter as she ran along a long dirt track between some trees beside the same young man. She looked happy. It was impossible to see her in those pictures as anything but happy, yet now she always seemed to have such a negative attitude to the whole world.

I suddenly spotted a bare foot sticking out from behind the couch beside the curtains.

"Miss Amber?!" I yelled.

It was dark, but I could make out that she was bleeding from a cut on her forehead.

"Are you alright?" I whispered, going over to check whether the wound was serious. It didn't look too bad, but I dialed 911 and gave her address. My medical knowledge was limited to taking painkillers for my period cramps. I looked around the living room and managed to turn on one of the standing lamps in a corner and, just as I turned round, I saw him.

The silhouette of a man was watching me from the dark passage that seemed to lead to the bedroom. He was motionless, a jewelry box in his hands, and I couldn't see his face or tell what he wanted.

"If you're looking for money, I don't know where it is," I said.

"Your cell phone," he shouted in a whining voice that sounded like a motorbike whose motor was about to give up.

I realized he was a desperate thief in search of easy money. It was the end of the month. Christmas was approaching. Criminals have gifts to buy, too.

I tossed my phone into the darkness and the silhouette crouched down to pick it up. My heart was racing however much I tried to hide it. Over time I'd discovered that part of me always went back to that park when I found myself in dangerous situations; that moment had left its mark on my soul forever and I had to live with it, whether I liked it or not. A moment like that changes you, it alters everything you are and try to be, although it's impossible to predict which way it will make you turn. In my case, that park led me to darkness and revenge. The image of a flaming James Foster was also burned on my mind, and my fear of going out had turned into the terror of not taking action.

"I've got a gun," I lied. It was at home. "Take the cell phone and that will be the end of it. Try anything else and I'll shoot you."

I noted an immediate change in his attitude, a slight tremor in his breathing as it floated on the air. Perhaps he noticed in my voice that inner rage I carried because of injustice. Miss Amber groaned in pain, and I looked towards her. She was alright. That moan confirmed that the blow hadn't been too hard. Then, as though he were merely a breeze that had blown in to put the finishing touches to my personality and plant enough fear in my life to leave me crying to the heavens for mercy, he made a break for the door and disappeared.

I spent an hour waiting for the ambulance and consoling Miss Amber while I thought about everything that was going on around me. The whole world seemed to be disappearing down the drain and nobody was doing anything to stop it: violence, attacks, corruption, fear of walking alone, rapists. It was depressing. I thought of Kiera, of the little girl I hadn't had the chance to look for recently, and I decided I would find time to do so. Late at night, in the small hours. There was no other way.

Miss Amber wept beside me, and I hugged her, imagining that it might make her feel better.

"Thank you, Miren. You're a good girl," she said faintly. The wound didn't seem too deep, although it was still bleeding and would need stitches.

"You wouldn't say that if you could see inside my head," I

replied, being honest for once. She looked at me seriously, then stayed silent for a while, looking at the photographs on the walls.

Then, without my asking, she began to speak:

"You know, Miren, I was alone like you once and… I fell in love without wanting or trying to. He was a wonderful man. One of those who just appear in your life and let you be who you are without trying to change you, loving every one of your faults, and filling your life with fireworks."

"You should rest, Miss Amber…" I interrupted her, "the ambulance is almost here."

"No… I want you to know. I think you're good and I don't want life to knock you about any more. I want you to be prepared."

"Alright…" I sighed. There are people who need you to listen to them from time to time, although the lessons they try to deliver often have unintended consequences.

"As I said… we were happy. So happy. This apartment is full of photos from that time. We dated for two marvelous years. One night, after leaving an amazing restaurant beside the river in Brooklyn, surrounded by fairy lights in the trees, he went down on one knee and asked whether I'd like to marry him."

"And what happened?"

"I squealed 'yes'. I was happy with him, you know?" She paused briefly to look at one of the photos. "He was called Ryan."

"Did he die?"

"Just ten minutes later," she said bluntly.

I held my breath. Pain seemed to be everywhere, lying in wait for exactly the worst moment to appear, so as to cause the most damage.

"A few feet on, while we were waiting for a taxi, a man with a gun told us to give him everything we had on us. Wallet, watch, engagement ring. I agreed, but Ryan was brave. Brave and stupid. Bravery is dangerous if you don't know how to judge the consequences. He died in my arms from a gunshot wound to the neck."

"I… I'm so sorry, Miss Amber."

"That's why I shouted. So that you wouldn't risk your life for a bit of jewelry. It isn't worth it. If the world's falling apart, it's because good people are leaving it before their time."

I nodded, letting that idea sit in my mind, but I still came to the conclusion that life is shit, and that violence is shit, but that it sometimes seemed like the only solution.

Once the ambulance had taken Miss Amber away, I went into my apartment and took out the box containing the file on Kiera. I knew I would find what I needed there.

A crazy idea had lodged in my mind. A photo slid out of one of the folders and landed by my feet. In the darkness I didn't realize which photo it was, even though I had gone through every single one in the box and the archives hundreds of times, and it wasn't until I bent down and picked it up by one of the corners that I realized who it was. At that moment, at that exact instant after what had happened to Miss Amber, I decided to search for the man who had raped me.

Chapter 52
June 14, 2002
Four years after Miren was attacked

The shadows move for fear of the light.

It was always hardest for Miren at night. At night, shadows became problems. People would walk around knowing that the lack of light was an advantage, and although there were hiding places, they were all full of other people trying to do the same. But everything changed when you had a weapon under your jacket. Since she'd started working at the newspaper, she had more free time at weekends, and since she'd bought her gun, she would use this time to keep an eye on someone. On just one person.

It wasn't somebody who was the subject of one of her articles; it wasn't anybody powerful, it wasn't a businessman or a politician. In fact, the person she was watching didn't even have a job. At least not a normal job with taxes to pay. He lived in one of the social housing developments built by the government in Harlem to provide low-rent accommodation for low-income residents. In theory it seemed like a good idea, but in practice what it had done was gather people with few resources in the space of just two or three streets, encouraging high levels of crime. There were also families living there who worked day and night just to pay the rent and to build a future for their children, but between these hard-working families hid a huge number of criminals and drug addicts who saw the subsidized rents as an opportunity to establish a territory for their muggings, robberies and drug dealing.

Miren lived on the edge of that neighborhood, on West 115th Street, and as the street numbers went up it was clear the potential problems did the same. Gangs would sit on the stairs of the 116th Street subway station, cars with tinted windows would cruise around slowly from 117th Street upwards. There was nothing dangerous about the area during the day; it had various parks where plenty of people took their children and stores of all kinds that were open until the sun set and the dangers began to emerge.

Miren was wearing a black hoodie and dark jeans, and she would have blended into the night shadows if it weren't for the light reflecting off her pale face. She waited for a whole hour on the sidewalk watching a row of windows in a building on 115th Street. She watched a couple arguing, moving from one side of the room to the other. The man and woman followed one another from one room to the next, gesticulating wildly. After a few seconds, the woman suddenly appeared at the window and leant out.

Miren jumped behind a parked car to hide. Seconds later a man came out of the doorway and the woman who was waiting in the window yelled "jerk" after him and threw a lighter at him that bounced off the asphalt. The man mumbled something back that Miren couldn't catch and then began to walk. She followed him at a distance.

He crossed two streets until he reached 117th Street. Miren stopped when she saw the guy go down the stairs into a bar, outside which was a group of four equally scruffy men. She waited, just like always. She kept wondering if it would be better to go home, thinking that maybe that day wouldn't be any different from all the previous days. Two hours passed before the man finally came back outside. For the whole time, Miren didn't take her eyes of the door. Every now and then, groups of young boys and girls would enter or leave, dressed up and ready to dance until they dropped.

Although she almost gave up several times, Miren knew that people like him needed a high level of vigilance. Or at least that was what she told herself, unsure of what that really meant. She found the situation so complex that she didn't even really know what she was doing there. She had fallen into the routine of doing the same thing every weekend, leaving her apartment and positioning herself opposite the guy's front door, following him wherever he went, without even knowing why. It was as though she only realized what she was doing once she'd spent several hours waiting, when a voice in her head whispered, "What are you trying to do, Miren? Why don't you go home?" But the hours always passed, and she would still be there until the guy set off home and she could leave calmly, feeling that she had fulfilled her duty.

However, on that occasion Miren was surprised by the sight of the man leaving the bar, dragging a young girl who was stumbling and could barely climb the stairs. The doorman asked the girl if she needed help and the man replied that she was his friend and that he would take care of her. Miren got to her feet in the shadows and watched carefully, as if she were a lioness about to hunt a gazelle in the middle of the savannah at dusk. The only thing different was that this time the gazelle was planning to snack on a lion cub.

The girl could hardly keep her eyes open, and the man pulled her along clumsily. She was wearing a short blue dress, similar to the one Miren had worn that night.

Miren followed them. Things didn't look good, but she didn't dare do anything yet. The image was so upsetting that for a good while she kept a safe distance behind them. On two occasions the man picked the girl up after her legs gave way, silently hauling her up by the waist. The girl, between giggles, thanked him for taking care of her.

They reached an alley and went down it. Miren lost them for a few long seconds while she caught up. She leaned around the corner and swallowed when she arrived.

The girl was slumped on the ground by a dumpster with her eyes closed and her head thrown back, leaning against a graffiti-covered brick wall.

"Please take me home... I don't feel well."

He didn't reply. He just looked down at her, his eyes those of a demon who had lured her into a trap.

"I think... I had too much to drink. Where are... my friends?"

"Your friends are just coming," he whispered as he undid his fly and threw himself on her.

"What... what are you doing? No...!"

"Shhh... you know you want this," he moaned as he began to kiss her neck.

"No... not this... please... no."

"Shut up!" he ordered with a muffled shout.

The man moved his hand away and pulled her dress up, tearing the fabric, and preparing a new trauma by the light of the moon.

"No... please... my friends... are... waiting for me."

"It won't take long," he whispered, as he continued kissing and touching parts of her he had no permission to touch while she was insufficiently conscious to protect them.

Suddenly a female voice burst into the alleyway, the echo making it sound louder than it really was:

"She said no."

The man looked up and saw Miren, a backlit silhouette.

"What the hell do you want? Get out of here. We're having a little fun."

The guy shifted his position and looked at her in confusion, not understanding at all.

Miren turned serious, almost standing to attention, trying to take up more physical space than she really did, like the defensive tactics of an animal that feels threatened.

"She told you to leave her alone," Miren repeated. Inside she was trembling with fear.

"Why don't you just leave? This has nothing to do with you."

"Oh, but yes it does," she corrected him.

At that moment, Miren pulled out her pistol and pointed it at him. The metal of the weapon reflected the light of the moon, the only witness to what was happening in that trash-filled alley.

"She said no, asshole."

"Hey, hey, easy," he replied, stressed. He jumped to his feet and raised his hands. His eyes widened with fear. Miren remembered how she'd felt as she'd run through the streets that night in her torn dress. "I'm leaving. I don't want trouble," he said. Then, when his eyes finally managed to focus on Miren's face in the darkness, he said, "Hang on, do we know each other?"

"Know each other?" she asked. "Know each other!? Don't you even remember me?"

That pushed Miren to the limit. She hadn't stopped thinking about what this guy had done in that park for a single day after he and his gang had beaten Robert up. That coward Robert who had never taken any responsibility and never helped her escape the darkness with his unreliable statement and his pathetic apology. Miren hadn't ever forgotten the face of the man in front of her. Sometimes she would see it with that devil's smile when she closed her eyes. The sad thing about life is that it's unfair, and it's unfair because it is forgetful. But Miren didn't forget. It was impossible for her.

"I don't know... girl.... you're not... ringing any bells. Do you want to lower your gun?"

"You shut up. Don't move."

"Hey... easy there..." the man stretched his hands out towards her, trying to calm her down.

Miren took her cell phone out of her hoodie pocket and dialed 911.

"Police?" Miren said into the handset without lowering her gun.

Suddenly, the man leapt at her and knocked her over. The gun slipped out of her hands and landed next to the girl, who had just passed out again.

Miren cried out in pain when she hit the ground and found herself beneath the man, who lay on top of her and trapped her between his legs.

"Well, well... it looks like the three of us are going to have some fun," he said.

Miren tried to fight and kick, but she could hardly move. She felt the man's weight on top of her and he was holding her by the wrists. Each of her attempts to hit him was parried, her kicks just hit his legs and didn't reach his back. She felt defeated, just like she had that night. A tear formed in the corner of her eye. Just then, as if she'd suddenly travelled back to the past, she felt the man pulling her hoodie up to reveal her bra and, again, all she could see was his smile dancing in the darkness.

Miren yanked hard with one of her hands, grabbed the man's hair and pulled him towards her.

"That's it... we're going to have some fun," he said, thinking he'd convinced her. "I like feisty girls," he whispered. His face was so close to Miren's they could feel each other's breaths. Miren's bottom lip brushed against the man's top one, but at that moment, the flash of a gunshot lit up the alley. The sound reverberated off the walls, causing some cats to yowl and several dogs to start barking. The girl was holding Miren's gun in shaking hands and the man's body instantly slumped on top of Miren, covering her in warm blood that seemed black in the shadows.

336

Struggling to breathe, Miren extricated herself little by little from beneath the body and both women looked at one another silently between gasps, making a promise that didn't require words.

Afterwards Miren helped the girl up and put the gun away. Neither of them spoke as they stumbled away from there as fast as they could. They stopped on a corner and Miren wiped the blood off her face with her hoodie. Then they got into a cab to Miren's apartment, the driver complaining about taking them such a short distance, and she let the girl sleep in her bed. Miren didn't sleep a wink all night, watching her, aware that perhaps this was the end, or a beginning. Neither girl asked the other's name, and the next morning, after Miren had lent her some old clothes and the girl had dressed to leave, she just said 'thank you' before shutting the door behind her. They never saw each other again.

Chapter 53
January 15, 2004–mid-2005
Seven years after Kiera's disappearance

The greatest virtue of a determined person is making their final attempts into penultimate ones.

Following the call from Miren Triggs, Agent Miller had agreed to meet her the next day. The day after the article, following the identification of the doll's house, Miren had updated him with all the most relevant information she had gathered and extracted from the images from the video: the model of the doll's house—Smaller Home and Garden by the Tomy Corporation—and the type of wallpaper, one of the most popular designs sold by Furnitools, a DIY chain with a nationwide presence.

For his part, Agent Miller had requested increased resources in the search for Kiera but had found himself facing a brick wall, which Miren still knew nothing about.

They had arranged to meet on the Bow Bridge in Central Park. Miren had asked to meet there because the stillness of the water and the autumnal views of the park and the San Remo building emerging above the trees helped her to think. After waiting for around fifteen minutes, during which a couple got engaged in front of twelve random by-standers, Agent Miller appeared at the other end of the bridge and Miren quickly went over to him, keen to get out of there.

"What progress have you made, Ms. Triggs?"

"That's why I called you. I've got... serious problems making progress by myself. I know you're looking for her too, but the next step requires a big push and... I can't do it alone."

"A push?"

"Look, Agent Miller, we've been investigating, and this particular model of dollhouse could have been bought from any one of two thousand toy stores and department stores across Manhattan, Brooklyn, Queens, New Jersey and Long Island. I have a pretty exhaustive list of toy stores. I know that lots of people come from further afield to watch the Thanksgiving parade, but I think the person or people who took her are from one of these areas."

"What makes you think that?"

"It rained that day. When it rains people tend to travel into the city via public transport. To travel in from New Jersey or Long Island using public transport takes between one and two hours. The parade began at nine. The kidnapping occurred just before midday. My theory is that the kidnapper arrived at the parade very early to find a spot near Herald Square. It's a very central area and it's almost impossible to get a spot if you don't get there early. If the kidnapper wanted to make sure he was in the area immediately around Herald Square, he would've had to arrive by around eight in the morning. Based on him arriving at the place where Kiera disappeared by eight in the morning, it's possible to establish a fairly straightforward map of distances and directions in which the kidnapper could live using the first trains of the day from each area and how long it takes to travel into the city center if you need to be there by eight in the morning."

"I get it."

"This limits the places the kidnapper might live to the areas I've already mentioned: New Jersey, Manhattan, Brooklyn and Long Island."

"And did you reach this conclusion by yourself?"

"It's a theory. I could be mistaken, but I've been reading the file and thinking about this girl for years. The job of an investigative journalist is to confirm theories, a good friend taught me that, and I think this theory is more valid than the idea that a guy travelled from some other part of the world to carry off a little girl in the middle of the most famous parade in the world."

Agent Miller nodded and sighed before speaking. "What do you need from me?"

"Could you organize a search of all the toy stores and model shops in the areas I've mentioned? Perhaps some of them have security cameras, lists of credit card payments, or even, the holy grail, lists of customers who bought a doll's house and left a written record of their address somewhere."

Agent Miller tried to get his head around everything Miren had just told him.

"Do you know how long what you're asking me for could take?"

"Yes. And that's why I'm asking you. I can't work on this story at the paper anymore, and it's impossible to do it all by myself."

"Are you leaving?"

"Leaving? No. It's just that... I can't stretch to it. It's impossible. Perhaps you have more resources to.... to keep pursuing this, Agent Miller. You guys are good at this and I... I'm on my own."

"Don't you believe it. My hands are tied. Everyone wants me to find Kiera Templeton, but they also want me to find all the other missing people. When you journalists focus on a case it seems to be the only one, but I can assure you there are others, hundreds of others, and you can't imagine the list of missing people I have that gets longer every day."

"Nor can you imagine my list," thought Miren, mentally reviewing the archive boxes full of the names of missing women she kept in her storage unit.

"But you have something new to work on," she said, aloud this time. "Don't let this family down, Agent Miller. Perhaps the FBI can find something. This tape will put us on the right track. I'm sure of it."

"I'll do whatever I can to find this girl, Ms. Triggs," he agreed at last.

"And so will I," she added. As they reached a fork in the path they were following around the park, she went on, "I know that information only flows one way, Agent Miller. That you don't need to share any advances you make with me, but I think you know as well as I do that I'm not going to stop looking for Kiera."

"You want me to tell you what we know, don't you?"

Miren didn't reply because she assumed the question was rhetorical. Miller snorted and looked up at a metal statue of a mountain lion hunting among the trees of Central Park; an elegant allegory for what this journalist had become.

"To be frank, we don't know much. There's no usable identikit portrait. We know it was a white woman with blonde curly hair, but nothing else. According to forensics, there are no fingerprints on either the tape or the envelope except for those belonging to the family and a boy from down the street, who was the one who delivered the envelope and who can't remember the person who gave it to him in any detail. We're at a dead end. We also know the make of the video recorder used to make the recording, a 1985 Sanyo VCR, based on the pattern it left on the video's magnetic tape. It's technical, but certain. It seems that each different model of tape head redistributes the magnetic particles on the tape in a specific way, leaving a recognizable print on the band. It's like a kind of fingerprint which doesn't allow us to identify the exact VCR used, but does identify the model. We have the footage from the security cameras on the day she disappeared, but there was nothing that stood out: people everywhere, but no sign of Kiera. They cut her hair, we know that much, but we can't investigate every single person walking by, holding a child by the hand. It was Thanksgiving. The streets were full of families like that. As you can see, it's a pretty messy selection of things and hardly any of them are much use to us."

"I see," Miren replied, her voice serious.

"If you find anything else, will you tell me?" asked Miller. "I... I'll try to follow up on the toy stores, but I warn you, it looks complicated."

"You can count on it. I don't want the credit, Agent Miller. At this point, my only concern is to find Kiera Templeton and get her home."

"Can I ask you why this is so important to you? There are plenty of other cases like hers."

"And who says I'm not looking for them, too?" she replied, just before saying goodbye.

When he reached the office, Agent Miller put in a request to trace and visit the toy stores in the areas outlined by Miren Triggs. If they could get hold of a list of all the customers who had bought a Smaller Home and Garden doll's house they could organize more focused searches. It wasn't a case of getting hold of the list and searching the homes of all those customers, something the parents would no doubt demand, but of investigating those who fit the profile of potential kidnappers. To his surprise, his superiors at the FBI's missing persons unit approved his request.

They assigned twelve agents to visit toy and model stores, but they soon found themselves facing a major barrier: almost none of them kept a record of clients who had bought one of those toy houses, and especially not those who had bought one between 1998 and 2003. Some toy stores had client details from 2003, some from 2002 and others even dating back to 2001. But the data was so basic and scarce that it wasn't much use. From a total of 2,300 toy stores, they only managed to get information from 71. From those they obtained the details of only 12 customers who had bought that specific model.

They visited all 12 of them and they were all perfect families with children who welcomed the agents with coffee and maple syrup cake, going on to give them a full guided tour of the house and garden where, of course, they did not find Kiera.

In 2005, the FBI officially cancelled the search once again, and Agent Benjamin Miller called Kiera's parents once more to inform them.

"Is there any news? Have you found anything?" Aaron Templeton asked as soon as he picked up the phone.

"Still nothing, Mr. Templeton, but we're getting close. We still have all our agents working on this. We'll find your daughter. We won't stop looking for her, I promise," he lied.

Chapter 54
Miren Triggs
2005–2010

The solution is often within plain sight,
waiting patiently for somebody to
wipe the dust off it.

I genuinely didn't expect much of Agent Miller. I could feel the exhaustion and depression in every sentence he spoke, as if each disappearance had taken something out of him. Time passed, and with the same speed at which the FBI had investigated more than two thousand toy stores, they called off the search and moved on to looking for someone else. I didn't blame them. They had to prioritize their resources, but part of me always travelled to Kiera's room and sat beside her, to watch her playing with her dolls for a few minutes. I liked to imagine what her voice would be like. I liked to imagine her smiling, her expression full of life, although I had the feeling that in the real world, her eyes must be dull, like a broken, distant lighthouse, causing boats to run aground on the rocks. Agent Miller and I were those boats, and her distraught parents wept not because the lost boats crashed into the cliff, but because the lighthouse no longer gave out light.

In 2007, four years after the first tape, the dark silhouette of a woman with blond curly hair left a second tape at Aaron Templeton's office and I felt more alive than ever. Work at the newspaper took up my days, reviewing missing persons cases consumed my nights, but for a while the fire to find her was reignited. I had become a searcher. Isn't that what journalism is? Searching. Searching and finding. Sometimes what you searched for wanted to be found; other times you had to be the one who seized hold of the thread of the truth and pulled on it to draw it out from the depths of the hole where it was trapped so that it came to light once more. Since Kiera's disappearance I had begun to compile information about active cases with strong evidence that something serious had happened: Gina Pebbles, a teenager who had disappeared in 2002 on the way home from high school in Queens and whose trail had gone cold after a mile or so when they found her backpack in a park; Amanda Maslow, a sixteen-year-old girl who was kidnapped in a rural town in 1996, and Adaline Sparks, a sixteen-year-old girl who disappeared from her home in 2005 despite the fact that all the windows and doors were locked from the inside.

I didn't manage to find anything following the second tape in 2007 either, although it triggered a media circus. I tried to distance myself from all that and immersed myself in Kiera's file once more, like I had done previously. I went through all the videos from the security cameras to find a trace of the woman, but the images weren't sharp enough to help. Kiera Templeton appeared again, this time in June, only to vanish again until whoever was sending the tapes decided to carry on the game.

I called Agent Miller to ask him whether they had drawn up a profile of the kidnapper. The use of VHS tapes was clearly a symptom of some psychopathic disorder unknown to me. That son of a bitch must be a mentally disturbed nineties fetishist, and it didn't take Miller long to secretly send me a brief paragraph provided by the behavioral analysis team in Quantico that read: "White male. Forty to sixty years of age. Works as a mechanic or repairman or similar. Drives a gray or green car. Married to a woman with a weak personality. The use of VHS tapes reflects his rejection of the current, modern-day world."

Nothing more. The FBI summarized Kiera's potential captor in a few brief lines that could describe anyone. Even my own father could fit that profile if it weren't for my mother's feisty personality.

The time between one tape and the next flew by at the speed of light. By the time the third one arrived in 2008, a few days before the presidential elections that would be won by Barack Obama, nobody except me paid it the slightest attention. I hated the media circus fueled by morbid curiosity that accompanied all dramatic cases, but also the fact that politics infiltrated everything. You saw the smiling faces of Obama and John McCain whichever way you turned, promising hope as though the world wasn't going down the drain.

That tape of Kiera upset me. She was wearing a bright and uncomfortable orange dress and she didn't stop writing in a notebook throughout the whole minute-long recording. She was a broken doll, just like I used to be. If you watched carefully, it didn't take you long to imagine her tears falling onto the paper. I'd been through a period like that, when I felt alone, a prisoner of the universe, and in fact perhaps I still was, however much I had stuck myself back together with a glue made from rage and desperation.

After seeing that tape, I felt the need to visit the Templetons. I don't know why, but I needed to share some light with them. I had come to consider myself a bit like Kiera, lost and vulnerable, and although they might see their daughter like that, I knew that if she came home one day it would be possible to move forwards. Of the two of them I only managed to persuade Aaron to go for a coffee and all I can remember of that conversation are his tears and the long hug he gave me before we said goodbye. He barely spoke. He was very different to how he used to be. We'd both had the same bad luck.

During that time, I managed to consolidate my position at the newspaper. I tried to meet the demands of the investigative team, which no longer included Nora Fox, thank God, and I must admit that Bob's flexibility made him easy to work with, so I built a friendly working relationship with him.

We spent the whole of 2010 working on an article that used a lot of resources and even more of Phil Marks' patience. It dealt with a case that wasn't public knowledge in which a dozen workers at factories in China owned by a famous cell phone company had died by suicide due to stress and poor working conditions. When the 12-page report hit the streets at the start of November, Phil called the three of us to his office to congratulate us and give us a couple of weeks off to rest.

But I didn't need rest, I needed to find the answer to a question that had been plaguing me for years: where was Kiera Templeton? Who had her?

I re-watched the digitalized videos of Kiera over and over again. I made myself a playlist of them using the VLC program so that, once one started, it ran straight into the next one. I spent an entire day like that, watching Kiera grow up, imagining her life. I even began to doubt whether she actually needed rescuing.

Then I had a mad idea: I would watch the tapes in the same way they had been recorded. So I decided to buy myself a 1985 Sanyo VHS machine. I found two relics on Craigslist that were being sold for parts and I arranged to buy one from its owner and see if it offered any solutions. At the corner we'd agreed on, I met a fat guy who ran an old video store and was selling off everything in the shop to close it down.

"It's one hundred dollars," he said, after saying hello and telling me his name, which I don't remember. "As I said in the listing, it's broken, but it should be easy to fix. You just need to change one of the tension arms for the magnetic tape and you'll get it working."

"Do you know where I could get the right part to fix it?" I asked, checking whether anything else seemed damaged from a quick glance at the outside.

"You can't get hold of them easily. There are only two or three places in the entire city that repair these old dinosaurs. It's almost not worth fixing them. Streaming is the future, that's what they say, isn't it? But hey, if you have old videotapes then this is the answer. There's no other option."

"Only two or three repair places?" A spark lit inside me.

"Yeah, sure. That's including New Jersey, where I live. I think the old VidRepair place downtown closed a few months ago, even though these old things break down a lot. Dust builds up inside and the plastic parts break. But, of course, hardly anybody uses them anymore. It's a business destined to disappear. Just like mine. It's sad, but there you are. Not even DVDs will be able to hold back the digital world that's on its way."

"Do you know the names of those stores?" I asked, my heart in my mouth as though I was about to uncover something important.

Chapter 55
November 26, 2003
One day before the first tape
Unknown location

Compassion always requires
love and pain in order to flourish.

The day before Thanksgiving in 2003 Iris spent the entire morning at home with Kiera.

"How do I look, Mommy?" asked Kiera, who was wearing an orange tablecloth as a dress.

"You're missing the best part, honey," said Iris, tying a bow of the same color around her waist.

Iris loved playing princesses with Kiera and although she hadn't bought many dresses so as not to arouse suspicion, Iris worked hard to improvise them with tablecloths that she tied around Kiera's little waist. This allowed them to play at dressing up in a thousand different ways, to develop the Kiera's imagination creating gizmos and accessories out of almost anything. This almost always turned out well, except when Kiera made herself a scepter using the toilet brush.

"I need one more thing. I'll be right back," said Kiera at one point and skipped happily to her bedroom, much to Iris's surprise. An hour later, during which Iris checked channel 8 twice to make sure she was alright, the little girl came out of her bedroom wearing a tiara made from macaroni stuck to a piece of cardboard.

"How about now? Do I look pretty?"

Iris smiled. "You look beautiful, darling," she replied, in a voice that betrayed a warm hint of pride that she was raising her well.

They spent most of their time like this: playing together, reading one of the old books they had at home and which they'd never really looked at before, or lying on the couch in the living room, watching VHS tapes from Will's movie collection.

Will's death was behind them. Iris went through a stressful, difficult period after he died. From time to time, she needed to go out to complete the paperwork registering her husband's death, and whenever she did so she begged Kiera not to open the door to anybody and not to even think about going out because she would get sick like the last time.

She tried to make these trips as brief as possible and, if necessary, she would spread them out, so they didn't group together. By running only one errand at a time she would be back more quickly, and she would sigh with relief as soon as she had checked Kiera was alright. Iris was very worried during those weeks, wondering how the two of them would get by in the future. Kiera couldn't stay alone all day while she went out to work to earn a living. She cursed Will again and again. She came to hate him so much that she didn't even go to his funeral or inform his distant family of the news. To her, Will was a coward who had left as soon as the situation had become complicated.

But she soon discovered that Will's accident had triggered an insurance policy worth around a million dollars. Without her knowledge, Will had taken out a life insurance policy through his job at the garage. To this was added the sum of the compensation offered by the local authorities for not providing adequate signage around the level crossing.

When Iris checked her bank account and saw the total sum resulting from the tragedy she wept for hours. Will's death had not been a disaster for her and her daughter, but a relief that allowed Iris to remember her husband as somebody special who changed her life for the better. In the end, it had been Will who'd given her Mila and who had also given her the opportunity to spend all her time with her.

Will's death also reinforced the idea that outside was dangerous, not just due to the mysterious waves that seemed to bring on her first fit, but also because it was possible to die out there, just like her father had.

They reached a point where Kiera was so convinced that going outside was dangerous that she would beg her mother to be careful whenever she went out. Gradually, Iris became brave enough to lengthen her outings to do the shopping, leaving the little girl at home, and she was surprised that Kiera would run and hug her when she arrived home, thanking her for coming back safe and sound. The little girl was almost as afraid of going outside as Iris was, although for different reasons, and this fight against a common enemy made them even closer, even if the enemy didn't really exist.

There was even one occasion when Iris reluctantly left the front door open when she came home laden with shopping and, to her surprise, Kiera rushed to close it and then said: "Please, Mommy. Be careful, I don't want to get sick."

Without Iris intending it to be, the process of Kiera's captivity had been like that of taming a wild elephant: initially tied to a post, unable to move without being beaten for trying. When the beatings cease, the elephant stops trying to escape because it feels happy and protected by its keeper, who, in its eyes, saved it from its suffering. Kiera no longer wanted to leave her safe environment because she linked going outside to her fit, just like the elephant felt safer with its cruel keeper.

After playing dressing up that afternoon, Kiera tried to style her mother's hair, yanking with a comb while Iris laughed with pain. Then they swapped roles, but Iris brushed softly and carefully. Kiera's hair was long and dark, and the brush slid through it as though she were caressing a silk handkerchief with her bare hand. Kiera found such caresses relaxing and enjoyed them for a while whilst watching *Matilda* on the television.

When the film finished, Kiera went to her bedroom to sing a Christmas carol she had learned from *Home Alone*. When she returned to the living room, she saw her mother holding the remote control and crying.

"Mommy? What's wrong?" she asked, shocked.

"Nothing, darling... it's just... a bad memory about something that happened."

"You mean about Daddy?"

"Yes, honey," she lied. "About Daddy."

"Don't worry, OK?" said Kiera, stroking her mother's face. "We're together. Daddy's OK up in heaven. Like in the film *All Dogs Go to Heaven*."

Iris laughed. Kiera often managed to simplify a problem and turn it into something light-hearted, and Iris found it impossible not to laugh at these witty sentences that she came up with.

"Are you comparing Daddy to a dog?" Iris replied with a smile as she wiped away a tear.

"No!" said Kiera. "It's just that... I don't like it when you cry. Do you want me to tell you a story?"

"Yes, sweetheart. I'd love you to read me a story," she replied. "But will you give me just ten minutes to myself? I need to do something here in the living room."

"Do you want me to go to my room?"

"Why don't you play with your doll's house for a while, and I'll be there in no time. OK?"

"Are you sure you're alright?"

"Yes, Mila. Really," she repeated.

Kiera went to her bedroom feeling confused and shut the door behind her. She wondered what was up with her mother and spent a few minutes trying to work out what it could be. She was young but observant, and she wanted to see her mother happy.

Meanwhile, in the living room, Iris turned the television back on, connected the antenna that allowed it to pick up channels and dropped the remote on the floor as soon as those images filled the screen again. In them two parents were holding each other and weeping opposite a photo of a three-year-old girl. She knew her well: it was Kiera. The parents stood embracing at a vigil that had taken place in Herald Square the day before, which had been attended by around two hundred people including friends and passersby who still remembered the case. Grace stood at the microphone, her eyes red from crying and her face worn from pain. Beside her, Aaron Templeton's gaze seemed lost, and his face distorted. They were both shadows of what they once were. Iris turned up the volume and, for the first time, heard the broken voice of the mother whose little girl she'd stolen.

"You're about to turn eight, my darling daughter," said Grace, to the group of people in front of her. The photo of Kiera seemed to show just how happy she'd been at her side. The image was different to the one that had been printed in the *Press* and on the adverts that had been shown on television years earlier. It showed Kiera giggling, or rather laughing hard, her dimples and the gap in her teeth visible. The little girl's eyes shone with a deep and pure happiness. "If only I could have watched you grow up, seen you fall over, taken care of your grazed knees, sung you your favorite lullaby every night, the one in which I told you nothing would ever happen to you," Grace

Templeton paused to steady her voice, which trembled between her vocal chords. "If only I'd had the chance to raise you with good values, my darling. If only I'd kissed you on the forehead way more often than I did, if only I had you here in front of me now so I could know you were alright, my darling. I ask mercy from the person who took you. If, on the other hand, you did something awful to her and my little girl is lying dead somewhere, I ask just one thing: tell us where she is, so…" she burst into tears and Aaron hugged her. Images of the old Templeton house surrounded by Christmas lights appeared on screen, while the voice of the newscaster reminded viewers that they had set up a hotline in that house during the first few days after the disappearance, but that they never received any leads.

Iris watched those images in floods of tears. She had never previously stopped to truly consider the pain she was causing. Although she knew the little girl had a family and that they were looking for her, she had never stopped to contemplate the amount of harm she was doing. Now she loved the girl with all her heart and that also made her understand how much the Templetons must love her too. Her bottom lip was shaking, just like Grace Templeton's had done as she addressed her daughter. She thought about Grace, about how much those parents had been through and about what she should do.

She tried to dry her tears, but her eyes were like a torrent of guilt. She changed the channel to try and rid herself of the image of Grace and accidentally pressed channel 8, which showed her Kiera playing peacefully with her doll's house, wearing the orange dress made from a tablecloth.

She laughed.

Iris gave a short, nervous laugh through her tears. Suddenly, without thinking about it, a crazy idea had lodged in her mind. One which would have disastrous consequences.

She rummaged through the shelf holding Will's VHS movie collection and found a box which held various brand-new TDK tapes. She spent a while wiping them down with a cloth, making sure they were clean of any fingerprints or anything else that might incriminate her. She put one into the VCR and, without thinking or knowing what she was doing, she pushed the record button and watched Kiera moving around the room as she recorded. She stopped the recording a minute later and, after writing 'KIERA' in marker pen on the label, she wiped the tape again to get rid of any potential prints. She put it in a padded envelope and knocked at Kiera's door, her heart in her mouth.

"What's wrong, Mommy?" asked the little girl as soon as she saw her mother again. "Are you really alright?"

"Yes, honey… it's just that… I have to go out and deliver a package for some friends tonight and… I'm afraid in case something happens to me," Iris said in a rush, without wanting to give too many details.

"Don't go, Mommy," replied Kiera, anxiously. "They can come here. It's dangerous and I don't want anything to happen to you."

"I have to go, darling. They're not well and… I'm sure it will help them. Will you be OK?"

Kiera hugged her and whispered in her ear:

"Yes, Mommy. I won't open the door to anybody, and I'll keep the lights off, but promise me you'll come back," she said in a sweet voice.

"I promise, darling."

Chapter 56
Miren Triggs
November 26, 2010
The day before the last tape

Did the past used to seem as strange to us as the present does now?

I arrived at the first VCR repair store early the next morning. It was in New Jersey and, according to the guy who had sold me my Sanyo VCR, it was the best repair shop in the entire city. If the boss, Tyler, couldn't fix a problem or find a solution, he would give you one of his hundreds of machines in perfect working order as compensation.

It was a long, narrow store full of metal shelving units on both sides with old VCR machines lining the way to the desk. As soon as I went in it felt as though I'd entered a cemetery for obsolete technology that had changed the lives of a previous generation only to be rejected when something better came along. But isn't that what evolution is? Changing as you go forward without worrying about what is left behind.

A man in his sixties suddenly appeared from behind one of the shelves and greeted me enthusiastically. He radiated a comforting warmth that seemed to be soaked in nineties films.

"How can I help you, ma'am?" he asked.

"Hello... my name is Miren Triggs, and I'm a journalist with the *Manhattan Press*."

"A journalist here? This store won't last much longer. The papers can't be interested in this."

"Well, if things keep on as they are, maybe there's a lot the media can learn from a store like yours," I replied with my best smile. I needed his help. This last shot might turn out to be useless, but I had to try.

"Well said," he smiled. "So, what do you need? How can this poor old man be of assistance?"

"I know what I'm about to ask is unlikely, but... have you fixed a Sanyo VCR from 1985 in the last few years?"

"A Sanyo VCR from 1985?"

"I know it's complicated. I'm looking for someone who owns one and this is my last attempt."

"Might I ask why?"

What the hell, I thought. Honesty can open doors, too. At least when it works to unite good people, and the owner of that store seemed to radiate goodness from deep inside.

"Do you remember the case of Kiera Templeton? The little girl who disappeared and then somebody sent some videotapes of her?"

"Yes, of course. How could I forget? Those tapes really caught my attention. Using them to do harm... people have lost their moral compass."

"We know they were recorded on a 1985 Sanyo VCR from the pattern of the tension arm on the magnetic tape."

"A Sanyo tension arm?" he asked, in a confused voice.

"That's right."

"Do you know that Philips VCRs have the same tension arm?"

"Seriously?" I asked, surprised.

"It's not just Sanyo VCRs that contain Sanyo tension arms. Philips didn't produce its own VCRS back then, or at least not entirely, and Sanyo manufactured them using the same tension arms as it used for its own brand. I don't know what kind of agreement they had, but it's something that any fan of VCRs from that era knows," he said, as if stating the obvious.

"Are you telling me I need to expand my search to include Philips videorecorders too?"

He smiled politely. "Yup, that's right."

"Please could you tell me... have you fixed a Sanyo or Philips of that kind?"

He nodded his head with a smile that almost made my heart stop. I closed my eyes and took a deep breath. Perhaps this would be useful. Perhaps this good-hearted man had the answer to all my questions.

"If my memory serves, I must have fixed ten or twelve of those models in the past three years. Their tension arms tended to break pretty easily. Some models that didn't have a high level of quality control barely lasted five years before the arm broke."

"Five years," I sighed, trying to think. "So if anyone is still using one of those, they'd have to repair it at regular intervals."

"Yes, if they had one of the initial run. Those early ones were the most defective, but that's always the case with technology, right?"

"And do you happen to have a list of clients for whom you've repaired VCRs?"

He smiled at me again. "It'll take me a while to go through my invoices, but... of course. Everyone who gets their machine fixed here leaves their details and a deposit. Give me a couple of hours to see what I can come up with," he replied, one of the most hopeful sentences I'd heard in recent years.

I waited impatiently by the door, watching the apparent peacefulness of the street. Perhaps Kiera, or one of the other people who'd disappeared never to be heard of again, was nearby in some dark corner. It made me panic when my mind went back to those old fears. Two hours later, Tyler came out of the door holding a page torn from his notebook with a list of eleven names and addresses. He had also made a note beside each name of the nature of the repair he'd carried out and anything else they'd bought in the store, along with the date he'd written down in his archaic handwritten accounts book. Spare parts, replacements, VHS tapes, repairs. According to what he told me, he kept a detailed record of every card payment because he didn't want any trouble from the banks. Who did?

"Thank you," I said. "If only the rest of the world was more like you."

"It already is, Miss. You just have to look in the right places," he replied before disappearing into his store once more.

Almost all the addresses were on this side of the river, so I took the opportunity to visit them before night fell.

I didn't have any kind of plan. I didn't know how to behave if I found anything suspicious. I considered the possibility of calling Agent Miller to tell him of my progress, but that would just waste more time.

I visited the first person on the list, a certain Mathew Picks, and a man in his seventies opened the door. When I asked him about the repair to his VCR, he didn't hesitate to show it to me, along with the rest of his home. He told me he loved the grainy quality on the screen you got with VHS tapes and the magic of waiting while the tape rewound. He also told me that his wedding was recorded in that format, and he would watch the tape of him marrying his wife, who had died ten years earlier, every night as long as he lived.

I left with a bitter-sweet feeling. I visited three more of the addresses before night fell, all with the same results: they were devotees of the format who didn't want to lose the ability to watch films that were still unavailable on DVD or Blu-ray.

Night had fallen when I stopped the car outside a small, white-painted wooden house with its lights on in Clifton, Passaic County, New Jersey. I wasn't expecting much. The day had begun quite hopefully and become more difficult in the afternoon. When I knocked at the door, a blonde woman with curly hair opened it with a worried look on her face.

"Hello," I said, trying to hide my nerves. "Does William... William Noakes live here?"

Chapter 57
November 27, 2010
The day of the final tape
Clifton, New Jersey

*Unspoken words meant
more than those that could be said.*

"Hello. Does William... William Noakes live here?" Miren asked, consulting a folder. It was ten at night and Mila was already in bed, as usual. Her mother still treated her like a little girl even though she was already fifteen.

Iris froze. Nobody had asked for him for years. She had managed to change the name on the telephone bill and the bank accounts, and the question left her feeling disorientated.

"Um... yes, he used to. He was... my husband. He died years ago."

"Yes... that's why I'm here. We've... noticed some irregularities in connection with his credit card."

"What's going on? Isn't it a bit late for... for that kind of thing?" Iris asked uneasily, thinking quickly. Mila was already asleep and there was nothing to hide in the living room.

"Um... yes. I know it's late, but I wasn't able to come sooner. You see... there's been a problem with your husband's credit cards. It looks like they've been in use since his death and that… is an error that the company needs to investigate."

"What problem? I pay all the bills regularly every month."

"Yes, yes. It's not exactly that there's a problem. I haven't explained myself very well. We just need to fill out a form and for you to answer a few questions related to certain payments made from your husband's account to ensure that nobody has stolen the card and that it's not being used by anybody without proper authorization."

"Somebody without proper authorization?"

"It happens more than it should. They make a duplicate of the card and by the time the holder finds out, the account has been maxed out."

"How awful. I've never… never seen any strange payments on the card."

"May I come in, please? This will just take a moment. It's cold out here."

Iris nodded, confused, but accepted that she couldn't leave Miren there outside. A powerful, icy wind was blowing that day. The woman didn't seem to represent a threat. She was smiling and her gaze was full of energy: she seemed a bit like an insurance salesperson.

Inside, Miren rapidly scanned the room, looking in all directions: table, couch, coffee table, television, Philips video recorder. The paper on the walls was a pattern sold by Furnitools, blue with orange flowers.

"Thank you very much, Mrs.… Noakes."

"You're welcome. Do you work for the bank? It's the first time I've seen you," asked Iris, sitting down and gesturing Miren to a seat.

"I'm from their card company. This will only take a minute, I promise."

"Alright," Iris finally agreed.

Miren looked around again: long hall, green cupboard with an unlocked padlock, window with sheer curtains. At the end were two doors, both shut.

"What do you do?" was the first question Miren asked as soon as she'd sat down on the couch. She took out a biro and made as if to note down the answer.

"Well... that's a difficult question. I... I take care of my home. When Will died he left us a decent sum of money. By living a frugal life, I think I'll be able to... live off my savings."

All Miren's alarm bells were ringing. That simple, unimportant word 'us' had caused her ears to prick up.

"Did you have children, Mrs. Noakes? It... it doesn't say on the form."

A shiver ran through Iris's body, starting at the back of her neck and running down to the tips of her toes.

"No... we didn't have children. But I've always really liked dogs and... they're like my children, you know?"

Miren smiled, accepting the answer, but inside she knew that something was wrong. She hadn't seen any sign of a dog kennel, and there was no smell of them in the living room. What she did notice was that the house smelled quite stuffy.

"Alright... Let's move on... to the spending. I've got a series of purchases I need to verify."

"Of course, go ahead."

"On June 18 three years ago, someone spent 12 dollars and 40 cents on your husband's card at Hanson Repair. It looks like it was to purchase several VHS tapes. Was it you?"

"Hanson Repair?"

"It's the electronics store about ten minutes away from here. Do you know Tyler?"

"Um... I don't remember... but if you have a note of it then I guess so," she replied.

Miren crossed off one of the lines on the list on her piece of paper and moved on to the next.

"On January 12, 2007, there's a payment of 64 dollars and 20 cents at... the same store, Hanson Repair. Is that correct?"

"2007? That's ... a long time ago. I don't remember. I've had things fixed there on several occasions but... I couldn't say for sure about 2007."

"That's fine, to be honest, in this case we just need you to confirm that it was you who made the payment. I've spoken to the store. They've confirmed that you're on their client list. On this occasion, it was for the repair of a Philips VCR."

"Oh yes. That sounds likely."

"It's that one there, right?" said Miren gesturing at the VCR with her biro and then smiling again.

"Oh... yes."

"It's a gem. How old is it? Twenty? Thirty?"

"I've no idea... Will... Will bought it when we moved in here. We used to use it a lot. Now... now what with DVDs and TiVo we... almost never turn it on."

That plural again. And the uncomfortable silence afterwards. Miren controlled herself this time.

"Perfect. I think that's all we need."

"Really? And I can keep using his account?"

"Well, you ought to... cancel it using the death certificate and transfer any funds to your own account. That would be normal procedure; it's a bit of a slow process, but it's for the best. That way... you can avoid complications," replied Miren, getting up. She had her. She was sure of it. Her mind was whirling, thinking of the best way to go about things. She walked towards the door, her mind comparing options, Iris behind her. And then she remembered Professor Schmoer's advice: "The job of an investigative journalist is to confirm theories, Miren. And yours only requires a yes or a no from Margaret S. Foster. And that's what you can get just by asking her and observing her reaction."

"Is that really all you need?" it was Iris who asked the question this time, smiling.

"Yes… I think… I think I've got everything…"

Iris opened the door and Miren went out and turned on the spot. She had to take the plunge, even if she came up against a brick wall. Her heart felt like it was about to burst into a thousand pieces.

"Well… there is one last thing," she said suddenly. Iris looked at her with an open, surprised expression.

"Of course, whatever you need."

"Did you or your husband buy a Smaller Home and Garden doll's house?"

Iris's expression turned from warmth to terror in an instant. The doll's house wasn't in sight. It was in Mila's room and there was no way the woman could know about it. Iris opened her eyes as though she needed to find something in the dark, clutched the edge of the door tightly, and her lips opened just far enough to let in the air she had begun to lack. She didn't answer for the time it took the question to answer itself and for the unspoken words to transmit as much meaning as if they'd been spoken.

"I… I don't know what you're talking about," she replied, after a long moment clinging to the door. "Now, if you'll excuse me, I have things to do."

She closed the door abruptly and Miren walked to her car, incredulous, trying to control the adrenaline she felt pumping through her veins, unsure of how to react. She got in, started the motor and drove to the end of the street, while Iris watched her from behind the fine curtains. When Miren finally disappeared from view, Iris screamed so loudly that Mila woke with a jump.

"What's wrong, Mom?" she asked sleepily, after opening the door at the end of the hallway.

"Get your clothes together, sweetheart," Iris said, her face covered in tears. "We're leaving in an hour."

"Leaving? Going out into the street? What are you talking about, Mom? I'll get sick."

"We don't have a choice, honey," she said between sobs. "We have to go. You'll be alright."

"Why? No!"

"Darling. We have to go. Truly. We don't have a choice."

"But where are we going, Mom?" asked Mila, shocked.

"Somewhere nobody will find us, sweetheart," said Iris, almost too weak to speak.

Chapter 58
November 27, 2010
The day of the last tape
Clifton, New Jersey

Once you've set out on that first journey
it won't be your last.

Mila had dressed according to her mother's instructions. She'd covered her head with a scarf and was wearing sunglasses, even though it was dark. The clothes she had on covered almost every part of her body, leaving only her pale hands, pink cheeks and full lips visible. The sunglasses meant she could barely see in the night, so she clung tightly to her mother as she walked, worrying she might suffer an epileptic fit at any moment.

She'd only had around ten of them throughout her life: after an argument with her mother, after watching a thriller on the television, after brushing her teeth. Following each of those attacks her mother had reinforced Mila's belief in the idea that it was caused by electromagnetic sensitivity, the result of electric currents, Wi-Fi, and mobile phone masts, and she had grown up fearing the outside world as though it were a radioactive environment that could kill her. That was why they didn't have cable TV at home—Iris would check it every so often, hooking up to the signal only to disconnect again when Kiera was around—and they only occasionally watched the VHS movies her mother bought in thrift stores.

While Mila had been getting ready and gathering her things, Iris had been considering where to go and what to do. They didn't have much time. The woman had asked about Mila's doll's house and that suggested they didn't have long. She filled her suitcase to bursting and managed to drag it to the car. It was a small, white Ford Fiesta, more than ten years old, which she had bought to do the shopping once Will was no longer around.

Iris helped Mila to the car. She experienced the icy air of the street for the first time in a long while. The further she went from the house, the worse she felt, and although this was purely the result of conditioning, her legs collapsed just before she got in the car.

"Wait here while I get a few more things," Iris ordered her.

Iris went back to the house and put one of the last untouched TDK videos she still had in a box into the VCR. As she had done on previous occasions, she recorded a minute of the now-empty room. She thought that perhaps this way those parents would understand that they would no longer receive news of their daughter. It was a goodbye, a wordless farewell, because it couldn't be any other way. Deep down, she sympathized with them. She couldn't imagine her life without Mila, and she often thought, regretfully, of how much they must be suffering. After all, that was how the first tape had come about.

Iris spent the entire night driving one way and the other, indecisive, meandering around the city. Mila didn't stop looking outside during the whole journey, captivated by an unfamiliar world.

Every so often she would ask what something was: a gas station, a bakery that was still open and preparing pretzels for the following day, a group of homeless people who'd set up a camping tent beside some dumpsters. Iris didn't have a fixed plan and when her watch showed five in the morning, she realized she had stopped the car in Dyker Heights, outside the Templetons' old house.

Some locals had begun to decorate the outside of their homes with lights, but they were still turned off at this hour. Every so often in the gardens it was easy to see reindeer, Santas, and six-foot tall toy soldiers.

Iris was uneasy, like every occasion when she had delivered one of the tapes, but this time was different. Beside her, Mila was watching her, her transparent skin partially covered by the glasses and a dark scarf enveloping her hair, unaware of what was happening.

"Mila, honey, could you leave this package in that mailbox, please?" she asked, once she'd taken several deep breaths to find her nerve.

Iris stretched her arm towards the back seat and picked up a brown padded envelope. Inside was the tape she had filmed while Mila waited in the car, shocked and uneasy about going out into the street in the middle of the night.

Iris had turned on the television, selected channel eight and waited for the screen to gradually display the image of that empty bedroom with its orange-flowered walls. She had been thinking of those parents, Aaron and Grace Templeton, who appeared on the news every so often, crying and begging for whoever had their daughter to let her go.

She felt deep pain for them. Every time she was reminded of their existence, she was afraid she might not be able to continue and might let Mila go so she could live the life she deserved with her real family and not the one she lived now: trapped between four walls, believing that something bad would happen to her if she went outside.

But Iris still couldn't do it. She loved Mila so much that she couldn't lose her. Mila had become the focus of her existence, the one thing that made her feel alive, and a child, even a stolen child, changes you forever. A smile after hours of crying and asking for her parents was a relief, a laugh between games was like a first kiss, and an 'I love you, Mommy' made nothing else matter. A child made you addicted to love and, for her, after building such a connection with Mila, the idea of saying good-bye to her forever was unthinkable. She had spent so much time with her, she had created such a deep bond with the little girl—now a teenage girl—that she couldn't bear the thought of being separated from her.

When Miren had appeared at her door the previous night, Iris hadn't known how to react and the only thing she could think of doing during the hours that followed was disappearing.

"Why are we here, Mommy? What's in this envelope?"

Iris gave the deepest of sighs and tried to control her heart rate as she gripped the steering wheel.

"I'll tell you later, alright sweetheart? We need to go on a long journey and… it's to say goodbye to some friends."

"OK, of course, Mom," Mila agreed, not really understanding.

Mila got out of the car, with the scarf still covering her head, but without her sunglasses, carrying the envelope labelled with the number four. She went over to the mailbox of that house with its lights out with a strange sensation running through her body. It was still early, and she could see a Christmas tree all lit up through one of the front windows. The place seemed familiar to Mila, as though she had seen it before for a few minutes but was unable to remember when. When she reached the mailbox she struggled with its door—she didn't know how to open it, after all she had never opened one before. As she struggled, she felt a shadow appear at her side and a female voice whispered to her:

"Let me help you, Kiera." Miren spoke in the calmest voice she could manage.

Mila jumped and let the tape fall to the ground. Iris, on the other hand, who had watched from the car as the woman hurried over to her daughter, felt as though what she loved most had been snatched away in a moment.

Iris quickly got out of the car and ran over to Mila.

"Kiera?" asked the girl, confused. "I think... you've got the wrong person."

Miren crouched down and picked up the envelope so carefully that Mila didn't feel at all in danger, despite the fact that her mother was hurrying over.

"Who are you?" she asked.

"An... an old friend of your parents."

"You know my parents?"

"Yes. I think maybe better than... you," Miren replied. Mila frowned, trying to work out what she meant.

"Do we know each other?" she asked, just as Iris arrived beside her and grabbed her tightly by the arm.

"Let's go. We have to go, darling. Get in the car."

"What's happening, Mom?" Mila asked her mother, confused. She didn't understand her behavior.

"We're going. Come on, get in."

"Do you know this woman?" she asked. "She says she's your friend."

"That's not true! Come on, just get in the car," Iris shouted, desperate.

Miren left the envelope in the mailbox and closed it. She saw that Iris was dragging Kiera towards the car, and ran after her.

"How have you been able to live with the guilt?" asked Miren, while Iris pushed Mila into the car and went round to get into the driver's seat. "How could you rob a little girl of her entire life?"

"You don't know anything!" Iris replied with a yell before opening the door and trying to get in.

"And you're not going anywhere," replied Miren, pulling out a gun and pointing it at Iris's head.

Iris held her breath for a few moments, looking at Miren sadly and finally begged, "Please… no. Mila doesn't…. she doesn't deserve this. She's a good girl. She doesn't deserve to lose her mother."

"I know. But she didn't deserve it before, either," declared Miren.

Iris sighed, powerless. A reddish line appeared at the corner of her eye.

"Get into the car and drive," said Miren, in the most menacing voice she'd ever used. She opened one of the rear doors and got into the back seat behind Mila, who was beginning to get scared. "Kiera needs to go back to her real parents."

Chapter 59
November 27, 2010
The day of the last tape
Central New York

Good friends are always there,
even when they don't seem to be.

Jim Schmoer had spent the entire morning teaching a group who, for a while, had just seemed to be a mass of Miren Triggses looking at him, asking awkward, conflicting questions and putting his critical thinking to the test. He was happy. The long years when he had attended classes enthusiastic but frustrated because there was hardly ever a journalist's soul among the students were finally over. This group was different. Every time he asked something, it turned out that his students had already discussed that same point on social media, taking part in lengthy debates on Facebook, Twitter, Reddit, or Instagram, forming opinions for themselves that were so diverse that the classes had become a marvelous place for people who enjoyed disagreement. The instantaneous nature of the internet had opened the doors to information and debate, and he had no doubt that this was the best group he'd ever taught. Of course, the social networks also spread misinformation, but this group in particular seemed not to trust anything they read if it wasn't backed up by an official source. He was so engaged, so fulfilled by teaching this generation that was growing up with a power and desire he had never seen before, that he spent entire days looking for ways to innovate so that he could satisfy the hunger of this mass of aspiring journalists with more guts than he'd ever had. He spent six hours straight teaching that morning and when he reached his office at Columbia University at three in the afternoon, he realized that there were various missed calls on his cell phone from an unfamiliar number.

He hesitated over whether or not to return the call, but he was a journalist, and he couldn't leave this question unanswered.

He dialed and waited for three rings before a female voice answered the call.

"Lower Manhattan Hospital, how may I help you?"

"Hello!" said the professor. "I have several missed calls from this number. Has something happened?"

"May I take your name, sir?"

"Schmoer, Jim Schmoer."

"One moment... let me check.... No... it must be an error. We haven't called anyone named Jim Schmoer from here," the person on the other end of the line said abruptly.

"An error? That makes no sense. I have four missed calls. Are you sure nobody called me intentionally?"

"Four? Alright. Let me just..." the voice moved away from the handset and seemed to address someone else: "Did you ring a man named Jim Schmoer, Karen?" A quiet 'yes' reached the professor and he was instantly worried.

"What's happened?" he asked, shocked.

"One second..." said the voice, to be replaced a moment later by a gentler, warmer one: "Are you Jim Schmoer? Professor Jim Schmoer?"

"Yes. What's going on?"

"You're listed as the emergency contact for… let me see… what's the name…"

"Emergency contact? What are you talking about? For who? What's going on?"

Jim Schmoer felt himself starting to sweat. His parents lived in New Jersey, and he thought perhaps something might have happened to one of them.

"Are my parents alright? What's happened?"

"Your parents? No, no. It's a young woman. She's called… Miren Triggs. Do you know her?"

Chapter 60
November 27, 2010
Twelve years after Kiera's disappearance
Dyker Heights, Brooklyn

And what if all that dark-
ness was nothing more
than a blindfold covering your eyes?

"What's happening, Mom?" asked Mila from the passenger seat, scared and on the verge of tears.

Mila was not prepared for the world. She was afraid and this situation was so new and strange for her that she blocked it all out.

Iris put her foot down on the accelerator and the car began to speed north as the first rays of the sun began to illuminate the city's skyscrapers, which stood like giant golden pillars on the other side of the river.

"Turn right here, towards Prospect Park," ordered Miren, pointing the gun at Iris, who had begun to weep. Grace Templeton lived beside that park. Iris was driving looking straight ahead, drying her tears from time to time, aware that everything was almost over. A dozen other vehicles drove alongside her, people starting their days, all a long way from that nightmare which was about to end.

"Who are you?" she asked. "Why are you doing this? Why do you want to take my little girl away from me?"

"Mom! What's happening?" Kiera raised her voice in a howl that was only audible inside the car.

"Your little girl? Kiera… this woman is not your mother," said Miren, raising her voice.

"What are you talking about? Mom, what does she mean?"

Iris suddenly sped up. She ignored Miren's directions and didn't turn right towards the park. She felt like she was about to explode. Once she'd accelerated, she made a hard left to join Belt Parkway, swerving at the last minute to avoid a truck that almost crushed the little Ford.

"What are you doing?!" shrieked Miren. "We're going to her real parents' house."

Belt Parkway was an elevated highway, skirting Brooklyn high above the ground. Office buildings and warehouses appeared small below them, in front of the impressive view of the approaching Manhattan skyscrapers, visible in the distance.

"Real parents?" murmured Kiera, confused.

"Don't listen to her, Mila. She's lying!"

"Do you want to tell her or shall I?" asked Miren in a threatening tone.

"Mom… what does she mean?"

Iris could hardly breathe. The pressure was too much for her. She couldn't take any more. The truth was always bound to come out one day, but deep down she had always clung to the illusion that this day would never actually come. She always thought that she was doing the best thing for her daughter, her little girl, her princess, the girl who was everything she'd ever wanted in life, that it was better to hide her origin from her, protecting her from a painful and bitter truth: that her mother was a terrible person who had kidnapped her and separated her from her real parents, the parents who would give her a better life than she could ever give. Iris had raised

Mila in fear, to be afraid of the world outside, with the single, selfish goal of preventing anyone from ever taking her little girl away. She was beyond fearing the consequences now. She wasn't afraid of jail, of a life sentence, she wasn't even afraid of the death penalty; she was afraid of being separated from Mila. This fear had dominated her entire life. Raising her at home, the disconnection from the outside world. Mila had only ever really known two people in her life: two fake parents who cared more about having a child than raising her well, and who had, through deceit and fear, turned a happy little girl into an isolated teenager, kept prisoner from the world. The biggest mistake a parent could make: clipping a child's wings so they couldn't fly.

"Do you want to tell her or shall I?" Miren repeated, her voice even more menacing this time.

Finally, Iris breathed through her sobs:

"I'm sorry… Mila. I really am sorry…"

"What are you saying, Mom?"

"You're… you're not my daughter," she admitted, her voice shattering. "You… you don't have an illness. You… you can go outside. You always have been able to…"

"What are you talking about, Mom? Why are you saying this? I *am* ill," Kiera objected, incredulous.

"I'm not your mother, Mila…" she went on. "Will and I… we took you home with us in 1998. You were on your own, crying in the street at the Thanksgiving parade and when I gave you my hand, you stopped. You smiled at me, darling, and I… I felt like I was already your mother. And then, I don't know why, you agreed to come home with us. While we were walking, I was expecting us to stop at any moment, that we would turn around and take you to your parents, but your little hand… your little steps, your smile… You were always such a cheerful little girl… at least, you were until we came along. I'm sorry, Mila."

"Mom?" said Kiera, who had begun to cry halfway through Iris's explanation, as if she was once more a little girl who had just lost her parents at a parade in 1998.

Several seconds passed before Iris composed herself enough to continue speaking.

"And one day… when Will was already gone… I saw your parents on television. I saw them crying in the footage of a candle-lit vigil they had organized the day before Thanksgiving in Herald Square, in memory of your disappearance. That day I saw your real parents crying for you, my little girl."

Miren didn't want to interrupt her. Kiera was distraught, listening to Iris with red eyes, moaning as she wept.

"Tell me all this isn't true, Mom. Please… tell me it's not true."

"It hurt me so much… I was so upset… I decided to tell them somehow that you were alright, that they didn't need to worry, that somebody was taking care of you, and you were alright."

"You sent them three videotapes over twelve years," Miren interrupted. "Why?"

"Yes… I used the camera that Will had set up… I recorded you and I left it at their home. I thought that would put an end to their pain… but every so often… they would appear on the news again and I would have to tell them again that you were alright, that they should leave you with me, that I would take care of you and raise you well, like you deserved. That there was no need for them to worry. I only wanted… them to know that… that nothing bad had happened to you."

"Mom…" said Kiera, throwing herself at her and hugging her, crying like she never had before. Her heart was full of contradictions, a conflict between love and sadness.

"Your name is Kiera Templeton, not Mila," Iris whispered between moans. "I'm… I'm sorry, darling… I… I only wanted the best for you."

After crying for a few moments, Kiera asked, "And what's going to happen now? I… I love you, Mom," she said, drying one of her mother's tears. "I want to stay with you, please."

The vehicle went down a ramp and suddenly entered the depths of the Battery Tunnel. Dawn over the city disappeared and was replaced by fluorescent lighting that flickered intermittently into the car.

"I know, darling… but, we can't stay together, do you understand? I can't… I can't look at myself in the mirror now you know what I've done. I can't carry on with this, Mila."

"But I want to be with you, Mom. I forgive you, truly. I don't care what you've done. I know how you've taken care of me. I know that you love me, Mom."

"You have to hand yourself in, Mrs. Noakes," Miren interrupted, uneasy. "If you do, perhaps they'll give you some kind of visiting rights and you can see each other." Miren tried to assess the situation in the hope of reducing the tension. Iris was trembling as she clutched the steering wheel and Kiera was behaving unpredictably. At first, she'd thought that finding her would mean rescuing her, but how could she do that when they had raised her in chains? "Her parents need to know where their daughter is. This isn't fair for them or for Kiera. Do it for her. Hand yourself in. The FBI office is near the exit from the tunnel. Hand yourself in and this will all turn out OK. Do you hear me?"

"You're not a police officer?" Iris exhaled, between sobs.

"I'm a journalist," Miren replied. "And I only want what's best for Kiera and for her parents to know the truth."

"I want the best for my daughter, too," Iris replied in a whisper. Then she sighed, trying to control the accumulation of feelings pounding in her chest. Kiera leaned towards her and hugged her again, perhaps aware that when they reached the FBI office, she wouldn't ever be able to do so again.

Iris wept and felt her daughter's embrace for a long minute

as she wept with her. She remembered all the times they'd played together, the times when they'd laughed while dancing badly to old songs from the films she put on for Mila. She thought of all the times she'd made up a story for her in which she played the witch and her daughter the princess. She remembered Mila crying every time they argued and her heartfelt hugs as she said sorry. She remembered how nervous she was every time she went out to do the shopping and left Mila alone at home, and how she would sigh with relief when she confirmed that Mila was still there, that she hadn't left, that she was waiting with a smile. With time they'd become complicit in her captivity, in a kind of game in which they fought together against an evil external force. She remembered how Mila would hug her when she got in after she'd been out to run an errand and the little girl would whisper to her that it was all over. They had lived through so many moments together that imagining being without her was worse than the thought of dying. And suddenly she understood Will's death. She understood that he'd done it because he felt empty without the little girl's affection.

"It would all have been so easy…" Iris whispered to Mila.

The light from the end of the tunnel illuminated Iris's face and just as they were about to come out into the harsh daylight, Miren realized that Iris had stepped on the accelerator, and that she'd overestimated her ability to make Iris see reason. She didn't want any more shootings, she didn't want for this woman to meet some kind of tragic end. But true heroes, those made of flesh and blood, can also make mistakes, and Miren was mistaken in thinking she had the situation under control. It's not possible to control a mind under such pressure, it's impossible to separate a mother from her daughter so easily, even if they aren't true mother and daughter.

"Brake!" screamed Miren, pointing the pistol at Iris's head.

"This all ends here, darling," Iris breathed to Kiera.

"Mom!" Kiera begged, pulling away from her mother. She braced herself on the dashboard as fast as she could when she felt the car lurch to the left.

"No!" yelled Miren, in a final attempt to avert the tragedy.

A shot rang out. The bullet grazed Iris's head and shattered the front windshield. At the tunnel's exit, where there were two lanes in each direction, the car suddenly crossed into the on-coming traffic at more than seventy miles an hour. By sheer good luck they narrowly missed a motorbike in the first lane. But bad luck was never too far away in moments like this, ready to appear and change everything, and saw to it that the Ford collided head-on with a squat, fully laden delivery van, which may as well have been a wall.

Chapter 61
November 27, 2010
Twelve years after Kiera's disappearance
Lower Manhattan Hospital

Just when everything seems to be over,
it's actually a new beginning.

Professor Schmoer walked along the hospital corridor with uncharacteristic speed. He could feel his heart pounding and walking any slower was inconceivable in that moment. He hadn't seen Miren Triggs for a few years, although he hadn't stopped reading her articles in the *Press*. Every time he did so he felt a proud smile lift his face, and for a while he even thought about contacting her again, but he always found an excuse not to.

He loved her in his own way, maintaining his memory of that night from a distance, and he felt like perhaps she also still felt that strange and unlikely connection between them. He pushed through several sets of double doors that he left swinging behind him and finally found himself in a new corridor that seemed much longer than the last. As he walked down it, he looked at the cards that displayed the different room numbers until he finally reached 3E, the room the receptionist had mentioned, and glanced through the window in the top of the door before going in.

He went to Miren's side and recognized her immediately, even though she was asleep and covered in bruises. She was being monitored by various screens that tracked her vitals and despite the obvious physical changes from the accident, in those closed eyelids and that dark brown hair he recognized the same energetic and strong-willed girl from all those years ago.

He sat down and let the hours pass by. From time to time a nurse would appear to check that everything was alright and then leave again, and then, just before midnight, Miren opened her eyes and smiled weakly.

"Oh... you've woken up..." whispered the professor in a warm voice.

"And you... you came, Professor Schmoer."

"You didn't have to go to such extremes just to see me again... and you're... you're not my student anymore. You don't need to call me professor. We could just go on... a regular date."

Miren smiled, her eyes half closed.

"They say you've been very lucky," the professor said, trying to encourage her. "You really are a tough cookie. According to what they told me, somebody died in the accident."

"I found her..." she said in a serious voice.

"Who did you find, Miren?"

"Kiera."

"Kiera? Kiera Templeton?"

Miren nodded stiffly.

"But... where is she? Who has her? Does this accident have something to do with it?"

Miren sighed, closing her eyes, then prepared to speak.

"Could you do me one more favor, Jim?"

"Of course... go ahead, Miren," he said in a gently, leaning carefully closer to her mouth to hear her better.

"Could you ask the Templetons to come to the hospital? It's very important. They need to know what's happened."

A while later, Agent Miller's cell phone rang in his pocket just as he reached Herald Square and saw the city suddenly light up with the Christmas lights. He had been walking along without knowing what to do or what next steps to take and, at last, he had found himself at the place where the story of Kiera Templeton had begun. The little girl had disappeared right by this spot, and a shiver ran down his spine at the thought that he would probably never find her. And even if he were to, she might not remember her parents. After all, Kiera had been just three years old when she disappeared, and he knew that memory tended to work in a very selective way during infancy. Agent Miller tried to remember the first memory he had and realized it was a series of snapshots of himself pulling a long a toy trailer when he was aged somewhere between five and seven, but it was something he couldn't be sure of.

He answered the call without looking at the screen and a male voice he didn't recognize greeted him:

"Agent Miller? Is that Agent Miller?"

"Yes. Who is this?"

"My name is Jim Schmoer, I'm a professor at Columbia."

"The University?"

"Yeah. I called your office and one of your colleagues gave me your personal cell number. He told me that you weren't based in the office at the moment."

"Yes... he shouldn't have..."

"Listen. I'm calling you on behalf of Miren Triggs. She asked me to contact you and the Templetons. Miren's phone is broken, she was involved in an accident, and she didn't have any other way of contacting you."

"Miren Triggs? Where is she? I need to find her. Her prints...

are on…" he hesitated over whether to tell him that Miren and Kiera's prints were on the envelope.

"Miren is fine. She just has a couple of broken bones and mild concussion."

"Where is she being treated?" Miller asked, uneasy.

"At the Lower Manhattan. Let the Templetons know. It's important…" Jim paused to make sure the agent was listening carefully. "She's found Kiera."

On arrival at the hospital, the Templetons met Agent Miller at the front entrance. Even the sliding doors seemed sharp as knives as they opened to let them pass and face one of the most dramatic moments of their lives. Aaron and Grace looked disconsolate, but they walked faster than you would have imagined from their appearance. Both their faces were marked by years of sadness, although they also showed a contained hope in the form of the tears gathering in their eyes.

Agent Miller greeted them with a warm hug as soon as they arrived.

"Ben… do you know what's going on?"

"Not yet. I've only just arrived. But it looks like Miren Triggs wants to tell you something. And she wants us all to be there. I haven't told anybody else. I don't want any kind of leak. It seems important."

Aaron reached out his hand and caught hold of Grace's. For the first time in years, she squeezed her ex-husband's hand and walked beside him, letting out a sigh every few steps.

"It doesn't look great," said Miller before setting off ahead of them, leading the way.

They went into the room and saw Miren sitting up in bed, wearing a hospital gown and sipping a glass of water. She was feeling a little better, but she was still weak. She had a bruise on her face, and her right arm was covered in bandages.

"Agent Miller," the professor greeted him, "I'm Jim Schmoer, it was me who called you. Mr. and Mrs. Templeton, I assume you already know Miren Triggs."

"My God, Miren... what happened to you?" asked Aaron. "Are you alright?!"

Grace stayed by her ex-husband's side, nervous and impatient following the entirely unexpected phone call. They both knew that Miren was still looking for their daughter, or at least, that's what she had told them when she visited to ask them for details about her or how she had disappeared.

Miren waited a few moments before speaking, searching for the right words. She had been thinking about this moment for years, envisioning the instant when everything would make sense, and she suddenly stood up. She did so carefully, placing a single foot gingerly on the floor, making sure that it didn't hurt, then she walked towards the Templetons, towing her drip behind her.

"Miren... you ought to rest," said the professor, moving toward her.

"I'm fine. It's just that... I can't find the words to explain to you all what happened to Kiera, everything that I've discovered about her."

Aaron and Grace hugged and hung their heads, closing their eyes so tightly that it made it even harder not to cry. They weren't prepared for this. To be honest, who could be? Not even Miren felt sure about what she was about to do. There seemed to be a slight note of desperation in her voice, but it was really the result of a life full of painful searches for the truth.

"I've found Kiera," she said, finally.

Grace covered her mouth with her hands, unable to take any more. She began to cry and, through her tears, asked in a desperate voice:

"Where is she?! Who has her? My little girl..." she exhaled between sobs. "My baby..."

Miren didn't reply. She, too, was struggling to hold herself together. In the end, for Miren, Kiera was like a part of herself and each time she saw her on one of those tapes she would imagine herself there, inside that room, surrounded by orange flowers, stroking her skin, as though she were looking for herself, as though she were still wearing that same dress from the night when everything changed forever. In that little girl she saw her own fears, her own vulnerability; she saw everything she was hiding in the depths of her heart: an enigma, an unsolvable puzzle, a jigsaw made from pieces of her own pain.

She realized she couldn't wait any longer. Everyone was waiting for a response, the shell-shocked parents, Agent Miller, looking nervous, and Professor Schmoer, who felt a kind of admiration for that wounded butterfly that only he had known before she had emerged from her chrysalis. She left the room and, turning around to speak to them, said:

"Please follow me."

She limped along, pushing her drip, its wheels squeaking slightly against the floor of the empty corridor. The parents watched her walk with such a mixture of emotions that they didn't know what to expect. Miren stopped a few feet on, in front of room 3K, and Kiera's parents looked at one another in shock, wondering what was going on, their hearts trembling instead of beating.

"Grace, Aaron, here's your daughter," Miren said finally, opening the door to reveal Kiera Templeton inside, asleep and with various monitors bleeping regularly as they tracked her vital signs. She had one leg in plaster and a bandage covered part of her head, but there was no doubt it was Kiera.

Grace covered her mouth with her hand and burst into tears as soon as she recognized the dimple in her chin. The dimple that she could never forget, that she'd stroked so many times when the little girl slept beside her all those years ago. She approached her gently, tears streaming down her face. Aaron did the same, following in his ex-wife's footsteps in silence so as not to disturb the painful and peaceful reunion they had waited for their entire lives. When Grace finally reached the bed she turned towards Aaron, hugged him tightly, weeping, and whispered something the others couldn't make out that was intended for his ears only.

A moment later, Miren closed the door, leaving the three of them alone in privacy so that the joy of the moment would remain exclusively inside that room.

Agent Miller put a hand on Miren's shoulder, and she nodded her head.

"Where has she been all these years?" he asked. "Who had her?"

"The wrong mother," she replied. "But let me tell you all about it in my room, Agent Miller. I think they deserve a little bit of time together as… a family," she said.

Professor Schmoer gave her an approving look and then caught up with her as he saw she was beginning to walk back to 3E. Miren groaned slightly at a sharp pain in her ribs, and Schmoer put his arm around her waist to help her walk.

"Are you alright?" he asked, feeling nervous and with a lump in his throat at finding himself so close to Miren.

"I am now," she replied, her voice hoarse with emotion and a smile on her face.

He let her lean on his shoulder and felt the warmth of her body beneath the hospital gown. That warmth took him back to a taxi ride, to the fire of a night that had never stopped burning inside him, to the understanding that perhaps that moment together would never be repeated. He swallowed, trying to contain his emotions, because he knew that the Miren at his side was very different from the one he remembered, that she was now the woman she should always have been.

"How did you find her?" he asked in a low voice once he had finally pulled himself together.

"I just followed your advice, Jim," she said, in a warm voice, taking hesitant steps beside him. "I never stopped looking."

Epilogue
April 23, 2011
A few months later

"So how is Kiera? Have you seen her again?" asked a woman from the back of the bookshop holding a copy of *The Snow Girl*.

"Well, yes," replied Miren, moving closer to the microphone. Her voice, which seemed hoarser and more delicate when amplified over a sound system, echoed against the spines of the books that stood on the shelves. Miren moved her biro from one hand to the other beneath the table in a movement she had begun to make during presentations when she was nervous.

"Kiera is fine, but I can't tell you anything more. She prefers… to stay out of the spotlight. She's trying to make up for lost time and that's something nobody should take away from her, however much the paparazzi stake out her house to try to get a picture or try to catch her out shopping."

The woman who had asked the question nodded happily. The bookstore had stayed open late, something they always did whenever they organized an event. It was a small store in a New Jersey suburb with barely enough space for twenty chairs in its largest room, so most of the people crowded in to listen were standing, all of them holding a copy of the book in their arms as though protecting a little girl in trouble.

The publication of Miren's book was a media sensation beyond what anyone had expected; it wasn't forced, it came about on its own. She'd taken advantage of the week she'd spent in hospital to write a final article on the case for the *Manhattan Press*, which ended up being the most important of her career. In it she explained how she had found Kiera Templeton and the end of that story which she'd spent years tied to by the family's pain. In that article, which she wrote on her laptop from her hospital bed, Miren Triggs provided the details of her investigation and how a family with problems conceiving had crossed the line that separates dreams from nightmares. Kiera Templeton had been found and the whole world wanted to know what had become of her, where she had been and what her life had been like. That front page of the *Manhattan Press* was as unexpected as ever and very different from the others. The headline that opened the paper read: "How I Found Kiera Templeton" and was under Miren Triggs' byline. The format of that day's paper was slightly different from normal: it had a full color front page with the photo of Kiera from when she was a little girl aged three and was printed on higher quality paper so it would withstand the test of time. That day's print run was increased to two million copies, anticipating high demand, but even that was not enough. People flocked to the newsstands as soon as word spread that a journalist from the *Press* had found her. The whole world wanted to know what had happened and how Miren Triggs had managed to solve the greatest mystery of the last twenty years.

While Miren was still in hospital, with her parents keeping her company until she was discharged, an elegant woman in a suit had come to visit her in her room. She explained that she was Martha Wiley, an editor from Stillman Publishing, one of the country's biggest publishing houses, and she offered Miren a million-dollar contract in exchange for a novel that recounted the details of the search for Kiera Templeton.

Having made her pitch, Martha Wiley said goodbye to Miren, leaving her with a telephone number to call if she liked the idea of expanding the article and the story. On the day she was discharged from hospital Miren arrived back at her studio apartment in Harlem, unsteady on her feet and accompanied by her parents, to find that her neighbor, Miss Amber, had taken advantage of her absence to fill her mailbox with advertising flyers.

She laughed. What else could she do?

Arriving upstairs she found that someone had broken the lock on her front door and cleared the place out, taking almost everything of any value. A while later she called Martha Wiley and confirmed her intention to write that novel, whose title was already reverberating in her head: *The Snow Girl*.

It was a kind of tribute to the article she wrote back in 2003. In the novel she told of her fears and insecurities, of her first contact with Kiera's case and how, gradually, that girl had become a part of her, until she found her twelve years later, finally fulfilling a promise she had made to herself: to never stop looking. She wrote the novel during the winter months, using the money from the advance to rent a cozy apartment in the West Village. It was a neighborhood that was less tough than where she lived before, much to her mother's relief. The only dangers in that area were the designer boutiques, which Miren never visited. When *The Snow Girl* was published it immediately became the best-selling novel in the country. Consequently, Miren, who didn't enjoy public speaking, had to emerge from the den where she had spent the previous months writing to attend the twelve public appearances and book signings that had been stipulated in her contract.

A girl in the front row raised her hand and, when she caught Miren's eye, asked:

"Have you given up journalism? Do you still work at the *Manhattan Press*?"

Miren shook her head with a genuine smile and began to speak: "It's something that's impossible to give up. I love journalism.

I don't think I'd know how to do anything else. My boss, who is very understanding, has given me a few months of leave right now. As soon as I feel ready, I'll go back to writing for them. I call him every week to make sure he's not let anybody sit in my seat."

She laughed, and so did the rest of the room. A dark haired young man beside the girl, who appeared to be her boyfriend, raised his voice without giving Miren the chance to identify who was speaking.

"Is it true that they're going to make a TV series about you? I read that one of the big production companies had bought the rights."

"Well, there's something in the pipeline, yes, although I can't give any more details at present. What I can say is that... it's not about me. It's about the search for Kiera. I'm not .... interesting enough for something like that. I'm just a journalist who looks for stories to tell. In this case the story was about Kiera Templeton."

The boy nodded with such a broad smile on his face that she knew her answer had been more than enough. She spent a while longer responding to questions as if playing a game of tennis, returning shots and getting through the session without sending any of them out. Then a woman who was standing asked another question without introduction:

"Is it true you carry a firearm?"

Her editor, Martha Wiley, who had accompanied Miren to each of these events, put up her hands and apologized:

"I'm afraid... we've run out of time for further questions if you'd all like to have your books signed. I know Ms. Triggs has loved answering your questions, but we need to catch a flight to Los Angeles tonight and we're running short on time. You can ask her whatever you like while she's signing your book."

"Don't worry, Martha," said Miren. "I think we've got time for a couple more."

Her editor clicked her tongue and the readers smiled in appreciation. She pointed to a man with a beard at the back of the room.

"So, do you carry a weapon or not?"

"You have a journalist's spirit," Miren smiled. "No, I don't carry a weapon. Let's say that was… a piece of dramatic license for the sake of the novel."

"And your fling with the professor? Was that dramatic license too?"

Miren laughed before replying and then added:

"Well, I won't say it was something that could never have happened."

"Come on… you can tell us. Nobody will find out."

The whole bookstore, which was packed with people clutching copies of *The Snow Girl*, burst out laughing, catching the attention of people passing by in the street.

"Let's just say that taxi ride seemed to fly by," admitted Miren subtly, trying not to laugh.

A satisfied sigh seemed to fill the room. Martha Wiley was the first to clap, eliciting a round of applause from the readers packed into the store. Miren remained seated while a line formed in front of her table. She took her hands out from beneath it and reached for the first copy with an excited expression.

"I really loved it. Don't stop writing."

"I won't," replied Miren as she signed.

One after another, Miren accepted the compliments, a little embarrassed. She felt like she didn't deserve so much affection and she focused on trying to give each person enough attention that they went home happy. She thought that perhaps they were there for Kiera and not her, and she felt that, in spite of the book's success, there was nothing of interest about her own story given that she was no Kiera Templeton and had not suffered that long ordeal. But as she spoke with everyone who passed her table with their copy of *The Snow Girl,* she realized that people only had kind words for her and for the good deed she had done. "You're a heroine"; "The world needs more people like you"; "Thanks for never stopping looking."

An eight-year-old girl wearing a red coat, who had attended the signing with her mother, said something that meant more to Miren than she could ever have imagined: "When I grow up, I want to be like you and find all the missing children." A tear formed in Miren's eye, but she managed to blink it away before anybody noticed.

Cards and gifts from some of the readers had been accumulating next to the table. There weren't many and when the signing finished and the store had emptied, the owner, a woman of almost seventy who had spent her whole life fighting for worthy causes, offered to put them in one of the cotton tote bags she kept for her best customers, thanking them warmly for having chosen her small bookstore for one of the book's events.

"You really don't need to thank me. On the contrary, thank *you* for giving me the platform," replied Miren, getting up and helping her put the parcels in the bag.

Among the gifts were a miniature copy of *The Snow Girl,* and a white rose left by a man who had been unable to speak while she signed his book and also his copy of the edition of the *Manhattan Press* from 1998 which featured Miren's first article on the front page alongside the image of James Foster in flames. She was surprised to see it again. The last time she had seen it was at her parents' house, where it attracted more dust than attention.

The letters, which she normally read when she got home or arrived at the hotel if she was travelling, were usually long messages that asked for help to find loved ones who'd been missing for years, romantic invitations that made her laugh or even requests for work that she was unable to accept. She tried to ignore them, although there were some requests for help that she would write down in a notebook so she could review the details in case there was anything about the story of their disappearances worth following up.

One letter stood out among the heap from this signing. It was a brown padded envelope with just three words written on the front in marker pen: 'WANT TO PLAY?'

"Did you see who left this?" she asked her editor, who shook her head.

Miren didn't remember anybody leaving this letter during the signing. In all honesty, she hadn't paid attention given that there were people milling around the table, taking photos and chatting while she concentrated on signing and thanking people for their support.

"It must be someone propositioning you. Open it and give us a laugh."

Miren snorted, but a strange sensation was making her uneasy. The writing was uneven and although it was in capitals, it transmitted an air of chaos that she didn't like at all.

"Perhaps it's a crazy fan. They say all writers have at least one," said the store owner in a jokey tone.

"That's what it looks like from the writing," Miren replied, serious. She didn't like this one bit. Part of her was telling her not to open it, warning her as it did from time to time, but the other part wanted to find goodness in those eyes that had been watching her with satisfaction for several hours. It had begun to rain outside, as if the clouds knew that this was the exact moment to create an atmosphere. Miren opened the envelope and reached inside. It didn't feel like anything dangerous, just a cold, smooth piece of paper. But when she took it out to have a look, she realized it was a Polaroid photo, dark and badly framed, with an image that was like a blow to her chest: in the center was a blond girl, gagged, in the back of what looked like a van. On the bottom border was a simple caption:
GINA PEBBLES, 2002.

Acknowledgements

This may seem to be the least interesting part of the book, but for the author, it's the most important part. For me, a book without thanks is a book without a soul. It's here, among these unfamiliar names, where you'll find the glue binding each page and follow each step it takes for an invented story to become printed sheets. Then you'll see how a book in a box travels to a bookstore and onto the shelves before ending up open on somebody's lap on a bus, subway, or plane; or perhaps being held for hours in the hands of a person who is looking for something, or for themselves, while sitting quietly on a comfy couch.

My thanks to Verónica, as always, because without her this book would have been written without any emotion. If you're going to try and write about feelings, you need to have some experience, and she has given me all of it. Each word of this book was born thanks to everything she makes me feel.

Thank you also to my little ones, Gala and Bruno, for all the paternal love that turns into panic at the thought that something might happen to you. I've realized that I write about my fears and about what I love, and they represent both together.

My thanks to Suma de Letras, which already feels like home, and to the whole team, who seem to be just next door in spite of the distance between us. My special thanks go to Gonzalo, who is not only my editor but has become a friend, one of those people who turns up in your life unexpectedly, and for whom you instantly consider buying beers to keep in the fridge just in case, even though you don't like beer or have a large fridge.

Thank you also to Ana Lozano for maintaining the perfect distance to encourage creativity and at the same time remain demanding, and for those eyes that make everything take on a new dimension. Thanks also to Iñaki, who is always there, even though he works hard not to make it obvious.

I have not forgotten Rita with her creativity, Mar with her determination, Nuria, the visionary, or the wise Patxi. Thanks to Marta Martí for giving me wings and a voice; to Leti, for always having the perfect words at the most special moments. My thanks also to Michelle G. and David G. Escamilla for opening doors on the other side of the world. Thank you to Conxita and María Reina for making my stories already available in more languages than I imagined existed, and for making my words travel to places I can only dream of visiting.

Thank you to all those booksellers who have welcomed me so warmly, for being so excited about my books, and for turning every signing in their stores into a party.

The best part, the final thanks, are reserved for you, my readers. It's difficult to put into words everything I go through with you and what you mean to me, and that's why, if you see me in person, you will hear me thank you for giving my stories the most valuable thing in life: the time you spend reading them.

Thank you from the bottom of my heart.

My thanks could go on, taking up several chapters complete with twists, surprises, and cliffhangers in the last sentence, but I think it's better to make each other a promise: for my part, I won't stop writing and, for your part, every time somebody asks you for a book recommendation, if you enjoyed it, recommend *The Snow Girl*, without telling them what happens